Also available from Alicia Hunter Pace and Carina Press

Sweet as Pie

Coming soon from Alicia Hunter Pace and Carina Press

Shine Like Silver

Also available from Alicia Hunter Pace

Gone South Series

Sweet Gone South
Scrimmage Gone South
Simple Gone South
Secrets Gone South
Santa Gone South (novella)
"Slugger Gone South" in *Take Me Out* (short story)

Nashville Sound Series

Face Off: Emile
Slap Shot: Bryant
High Stick: Jarrett
Body Check: Thor

SMOOTH AS SILK

ALICIA HUNTER PACE

carina press

carina
press®

Smooth as Silk

ISBN-13: 978-1-335-42485-3

For questions and comments about the quality of this book, please contact us at CustomerService@Harlequin.com.

Carina Press
22 Adelaide St. West, 41st Floor
Toronto, Ontario M5H 4E3, Canada
www.CarinaPress.com

Printed in U.S.A.

For Tara Gelsomino,
the best agent and mentor a writer could hope for.
It is a pleasure to walk this road with you.

SMOOTH
AS SILK

Chapter One

One of the best things about living in the American South was that you could eat ice cream in November. Not that it was banned in the Highlands of Scotland where Robbie McTavish was from, in Switzerland where he'd gone to prep school, or in New England where he'd played junior and college hockey. You just wouldn't be as inclined.

"Best one yet." He raised his towering cone of mocha praline fudge and smiled to Constance, the owner of Double Scoop.

"That's what you say every day."

"Not *every* day." He licked his cone and headed for the door.

"Near enough." Constance laughed. "Not that I'm complaining."

He was probably eating too much ice cream, if there was any such thing. Double Scoop made their own and had new flavors every week. The cheery little bell chimed behind him as he stepped out onto Main Street. The Laurel Springs shopping district didn't look too different from his village in Scotland—nice storefronts with harvest decorations on the sidewalks.

The other thing he liked about the American South

was Southern women. Really, he liked all women, but there was something intriguing about how Southern women wore pearls with blue jeans, drank straight bourbon, and put their initials on everything they owned.

And the sunglasses. Never had he known women who had sunglasses appear like magic in their hands the second they put foot to threshold. Maybe it wasn't magic. Maybe it was more like those claws that shot out of Wolverine's hands when he needed to fight, only these women were fighting the sun.

He hadn't had much female company of late—at least not like he'd had when he was playing professional hockey in Nashville. He'd left the Nashville Sound for the new Birmingham, Alabama, team when his best friend Jake had, figuring they'd continue on as they had before—keeping company with charming companions, exploring bars, and shutting down parties.

It hadn't turned out that way.

First off, Jake had, for reasons Robbie still wasn't all that clear about, decided he was tired of his partying ways. Then, before the season started, the head coach had been fired for sexual harassment, and Nickolai Glazov, the acting head coach, had threatened them with benching if their bad boy ways showed up on the pro hockey gossip blog, *The Face Off Grapevine*. Even if those things hadn't happened, night life wasn't exactly hopping here. The Yellowhammers' practice rink and offices had been built in this little outlying village rather than in the thick of downtown Birmingham. Consequently, most everyone connected with the Yellowhammer organization had settled here in Laurel Springs because it was more convenient.

And now, Jake had started keeping steady company

with his childhood pal, Evans—and he was fair besotted, too, from the looks of things. Sure, Robbie could have scared up some excitement if he'd wanted to, but it was too much trouble. He'd lost his running buddy and, after skating and working out, he never felt inclined to drive all the way downtown to hunt a good time that was likely to get him in trouble anyway.

So he was bored.

Apart from some right fine victories on the ice, the most fun he'd had lately was a mandatory team volunteer job, and how sad was that? He'd played piano at the bridal shop for the Laurel Springs Fall Festival last month. The owner, Hyacinth, had gotten her dander up at him for not exactly following everything on her exhaustive lists, but that had just made it interesting. He'd gotten a right fine tongue lashing from her, too. He smiled at the memory. It brought to mind that phrase from old movies— "You're cute when you're mad." But he'd known better than to say it. He hadn't seen her since that night and wondered if she'd gotten over it yet. Her shop was just up ahead. Maybe he'd pay her a little visit, see if she was still all het up—and see if she was still as pretty as he remembered.

He didn't have anything else to do. Tomorrow was Thanksgiving and Glaz had called practice off this afternoon to give a head start on the holiday since they had to report back midday on Friday. Hockey didn't pay much mind to Thanksgiving and the Yellowhammers had a game Saturday afternoon.

He crossed the street right in the middle. You could jaywalk in Laurel Springs without getting run over.

The window of Trousseau needed a little work. There were two headless mannequins wearing wedding dresses, and that was the first problem. He hated headless bodies—gave him the heebie-jeebies. The pumpkins and leaves were okay for this time of year, but she needed something that would catch the eye, like blinking lights and an animated scarecrow. Maybe a turkey or two, though he could never understand why Americans decorated with the thing they were going to kill and eat. Santa Claus had better look out. Cannibalism might break out any time.

Speaking of the right jolly old elf... If Robbie put his mind to it, he could think of some really good window decorations for Christmas—silver trees, twinkling stars, and maybe a snowman or some unicorns with flashing horns. People loved unicorns these days. His little nieces fancied them above all else.

Some motion beyond the display caught his eye. What on God's green earth was that and why was Hyacinth allowing it?

There was a woman on a little platform in front of a three-way mirror. Hyacinth and Brad—who Robbie had palled around with some lately—were hovering around. Hyacinth had her usual all-black duds and trussed-up hair in a bun Professor McGonagall look going—but that wasn't what horrified Robbie. It was the bride.

That dress absolutely did not belong on that woman. Robbie knew everything about weddings that was worth knowing, and not only because he'd been involved in all of his married sisters' weddings—five so far, and two to go, unless Sophie or Ella went to the convent like his granny hoped. He'd seen hundreds, maybe thousands, of brides and he'd never encountered one in such a train wreck of a frock.

She was wearing a straight dress with a dropped waist

that was meant for a tall, very thin woman with not much up top or in the bum area. This bride had a lovely hourglass figure with a small waist that was made for a ball gown. Now that he thought about it, her shape wasn't so different from Hyacinth's. Hyacinth had to know this dress was all wrong, so why had she allowed the bride to try it on? Hyacinth smoothed the skirt, smiled, and said something to the bride when she ought to be hauling her back to the dressing room and getting her out of that dress. If his granny were here, she'd march right in there and tell Hyacinth that she was about to ruin this poor woman's wedding day.

Holy family and all the wise men! Just when he thought it couldn't get worse, Brad settled a jeweled band with feathers coming off it around the lass's head. It suited the dress but, given that the dress didn't suit the woman, they ought not to encourage her with that little bit of frippery. If somebody didn't put a stop to this, Hyacinth was going to run herself out of business.

He had to go in there. It was his duty as a wedding authority and citizen of the Universe.

"Are you sure you wouldn't like to try a ball gown? Or an empire? Both would be so lovely on you." Daisy Dubois, who identified with Daisy Buchanan and was set on having a Gatsby-themed wedding, did not have the body for this flapper-style dress. But, so far, Daisy had ignored Hyacinth's suggestions.

"No," Daisy said firmly. "Especially not a ball gown. I refuse to look like a parade float."

Lois, mother of the bride, bit her lip and looked at the floor, probably wishing she'd never named her daughter Daisy. The four bridesmaids lined up on the sofa were no more enchanted with the dress than Lois. This had been going on so long they had gone from sneaking peeks at their phones to blatantly scrolling and texting while they knocked back the cheap champagne Hyacinth served.

There was no chance any of them were going to be honest with Daisy. Hyacinth had been down this road enough times to know that there were two kinds of unfortunate bridal posses: the overly vocal and critical ones, and the ones who made the consultant be the bad guy. This bunch was firmly in the latter category. Hyacinth would be the bad guy if it came to that, but everyone would be happier if she could gently nudge Daisy into wising up on her own.

She'd also been down this road enough to know that, given time, Daisy *would* wise up. Then she would take some suggestions and everything would turn out lovely.

Daisy turned and pulled at the fabric around her hips. "Is it too small? It doesn't feel right." Good. She was getting there. Hyacinth felt the first hint of the sparkling happy little cloud that always formed when a bride found the dress of her dreams.

But there was still work to do. Hyacinth pretended to study and waited a few beats to say what she already knew. "Not too small. A larger size would swallow your shoulders and waist. This is just the nature of a column dress." Altering wouldn't fix the problem. "Let's try something with a flared skirt." There were a dozen on the rolling rack in the workroom that Hyacinth had already put aside just for Daisy.

"Would it have the Gatsby look?" Daisy asked. Hyacinth exchanged glances with Brad. They both knew there was no way to sell that.

"To be honest, no," Hyacinth said, "but it would show off your beautiful small waist."

"And we could do some accessories that would give the feel of the period." You had to hand it to Brad. He always gave it the old college try.

Lois nodded and the bridesmaids looked up from their phones, hopeful.

"No," Daisy said stubbornly. "I don't want the *feel*. I want to look authentic. I want to try another drop waist."

They'd already been through this three times with three different dresses and there were only two more in the right price range. Maybe that would be enough. If not, Hyacinth might have to be blunt—but she wasn't going to borrow trouble yet.

"Of course. Let's get you back to the dressing room." Hyacinth held out a hand to help Daisy from the pedestal when the bell above the door jingled.

Hyacinth looked around, set to greet the newcomer, but she froze.

Robbie McTavish. That was the last thing this room needed right now.

It had been almost a month since she'd seen him, but that nightmare fall fest was still fresh on her mind and probably always would be—and all because of him. First, he'd shown up wearing a ragged kilt—much like the one he was wearing now. Next, he had ruined the centerpiece of her refreshment table when he cut her fabulously expensive haunted house wedding cake before the festival even started. Then, he'd ignored her carefully compiled playlist and banged out whatever he pleased on the piano, often singing along. Admittedly, he played well and had a pleasant voice, but how could he have thought "Monster Mash" and "Werewolves of

London" were acceptable when she'd wanted "Pachelbel's Canon" and "The Bridal Chorus"? And she hadn't been able stop him. Every time she'd tried to get him back on track, he'd said, "Yeah, yeah, lass. For sure," and plowed right on doing what he wanted.

Her brain began to smolder at the memory of it all.

It was her own fault that he was here today. He'd left his grubby kilt and shoes in the dressing room the night of the fall festival when he'd changed into his not-at-all-grubby formal kilt for the festival after-party. If only she hadn't procrastinated about calling him to pick up his things, she could have directed him to come here on her schedule. Now, not only was he here in the middle of a difficult bridal appointment wearing a faded I heart New York T-shirt with yet another worn out kilt, he had a chocolate ice cream cone the size of the Statue of Liberty's torch.

Hyacinth did not allow food in her store beyond the champagne and cheese straws she served clients. She had a little whimsical sign outside over a trash can that said, "Check Your Coffee at the Door! Someone's Silk Dream is Inside." Apparently she needed to add ice cream to that sign.

"Hey, Robbie," Brad said.

Robbie nodded. "Brad, my friend. You owe me a *Mortal Kombat* rematch."

"And you owe me a burger. I paid last time because you didn't have your wallet."

Organized, dependable Brad had befriended this soup sandwich of a man? That was news to her, but none of her business. They were just an unlikely pair. Robbie settled his eyes on Hyacinth and pushed his messy copper hair out of his eyes—the greenest eyes she'd ever seen. "And the lovely Hyacinth." He gave a nod to Daisy and then to her entourage. "Ladies."

"You must be here for your shoes and kilt," Hyacinth said. "I'll get them for you."

Robbie looked surprised. "This is where I left them? I wondered where they got off to. I had to get new gutties." He held up a glow-in-the-dark green running shoe. His socks didn't match and he had a scrape on his knee that needed some Neosporin and a bandage. It was when she was wondering idly how he'd hurt himself that she noticed his leg—and then the other one. They were chiseled, strong, and very attractive. How had she missed that before? "Do you like them?" She might have thought he was referring to his legs if he hadn't pressed a button on the shoe, causing the soles to burst into a light show. "Fancy, huh?"

"I didn't know they made those for adults." If he wasn't here for his belongings, *why* was he here? Not that it mattered. Good legs and green eyes or no, she had to get rid of him. Bridal parties were notoriously protective of their time. But when Hyacinth turned to gauge the mood of the room, Daisy and Lois were smiling so bright you could practically see moonbeams swirling around them, and the bridesmaids sat a little straighter and had put down their phones. One crossed her legs and another licked her lips.

Okay, so he was hot. Annoying, but hot.

"Excuse me a moment," she said to the bridal party. "I'll be right back." She turned to Robbie. "Come with me. I'll get your things." Once they were out of earshot, she added with a hiss, "You need to take that ice cream and get out of here."

"What?" He licked the cone.

"The ice cream. I don't allow food in the shop."

"What about those little cheese things those women are eating?" He continued following her as she turned the corner and advanced toward the counter—licking as he went.

"That's different." She turned around. "Stop right here. Stay clear of that dress display."

But she stopped too quickly and he was too hot on her heels. She knew what was going to happen by the look on his face before the huge scoop of chocolate sailed off the cone, over her shoulder, down the front of the new Rayna Kwan that she had put on display just this morning.

His mouth formed an O.

"Fuck." She never said *fuck*—or even thought it. Apparently this man brought it out in her, but nothing called for bad words like eight thousand dollars' worth of ruined beaded silk.

"Holy family and all the wise men," he whispered, his brogue more pronounced.

They were both frozen in time.

He went into action first. "Sorry. I'll fix it." He removed the paper napkin from around his now empty cone and started to dab at the stain—and what a stain it was. There was a four-inch-wide band of chocolate from shoulder to waist—not unlike a royal sash—and splatters peppered down the front of the skirt.

"Stop! You can't fix it."

"I'll pay for it." He scooped up the ice cream from the floor and stood looking at it melting in his hand. She grabbed the small trash can behind the accessories counter and held it out to him. "Here," she said wearily.

He looked at the ice cream mournfully before he dropped it in. "I'll pay for it," he repeated as he wiped his hands on his kilt.

"I just put that out so it would be ready for an appointment I have on Black Friday." After numerous conversations with Connie Millwood about what she was looking for, and many hours of exhausting searching, Hyacinth had deemed this perfect for her. "The bride is coming from Georgia for the appointment."

"Did she ask for this dress?" He pointed at the ruined gown. "*This* particular one?"

"No…" she had to admit. But it had everything she wanted—the corset bodice, sweetheart neckline, mermaid skirt, crystal embellishments, and all the rest… Now it was a chocolate mess.

Robbie McTavish had the audacity to smile. "No problem, then. There can be another. I promise I can afford it."

"Not the point. Do you have any idea how much time and effort I put into finding dresses that fit this particular bride's body type, vision, and budget? How many hours I spend finding the perfect thing for every bride who walks through my door? You can't put a price on that."

"Well." He gave a backward glance to where Brad was helping Daisy onto the platform in yet another unflattering flapper dress. Robbie looked at her and raised an eyebrow. "That right there is, indeed, a product of genius."

Her smoldering head turned into a burning bush—

though to be fair, this might not have been the best time to point out her styling skills.

"You need to leave. Now. Out the back door. You've done enough here."

But did he do that? Of course not. He shrugged, threw a smile over his shoulder and advanced on the bride. Hyacinth had to practically run to keep up with him.

"Lass, aren't you a vision. You're getting married. I fair love brides."

Daisy blushed. "I am. In eight months. It's going to be a Gatsby theme wedding. I want it to be like the party in the movie—the one with Leo DiCaprio. I love that movie."

"Aye," Robbie nodded. "So do I."

Hyacinth would bet every inch of lace in the place that he'd never seen it.

"You want to look like Daisy? A flapper girl?" Robbie asked.

All right. Maybe she would have lost her lace, but she had trouble trusting haphazard people—and she knew haphazard. Before coming to live with Memaw, she had cut her teeth on turned off electricity, lost keys, and chronic, habitual tardiness. But no more. She'd fought to stay away from chaos all her life—fought hard—and now it had invaded her ordered little pristine world in the form of red hair, a faded kilt, and neon flashing shoes. And good legs.

Her heart raced.

The bride of the moment, however, had no sense that chaos was swirling about her and was enchanted by him. "My name is Daisy." She blushed some more.

"Ah, a beautiful name. Did you know it's sometimes a nickname for Margaret?"

"No. I'm just plain Daisy—named for my grandmother."

"Not just plain. You could never be that."

He was getting more Scottish by the second and Daisy was eating it with a spoon. Hyacinth's heart raced even more. It was fall fest night all over again. She'd lost control and had no idea how to recapture it. But she had to try.

"My name is Robbie, named for my grandda." His attention was fully on Daisy.

"You're from Scotland." Daisy stated the obvious.

"Aye. My family has a wedding business. Our ancestral castle's the most popular spot for hitching in the whole of the country. We've had more weddings than Gretna Green." That was interesting, but was the mayor of Haphazard City telling the truth? He had no reason to lie, but neither had Hyacinth's dad had a reason to say he'd played guitar with Eric Clapton. "I've seen more brides than stars in the sky, but none more bonnie than you." He pronounced *stars* like a cross between *stirs* and *stairs*. Under other circumstances, that might have been charming.

Then, he reached out like he was going to take Daisy's hands in his—hands he had not washed.

Chocolate hands!

One ruined dress was one too many. She would be damned if there was going to be two.

"Stop!" It came out louder than she intended. She grabbed the champagne bottle from the bucket on the table, tore off the damp cloth napkin, and slapped it in Robbie's hand.

"Ice cream," she said as if that explained everything. She scrubbed first one hand and then the other. It was impossible to ignore that his hands were big, strong, and warm. But she didn't care about any of that. She only cared that they were clean before they touched another thing in her shop.

But then...but *then*...he circled her palm with his thumb. Slowly. And her body betrayed her by wanting him to do it again. She didn't plan to raise her face to look at his, but it happened anyway. He dropped his eyelids to half-mast and smiled like he had a secret. Her stomach turned over. And no wonder. She hadn't been touched by a man except in passing in nearly two years.

And he squeezed her hand—but she would not squeeze back. Hell, no. She couldn't control everything—or really, maybe much of anything—but she could control this.

She jerked her hands away.

The silence in the room was deafening. Clearly they all thought she'd lost her mind. Well, let them think it. They weren't the guardians of thousands of dollars' worth of silk, satin, and lace.

"Thank you, lass." There was an edge of laughter in his voice. "It's been a while since I've needed someone to clean me up."

Before she could suggest that he run along now, he took right up where he'd left off with Daisy. This time, he succeeded in taking her hands, and he spread them wide as if to get a better look at her. Someone from the bridesmaid gallery sighed.

And all Hyacinth could do was stand there clutching a chocolate-stained napkin and watch it happen. Daisy smiled like smiles had been invented for him.

Best case, he was going to convince her that dress had been made for her. Worst case, she was going to throw her engagement ring against the wall and follow him to the ends of the earth. And it would be preserved for posterity because one of the bridesmaids seemed to be videoing now. She wondered vaguely how long that had been going on.

"There was a Scottish queen called Margaret—Margaret Tudor, wife of James IV of Scotland. She was Henry VIII's sister. Her marriage was a love match and James called her Daisy."

"Oh…" Daisy put her hand to her heart. More lies, more eating up by Daisy.

"She was a princess when she got married. Every girl ought to be a princess at her wedding, don't you think?" Daisy nodded, wide-eyed.

"I know you're going to get married in a flapper dress, but you know what I'd love? To see you in a real princess dress. Would you like to try one on, for fun?"

"Well…" Daisy cocked her head to the side and chewed on her bottom lip. It was all too obvious she wasn't going to tell him no. Hyacinth suspected that few did.

"Hyacinth won't mind, will you, Hyacinth?" Robbie gave Hyacinth a crooked smile.

"Not at all." What else could she say? Besides, maybe this little development would turn things around. Here was the chance to get Daisy in the ivory A-line with a tiered skirt and portrait back. But she had to get rid of him, without sounding like a bitch in front of these people. She bit her lip and tried hard to channel her friend Ava Grace, who was every inch a lady. "I know of just the thing. But I can take it from here, Robbie. I know you are a busy, busy man. Thank you oh-so-much for your assistance. Daisy, come with me." Hyacinth held out her hand.

"But Robbie wants to see me look like a princess."

Mother of pearl. She was living in Nightmare City—but she clung to the small bit of cloud that remained.

"Yes, Hyacinth." I never miss a chance for a princess sighting. I go to Disney World twice a year for that particular pleasure."

Every woman in the place burst into delighted laughter. And so did Brad. Traitor.

"Of course," Hyacinth acquiesced through gritted teeth. No getting rid of him yet. "Daisy?" She held out her hand again. "Let's see what we can find."

"Brilliant!" And before Hyacinth could stop him, Robbie went tearing around the showroom flipping through dresses. "I'll find something."

Lois and the bridesmaids chattered and giggled. Hyacinth picked up a word here and there—*charming, so funny, isn't he the the sweetest?*

She stomped off after Robbie. "Stop it," she called after him. "That's the ball gown section. Daisy has made clear she will not have a ball gown. I've tried!"

By now, she'd caught up with him and she was close enough for him to whisper. "Daisy doesn't know what she wants. She only thinks she does." And he continued to flip through the dresses.

"What do you know about wedding dresses?" she hissed at him.

"More than you think. Ah!" He didn't look at Hyacinth, but turned back to Daisy and her posse. "This! This! I've got it!" he called across the way. And he presented Daisy with the biggest, blingiest ball gown in the shop—the Simone Donatella with the silver beaded bodice and hem.

Daisy put her hands on her cheeks. "I could try it on—you know. Just for fun. But is it my size?"

"No." Hyacinth put her hands on her hips. This dress was a six and Daisy needed an eight.

"It'll fit," Robbie said. "Numbers don't matter. I have an eye for these things."

Brad took the dress from Robbie. "I'll take you back. Patty's waiting to help you."

The dress was two thousand dollars over Lois's budget; it wouldn't fit and Daisy wouldn't go for it anyway. Yet, this could be productive. Maybe Daisy had begun to think outside the box a little. While a ball gown was too far in the extreme from Daisy's vision, there was a good chance they could get her in a romantic lacy empire or the ivory A-line.

Meanwhile, Robbie was leaving the minute he saw Daisy in this dress—and she intended to tell him that right now. Having collected herself, she walked back toward the seating area, where Robbie had made himself comfortable in the chair across from Lois.

"You truly have a real, live castle?" one of the bridesmaids asked as she handed him a glass of champagne—champagne meant for customers. "Does it have a name?"

"Aye. A wee one, as castles go. Thank you, lass." He accepted the glass and took a sip. "Wyndloch's the name, though my mum calls it Castle Crumble."

No way was he telling the truth. He'd happened in her shop, started wreaking havoc, and now his family was in the wedding business? That was all too convenient. Besides, wouldn't he have mentioned it when he was here for fall fest?

But apparently these people believed him. "And how did your family castle ever end up turning into a wedding venue?" Lois asked.

"Came a time when keeping sheep didn't pay the bills. My great grandma had the idea to let out the homestead for parties and weddings. Now, Wyndloch is right popular."

Time to call his bluff. "Where might I have seen it advertised?" Hyacinth asked.

He shrugged. "Maybe you wouldn't have. We don't have to advertise."

"Mmmm. I see," Hyacinth said. "Waiting list?"

"Four years."

Despite herself, Hyacinth found herself buying into this—and she wasn't sure why she wanted so badly for him to be lying.

She could find out, here and now. She whipped out her phone and googled Windlock Wedding Venue Scotland. The site came up, despite her incorrect spelling. So he wasn't lying. She might have still doubted him had there not been a picture of the McTavish clan—including Robbie—standing in front of the "wee" castle—which had to be 40,000 square feet at the smallest. There were at least thirty of them and they were all wearing tartan—the men in kilts, the women in skirts. She squinted. A small redheaded girl stood in front of Robbie, totally obscuring his legs. He had his hand on her head.

Hyacinth enlarged the photo and zoomed in on Robbie to get a better look. His kilt was nothing like the ragged, wrinkled one he wore today. He was in full formal Scottish attire. He had it right, too—Prince Charlie jacket, hose, flashes, sporran, ghillies, and everything else that went with the fine wool kilt. Hyacinth knew this because she'd dressed a bride last year who'd had the men in the wedding party wear formal kilts. She'd thought it pretentious, but Robbie McTavish did not look pretentious. You had to hand it to him; he looked completely comfortable—and magnificent.

"Look at me, Mama!" Daisy swept into the showroom with Patty and Brad carrying her massive skirts.

Everyone—even Robbie—went silent as Brad helped Daisy onto the platform.

It was the perfect fit.

Daisy beamed at Robbie. "It feels…right." Lois and the bridesmaids gathered around her. "I could still have my Gatsby wedding, couldn't I? It wouldn't ruin it if I wore this dress, would it?"

"Of course not," Lois said, with the bridesmaids backing her up like a relieved Greek chorus.

"I think a princess does what she likes," Robbie said.

"But how much does it cost?" Daisy asked.

Now for the bad news. Maybe Robbie would buy it for her. It would serve him right to have to pay for this dress *and* the Rayna Kwan. He'd started this. Hyacinth never showed a bride a dress out of her price range.

"Your grandma Daisy said if you found *the* one she would pay the extra, up to four thousand dollars." Lois cast a questioning look at Hyacinth.

Relief settled over Hyacinth. It would probably take that. A veil to go with a dress like this was considerably more than a feathered headband.

Daisy smiled at herself in the mirror and the sparkly cloud moved in—though this time it was tinged with a touch of gray because it happened in spite of Hyacinth rather than because of her. Still, the important thing was that Daisy was happy.

"That will cover it," Hyacinth said. "How about we try some veils?"

"And a tiara?" Daisy asked breathlessly. "Could I have a tiara?"

"You *must* have a tiara," Hyacinth said.

"And I think a crystal and silver beaded belt to accentuate your small waist," Brad said.

This was the best part of a bridal appointment—when the dress had been chosen and the bride was truly delighted. The choosing of the veil and accessories and making appointments for fittings was all high-spirited fun—sort of like picking up last-minute stocking stuffers on Christmas Eve after the hard holiday things had already been done. Or at least that's how Hyacinth imagined Christmas was for most people. Since her grandmother had died, she only had her staff, her mentor Claire, and her friends Evans and Ava Grace to buy for. That had been done since August.

It was almost closing time when Lois slipped her credit card to Hyacinth. "Tell Robbie thank you," she whispered. "I don't think we'd have a dress if he hadn't charmed her into trying it on. It's almost as if you planned it."

Hyacinth barked a little laugh as she ran the card. "I can assure you that I did not plan for Robbie McTavish."

Where was he, anyway? She'd all but forgotten him. Evidently he had no opinions on veils because they hadn't heard from him in a while. Her eyes cast quickly about the store—he was nowhere to be found. Thank goodness he'd left. She let out her first full breath in a half hour.

But after she'd ushered Daisy and posse out, Hyacinth caught sight of him leaning against the accessories counter, eyes cast down, looking as sad as she'd ever seen a man look. A chord of sympathy chimed inside her, though she had no idea what she was sympathizing with. Maybe Trousseau made him miss home. Maybe Daisy had reminded him of a lost sweetheart.

"You're still here." She came up beside him.

He turned. "Hello, lass. All well with Daisy?"

"Yes." She was considering asking him why he seemed sad when she caught sight of where he'd been looking—the small trash can that contained the remains of his ice cream cone. The little sympathy chime turned into an iron clanging bell. "Please tell me you weren't considering eating ice cream out of a trash can."

He rubbed the back of his neck and squinted his eyes mostly shut. "Naw," he said around a yawn. "It's melted."

"It's melted? And that's the only reason you didn't consider eating out of a trash can?"

He shrugged. "How dirty could it be? It's not like you're butchering hogs in here. You're selling wedding dresses." He looked down at the can one last time and ambled to his feet. "It was excellent."

"If it was that excellent, why didn't you just go away and eat it instead of coming in here ruining dresses and causing chaos?"

"That girl needed help. *You* needed help." His green eyes bored into hers and he took a step closer.

Every hair on her body stood on end.

"*I* needed help? How do you figure?"

"How do you figure that you didn't? The dress was all wrong for her. In the wedding business, your reputation is everything. And there is no repeat business—or at least not enough to count. What would people have thought if you'd let Daisy go down the aisle wearing that dress?"

"If I had let her? *Let her?*" She wanted to scream. "For your information, I knew the dress was unflattering. I had done everything I could to steer her in a different direction. At that point the best thing to do is let the bride try on dresses until she figures it out on her own."

"She wasn't showing any signs of it."

"How do you know? You'd been in here all of fifteen seconds before you insinuated yourself in the situation."

"I was right, wasn't I?"

"She knew it wasn't right." That was true. "She was coming around." Probably.

"Would you have sold it to her?" Robbie lifted his chin. "No matter how bad it looked?"

"Not without telling her point blank that it wasn't flattering."

"Have you ever done that?" He took another step closer to her, all the while looking so smug, like he knew the answer.

"A few times. Most of the time the bride will see it on her own and I can guide her toward something more suitable." He was close enough that she felt his body heat, but she would *not* step away. No way would she give him the satisfaction of thinking she had noticed.

"But if she hadn't?" He dropped his face closer to hers. Damn. He smelled like chocolate, probably tasted of it. "Would you have sold it to her?"

"You say that like you wouldn't have. In the end, it's not my decision."

"Reputation."

In truth, she'd never sold a dress that was truly hideously unflattering. She would have rolled in the mud wearing the most expensive dress in the shop before she would have admitted it.

She changed the subject. "You showed her a dress that was way out of her price range."

"Clearly not. They bought it." He narrowed his eyes and didn't quite close his mouth when he finished speaking.

"It's cruel to show someone something they can't have."

The moment froze. They locked gazes for what seemed like a long time.

Then the spell broke. "You're right." Robbie closed his eyes and stepped back out of her space. "But it worked out."

"This time."

He came across with that damned cocky crooked grin again. "I have some other ideas for you. Your showcase window could use some livening up. I'm going away for Thanksgiving, but let me take you to dinner next week and I'll share my ideas."

Hyacinth stopped cold. He did *not* say that to her!

"This was kind of fun. The next time you have a difficult bride, call me. I'll be glad to come help you."

He frowned like he was trying to work something out, then brightened. "I know. I'll get you some game tickets. You can come see me play. Then, we'll have dinner."

There weren't enough deep breaths in the universe to bring her back from this.

"I don't like hockey. I don't have time for it." Never mind that Claire, her mentor and silent business partner, who also owned a small part of the Yellowhammers, had given her a whole set of season tickets.

"You don't like hockey?" He said that as if she'd said she didn't like breathing. "Well, just dinner then. I can still help you out with your windows and I might change your mind about hockey."

"Tell you what, Robbie, let's *not* have dinner. I can tend to my own windows and my own brides. You tend to your hockey and leave me out of it."

"I can tend to more than one thing."

"Here, tend to this." She reached under the counter and got a bag that contained the kilt and shoes he'd left. "I mended the hem." She hadn't been able to help herself. She'd washed it, too.

"That was good of you." He looked inside the bag. "It looks like it's been ironed."

She gave a half nod. "Only sloppy seamstresses don't press their work." Memaw had taught her that.

"Then I *do* owe you dinner." He held out his hand.

"What do you say?"

"I say no thank you."

"Have it your own way," he said.

"Believe me, I try, but that seems nigh on impossible when you're around."

He laughed. "Goodbye, lass, I'll be going now. Need to pack for the little trip I'm taking. You have yourself a fine Turkey Day." He gave a little salute as he left.

She, like Robbie, was also taking a short Thanksgiving trip. Unlike him, she was packed and ready.

She locked the door after him and sighed with relief. Never had she known a human who wore her out like Robbie McTavish.

What a ghastly day. She closed her eyes and leaned

against the doorjamb, afraid if she moved, something else would happen. She wasn't sure how long she'd been standing there when she heard the pecking on the glass. Dread washed over her. Couldn't she catch a break? It would be him again, perhaps with a taco truck and brass band.

She opened one eye and relief and joy overtook her. Not Robbie, but sweet Chloe Harper, who'd gotten married last month and moved to Memphis. Hyacinth opened the door and Chloe flew into her arms. Getting Chloe married had been quite the adventure. She'd kept gaining weight and Hyacinth had had to alter her dress twice. Even at that, she'd burst a seam at the wedding and Hyacinth had rushed over to sew her back into her dress.

"I know you're closed," Chloe said, "but we just got into town for Thanksgiving. I had to come by and bring you a picture." The girl dug into her tote bag and pulled out a framed photo of them both, with Chloe wearing her wedding dress.

"Thank you, Chloe. This means a lot to me. Seeing your happy face is just what I needed today."

"It's nothing," Chloe said. "But I had to stop and tell you that you saved me—saved my wedding from being a disaster."

"Oh, that's not true," Hyacinth said.

"It is," Chloe insisted. "You just don't know. I've lost it now, but you remember how I kept gaining weight after the dress was altered? I was a nervous wreck and couldn't stop eating."

Impossible to forget. "It happens sometimes. Getting married is stressful."

"But you never once lost patience with me. You just

kept telling me I was a beautiful bride and fixing my dress."

"You were a beautiful bride." Hyacinth gestured to the picture. "The proof is right here."

Chloe closed her eyes and shuddered. "And then, right after the ceremony, I burst that seam. I hated myself so much right then. I was sure that Gunner would be disgusted with me. I wanted to run away. I almost did. But you came and fixed my dress. You were so calm, you just kept saying I was gorgeous, and I wasn't to worry about a thing, that you would sit right there in that dressing room, ready to take care of any problem I had, even if I wanted to dance all night. You said you hoped I *would* dance all night because it was my special night—and it ended up being just that, and all because of you. If you hadn't done that for me, I would have had nothing but awful memories of my wedding."

"Oh, sweetheart." Hyacinth's eyes filled. "I'm so glad it was a happy night for you."

Chloe nodded. "And Gunner and I are so happy. Maybe we would have been anyway, but I can't think having a bad start would have done us any good. You're the best fairy godmother a bride could ever have."

And just like that, Hyacinth was centered again, wrapped in that warm, sparkly cloud. "Thank you, Chloe. You have no idea how much I needed to hear that today."

She locked the door and waved goodbye to Chloe through the window.

She needed to remember that a day like today didn't wipe away all the happy brides she'd sent out her door. Chloe and all the other brides who came to her to help make their day perfect were the reason she loved her job and loved this shop.

And she did love Trousseau—so much.

She still couldn't quite believe her luck that it was hers. She'd visited Trousseau for the first time when she was twelve years old, shortly after she'd come to Laurel Springs to live with her grandmother. Memaw had been that renowned and sought after seamstress that every community has, and in addition to sewing for the public, she'd done alterations for Trousseau. It was here that the first seeds of Hyacinth's ambition to design wedding gowns was born. Memaw taught her to sew, and by the time Hyacinth was fifteen, she was helping with the alterations and making some of the simpler garments for Memaw's clients.

After graduating from design school, she had planned to get a job in a bridal shop to learn the business, save some money, and get some contacts. By then Memaw had died, and she'd had little reason to return to Laurel Springs.

But shortly before graduation, Claire Watkins called her home—and when Claire called, you went. She had old money, new money, and amazing business sense. It had been looking good for Birmingham to get the pro hockey team franchise they had been wanting, and Claire was on a mission to put some spit and shine on the suburb of Laurel Springs Village to make it attractive to the hockey crowd. Trousseau was looking a little dusty, a little tired, a little last century and the owner wanted to retire—and, like many things in Laurel Springs, Claire owned the building. Was Hyacinth interested? Claire would invest and mentor her, if she thought she could breathe some fresh life into it.

And she had accomplished that.

She had forgotten that for a little while today. Memaw had always said there was nothing that had ever touched this Earth that was perfect except Jesus Christ and the Alabama Crimson Tide, but she hadn't lived to see Trousseau, all revamped and shiny. She would be proud of Hyacinth.

It was too much to hope for that she would never see Robbie again. This was Laurel Springs, with connections like the fibers of a spider web.

Claire had invested in two other businesses. Along with Hyacinth, Evans Pemberton, of Crust pie shop, and Ava Grace Fairchild, of Heirloom Antiques, made up the trio of "Claire's Girls." Evans and Ava Grace were Hyacinth's best friends and Evans had landed in a relationship with Robbie's best friend and teammate, Jake Champagne.

So he would be around—as would she. But hopefully it would be a while before she had to see him again—a long while.

Chapter Two

Robbie stuffed his backpack with a couple of T-shirts, two pairs of underwear, and his toothbrush. That ought to do it. He could use Jake's shampoo, soap, and such.

But wait. He needed a kilt. He sniffed the one that Hyacinth had mended. It smelled good, like some kind of flowers. Or fruit. Anyway, good.

Hyacinth. Never before had he known a woman who lived so completely immersed in a perpetual state of panic.

True, the incident with the ice cream and the dress was unfortunate and he was sorry for his part in it. But if she hadn't been mad to begin with, and hadn't been all het up, ordering him around and stopping too quick right in front of him—*after*, mind you, demanding that he follow her—it wouldn't have happened. He saw no reason to point any of this out, as she was not a woman to be reasoned with. Nor was she one to be appreciative of his willingness to pay for the dress and make it up to her by helping out with Daisy.

Still, it was his ice cream and he would do the responsible thing. McTavishes always did. But it looked like he wouldn't be taking her to dinner or helping her with her windows. Not that he wanted to, not really.

Crabby was what she was—even crabbier than that Peanuts girl, Lucy. She wasn't one bit impressed that he was a pro athlete. That was good news and bad news.

Yet, he liked her. Everything else aside, she was clearly, like everyone in his family, a hard worker. If she was a little too uptight and unbending, he had to admire how organized she was. It was all he could do to keep milk in the refrigerator and get to the rink on time.

He shouldn't have asked her out. He wouldn't have, except for that little moment they'd had with their hands all tangled up together. Wasn't it just his luck that when he'd finally, after all these months, felt a connection with a woman, it was with one who didn't like him? He wasn't used to not being liked or being turned down. And then there had been that moment when it seemed like they ought to kiss. She'd deny it, but there had been some heat for her, too—enough that it rattled her.

Which reminded him—condoms. The chances he would have sex while in Cottonwood, Mississippi, were all but nil, but sometimes the unexpected happened. A condom wasn't something he would borrow from Jake, regardless of how close they were—and they were close. That bond had been sealed their rookie year the second day of training camp. Robbie had gotten a knock on his noggin and Jake had slept in the same room with him and wakened him every two hours. That wasn't something a man would soon forget.

When he fetched the condoms from the bathroom, he caught sight of his phone charger on the nightstand. He'd need that and he was down to his last one. He'd bought three last time, but his car and condo seemed to eat them.

That Hyacinth had probably never lost a phone charger in her life.

The doorbell rang. That would be Jake and Evans. But when he opened the door, it was Jake alone.

"She throw you over, did she?" Robbie asked as he stepped aside to let Jake enter.

Jake closed his eyes and shook his head like he did when somebody said something that didn't agree with him. "No. She did *not* throw me over. She needed to go back to her house for some things. We're picking her up there."

He'd forgotten Evans even had a house. She *was* pretty much living right across the hall with Jake these days.

"I'm all ready." Robbie slung his backpack over his shoulder. "Ready for some Mississippi Turkey Day adventure."

"Did you pack socks?" Jake asked. "The last time you went home with me, you didn't pack socks and I never saw the ones I lent you again."

Hell. "I'll be right back."

Having freshened up and changed into jeans and a soft, autumnal amber sweater, Hyacinth sat down, reached for her phone, and let her mind drift to the big thing she had cooking—the chance to get *Trousseau* on the reality show *All Dressed in White*, where they filmed a bride choosing a dress. All she needed was a celebrity bride or groom, and a pro hockey player was close enough.

And she was close, so close.

Jake and Evans were Hyacinth's best chance yet to get on *All Dressed in White*.

Also, her first chance. Her only chance so far. If only they would get engaged.

It was due to tenacity and perseverance that she had Alex Leman's personal cell number. Most of *All Dressed in White*'s episodes were shot in upscale, established bridal shops in big cities with ordinary, everyday brides. But occasionally, there would be a special show with a celebrity bride or groom. When she'd first contacted the show three years ago, they'd had no interest in a fledgling shop on the outskirts of Birmingham, Alabama, with an inexperienced owner. They'd been polite, yet firm. But she kept calling—pestering them, her memaw would have said—and they had gotten less and less polite. Somebody's assistant to somebody else's assistant had gone so far as to tell her that shops like Trousseau were a dime a dozen and *All Dressed in White* was only interested in the unique and the elegant. But that didn't discourage Hyacinth. If anything, it fueled her.

Alex was an assistant director and Hyacinth was reasonably sure she'd gotten passed on to him because he was the new kid on the block and he'd been given the task of doing what no one at the clerical level had been able to do—get rid of her. Only too bad for them, the day they patched her through to him, Alex had some time on his hands and they had a conversation.

Turns out they were kindred spirits—*ambitious* kindred spirits.

She checked the time. Jake and Evans were due in twenty minutes. She had plenty of time to call Alex, even if they weren't late, which they usually were. Ava Grace would have said she ought not make a business call on Thanksgiving Eve, but Hyacinth wasn't practically engaged to Skip Landry and his trust fund, nor did she have the Fairchild money to fall back on. The holiday hadn't been invented that was going to get in the way of her goals.

The phone rang. Alex wasn't always glad to hear from her, but he always took her calls.

"Hyacinth Dawson. As I live and breathe." He tried to fake a Southern accent and she relaxed. This was not one of those days that he wasn't glad to hear from her. "Here on the eve of this great country's harvest and gluttony celebration, I would have thought you'd be out digging sweet 'taters and grinding cornmeal."

"I did that yesterday. You know how I like to stay ahead of the game. Have you shot your turkey yet?"

"My wife's taking care of that. I bought her a brand-new ax to chop the head off."

"How generous."

"You got anything for me?" His tone went to business. "I might."

"*Might* isn't going to make Trousseau into the Hyacinth Dawson Design Studio."

Alex knew what she wanted——to grow her business so she could realize her dream of designing wedding dresses. She would never give up Trousseau; it meant too much to her, but there was room to expand the building. She dreamed of a big, airy studio with state of the art sewing machines and the best seamstresses to help bring her creations to life. She wasn't fool enough to think that having Trousseau featured on *All Dressed in White* would get all that for her, but it would be a damn good start.

However, that wasn't half of it. She had not told Alex part two of her *All Dressed in White* ambition. There were a few—five to be exact—bridal salons that had become so popular with the audience that they were featured regularly. *If* she could get this opportunity, *if* it went very, very well, maybe Trousseau could join that rank. The ultimate would be letting the audience watch Trousseau evolve to include the studio.

"I don't like *might*," Alex went on.

"*Might* won't get you what you want either," she countered, "but my *might* is really more of a *probably*. I'd go so far as to say almost a sure thing."

"Tell me more." Alex had some dreams, too—to become a senior director with assistants of his own. If she could get a celebrity customer, he thought he could sell the idea—and be allowed to direct the episode himself. While someone from the entertainment industry would be ideal, a pro hockey player would do. It didn't hurt that Alex was a hockey fan, though his team was from New York. Or maybe New Jersey.

"Do you know who Jake Champagne is?" she asked.

Alex answered immediately. "Nashville Sound. Championship cup. Damn fine D-man."

"He's a Yellowhammer now," Hyacinth said.

"That's right. I heard that."

"He's dating one of my best friends."

"Oh, well." Alex sounded disappointed. "He *dates*—a lot."

"Not anymore, he doesn't," Hyacinth said. "He and Evans go way back—childhood friends. Her parents are his godparents. He's not messing around here. You'll love her. She's pretty, smart, and—get this—an artisan pie maker. Owns her own shop."

"That *is* the kind of thing the audience eats up." He

sounded hopeful. "But are they engaged? That's kind of important."

"Not yet. But, I'm telling you, it's coming. They've got it bad. And," she added, "I'm about to take a four-hour car trip with them to Cottonwood, Mississippi, for Thanksgiving. I guarantee I'll have a better idea of when that ring will land on her finger at the end of this weekend. My guess is Christmas. Valentine's Day, at the latest." If she could report that it happened this weekend—all the better.

"Will they do the show?" he asked.

"They'll do it, all right. As I said, Evans is my bestie. She'll do anything for me. And he'll do anything for her."

"I admit, Dawson, sounds like you might have us something."

"I do. I feel it in my bones."

"Keep me in the loop."

"Are you kidding? You are the loop." The doorbell rang. "I've got to go. That'll be the happy couple now."

"Have a happy—and productive—Thanksgiving. And send me a picture of her—better yet, them together."

When Hyacinth opened the door, it was only half of the happy couple—Evans.

"Where's Jake?" Hyacinth looked over Evans's shoulder.

"I needed to come home and get a couple of things. They're meeting us here."

"They?" Hyacinth got a bad feeling in the pit of her gut.

"Here they are now!" Evans said happily and turned to watch the big black Suburban Jake had bought specifically for this trip roar up and stop. As quick as a star can twinkle, Jake was out and on the porch, headed straight for Evans.

"Hey, you," he said, eating Evans up with his eyes.

Hyacinth had a fleeting thought that the way he looked at her would play well for the camera, but it was obliterated when Robbie McTavish appeared out of the passenger side.

Mother of pearl! It couldn't be.

"Is he going with us?" She tried to keep the hiss out of her voice, but didn't entirely succeed.

"Uh-huh." Evans was headed straight for Jake's arms.

"You didn't tell me that."

"Did I not? I meant to." Evans clearly did not care that she had failed to provide Hyacinth with vital information. She was only concerned with Jake's mouth descending on hers.

Robbie stepped onto the porch, looking as surprised as Hyacinth felt, but amused, too. "Long time no see, lass."

"Why didn't you tell me you were going on this trip?"

"I told you I was taking a wee trip. I didn't think you cared where. And I didn't know you were going."

Four hours in the back seat with Robbie. Had she not been on engagement watch, she might have considered staying home.

She took a deep breath and called back her conversation with Chloe. She was competent, caring, a fairy godmother. Good. She was centered again.

"I can't believe they didn't tell us," she said.

"Can you not, now?" He jerked his head toward Jake

and Evans, who were kissing like they hadn't seen each other in months.

He had a point. Between the two of them, those two only had three things on their minds—hockey, pie making, and each other.

Might as well get on with it.

She turned toward Evans and Jake. "Hey, lovebirds. Are we going to Mississippi? Or do I need to go buy a turkey?"

They parted—reluctantly. "We're going." Jake didn't take his eyes off Evans and dropped a kiss on her nose.

"My suitcase is already in the Suburban," Evans said, "but I have pies to take and a tote bag with some shoes and things."

"I'm on it," Jake said. "Robbie, why don't you get Hyacinth's things?"

"Sure thing," Robbie said as Jake and Evans left. But he leaned on the porch rail and crossed his arms over his chest. "I see you changed clothes. That color is becoming on you."

Was that a compliment or a dig because she usually wore black? She decided to take it as a compliment.

"Thank you. I see you didn't change clothes." Though the chocolate spots where he'd wiped his hands on the kilt were a bit faded. He'd probably scrubbed at them with a wet paper towel, if he owned paper towels.

"I'm clean. Especially my hands." He raised his hands, wiggled his fingers, and gave her a smoky look.

Her stomach did a little flip, but she wasn't playing that game. "Let's call a truce and have a pleasant holiday."

He shrugged. "I don't have anything to call a truce

about, but I'm all for a pleasant holiday. Let's get your suitcase."

She led him into the house. "I have everything together, right here by the door."

He caught his breath when he saw it. She half expected him to ask if she were moving to the Delta permanently, but he didn't.

He wasn't the kind to understand that she needed a large bag for all the *what ifs*. What if she planned on a skirt for Thanksgiving dinner and everyone else had nice pants? Or were completely casual in jeans? What if she needed clothes for helping with the cooking? What if it rained? What if it turned colder——or warmer—— than expected? (Which was clear skies with a high of seventy-two and a low of sixty-one. She'd checked.)

Robbie swung her laptop case over his shoulder and lifted the suitcase and cosmetic bag——which left her coat and the canvas boat bag with her extra shoes, hairdryer, and the hostess gift she'd gotten for Evans's mother.

"I guess it will take both of us to load your things."

But it wasn't a jab. He smiled when he said it.

Did it have to be such a nice smile?

Chapter Three

These people did not travel like Hyacinth. They hadn't been gone two hours and they'd already stopped twice.

First, though no one else seemed to think it odd that he hadn't already taken care of it, Jake announced a half hour down the road that he needed gas. Hyacinth stayed buckled into her seat, but Robbie and Evans went into the store and didn't appear again for fifteen minutes, Robbie with a bag of beef jerky, HoHos, and a baseball cap with a bird dog on it. Who knows what Evans was doing all that time, but she wasn't using the restroom. At least Hyacinth hoped not, since the second stop thirty minutes later was to let her take care of that. This time Robbie bought a giant insulated coffee mug imprinted with Sweet Home Alabama and a bag of M&M's.

Hyacinth held her tongue through all this, though she had to remind herself that this wasn't her vehicle, nor was their destination her childhood home. But it was hard not to take control of the situation. This was like traveling with her parents, who had never let where they were headed or when they were expected to arrive impact their travel plans. She hadn't been able to get control of that either, which is why she usually insisted on taking her own car.

But she couldn't watch Operation Jake and Evans Engagement from her own car.

Only after they'd crossed the Mississippi line did Hyacinth begin to relax. At least they were in the state of their destination now.

"Who's hungry?" Jake asked.

"Me," Evans said.

"I could eat," Robbie agreed, but she didn't see how considering how many HoHos he'd consumed.

"I am, too," Hyacinth said—and she had to admit this was a necessary stop. People did have to eat.

Jake swung the car off the interstate, but instead of turning toward the row of gas stations and fast food, he veered in the direction of what looked like nowhere.

"Oh!" Evans clapped her hands. "We're going to Cook's, aren't we? I haven't been there in forever."

"You know it, baby." Jake covered her hand with his.

"I never come this way without stopping by."

Stopping by? There was no stopping *by*. There was going to—and going way out of the way, at that. Who did that? Hyacinth and Memaw had the same philosophy about eating on the road—get in, get out. That meant Arby's, McDonald's, or—if they had a little more time—Cracker Barrel.

Yet, Jake drove on and on, into the wilderness.

Robbie opened a pack of beef jerky. Evans switched the music to Adele. Jake drove some more.

Mother of pearl. They were on a gravel road now. Where were they taking her?

"I'm so excited!" Evans said.

Maybe Evans wasn't her friend, after all. Maybe she was part of some cult that sacrificed bridal shop owners to their goddess. Or maybe any person connected with the bridal industry. That would make Robbie a prospective victim, too.

At long last, there were lights up ahead and a building surrounded by cars.

"Careful, lass," Robbie said as Jake parked the car. "There are chickens about. You don't want to step in poop."

Well, why not chickens? And, of course, Robbie had been here before, too, being Jake's brother from another mother.

The restaurant was built of turquoise cinderblocks with a tin roof. The sign said Cook's—We Cook It. You Eat It. Est. 1947.

Inside the floors were creaky wood and the walls covered in pictures of beauty queens and football players. The bar was in a separate room toward the back. The music wasn't live, but that hadn't stopped the people who wanted to dance. The place was huge and nearly every white paper-covered table was filled.

"Over here." Jake steered them toward the wall to a table for four. "Robbie has to sit with his back to the wall."

"Aye." Robbie pulled out a chair for Hyacinth before taking his seat. "You never know what's coming."

Immediately, a waitress wearing shorts and a Cook's T-shirt appeared.

"Evening, folks."

"Evening," Jake said. "We'll start with half-and-half and a half pound of boiled."

What? That was a lot of halves. And of what?

But apparently the waitress knew because she nodded.

"Make that a pound of boiled," Robbie said. "And I'll take the check."

Hyacinth opened her mouth to protest, to say that she wanted a separate check, but it was already a done deal. Jake and Evans hadn't reacted at all; they wouldn't have. Dinner for four was pocket change to Jake—and Jake and Evans were a single entity. But moments like this were awkward for Hyacinth. It made her feel like others thought she couldn't afford her food.

"What can I get you to drink?" the waitress asked.

"Sweet tea for me," Jake said. "I'm driving, Ladies? A glass of wine?"

"I like beer with my half-and-half," Evans said. Presumably she wasn't going to mix cream and Michelob Ultra. "I don't care what kind."

"Beer is fine," Hyacinth said, mostly because it was easier. Everything about this place was electric, hurried, frenzied. Breathe and you'd be left behind.

"Then we'll have a pitcher," Robbie said. "Miller Lite? Good."

"I'll be right back with your apps and to get your order," the waitress said.

"She means it, too. Everybody decide." Jake passed out the plastic laminated menus that were propped between the napkin holder and sauce bottles. "They don't like to wait around."

Mother of pearl! The prices on this menu did not match the décor or the chickens in the yard. But before Hyacinth had time to take it all in, a huge platter of oysters appeared—half fried and half raw, slimy, and nasty—along with a basket of boiled shrimp.

Robbie poured beer and the waitress demanded to know what they wanted to eat—as if there wasn't enough food for ten people already on the table. Not that Hyacinth was going to eat any of those oysters. No, sir.

She liked seafood, but oysters weren't seafood. They were an abomination.

Jake, Evans, and Robbie set about ordering fifty-dollar plates of assorted seafood and steak with extra crab legs.

Crab legs. Did they know how long it took to eat crab legs? If they hadn't been dead, Hyacinth would have sworn Brian and Angela Dawson were driving this crazy wagon. Evans had never been as exacting as Hyacinth, but had she been completely assimilated?

Hyacinth ordered a bowl of gumbo and a side salad. Never let it be said that Hyacinth Dawson ordered the most expensive thing on the menu because someone else was paying.

She had to hand it to this place. They were fast. Not fast enough to make up for the off road excursion, but it could have been worse. They'd barely had time to touch the shrimp and the slimy platter of hell before the entrees arrived.

And the eating commenced, though not a lot of talking beyond "pass the cocktail sauce," and "anyone got an extra lemon?" It was a full-time job to eat such a vast quantity of food.

At one point, without discussion, Jake scraped his coleslaw onto Robbie's plate and Robbie gave Jake his hush puppies. Clearly they'd done that, or something like it, a hundred times. There was no one Hyacinth had ever had that kind of relationship with.

The gumbo and salad had been a mistake. Though she ate slowly and peeled her share of boiled shrimp, Hyacinth was long done while they were still slurping oysters and cracking crab. The table looked like a warzone.

"Are you sure you wouldn't like some of my scallops, lass?" Robbie asked.

"No, thank you. I'm full." She had to admit, he hadn't given her any trouble tonight—though come to think of it, it seemed she'd gone to dinner with him after all.

"Then let me refill your glass." He poured her another beer.

She sipped it for something to do.

Finally, Jake tore open a wet wipe and swiped it over his hands. That must mean the meal was over. Evans had stopped eating a while back and there was nothing left on Robbie's plate.

"Pass me one of those wipes, would you, Sparks? I need to clean up my hands, too."

Robbie gave her a sidelong look and grinned, but he didn't say anything. Was that a tingle Hyacinth felt in her own hands? And why was it working its way up her arms and down her spine?

The waitress appeared—a good sign. Robbie would pay the monster bill, they would all pee, and get on the road. Surely, there was nothing else between here and Cottonwood that needed exploring.

"What can I get you folks for dessert?"

Dessert? No. Surely to Lucifer not.

"I'll have that banana pudding that I had last time I was here," Robbie said.

"Me, too," Jake chimed in and reached for Evans's hand. "I can only eat your pie."

Evans beamed. "None for me." Finally someone with some sense. "But I'll have a cup of coffee." Scratch that.

"I don't want anything," Hyacinth said.

"It'll be just a few minutes," the waitress said.

"There's fresh coffee brewing and I'll send a busboy over to clear the table."

"Sounds perfect." Jake rose and pulled Evans to stand beside him. "Just enough time to take my girl for a spin." And they headed toward the dance floor.

Oh, no. Robbie was getting to his feet and grinning like he was about to bestow the Hope Diamond on her.

He extended his hand. "Dance with me, lass." Wasn't the Hope Diamond cursed?

The song pouring out of the bar room was slow and mournful, Bonnie Raitt's voice sandpaper and silk. No way was this going to happen.

At her hesitation, Robbie inclined his face the barest bit toward hers and smiled a sweet schoolboy smile.

"Come on. In the name of a truce. In the name of having a pleasant holiday."

"I can't," Hyacinth said. "Raised Baptist. Baptists don't dance." Though that wasn't her reason. She was too inhibited, too afraid she'd be clumsy and awkward.

He raised an eyebrow. "A religious conviction then?"

She shook her head; she wouldn't lie about that. "No, but I never learned."

"Ah, then." His smile widened and he took her hand. "Dancing isn't for learning. It's for doing. Every good Catholic boy knows that."

"I told you, I don't know how." But for some reason she let him draw her to her feet and lead her to the dance floor. Maybe it was the beer. Maybe it was his hand, warm and strong, and the memory of their hands together earlier. But he wasn't bulldozing her and refusing to take no for an answer. He was only coaxing her. So she went with him.

He drew her to him. "Just fall into me. I'll take you

there." Words from a storybook, but this wasn't a storybook; this was a bad idea. She was the tin man left out in the rain. "Relax, lass," he whispered. "Lay your cheek just so." When he reached to guide her head to his shoulder, he stroked her hair, sliding his hand downward until his fingers caressed her ear and his palm cupped her cheek. He barely moved the heel of his hand in a circular motion against her clenched jaw, until she allowed the tension to melt away and her face to press against his neck. Only then did he begin to dance slowly to the music, gently guiding her to move with him. It was a nice place to be. Warm. Safe. Just this side of exciting. He smelled like soap, pine, and—to be honest—beef jerky and clean sweat. She laughed a little at the thought.

"Who says a Baptist can't dance?" he teased.

She looked up at him. "Maybe it takes a Catholic to take her there."

He laughed low and sweet. "I'm going to buy you a St. Vitus medal."

"A who?"

"St. Vitus—the patron saint of dancers."

"Baptists would never have that—if they had patron saints at all."

"Catholics have a patron saint for everything. Some do double or triple duty." He sounded a little chagrined. "It's only fair to tell you that St. Vitus is also the patron saint of those with nerve afflictions. Maybe you wouldn't want that medal after all."

"We can all use all the protection we can get."

He laughed. "True enough. For a while there I thought I needed protection from you."

"Or I from you."

"You know, lass, I really did mean well this afternoon. And I am sorry I ruined the frock."

Hyacinth had never given out a lot of points for meaning well, but why take it up again? "Well, as you said, it worked out. It's over." It felt good to say that, mellowing. Mellow wasn't something she usually kept a lot of company with.

Robbie cocked his head, seeming to listen to the music. "Do you think it's true? What the lady is singing about? *Does* love have no pride?"

In Hyacinth's experience, people asked philosophical questions because they wanted to express their own opinion—not hear yours. She would just go ahead and let him get on with it.

"What do you think?"

"I don't know. That's why I asked you." That was a surprise.

She considered. "I don't think you can love something you don't have pride in. I have pride in my shop. I assume you have pride in your hockey. You seem to love it."

He shook his head. "I do, but not the same. She means she'd throw away all her pride, do anything for his love. Do you see yourself doing that?"

"*Anything* covers a lot of ground. I'm not likely to rob a bank, or love someone who would want me to."

"Anything within reason," Robbie said.

"That can mean a lot of different things."

"Within the law, then."

She didn't know how to answer that. Truthfully, the question confused her so she asked one of her own. "Have you ever loved someone enough to do that? Throw away your pride?"

"Not even close."

"Not even as a teenager, with hormones raging?"

"I didn't need to. I had a hockey stick and dynamite slap shot. How about you?"

"Not even close."

"But I've seen it in action—the no pride," he said.

"Directed at you?"

"No, no. Thank the good Lord, not. But I had a friend since I was a boy. Leith. From the time we were tots, Kyla loved him. She wore her longing like a veil and bore her love like a cross. I used to think it was pitiful, but now I wonder. Maybe that's what real love is. Willing to do anything."

"Sounds more like obsession to me," Hyacinth said.

"I think love is more about compatibility."

He grinned. "Finding someone just like yourself? No wonder you've never been in love. There's no one like you."

Hyacinth didn't know if that was a compliment or a dig, but she let the mellow wash away the wondering. And Robbie was wrong. She had found someone she'd been completely compatible with—twice, in fact. Chris and Sean. She thought of them as the Could've Been Maybes. Same goals, same attention to detail, same outlook on life—but she'd gotten bored with Sean and too busy for Chris. She didn't want to talk about that.

"So this Leith and Kyra—did they have a happily ever after?"

Robbie shrugged. "After a fashion. He married Finola. They seem content. Kyla took the veil."

"What? She literally became a nun?"

"She did."

"Seems a bit dramatic, don't you think?"

"Who knows? Maybe she was meant for that all along, which is why she longed for someone out of her reach."

"Why was he out of her reach? What was wrong with her?"

"Nothing, but Leith didn't return her feelings. She scared him. To be loved like that is a hard job, I'd wager."

And with that he tightened his arms around her and brushed his cheek against her forehead. The conversation was over and they melted into each other, and the tingle in her became a hum. She could have stayed like that for a long time.

Except the song abruptly ended, and was immediately replaced with the loud first strains of "Uptown Funk." Jarred back to reality, panic shot through Hyacinth. "I really can't do that!" She gestured to the couples around them who had broken apart and began to dance in fast rhythmic steps.

Robbie circled her shoulders with his arm. "You don't have to, lass. Maybe after you have your medal?" He led her away. "Come on. I'll give you some of my banana pudding."

They didn't speak any more about love, compatibility, and pride, but she had the feeling they'd been exploring something neither of them knew a thing about.

It was way past midnight when they pulled into the circle drive in front of the big brick house where Evans had grown up, but every light was on.

Robbie stretched his legs and yawned. They had driven though the little town of Cottonwood, but now they were in the middle of nowhere, surrounded by fallow fields. The plan was to leave the women off here and then for Robbie and Jake to carry on to the Champagne farm, just a mile or so up the road. Robbie and Hyacinth had gone to sleep a while back. Robbie gently shook her shoulder.

"What?" She jerked her head up.

"We're here. I didn't think you'd want Evans's parents to catch you sleeping."

"I wasn't asleep."

There was no time to reply, but Robbie didn't want to anyway. Things seemed to have settled between the two of them and he didn't want to argue with her anymore. What he really wanted to do was smell her hair again, like he had when they'd danced, and press her against him just so.

Before Jake cut the engine, the front door opened and Keith and Anna-Blair Pemberton stepped out. Much happy noise and hugging ensued—Robbie the recipient of some of it himself, as he'd met the couple when they'd come to Laurel Springs for a Yellowhammer game. It was nice. He also came from a family of huggers and he missed it.

"Now," Anna-Blair said once the hugging was over. "Does anyone want a snack or something to drink?"

They all declined. "I'm saving up for tomorrow," Jake said. "Robbie and I will be back over early with Dad. Gotta get those turkey fryers cranked up."

"Great," Keith said. "We need to move the tables from the barn to the backyard. Anna-Blair is determined to have our Thanksgiving outside."

"If," Anna-Blair said, "the weather is good to us and I think it will be."

"It's kind of you to have me for your holiday meal," Robbie said.

"Our pleasure," Anna-Blair said. "Jake and Robbie, if you'll get the girls' things and take them up, Keith and I will take Evie's pies to the kitchen. Hyacinth, you're in the rose room at the top of the stairs on the left, across the hall from Evie. Let me know if you need anything."

Fat chance of that. If the weight of her varied and numerous bags was any indication, she'd brought everything she owned—and maybe some stuff she'd borrowed and stolen.

Robbie and Hyacinth left Evie and Jake fiddling with pies and went inside.

"Lead on," Robbie said. Watching her jeans-clad bottom bounce up the stairs in front of him was not an unpleasant task.

"First door on the left," Hyacinth murmured to herself and entered the room. "I guess this is it."

"Pretty fancy." He put her things on the bench at the end of the tall canopied bed. The walls were pinkish—rose, he guessed—and there was a velvet couch and a lot of shiny crystal stuff on the dresser.

"Says he who grew up in a castle." She put the monogrammed canvas bag she carried on the couch. He would have given a lot to know what all she had brought and why she needed it.

"We just live above the shop. The public rooms are fit for company, to be sure. Where we sleep and take our tea are not nearly as grand as this. Besides"—he grinned at her—"it's just a wee castle."

"Not that wee." She pushed her hair off her face. "I googled it."

"You did?" He wouldn't have thought she'd be that interested in his family's doings.

The corners of her mouth turned down and she swallowed. "I didn't believe you. I was checking out your story." She laughed a strained little laugh. "But there you were. Standing in front of your 'wee' castle with your not so 'wee' family. All matching." She smiled sheepishly.

He hated having his word questioned and he waited for the anger to set in, but it didn't. He supposed it was because there was something sad and apologetic in her manner. And she hadn't had to tell him. What had happened to her to make her question everything that came her way?

"We all have faults, lass," he said quietly. "I've got a lion's share. But I'm not a liar."

She nodded and abruptly changed the subject. "You and Jake are close."

"Ever since our rookie year with the Sound. We hit it off straight away. He took care of me when I got hurt and brought me to his family home for holidays. I like to think I was of some help to him during his divorce. I have seven sisters, but never a brother until Jake."

"Do you think he and Evans will get married?"

"Absolutely. Without a doubt."

She smiled, excited like.

"After all," he rushed on. "Almost everyone does. Now, whether they marry each other—we'll have to wait and see about that, won't we?"

"Oh, you!" She half closed her eyes, looked toward the ceiling, and shook her head. "You knew what I meant." She picked up a small pillow from the bed. He was certain she was going to fling it at him but, at the last moment, she laid it back on the bed. "Better leave that alone. Looks like it was probably embroidered by somebody who's long dead."

"Right. Wouldn't want any ghosties to haunt you tonight."

"Thank you for bringing my things up." She stepped toward the door and put her hand on the crystal knob.

"My pleasure," he responded to her exit line. "See you tomorrow."

He didn't plan it, but natural as could be, he encircled her shoulders with one arm, her waist with the other, and brought her to him. She went rigid, but then almost immediately relaxed. It felt like she belonged there.

He wanted to kiss her—had ever since he'd held her on the dance floor, maybe before. But, even more, he didn't want to ruin this moment. It was a given that he liked sex—who didn't? But he also liked kissing, hand-holding, sweet embraces—like this one.

A kiss would have meant nothing to most of the women he'd known lately—to him either. But this was different. He got the feeling that kisses would matter to Hyacinth, and he doubted if she gave them out like candy tossed from a parade float. A kiss with her might mean something to him, too. Maybe too much.

This woman had some fire in her, for sure. She could burn him to nothing and he'd thank her for the pleasure of it all. But, make the wrong move, and she was all too capable of screaming the house down and beating the hell out of him with one of her many travel bags.

Nobody needed that.

So he didn't tilt her face up and lower his mouth to hers, like he wanted. He did, however, let his hand drift up, his fingers trailing her neck before they settled in to stroke her cheek. She sighed and smiled. He hadn't seen that smile many times and maybe never directed at him. He saved the image and packed it away.

"Goodnight, lass." He loosened his hold on her.

"That was a nice moment, don't you think?" Maybe there could be more of them.

She didn't say yes, but she didn't say no. She just widened her eyes and reached for the crystal doorknob again. "Thank you for carrying my things up," she repeated, all prim and proper like. But she had been thinking about a kiss, too—at least he thought so. Hard to read, this one was.

He dropped a little peck on her temple. "Sweet dreams."

He had to pause outside her door to give himself a chance to settle down before he was fit to be seen in polite company.

Then, he whistled a little tune as he bounded down the steps in search of Jake.

Chapter Four

When she woke the next morning, Hyacinth's first thought was of what had passed between her and Robbie last night—or maybe it was just a continuation of the thoughts she'd fallen asleep with, after she'd *finally* gone to sleep.

What in the ever loving hell had come over her?

She'd, one, danced with him, when she'd never danced a step in her life. Two. Not only eaten half his banana pudding, but let him feed it to her. Three. Almost kissed him last night.

How had she—Hyacinth Dawson, who never deviated from the plan—gone from hoping to never see him again to wanting to kiss him?

She actually knew the answer to that. It had been a long time since she'd dated anyone. She hadn't even wanted to. So why now and why Robbie McTavish, of all people, those fabulous legs notwithstanding?

She was no virgin, but she hadn't been around the block all that much either. One of her long-term goals was a husband and two children. While she wasn't exactly actively seeking that yet, she considered it a waste of time to dabble with a man who was not husband material— and Robbie definitely was not. Not even boyfriend material. No. She knew exactly the qualities she wanted in a man: goal-oriented, organized, neat, punctual, willing to be an equal partner in child-rearing and home maintenance, respectful of her career because she was *never* giving it up or letting it take second place to his.

And yet...yet. The Could've Been Maybes—Chris, and before him, Sean—had been all those things, but they hadn't clicked.

But with Robbie, there was something there, something different. He was a flirt, but that was nothing new. She'd been flirted with, though she wasn't very good at returning it.

Evans and Ava Grace were always telling her to loosen up. Even Claire hinted at it. But there was never enough time—bridal appointments, alterations, keeping up with the market. Those were the important things, the things that made her life work. One success at a time. Flirtation and uncomplicated fun hardly seemed worth the time.

But then it hit her—what was different. Robbie made her feel special. She hadn't felt special in a very long time and never to a man. Was she an idiot to bask in it, to hope for more? Maybe. But she understood the power of that feeling. No bride ever walked out of a bridal shop with a dress without feeling special. And she gave it to them. She never lied, but she found a way to make every one of them feel exceptional.

What was wrong with wanting a little of that for herself?

She wasn't looking for serious, let alone long term, but if he asked her to dinner again, she would go. She might even ask him.

Deep thoughts for Thanksgiving morning.

Mother of pearl! *Was* it still morning? Had she slept until noon in somebody else's house? She grabbed her phone from the bedside table. Almost nine o'clock. Was she late? And if so, late for what? Breakfast? Onion chopping? Table toting? She had no way of knowing. She had intended to go downstairs last night, give Anna-Blair her hostess gift, and ask about today's schedule. But after Robbie had left, all she'd been able to do was sink down on the bed and sit there like a fool until Evans and Anna-Blair knocked on her door to find out if she needed anything. Even then, she'd been so distracted she hadn't asked.

With any luck Evans would still be in her room. Hyacinth slipped on her robe and stepped across the hall. *No* luck. Evans's door was open, the room was empty, the bed made. Probably had been made for hours. She would text her and see if she could get some direction.

Then she caught sight of Evans's phone, plugged into the charger on the bedside table. Nothing to do but get dressed and go downstairs, but she didn't even know the dress code—something she'd intended to ask Evans last night before she'd gone brain dead.

But wait. As she was crossing the hall back to her room she noticed the door on the landing. It would lead to the balcony across the front of the house. She'd take a peep. Maybe someone would be milling around and she could at least get an idea about what people were wearing.

She heard the voices before she saw anyone.

"You do know you can buy nuts already shelled, don't you? In a bag at the grocer's." No mistaking that Scottish brogue.

Female laughter. "I've been saying that for years.

Mama says we aren't buying pecans as long as we've got pecan trees."

A little chill went through Hyacinth as she stepped to look over the rail where Robbie and a blonde—maybe Jake's sister—were sitting on the steps shelling pecans. They had their backs to her, but she could see that Robbie was wearing the kilt she'd washed, mended, and ironed.

He ate the pecan that he'd just shelled.

"Stop it, Robbie!" The blonde playfully slapped at him. They were sitting close enough together that she didn't have to reach far for that slap. "If you don't stop eating half of what you shell, we'll never get enough for the sweet potato casserole."

He caught her hand. "If you weren't so worried about ruining your manicure, lass, we'd have had enough long ago."

Lass.

Then he gave her a one-armed hug—like he'd given Hyacinth as they were leaving the dance floor last night.

She shattered.

Which made no sense. It wasn't much of a hug and *lass* wasn't his own private term of endearment for her. He'd called those girls at Trousseau yesterday *lass* and it hadn't bothered her. But that was before, before she'd gotten confused and thought Robbie had treated her differently—special.

But she wasn't confused anymore. She'd been a fool—an affection starved fool, picking up crumbs from a man who scattered them like Hansel in a spooky forest.

Well. This was productive in more ways than one. Robbie was no help in the dress code department, but the girl wore black leggings and a tunic the color of an orange autumn leaf. Hyacinth could work with that.

The girl stood up. She was tall, thin, and long-legged. She would be.

"I'll be right back. I'm going to get a refill on my coffee. Do you want some?"

Hyacinth ducked back inside before she could be discovered. She'd never know if Robbie wanted coffee.

Not that she cared.

Thanksgiving in Mississippi wasn't very much different from a wedding day at Wyndloch. The work started early and, Robbie suspected, would go late. Not that he minded overmuch. Jake's family treated him like family.

He, Jake, and Jake's dad, Marc, had started the day by carting crates of dishes and food to the Pemberton house, and the chores hadn't let up for hours.

Though he'd kept his eyes peeled, Hyacinth had not been around for any of this.

Now he was on the front porch with Jake's sister Addison, shelling pecans.

"That's enough," Addison pronounced, putting aside her nutcracker.

"Is it?" He glanced at the bucket that was still half full of unshelled nuts. "There are still nuts to be shelled."

"Not by us." She stood up. "Mama said four cups and we've got at least that. Let's go inside and see what's on the buffet. I haven't had anything to eat this morning."

"You're the boss." He had eaten, but he'd done a lot of hauling of tables, benches, and table decorations since then. He could use a wee bite of something. Besides, surely Hyacinth was inside.

But when they entered the Pembertons' dining room, only Jake and Evie were sitting at the long shiny table. The house smelled like all kinds of good things to eat—onions, cinnamon, and bread. Maybe Hyacinth was in the kitchen tending to some of that—bossing people around.

Evie looked up. "Ah, there you are."

Robbie thought she was talking to him and he was about to answer when he heard Hyacinth's voice behind him.

"I'm sorry. I overslept."

He turned to get a look. No Hogwarts clothes today. She wore rust-colored pants and a silky brown blouse—which he thought was a lot smarter than the sweaters Evie and Addison wore. It was already muggy out there.

"Good morning, lass."

She did not return his smile, though her mouth did tighten up like she was trying to fake one.

"Morning." She cast her eyes down. Well, hell. He had hoped for a bit of warmth. But maybe it wasn't personal. Maybe she wasn't a morning person.

"I didn't mean to sleep so late," Hyacinth said.

"You're good." Evie got up, moved to the buffet, and filled a coffee cup from a silver pot. "Nothing to get up for. I'm glad you got some rest." She set the coffee cup at the place on the other side of Jake and moved the sugar and creamer within reach. "We don't eat much on Thanksgiving morning. There's fruit and muffins here, but I'll be glad to make you some eggs if you want them."

"No, no. I don't need eggs." Hyacinth sat down and reached for the cream. "I'll start with the coffee. I might get a muffin later."

Robbie had intended to get a muffin himself, but he quickly moved to sit at the end of the table next to Hyacinth.

"Hi. I'm Addison." Jake's sister advanced on Hyacinth and stuck her hand out like a politician gathering votes. "So pleased to meet you, Hyacinth."

"Hello," Hyacinth said.

"I'm sorry." Evans slapped her hands to her cheeks. "Where is my head?"

"On my brother, apparently," Addison said wryly.

"And that's the way I like it." Jake took Evans's hand, pulled her in for a brief kiss, and then guided her back to sit beside him.

"I'm going to take these pecans to the kitchen and get a yogurt," Addison said. "Anybody else want one?"

"Me," Jake said. "Peach, if there is any."

"Gotcha." And Addison drifted through the swinging door to rifle through the refrigerator, just like it was her own house. That was nice. He wouldn't do it here, but felt at home like that at the Champagnes'. "Where is everybody?" Hyacinth asked. "Seems quiet."

"Lunch is at two," Evans said. "Most everyone will come then, but my sisters and their families will be here in about an hour. My brothers-in-law can't miss the macho turkey frying. I guess Dad and Marc are out setting up the fryers." She looked at Jake for verification.

Jake looked up from his iPad. "Down by the barn. And they're icing down the beer. We start drinking early in the Delta."

Evans went on. "Mama, Christine, and Miss Althea—Jake and Addison's nana—are out setting the tables."

"Should we go help them?" Hyacinth half rose from her chair.

"No," Evans said. "They don't trust us with their McCarty pottery."

"It's the decorating they don't trust us with," Addison breezed back in holding three containers of yogurt, with a newspaper under her arm. "They trust us with the dishes well enough when it's cleanup time." She handed two of the yogurts to Jake and sat down across from Hyacinth.

Evans laughed. "True. Can't throw those pumpkins and dried corn on just any which way."

"I feel like I should do something to help," Hyacinth said.

"Don't worry about it. You'll get your chance later." Addison opened the newspaper. "Anybody want part of the Black Friday ads?"

"No, thanks," Evans said. "We have to leave early. The guys have practice and Hyacinth and I have Black Fridays of our own to get back to."

Robbie laid a hand on Hyacinth's arm, glad for the chance to touch her. "I'm going to get one of those muffins, lass. Can I bring you one?"

She looked at his hand on her arm then back at his face. "Sure. And—"

"Oh, hell," Jake said almost under his breath.

Everyone looked his way.

"What?" Addison asked.

"Give me a second…" He scrolled his iPad screen, frowned, and looked up at Robbie. "Looks like you made *The Face Off Grapevine*."

Holy family and all the wise men! "That can't be right! I haven't done anything…lately." Had he? On the day he'd taken over as head coach, Nickolai Glazov had sworn that Robbie's and Jake's Wild Ass Twin days were over and they'd better not show up in a bad light on that online hockey gossip rag unless they wanted to ride the bench. "I can't think of anything—"

"Hold on," Jake said. "It might not be that bad. Everything on that site isn't about hell-raising." Then Jake began to laugh. "Is there something you forgot to tell me, Robbie? Are you getting married?"

Married? Me? No... I..." Where the hell could that even have come from? It's not like he'd even had a date lately. "What does it say?" He stretched out his hand for Jake's iPad.

"No." Jake gripped the device. "Listen. 'Is Yellowhammer forward Robbie McTavish tying the knot? We wouldn't have thought so until we ran across this video. We can't think why else the kilt-clad Scot, known for his charming and heartbreaking ways, would be prancing around a bridal boutique giving fashion advice to a bride-to-be, since he has no relatives in this country. The jury is still out, but take a look and decide for yourself. Hey, Robbie! You're not supposed to see her in the dress before the wedding.'"

Annoying, but still, not so bad. No ice girls, debauchery, or public drunkenness involved—nothing that should get him benched.

"Prance," he said. "I don't prance."

He looked around the table. Addison was biting her lip and looking down—clearly trying hard not to laugh. Evans was wide-eyed with her hand over her mouth.

"This was in Trousseau, I take it?"

"Aye," Robbie said. "I dropped in for a wee visit. Yesterday." He looked at Hyacinth, whose expression was mostly neutral, but a little grim around the edges.

"There's a video?"

"One of the bridesmaids was recording, I noticed, but I never thought—" She trailed off and tightened her jaw.

Tension crept through the room and everyone was quiet for a beat.

Hyacinth gestured to the iPad. "No point in waiting. Let's see it."

Jake turned the iPad where everyone could see and hit play.

That bridesmaid was no cinematographer, that was for sure. The picture was shaky, the sound quality bad. The video started when he was waving his shoe in the air, demonstrating the light-up soles. She'd gotten the part where Hyacinth had demanded that Robbie follow her, but the girl hadn't left the sofa and pursued them around the corner—so she hadn't gotten the actual soling of the gown, a good job of that, too. There was no doubt that would have sent Hyacinth into orbit. He cut his eyes without moving his head so she wouldn't see him checking her reaction. She looked calm—even took a sip of her coffee.

Next onscreen was Robbie talking to Daisy about how she wanted to look like a flapper girl, and Gatsby, and all that. Then quick as Thor throwing his hammer, Hyacinth went out of her mind, yelling at him not to touch Daisy. She must have been pretty loud because it came across clear. Then there was the hand washing bit. And there was a moment—barely that—when they stood looking at each other in a certain way.

Ah, here came the part that might make it look like he was the groom, the way he held Daisy's hands and smiled at her. Then he was running around looking at dresses, with Hyacinth stomping after him, yelling at him that Daisy didn't want a ball gown.

He supposed he should call Miles, his agent, and have him make a statement that he was not getting married.

Now, he was showing the dress to Daisy and Hyacinth was shaking her head no, no, no. If he recalled correctly, that was one of the many times Hyacinth had tried to make him leave. Then he said the thing that had made everyone laugh. "I never miss a chance for a princess sighting. I go to Disney World twice a year for the pleasure."

It wasn't that funny, but everyone—at least Evans, Jake, and Addison—laughed like he was a rerun of *The Big Bang Theory*. He got the feeling it was laughter they'd been holding in and were relieved that there was a moment acceptable to let it out. He chanced another peep at Hyacinth. She lifted the corners of her mouth and shook her head a little, but he knew better than to think she was amused.

Next, Brad led Daisy off to try on the fairy princess dress and Robbie sat down with the mum and the girls and told them about Wyndloch. Probably because he was close by and sitting still, that got captured good and proper.

Uh-oh. Now Hyacinth was standing there, full screen, with her arms across her chest—not unlike a pissed off hockey coach—barking questions at him about Wyndloch. He could see now that she had thought he was lying.

Thank the stars in the sky that Daisy appeared wearing the dress, and everyone gathered around her to ooh and ahh.

And the video ended.

"Well, how about that?" Jake said.

Robbie said the first thing that came to his mind. "Did you see where that gossip rag showed how stupid they were? How could anyone think I was marrying Daisy when her own mum didn't know anything about my family home and business? They just threw it up there with hashtag this and hashtag that to get attention."

Again, not that funny, but more laughter.

This time Hyacinth didn't even pretend.

"Excuse me," she said. And she was gone.

"Oh, no…" Evans made to rise.

But Robbie was on his feet first. "No. Let me go."

Hyacinth took five deep breaths.

I refuse to let this get the best of me. But she was shaky, and with good reason. However, she'd never been one to overreact and she wasn't going to start now.

This was bad, but she'd seen bad before and lived to tell it. She'd live through this, too, no matter how utterly humiliated she was.

But she wanted to go home—home to Trousseau, where she could feel centered and empowered. She needed to open the doors herself in the morning and maybe do some damage control—or maybe not, depending on how many people had seen it.

Since she'd broken her rule to never go anywhere without her own car, that wasn't going to happen, but she could at least get away from her laughing friends, harum-scarum Robbie, and that iPad from hell.

When faced with the front door or the foot of the stairs that would take her to her room, the choice was easy. The stairs would only take her so far and box her in, while the door would lead to the far reaches of the earth, would take her to Tibet if that's what she decided.

Now that she stood on the front porch, she wasn't so sure. She was in the middle of nowhere, with nothing around but a manicured lawn alive with fall flowers and acres of plowed earth. Jake's giant black SUV sat in the circular driveway but, even if she had the keys, she couldn't start stealing cars—no matter how bad she wanted to go home.

She needed a place to sit and collect herself, and it wasn't going to be in one of those rocking chairs or swings on this porch that was as big as her whole house. She ran past the mums and piles of pumpkins on the steps and around the corner until she came to a little porch on the side of the house.

She would have liked a more secluded place to hide, but it was better than nothing. The backyard, where all that beer icing and table setting was going on, wouldn't do. Maybe nobody would find her here. Maybe nobody would look for her. They were probably in there watching the video again, this time laughing as much as they wanted instead of biting their lips and nervously fidgeting to keep from looking at each other.

She sank down on the steps and took out her phone.

She, on the other hand, was *not* going to watch it again—ever. All kinds of *hell*, *no* stomped through her on that subject. She didn't need to relive it to know how ridiculous, how out of control she'd looked—screeching like a banshee at Robbie, who was darting around like everybody's favorite Peter Pan in a kilt.

But she needed to know how many people had seen it. She called up *The Face Off Grapevine* and followed the link back to YouTube, praying that a hundred thirteen people and their dog had seen it.

But no.

Almost four hundred thousand views in fourteen hours.

Fourteen hours ago—when she'd been dancing with Robbie, letting him feed her banana pudding, and feeling all special. Just then the bridesmaid—or maybe Daisy herself—had been posting the video that would crash her life into a pigsty after a rainstorm. They would have tweeted it, too. Shared it on Instagram, Snapchat, and wherever else people who didn't have anything better to do went to infringe on the privacy of others and ruin their businesses.

Evans and Hyacinth would laugh at her, say she was being dramatic, but she wasn't. There was a thin line between a thriving business and a ruined one. Claire knew that, too. Trousseau was well in the black right now, because she sold wedding dresses and lots of them. But nobody was likely to come to her for a wedding dress after seeing her run around like a Keystone Cop in bad need of a nerve pill. As for *All Dressed in White*—she could forget that, no matter how good things seemed to be looking with Jake and Evans. They wanted *the unique and the elegant*.

No question that little display was unique, but about as far from elegant as a barn dance was from Buckingham Palace. Though if Jake and Evans would only act quickly, maybe it could still happen. That was the only chance she had to redeem her dignity and reputation—but it wasn't much of one. She might as well call Laurel Springs Dry Cleaning and tell them she was available to do alterations.

Don't overreact! she admonished herself. Then, with a sick feeling, she realized she wasn't. She was simply reacting to what was true.

"Hello, lass."

No, no, no. Not now. Anything but this.

He sat down beside her on the step without asking. "Are you all right?"

Her head went to a burning bush, then, to a forest fire. What she needed was Wonder Woman's golden rope. She'd strangle him with it, then lasso herself out of here onto her invisible airplane.

"Let's see, am I all right? Yes, yes, I am, in that I don't have a debilitating disease or a rattlesnake crawling up my pants leg. But I wouldn't say I'm in a very good place emotionally or mentally. In fact, I'm feeling a little punk—wondering what I'll do for a living when I have to shut Trousseau down."

"Come, now. It's not as bad as all that. Everyone gets embarrassed on the Internet from time to time."

Had she heard him right? *Everyone? Everyone?* No, I don't believe that's true. I think rich, professional hockey players who go around acting a fool do, and they have it coming. But shop owners who are just trying to earn a living and make a woman's wedding day be all she's dreamed of, as a rule, do not. Not unless a hockey player gets involved. Then she ends up the laughing stock of the whole country—not to mention her own friends."

"I don't understand why you're talking to me like this." Some of the light went out of his face. "I thought we had a moment."

"Yeah, well. We've had lots of moments, Robbie. More than we should. Most of them bad."

He looked sad, but smiled a little anyway. "Let's get you something to eat. You only had a bit of coffee. Your blood sugar is bound to be low. I'll borrow Jake's car and we'll go for a little ride—you and me. Stop and get you a snack."

Now, along with her head, the whole world was on fire. "A snack? You think low blood sugar is the reason I'm upset? That a ride will make me feel better?"

"Then tell me what I can do."

"I can't, because there's nothing to be done, but I'll tell you something else, Robbie McTavish. I *thought* I was humiliated on parents' day when I was in the fourth grade and mine came to school smelling like pot and dressed in flannel pajama pants and T-shirts. I *thought* I was humiliated when I was in design school and my instructor, who I admired, said in front of the whole class that my project was boring, predictable, and that I must have gotten my inspiration from a Lands' End catalog. But this." She waved her phone in the air. "*This* takes the cake. I'm tough. I've had to be. People say I'm singled-minded. Fine. I've had to be that, too. But I don't even know how to start picking up the pieces of this."

"Probably not that many people have seen it, and nobody you'd know. Probably only a few hockey fans."

"Do you think I'd be reacting like this if that were true? Do you think that's not the first thing I checked? It's gone viral, Robbie—big viral. I'm sure because of hashtags like *RobbieMcTavishBridalShop*, *YellowhammerHockey*, and, and… I don't know what else." She would not cry, hadn't cried in forever. She didn't do tears. Especially not in front of him.

There'd be plenty of time for tears in private later,

after she'd lost the one thing she'd ever wanted, the thing that defined her.

He closed his eyes and looked down. "I wish I could help."

"You can't. Nobody can. Why don't you go in the house and start tweeting that you're not getting married. Chop some celery with Addison. Take a selfie with her and post it."

He looked up and wrinkled his forehead. "I'm not understanding you, lass."

"No? Understand this. Don't call me *lass*. Don't try to help me. And above all else, stay away from my shop."

He looked at her for a long moment. All the color went out of his face.

He stood up, gave his head one quick nod, and walked away—without saying a word.

Chapter Five

Stung, Robbie followed the smell of frying fowl and the sound of male noise—talking, laughing, and banging stuff around. He knew from his previous visits what these men would be talking about: college football, duck hunting, the price of cotton, and their bird dogs. And—though none of it had anything to do with him—Robbie was great with that. There would be no trying to guess what was on their minds, no yelling, and no questioning his intentions. Above all, they wouldn't say things he didn't understand. Or if they did, he'd ask and they would explain.

"There's Robbie!" Marc Champagne looked up from where he was lowering a turkey into one of the three fryers. "Come on around, son. Jake, get him a beer."

Robbie entered the circle of Ole Miss red and blue folding canvas chairs. "Hello, all. Smells great."

"This is going to be some fine eating," Keith Pemberton said. "These are wild birds. I brined them for sixteen hours with bourbon and maple syrup."

Two men from different sides of the circle advanced on him, their hands out to shake.

"Yancey Mayhall," the first one said.

"And I'm York Mayhall. We're Evie's brothers-in-law."

Sure he was seeing double, Robbie blinked and shook his head. Then he realized Evie's sisters had married twins. One more bizarre thing on a bizarre day in the land of the bizarre.

"Happy to meet you." Robbie would have liked to think, at their age, that they hadn't dressed alike on purpose but, then, all these men—including Jake—were dressed pretty much the same. Ole Miss shirts and ball caps, shorts in varying shades of khaki, and leather loafers without socks. Keith Pemberton had on a wrinkled blue shirt, worn open over his T-shirt, but that was about the only difference. Though, come to think of it, Robbie didn't have much of a stone to throw, with the way his family liked to get decked out in their plaids. He supposed this was the tartan of Clan Ole Miss.

"Here you go." Jake handed him a beer.

"Thanks." Robbie uncapped it and settled into the chair next to Jake.

"Stop!" Suddenly, York Mayhall was on his feet, pointing. "Layton, Carson. Go play. You know what your mama said. No coming around frying turkeys until you're twelve."

"Can't see what it would hurt," Keith Pemberton said. "We'd watch them."

"You're not wrong." York took a drink of his beer. "But I have to live with her."

"Been there," Keith said. "Guess she doesn't remember that I managed to keep her and her sisters alive."

"This generation—too protective of their kids," Marc Champagne said. "I'd been duck hunting two years by the time I was twelve."

Then they were off—talking about how they'd roamed the fields, swam in the river, and traveled to Mars on the back of a catfish, all before they were out of diapers, with no adult supervision.

Jake leaned in. "How was Hyacinth?"

Robbie took another sip of his beer. "Madder than hell."

"Was she mad? Or was she upset and embarrassed?" What kind of question was that? "What's the difference?"

Jake laughed and shook his head. "There's a difference. Believe me."

"So all of a sudden, since you're with Evie, you're an authority on women and their moods?"

"It wasn't all of a sudden and I'm no authority. But I've learned some stuff, yeah. And I wouldn't call it a mood—not to her face."

No problem, brother. I won't be saying anything to her face. Or touching her face, or any other part of her. "It seemed like mad to me. And she blamed the whole thing on me."

"I can see that," Jake said.

"What?" Had he gone completely over to the pink side? There was a time Jake would have defended him if he'd been caught leaving Edinburgh Castle with the Honours of Scotland under his kilt. "I wasn't the one doing the filming or posting to YouTube. Do you think I like half the hockey world gossiping about how I might be getting married?"

"What possessed you to go into Hyacinth's shop, anyway?"

"I don't know." He rolled his beer bottle between his

palms. "I was at loose ends. I looked in the window and saw that girl in a dress all wrong for her, so I thought—"

"Yeah, yeah." Jake nodded. "That you'd go in and help her out."

"What's wrong with that?" Robbie demanded. "With trying to help a la—lady out."

She'd told him not to call her *lass* anymore. He couldn't fathom why, but fine.

"You tell me."

"It didn't work out so well," he admitted. "It was actually worse than the video showed."

"The hell you say. What'd you do? Set fire to the veils?"

"Close. I dropped my ice cream on a dress."

"You did what?"

"It was an accident. And Hyacinth had her part in it. If she hadn't been yelling at me, pointing here, pointing there, and stopping right in front of me..." It sounded lame even to him.

Jake laughed, though Robbie didn't get the impression he really thought it was funny.

"I can't believe she let you live."

"She may not, still. The day's not over yet. Let her catch you laughing, and you'll soon follow. She does *not* like laughing. Besides, I said I'd pay for the dress. What else can I do? There's no pleasing that woman." Though he'd come close last night, for a short while there.

Jake got a funny look on his face. "Robbie, do you *like* Hyacinth—as in, do you *want* her?"

Who the hell knew anymore? He had last night, but now, not so much. Not that it mattered. She'd made that clear enough—and that was fine. Being attracted to her made no sense anyway. She was the most confounded woman he'd ever run across and she didn't even like hockey. Maybe he wasn't really attracted. Could be that he was just lonely and he'd looked up and there she was.

But her hair did smell good.

"Do you?" Jake demanded again. "Answer me."

"Why wouldn't I?" He passed it off like joke. "I want all women."

"Then go get one of those other women."

"Why do you care?"

"Let's talk about the Bro Code."

"I know it well enough. 'Thou shalt not cast a lustful eye toward thy teammate's sister, ex-wife, ex-girlfriend...'"

"I think we need to add 'his wife's best friend.'"

"Evie's not your wife," he pointed out.

"No," Jake admitted. "Not yet. But she will be—maybe. If I can get her to have me."

Considering their conversation about this very thing last night, that was a nugget that would have interested Hyacinth. If she hadn't been so mean to him, he might have shared.

"How is it in Scotland, Robbie?" York (or was it Yancey?) asked. "Are there lots of helicopter moms, like our wives?"

He didn't know what that meant, but since he wasn't interested, he didn't ask for clarification.

"No, no. Not so much. But your wives are *very* bonny."

He hoped that was so. He had not met Evie's sisters.

Back in her room, Hyacinth knew what she ought to do—collect herself, freshen her makeup, and go act like the good guest she knew how to be.

It was the collecting herself that was the problem. She'd always believed if something worked on paper, it would work in reality—hence, all her lists, spreadsheets, and charts. She still kept a paper calendar as a backup to her electronic one, and it was a thing of beauty. It wasn't as if nothing ever went wrong. That would be too much to hope for, but it was never anything that Plan B—or occasionally Plan C—wouldn't take care of. But when Robbie McTavish was around, it was as if there were no plans. Just chaos.

Back in the yard, Robbie walking away without having the last word was a first. Though he hadn't walked so much as stalked.

And Hyacinth knew why. She'd hurt his feelings—but damn it, hadn't he had it coming? He couldn't learn when to back off. Still, a germ of regret joined the swirling halo of other complicated emotions swirling around her head.

Nothing had happened in a very long time that was so beyond her control as this.

She sank down on the velvet settee, booted up her laptop, and opened a file. Since she couldn't get home, she needed a plan—a list of steps for how to come back from this. "Begun is half done," Memaw used to say. All she had to do was begin—get the first step on paper. She typed, "How to respond when asked about the incident."

The cursor blinked, mocking her—and it was still blinking some time later when the knock came at her door.

Hyacinth closed her laptop. Might as well. She didn't even save the file. With resolve, she marched across the room. If it was Robbie, he'd better cowboy up, because she was ready for another round.

But it wasn't Robbie. "Can I come in?" Evans asked.

"Sure."

Evans shut the door behind her slowly and carefully, like she was entering a room where there was a baby sleeping—or a death watch going on. Then she went to sit on the edge of the bed across from the settee.

"I'm sorry about this morning," Hyacinth said. "And sorry I disappeared. It was...a lot. It's not like me to not pitch in and help."

"You don't need to be sorry," Evans said. "It *was* a lot. And there wasn't that much to do. Hattie and Louella did most of the prep before they got off work yesterday."

Hattie and Louella worked for Evans's and Jake's families. Hyacinth wondered idly how many people it took to run a castle—even a wee one.

"Mostly, we've only had to put things in the oven," Evans continued. "And you already know we weren't allowed to help set the tables."

"I haven't been a very good guest." She hadn't even given Anna-Blair the scented candle she'd brought for her. "Hiding out like this."

Evans swiped her hand in the air like she was shooing away a fly. "No one's thought a thing about it. The important thing is—how are you?"

Hyacinth opened her mouth to say she was fine, but what was the use? This was Evans. She took a deep breath. "I'm angry, embarrassed, and I don't know how to make this go away. I can't even imagine what Claire will say."

"I think Claire will say you shouldn't spend energy on things you can't do anything about—that it's done. And, Hyacinth, it's not like you were running around naked, cursing, and kicking puppies."

"Yeah, well. If that phone had had better audio, you might have heard some cursing. It was in my head and I wouldn't rule out that it came out my mouth."

"Did you and Robbie…argue?" Evans asked tentatively. "Today, I mean."

"Argue? Yes, I guess you could say we argued. You know what he wanted to do? Take me for a ride! And get me a snack—like a pack of peanut butter cheese crackers would set all this right."

Evans shook her head. "Men don't always know what to do, so they try to distract you with presents and food. Rides too, I guess." She paused. "This might not be the best thing to say right now, but Robbie *is* a good guy. I mean, he wouldn't have gotten up in the morning and said, 'I think I'll go cause some trouble at Trousseau today.'"

"I know that, Evans. But that's the point. He doesn't think. He just *acts*. He's like a cat! He does what he wants. How would you like it if somebody came into Crust and started adding stuff to your apple pie filling? Or making pie dough with any old butter and flour?" Evans set high store by her crusts and was particular about ingredients.

Evans shuddered a little. "I get it. I do. I would be upset, too. But I promise you, it's not as bad as it seems."

"This is going to ruin my business."

"Oh, Hyacinth, no! It's not like you to be dramatic."

She knew Evans would say that. "I'm not. I'm being realistic."

"Let me remind you of what Claire said at our last meeting. Your business is doing great, better than Crust or Heirloom. Your profits are up, even from last year, and they were good then."

"Yes. Now." She was loath to repeat Robbie, but he'd been right. "In the bridal business, reputation is everything. There's no repeat business. It's a one-shot deal. Women don't just walk down the street, see my shop, and think, 'Oh, look. How cute. I'll go in and buy a wedding dress.' They're planning a wedding. Their time is limited. They do their research and choose carefully before making an appointment. No one wants to depend on an out of control consultant to help them with the most important dress they will ever buy."

Evans nodded. "I do understand that your business is different from mine and Ava Grace's. You don't get impulse purchases like we do, but I still think it won't seem so bad tomorrow."

No. It would be every bit as bad, probably worse. But there had been enough drama and Hyacinth wasn't going to argue with Evans. She would never understand that losing Trousseau would be like losing Memaw all over again, not to mention throwing away what her grandmother had sacrificed to make sure Hyacinth went to design school. And then there was Claire's investment—and her own. Gone.

She shouldn't have sold Memaw's house. At least she would have had a roof over her head. Though she was still grieving for her grandmother when Claire's offer came, Hyacinth hadn't hesitated to sell the house to raise some capital. Memaw's spirit was more at Trousseau than it had ever been at that little clapboard house. Hyacinth could rent a place to live. If she couldn't pay the rent, she'd put a cot in her workroom.

Before her parents died, she'd slept in worse places. Once, they had lived in their ancient van for a week before going to stay with eight other people in a two bedroom apartment. Maybe she should trade her Mini Cooper for a van while she was still solvent.

That thought brought her up short. Evans was right. She had crossed over from realistic problems to melodrama. She needed to put her energy into fixing this rather than assuming the worst. How could she possibly get control of this situation if she couldn't get control of herself?

Damage control. That's what she had to do.

"You're right," Hyacinth said. "I work hard to avoid surprise, so it doesn't happen that often. I always have a plan B and a plan C—but this is like plan triple Z."

"Maybe so," Evans admitted, "but you'll find that plan and make it work. If there's anything I can do to help you, say the word. I promise I'm here for you. *Anything*."

Her words made Hyacinth feel better and she couldn't help but smile a little. That promise might come in handy.

Evans would look so scrumptious in the Giorgio Sabelli with the beaded Alençon lace and chapel length train.

Hyacinth rose. "Let's go down. It must be getting close to time for lunch. I can at least help with the drinks."

Evans looked relieved. "Give me a minute. I need to change out of this sweater. It's almost seventy degrees. Of all people, Robbie told me earlier I'd be too hot in a sweater."

Robbie McTavish, fashion consultant. What *would* they do without him?

With her luck, he'd want to help Evans choose her wedding dress. Just to be safe, Hyacinth would be sure to book Evans's appointment when the Yellowhammers were on the road.

Chapter Six

Thanksgiving lunch, which had looked like a photo shoot from *Garden & Gun*, was in the books. Hyacinth and Robbie had not spoken. She had sneaked a peek or two at him to see if he still seemed hurt, but she needn't have worried. As usual, he was having the time of his life, charming the women, laughing it up with the men, and teasing the kids—all while eating vast quantities of food. He had seemed particularly fond of the strawberry pretzel salad.

But that meal had not been the high point of the weekend. Oh, no. The Egg Bowl party—being held at the Champagne home—to watch the state rivalry football game between Ole Miss and Mississippi State—took that distinction. Having failed to think of a way to avoid it, Hyacinth was right in the middle of it.

"All right, girls, let's put the makings for the turkey sandwiches on this end of the table," Christine Champagne said. "Addison and I will put the salads, chips, dips, and other snacks at the other end. Sweets on the buffet. Drinks in the kitchen."

Hyacinth was helping Evans's sister, Layne, put out the food in the Champagnes' dining room, though how anyone could eat another bite, Hyacinth did not know.

Anna-Blair entered the room frowning at her cell phone.

"Evie still isn't answering my texts. I can't imagine where she and Jake are."

Hyacinth would have liked to know that, herself. During cleanup earlier, Jake had entered the kitchen and asked if he could steal his girl for a little while, and off they'd gone with everyone's blessing. But that was hours ago. When it was time to leave for the Champagnes', they'd loaded up into various vehicles with Anna-Blair mumbling all the while something about how she was sure they would have been back by now—from wher- ever they'd gone.

And now Hyacinth was here. Regardless of how warm and welcoming these people were—and no one could deny that they were that—she was a stranger in a strange land, with the only person she knew much beyond nodding acquaintance refusing to look at, let alone speak to her.

"Christine," Anna-Blair said, "you haven't heard back from Jake?"

Christine pulled her phone out of her pocket and checked it. "No. Not yet."

"Mama, don't worry about it." Layne arranged sliced cheese on a platter. "They're fine. They'll be here by kickoff."

"I just wish I knew where they were."

"I don't know *where* they are," Layne said out of the side of her mouth to Hyacinth in a little singsong voice, "but I bet I know what they're doing. No bed sharing in the Cottonwood, Mississippi. Been there."

"What did you say, Layne?" Anna-Blair asked.

"Nothing! Just how kickoff is important to them."

"If they're going to make that," Christine said, "they haven't got long. About twelve minutes."

"Really? That close?" Layne's head snapped up.

"That's plenty of cheese." She started closing up the deli bags of Swiss, cheddar, and provolone.

"Go ahead," Hyacinth said. "I'll finish up here." There were still pickles and condiments to put out. Maybe if she dawdled over the mustard long enough she could slip off to another room and avoid the ball-game entirely.

No such luck. These people were too well-mannered.

"Come on, Hyacinth!" Addison handed her a glass of wine and slipped an arm around her. "You don't want to miss this."

She did, in fact, though she appreciated Addison's kindness. There was nothing to do but follow Addison into the big cave of a room that seemed to have been designed for watching football. Hyacinth had never seen so many squishy chairs and sofas in one room or a television that big. It was even bigger than the one at Ava Grace's house. The pregame show was winding down.

Robbie sat on the floor at Marc Champagne's feet with Jake's teenage cousins, Adam and Nicole. They were having quite the high old time. From where she stood, it was impossible to tell what they were laughing about, but clearly Robbie was driving the fun bus.

Unless she missed her guess, Nicole had a crush on Robbie.

But didn't someone always? Hadn't she come close herself?

"Hyacinth, Addison," Jake's grandmother called from where she sat in the middle of a loveseat like a queen on her throne. "Come sit with me."

Hyacinth relaxed and smiled. Miss Althea was a bit eccentric, but she was the kind who made it her business to make sure everyone felt at home. She was the soul of propriety, but she wasn't the sort to let rules interfere with what she wanted to do. Before lunch, she'd circulated with a basket and taken everyone's cell phone, only returning them when the last bite of dessert had been eaten. As far as Hyacinth could tell, no one had argued with her.

Hyacinth certainly hadn't.

The petite, elegant woman was still dressed in the moss green pants and blouse she'd worn earlier. Unlike earlier, she was wearing a hat—a little felt bowler. It was the only hat in the house since all the men had removed their baseball caps inside.

"Are those real flowers on her hat?" Hyacinth whispered.

"Yes," Addison said. "That's a thing she does—takes her hats to the Flower Box to have them decorated for important occasions."

By now, they'd reached the loveseat-throne. "I like your hat," Hyacinth said. "And the flowers."

"White asters—the Omega Beta Gamma flower." She touched the button on her lapel imprinted with Greek sorority letters and the words Hotty Toddy. "I wear them for every Egg Bowl game. I always have, ever since we won the game in overtime my sophomore year at Ole Miss. Anything goes these days, I suppose, but there was a time when a woman wasn't supposed to wear a hat at night, but I did it even then. Some things are more important than the rules, don't you think?"

"Of course." Hyacinth settled in beside her.

"I suppose you're an Alabama fan?" Miss Althea asked.

"My grandmother certainly was."

"As long as you're not a Mississippi State fan." Miss Althea patted her arm.

"I don't have time to follow football." The instant it was out of her mouth Hyacinth knew from the looks on Miss Althea's and Addison's faces that she'd said the only thing worse than "Hail State." They wouldn't have liked that, but they would have at least understood it.

Worse and worse.

"It's time!" Keith Pemberton called out. "Coin toss." And in that instant two cell phones rang, simultaneously.

One of those twin men groaned. "Who would be calling *now*?"

Anna-Blair was on her feet. "It's Evie!"

Christine also rose. "And Jake." And they headed out of the room.

No one seemed concerned and turned back to the television where football players were lining up, kicking, and running. From the response in the room, whatever happened must have been good for Ole Miss.

Then Anna-Blair and Christine stole back into the room—both wide-eyed, both pale, both looking shell-shocked. And they were holding hands.

Dread covered the room like a creeping black cloud. Hyacinth could smell the fear—smell it on herself. Maybe it hadn't been Evans and Jake calling at all; maybe it was whoever had found their phones in some horrible wreckage calling their in-case-of-emergency contacts.

"Mama!" Ellis cried out.

Keith stood and took a step toward Anna-Blair. "Evie?"

Marc was right behind him. He took Christine by the shoulders. "Christine? What has happened to my boy?"

Christine seemed to snap out of it, to a degree. "Oh! No, not what you think. He's all right…they're all right."

Sounds of relief resonated through the room and Hyacinth felt it to her core. Beside her, Althea Champagne wiped her eyes and Addison covered her face with her hands.

Then Anna-Blair spoke before anyone had time to wonder what had caused their reactions.

"Jake and Evie are halfway back to Alabama. They have eloped."

Everyone started talking at once.

Well, not everyone.

Caught up in a swirling tornado of fear that Evans was dead, blessed relief that she wasn't, and the horror of her *All Dressed in White* dream burning to the ground, Hyacinth couldn't have spoken if she'd tried.

"Married! On *Thanksgiving?*" Layne's voice overtook the other voices in the room and the sounds of football. "You can't get married on Thanksgiving. Where would you even go? You have to have a license."

Had Robbie known this? Known it when they'd talked last night? Hyacinth sneaked a peep at him. No. He looked as surprised as she felt.

"They aren't married yet," Anna-Blair said.

"What did you say, Anna-Blair?" Jake's aunt Olivia asked.

Anna-Blair let out a frustrated sigh. "Will somebody mute that television?" At last, something that was more important to these people than the Egg Bowl. "I said, they're not married yet. They're going to the courthouse first thing in the morning."

"Courthouse!" Ellis exploded. "She can't go to the courthouse. We need to go." She jumped to her feet. "We've got to talk some sense into her. Put a stop to this. Have they even got any rings?"

"Hey!" Addison jumped to her feet. "That's my brother you're talking about and he loves her. And she's always loved him. We all know that."

"No, Addison," Ellis said. "I don't want to *stop* it. I want to put it off. You know, so we can—"

"Her mind's made up," Anna-Blair interrupted.

"And so is his," Christine put in. "Apparently, they went to get tamales, but decided to go back to Alabama and get married instead."

"That makes a whole hell of a lot of sense," one of those twin brothers-in-law said. "What do you want to do, Evie? Get a tamale, or go get married?" "Well, Jake, a tamale sounds mighty good, but I believe I'll take the wedding. We'll get tamales next time.'"

"Shut up, Yancey," Layne said.

"I tried to talk to her about a real wedding." Anna-Blair looked dazed. "Flowers...a band...all the nice things. She said she doesn't want all that—she wants to get married. Now. And you know how she is once she decides."

"I guess I owe her ten thousand dollars," Keith Pemberton said. He didn't seem overly concerned. "That's what I offered Ellis and Layne to elope."

"What?" the other twin said. "We could have had ten thousand dollars?"

Anna-Blair gave Keith the stink eye. "You haven't saved any money yet. She did agree to a reception, a party. Sometime when we can work it around Jake's schedule. Maybe when the season ends. She even said she'd wear a wedding dress." She whirled around and met Hyacinth's eyes. "Hyacinth!"

"Yes?" *Hyacinth reporting for duty!*

"Can you start looking for a dress for Evie? Something simple, but not too simple. Short—though not really short. You know what I mean. Tea length—or maybe waltz. Not one of those awful high lows. No veil, of course. But something for her hair. I don't know…"

No veil. No Giorgio Sabelli with beaded Alençon lace and chapel length train. No *All Dressed in White*. No coming back from utter humiliation. She vaguely wondered if *All Dressed in White* might be interested in an after-fact party dress. But she knew the answer. That was grasping at straws.

"Maybe a tasteful little jeweled headband—though not a tiara," Anna-Blair carried on.

"Yes, of course," Hyacinth replied in a perfectly normal voice, as if she weren't going to have to start taking in sewing like Memaw had done. "We'll find something pretty."

"I think we should go anyway," Layne said firmly. "If they're determined to get married at the courthouse, fine, but we should be there." She got to her feet, like she was going right then.

It only then occurred to Hyacinth that she had no way home. Maybe they *would* go tonight. She could hitch a ride and be there to open Trousseau in the morning.

"I don't know," Christine said. "I told Jake we'd come and he insisted that we not. But I'm not so sure."

"I think Layne's right," Anna-Blair said. "My baby

is marrying my godson. How can I miss that? Keith, don't you think we should go?"

Was it Hyacinth's imagination or did Keith Pemberton look longingly at the television before answering?

"Whatever you think, Anna-Blair."

"I want to go!" Nicole piped up.

"Hush, Nicole," Aunt Olivia said. "This isn't our business."

"But are we going? If they go?" the girl persisted.

"I don't know."

"I want to ride with Robbie." That child was truly obnoxious.

"Here's the thing, lass." There was some amusement in his voice. "Robbie's got no way to give you a ride. Seems I lost my own way back to Laurel Springs." He didn't even care. He wouldn't. Everything was one great big adventure for him, and his favorite part was seeing what would happen.

"Oh, that," Christine said. "Jake said to lend you and Hyacinth a company vehicle in the morning."

Hyacinth wondered if they could spare two. Not that she'd really ask. Riding back with Robbie would be no picnic, but maybe she wouldn't have to. If there was a whole caravan headed east, surely there'd be room for her in another car.

"I don't know why they wouldn't want us there," Hyacinth wasn't sure who said that.

Marc Champagne asked, "If we wait until morning, what time would we have to leave?" Then he looked back at the silent TV.

More voices—so many that it was hard to tell who was saying what. Some were calculating the time. Others were saying no, it had to be tonight. Layne and Ellis seemed to be discussing leaving the kids with their husbands and riding to Alabama with Keith and Anna-Blair. That would be a full vehicle.

Althea Champagne got to her feet. "Silence!"

Miraculously, everyone heard her and obeyed.

"First, is there anyone here who objects to this marriage? No. I didn't think so. The only reason to hie off to Alabama would be to stop this wedding, and we aren't going to do that. Jake and Evie are not two sixteen-year-olds running on hormones and stupidity. They're two adults who decided to get married. It's not that they don't want us there—they just don't want to fool with us right now. That's all right. They're going to have to fool with us for the rest of their lives. They'll barely have time to get married before Jake has to be at practice. There'd be no time for brunch, lunch, champagne, and confetti—which you know you'd all want to do." She stopped and looked around the room. "Agreed? Good." She sat back down. "Now someone put the game back on."

Hyacinth had had all she could stand. She was done with football, and done with Thanksgiving, done with the Delta.

Unfortunately, it looked like she wasn't as done with Robbie as she'd hoped—not if she intended to go home tonight. And she did. She'd even worked out how.

Jake was on the matrimony trail. Robbie hadn't seen that coming—at least not this quick. But, good for him. That didn't mean Robbie wasn't going to give the new groom hell for leaving him stranded in Mississippi, but he was happy for him.

"I wanted to go," Nicole said.

"Did you?" Robbie teased. "I couldn't tell. Maybe you can come over for a Yellowhammer game soon. Adam, we could knock a puck around—you, Jake, and me. Maybe a couple of the other guys."

"That would be great!" the boy said.

"How about me?" Nicole asked. "I can skate. I want you to skate with me."

How to answer that? Clearly the crush the lass had on him was only that, and harmless, but a fellow didn't want to encourage her—or hurt her feelings.

As he pondered that, who should appear behind Nicole like a demon rising from hell but Hyacinth? She pursed her lips, waved at him, and jerked her head for him to follow her.

Why not? He could use an out here—besides, he was curious at what manner of torment she was going to rain down on him now.

"Excuse me." He rose from the floor and followed her into the dining room.

She whirled around and widened those whisky-colored eyes. "I want to go home."

"Aye. I guess you'll have to suffer me to get there."

Even after all that had happened, she had eyes that would make a man want to jump on a stage and sing "Brown Eyed Girl." He didn't need to see that right now. He turned away from her and studied the food on the table. "You heard Christine. They'll fix us up with a vehicle in the morning. I'll pick you up early, like we planned to begin with." He took a chip and dipped it into some kind of cheesy tomato concoction. It was spicier than he'd expected.

"No. I want to go tonight. Right now—so I can be there

to open my shop in the morning. Robbie? Are you listening to me? Don't go down a bunny trail. Look at me!"

He did, but he took his time about it, wrapping a morsel of turkey with a slice of cheese and popping it in his mouth first.

"I thought you were set on being there by noon, for some appointment."

"That was *before*," she said. "Before I became a video star buffoon."

He wished she'd close those eyes. They looked panicked and it was hard not to feel a bit sorry for her—not that he could do anything about what she wanted. It wasn't like he had a magic carpet he could toss her on and command, "To Laurel Springs, Shaggy!"

"Even if you could leave—and you can't—what excuse do you think you would offer for leaving early?"

At that moment a cheer went up from the media room. "You hear that? They don't care. Besides, I'll tell the truth—that I need to be there for my staff, to do damage control and to show that I'm not hiding out, humiliated."

Her face turned pink. Whether she ought to be or not, she was humiliated. He had to admire that she was willing to meet it head-on.

"So I have to go."

"It's a long walk. I wager I'll beat you back to Laurel Springs." He wandered over to the buffet and studied the pies. He'd had pumpkin at lunch, but the pecan looked good.

Hyacinth followed. He could smell her right behind him—like flowers, but not the heavy, sickening sweet kind. Light and pleasant. Like her hair had smelled when they danced.

"Do you want some pie?" he asked.

"No. I want you to turn around and look at me—take me seriously."

He turned. "I do that. There's no more serious person to ever put shoe leather to earth. There's no other way to take you. I just don't know what you think I can do about what you want."

She took a deep breath and lowered her eyes. "I want you to take me to the airport. I'm sure the Champagnes will lend us a vehicle tonight, but I don't want to ask any of them to take me. I thought of an Uber, but we're in the middle of nowhere. So, yeah." She raised her face to meet his eyes. "It has to be you."

"Hmm. That's interesting. But, how can I? I've been asked not to help you."

She looked sheepish. Good. Maybe she'd think next time before she opened her mouth and said nasty, mean things.

"I was upset when I said that."

"Ah, so you *do* want me to help you?" Damn it, she was going to say it.

"No. Well, yes. But only this. These aren't ordinary circumstances."

"The circumstances are never ordinary, Hyacinth, when you need help. Anyway, you plan to fly back? Land at the airport with no car? Have to take an Uber or call someone to fetch you?"

"Not flying. I want to go to the airport to rent a car, so I can drive back."

"Tonight? Alone?" Not happening. "I can't let you do that."

"*Let me*? You can't *let* me? Who are you to let me do something or not?"

No one. He knew that, but it still wasn't going to happen. He read the papers. Things happened on the road, especially to women traveling alone—flat tires, kidnappings, murders. His da's voice echoed in his head. *"We take care of our women, son. Watch after them. Keep them safe."* Hyacinth wasn't his, but still. None of that was going to happen to her, not on his watch.

"All right," he said. "But not to the airport. If you're determined to go tonight—"

"I am."

"Then I'll arrange with Marc for a car and we'll both be going tonight."

She looked skeptical, but she nodded. "Thank you. I'll go make my apologies to Anna-Blair."

"Hold up there a minute, Hyacinth."

"What?"

"I've no mind to interrupt that ballgame to ask Marc for a favor. It'll wait until halftime. I suggest you speak with Anna-Blair then, too."

She grimaced. "How long will that be?"

"I'd say an hour. Maybe a bit more."

She opened her mouth, but then closed it again. He wasn't proud of it, but then there was some satisfaction there.

"Sure you don't want some of this?" He sliced himself a slab of pecan and then added a bit of apple, too. It was going to be a long night.

Chapter Seven

Back at the Pembertons' house, Robbie lifted Hyacinth's bags into the back of the white SUV with Champagne Cotton Brokers painted on the side.

"I'll take the key and put it back in the hiding place," he said.

Hyacinth hesitated. She should do it herself. After saying she hated to see Hyacinth go, but that she certainly understood, Anna-Blair had told Hyacinth where the key was hidden and then went back to watch the second half of the game. Hyacinth wouldn't want Anna-Blair to come home and find the key in the wrong place. On the other hand, she intended to drive, and it would be better if she could get behind the wheel without any discussion with Robbie. Besides, she could watch from here to make sure he did it right.

"Under the right planter by the front door," she told him. "*Right* as you're facing the door, not as you're coming out."

"I got it, Hyacinth. I was standing there when you got it out."

As he bounded up the porch steps, she slid into the driver's seat, fastened her seat belt, and adjusted the mirror. Good. He'd left the key in the ignition. Satisfied that he'd put the house key in the correct place, Hyacinth started the engine and felt for the button to adjust the seat.

The car door flew open. "What is that you think you're doing here?" Robbie demanded.

"I thought I'd drive," she said nonchalantly.

"You did, did you? I thought you wouldn't. Move."

She'd expected this and she was ready. "It's the least I can do. You have practice tomorrow. You can sleep on the way back."

He leaned on the door and gave her a lazy look. "Yeah? It's got a good beat, but you can't dance to it. No. The real reason you want to drive is because you're afraid I'll drive too slow, or too fast, or I'll stop too often, or God forbid that I should take a route not mapped out and sanctioned by Hyacinth Dawson. You want to be in charge."

There was no denying it. He'd practically read her mind. "So what? What if those are my reasons? Why do you care? You get to drive. You get to sleep. Win, win."

"Wrong. Marc Champagne lent me this vehicle. I'm responsible for it and I'm going to drive it."

"He lent it to *us*."

"No. He lent it to me, so *we* can go home."

"What's the difference?"

"Did you ask him for it? Did he put the keys in your hand? Do you know what's going to happen with it when we get back to Laurel Springs?"

She hadn't thought about that last part. "What *is* going to happen?"

"I'm going to fill up the tank, have the oil checked, and have it washed. Then, I'm going to give the keys to Jake."

"Jake's dad said to do all that?"

"Does Marc Champagne seem like the kind of man who would order a grown man around like he was a toddler?"

He paused and gave her a squinty-eyed look. He might as well have added "Like you do." That was fair, but she didn't care—though "order around" was such a harsh way to put it. Some people needed to be given direction and Robbie McTavish was one of them.

Robbie went on, "Marc only told me they were coming to Laurel Springs soon for a Yellowhammer game, and he'd pick up the car then. The rest, I figured out all on my own because—regardless of what you think of me—I've had good home training. I know that if you borrow something, you return it in better condition than when you got it. Just because I don't do what you say—your way—doesn't make me irresponsible. Now, get in that passenger seat."

She hesitated, searching for something to say, but couldn't find anything. It seemed he wasn't budging, but neither was she.

He took a deep breath. "You've got two choices, Hyacinth. You can go home tonight or go in the house, go to bed, and wait for me to pick you up in the morning. As long as I'm on the ice at one o'clock tomorrow, I don't care. I can eat turkey sandwiches and watch the rest of the Egg Bowl as good as I can drive to Alabama tonight. But understand this: no matter when you go, you're not driving."

She got out and got in the passenger seat.

It was with no small amount of satisfaction that Robbie watched Hyacinth surrender the driver's seat. To be honest, he didn't really care who drove, and Marc wouldn't have either. This was just a battle he had intended to win. Now that he had, he wondered why it had mattered so much. This was another case of him being easygoing—until he wasn't. And damn it, he'd had enough of Hyacinth's highhandedness.

From the time he was a lad, it had been Robbie's natural inclination to let emotion overrule his head when he was being scolded—so much so that he rarely picked up on the fine points of the scolding. Many had tried to break him of this—parents, grandparents, and nuns, to name a few. But Robbie had remained unchanged until his first year of boarding school when his coach had turned out to be an old-school kind of guy with a skate-until-you-puke philosophy. It had only taken about three rounds of that to make him bat back his emotions and engage his brain.

After that, he was a changed man—or had been until today.

What he'd taken away from Hyacinth's tirade was, one, not to call her lass. Two. Not to help her. Three. Stay out of her shop. The rest of it had been lost in a cloud of anger, frustration, and—he could admit it—the kind of hurt feelings that started in your gut and made your eyes sting. After all, he had meant well.

But now, driving through the night with Hyacinth pretending to sleep—he was sure it was a pretense—it started to come back to him.

It was ridiculous that she thought she'd lose her business because of that silly little video. Did she think people were going to stop getting married? Brides were going to stop wanting dresses? And he'd never known anyone to go so completely off the rails at being offered a snack and a bit of a drive around. It was a good thing she hadn't given him a chance to point out that she'd been cute in the video—and amusing. She seemed to be against all manner of amusement.

Fine enough. She'd see in time nothing would change with her shop. Women would continue to walk down aisles in expensive dresses and some of those dresses would come from Trousseau. And she didn't have to take a drive, have a snack, or laugh. Or kiss him—more's the pity and good riddance.

There was something from the conversation that niggled at him, though—what she'd said about being humiliated. Not the part about her teacher. If he had a penny for every time a coach had come down on him in front of his teammates, he'd own Australia.

But the other part... Sure, every kid was embarrassed by their parents from time to time, but unless she had exaggerated, they were over the top. And Hyacinth didn't exaggerate. He might not know much about her, but he knew that.

"Hyacinth." No point in pretending she was asleep.

"What?" Apparently, she agreed because she answered right away in a clear voice.

"Your parents really came to your school high? And wearing pajamas?"

"They really did." She sighed. "All the other mothers were dressed like they were ready for a Junior League luncheon, and there were mine, looking like they just rolled out of bed. Same with the dads. My parents weren't even potheads. It might have been easier to take if they had been. At least I would have been expecting it. But they had to pick that day for a special good time. To top it all off, they had the munchies and came in with a party size bag of Doritos and a carton of malted milk balls."

"Sounds like they were young and needed to grow up some. Surely they wouldn't embarrass you by doing that kind of thing now."

"No. They don't do anything anymore. They're dead."

"Holy family and all the wise men!" That was a shock. He knew people their age with a dead parent, but not both. It wasn't natural. It should have occurred to him to wonder why she had not been with her family on Thanksgiving. Thanksgiving was almost as sacred to Americans as Christmas—maybe more so, since not all religions celebrated Christmas. "Both of them? Gone?"

"Both. They died in an industrial accident when I was twelve."

"Oh, la—I mean, Hyacinth. I'm sorry." He had to stop himself from reaching for her hand.

"It's been a long time."

"And your other family?"

"I don't have any—at least none I know. My dad's family is in California, but I've never met them. My grandmother, who raised me from the time I was twelve, died a few years back. I was an only child of an only child of an only child. That doesn't make for a lot of family. I never knew my grandfather, but he was from Arkansas. He had one brother."

"I can't imagine."

"I'm sure. Remember, I've seen the picture of your family. Do they all live there? At Wyndloch?"

"Mostly, though some in cottages on the property. Always something going on."

"There was a time when there was always something

going on where I lived, too. There were always people coming and going, sleeping on the floor, staying up all night." She shuddered. "But then I went to live with my memaw. She was the best parent anyone could have. Everything was clean, orderly, and I knew what to expect. I never had to wear the same thing to school three days in a row because nobody had remembered to go to the washateria. She was also fun to be around."

Robbie had to wonder what Hyacinth considered fun. Maybe making grocery lists and organizing the Tupperware lids.

"This is none of my business, but I have a question," he said.

"I doubt that ever stops you. What?"

"Did your parents hurt you? I mean—"

"I know what you mean and, no. Not the way you mean. They never hit me, never even yelled at me, but it wasn't a normal life."

"What's normal?"

"Not my childhood. They were free spirits—and dreamers. That's what my grandmother always said. And I guess I was their mascot." There was something about her tone—almost like she was talking to herself instead of him. "They met when my mom was in college. He was a musician, playing in some local dive. She quit school and they went chasing around the country. I was born in Oregon. It didn't occur to them to send me to school until someone reported them. We were in Montana then. I don't know how many places we'd been in between. That's when we moved to Nashville. My dad thought he'd try to break into the music business for real, and they put me in school. I guess by then, even they realized they weren't going to homeschool me like they planned. By the time I started kindergarten, I was a year older than all my classmates."

That was probably when she'd learned to be in charge. The image of a tiny Hyacinth wielding a chip-board and giving directions to all the other little chil-dren made him smile.

"Anyway, my parents held out against the wander-lust until I was twelve—I'll give them that. They sent me to stay with my grandmother in Laurel Springs and headed to Colorado, but they ran out of money along the way. Stopped in Oklahoma and went to work in a factory. It blew up, them with it. And that's it. It was Memaw and me."

"They abandoned you—before they…they…passed away, I mean?"

"No. It wasn't like that. Not quite. They left intending to get settled and send for me. Who knows if their inten-tions would have come to fruition? They often didn't. But my grandmother wasn't just my safety net. She made who I am. She was an excellent seamstress. She took up sewing to earn money. And she taught me."

"You sew? Beyond stitching up a rip here and there?"

"Yes. I do all the alterations on the dresses I sell. And I went to design school. There was a settlement from my parents' accident and Memaw wouldn't touch it, though there were times we sure could have used it. But she said it was for my education. I never sew a stitch that she isn't right there with me."

All this explained some things. She had to have been a mess of grief—and relief, and guilt. Clearly she had been much happier with her grandmother and that would have brought on the guilt. That was a lot for a kid to live with. She hadn't grown up with the security he had. While his family wasn't wealthy, they all worked hard. There had always been enough money for everything they needed and a good deal of what they wanted, including a Swiss boarding school for him with a good hockey program.

No wonder she was concerned about losing her business. Maybe he could help her feel better about that, at least.

"Hyacinth, I know you think the video is going to hurt your business." He knew better to use the word *overreaction*. "It was fresh and you were embarrassed. I understand. You'd know why I get it, if you'd ever read *The Face Off Grapevine*. You aren't going to lose Trousseau."

"Maybe. I'm trying to get it in perspective, but I can't pretend it didn't happen. People are funny, especially brides. I can promise you there are some who wouldn't trust a screeching, out of control lunatic with the most important garment she'll ever buy. And that's who I was in that video."

"I think most will think it's funny."

"I don't like being laughed at." She'd probably had her share of that as a child. "And believe me. A wedding dress is no laughing matter to a bride—or her mother, who most of the time controls the purse strings. I just need to figure out what to do next. Being there to open my door in the morning is a start."

"Even if that's true, it'll blow over."

"Nothing blows over, Robbie—not without some help."

She might be right about that.

"Anyway, I'm not throwing my big picture plan in the trash without a fight."

Not a bad thought. Maybe he shouldn't be so quick to assume they couldn't take up where they'd left off in that rose room the night before Thanksgiving. There were lots of layers to this woman.

"What's your big picture?"

"My long-term plan. I don't want to just sell wedding dresses for the rest of my life, though I don't want to give up Trousseau. I *love* my shop. I want to open a studio and design, as well as work with my brides. But I need to be able to hire seamstresses and more staff to help run Trousseau. This is such a setback."

"That's a cool ambition, but why the setback?"

She sighed. "The next part of my plan—the short-term goal—is to promote my shop, by getting on *All Dressed in White*. That's—"

"I know what it is."

"You do?"

"What can I say? I'm a fool for reality TV. And, you know. Wedding business. My favorite is when they go to the shop in Charleston—with Sarah and Robin."

"I'm familiar. They've all but promised me a spot if I could get a famous client. I had even hoped Trousseau might become a repeat venue like Ever After in Charleston. But they like elegant. Now this happened. But even with all that, I thought there might be a chance. I thought Jake and Evans would get engaged and then—"

He caught his breath. "And now that's over." Wanting to preserve her livelihood was one thing, but this was a whole different matter. Not that there was any sin in being ambitious. If that were so, he'd bust hell wide open. Something didn't seem right, but he couldn't quite put his finger on it. Had she been planning on using Jake and Evans?

"Yes. So this has been nothing short of the holiday from hell," she said.

"I doubt if Jake and Evie would see it that way. Is that why you were asking me if I thought they would get married?"

"I hoped you might have some inside information. I believed it would happen, but I was trying to get some idea of when." She let out a long breath. "I guess now I know."

"I see." Cold moved through his gut. Yes, she had layers. This was one that he didn't like. "You aren't even happy for Evie and Jake, are you?"

"Of course I am." She sounded shocked, but it wasn't enough. His gut remained frozen. "Especially Evans. She's my best friend—she and Ava Grace."

"But it would have been better if they had gotten engaged first and got you on *All Dressed in White*?"

"They would have still had each other. Anna-Blair, Layne, and Ellis would have had the wedding they wanted. And as for me—"

"Yes. As for *you*." This was what sick disappointment felt like, just when he'd thought there might be a way to put behind them all the bad that had happened.

"It's a moot point, but I don't see what's wrong with that," she said defensively.

"If you don't, I can't explain it to you." There were few things more important than loyalty. Hyacinth might even believe that. The trouble was, she was loyal to herself first, and that was no loyalty at all.

They didn't say another word all the way home. After a time, she really did go to sleep.

Chapter Eight

Hyacinth put the sign that said Select Bridesmaid Dresses $99 in the window.

Brad had urged her to do more for Black Friday—a free veil with the purchase of a bridal gown—but she'd resisted. As a rule, Black Friday wasn't a huge day for bridal salons, and a giveaway was risky. Veils were high-dollar items.

She'd thought that such an offer wouldn't bring in business so much as it would have caused brides who had bought recently to delay their purchases until today. But maybe Brad had been right and she'd been wrong. She hadn't questioned her decision until now. Come to think of it, she hadn't questioned many of her decisions until two days ago.

And she didn't like feeling unsure worth a damn.

The truth was Robbie befuddled her at every turn. After their tug of war last night over who was going to drive, he had ended up putting her so at ease that she found herself telling him things she hadn't talked about in years, and other things she'd never told anyone. Surprisingly, it had been very comforting—maybe because he was easy to talk to or maybe because it had been easy to talk in the dark while speeding down the highway.

It didn't matter. In the end, it had all crashed with no more talk between them aside from his curt goodnight after he'd carried her bags in.

That had left her feeling emptier than she would have expected.

She moved the rack with the sale bridesmaids dresses to a more prominent place. Brad might have been right. This sale wasn't going to do anyone any good if there were multiple bridesmaids in the wedding. She added a few more dresses to the rack—not that it was likely to bring in more foot traffic. Maybe a few teens thinking ahead to the high school Valentine dance or prom. But that was fine. She'd have more time to concentrate on the appointment with Connie Millwood.

Brad had put an Odette Pascal that met Connie's criteria on the mannequin, and Hyacinth was double-checking the other dresses she'd pulled as possibilities for Connie when she heard the back door open. It was still almost an hour before opening time, so that would be Brad. Patty would follow soon.

"There you are." He entered the storeroom, carrying a cardboard tray of three coffees, like he always did.

"You say that like you were expecting to find me here this morning."

"I was." He set the tray on the counter. "Your car outside would have tipped me off, but I knew you'd be here this morning anyway, which is why I got you your usual." He handed her a tall, insulated cup. It would take more than a nonfat mocha latte to prop her eyes open today, but it was a start. She'd hardly slept after getting home last night.

She took a sip of her coffee. "And you knew this how?"

"I saw the video."

He'd pegged her reaction. No surprise. She groaned. "Do you think a lot of people saw it? I mean people we know?" she asked hopefully. She'd been so sure yesterday that the world had seen it, but maybe she was wrong.

"Hard to say. I did, but I'm a social media whore and I read *The Face Off Grapevine* every day. But so what if every person on the planet saw it?"

"Reputation, Brad. It's important in our business. And that video didn't exactly present Trousseau as an elegant dream dress sanctuary or me as an organized, dependable professional who can be trusted to guide a bride to that one enchanted, predestined dress." She unlocked the register and began setting it up for the day.

"You don't believe that. I've heard you say a thousand times there aren't any magic dresses." He removed some jeweled belts, tiaras, and earrings from the jewelry case and went to hang them on the silver Christmas tree Hyacinth had put up last week. "You didn't put enough on. It looks skimpy."

"Whatever. It doesn't matter what I believe. It matters what they believe. You've heard them go on and on about that bridal moment, when they just *know*. Does it ever make you wonder if they put as much thought into the groom?" She slammed the register drawer shut.

"I've never heard you sound so cynical."

"Yeah, well. I'm tired. And I've made a fool of myself." She retrieved the Windex from under the counter and went to polish the jewelry case.

"You're overreacting. Let's say a few tight asses decide to take their business to Warehouse Dresses by the Pound. Good riddance. Most people who would shop here probably haven't seen it, don't care. It'll blow over."

He removed the tiara she'd used as a tree topper and replaced it with a more ornate one.

"You sound like Robbie and Evans," Brad knew she wanted to be on *All Dressed in White*. Everyone did, but unlike Robbie, Brad didn't know she hoped to become a repeat venue for the show.

"I'll take that as a compliment," Brad said. "Robbie's a good guy."

Yeah, I thought so for a while, too. "Not the best time to say that, Brad. Remember, if he hadn't wandered in off the street that day..."

"He may not think before he acts all the time, but that doesn't make him a bad guy. He's just a free spirit."

Free spirit. Like her parents. Her gut clenched.

"You, know," Brad went on, "he and I hang out sometimes—play video games or go out for a burger and beer. There aren't that many men like Robbie who are willing to pal around with an openly gay man."

"What do you mean by men like Robbie?"

"Straight, good looking, rich. He's not one bit concerned that people might think he's gay." He took the Windex and rag from her. "I'll do the door."

"Do y'all ever talk about me?" Why had she said that? She never spoke without thinking. Besides, she didn't care. But did they? And if so, what had they said?

Brad laughed. "Not that I recall. We mostly talk about hockey, Scotland, and how a wedding can make normal people go absolutely bark-at-the-moon crazy."

This was solving nothing. She took another drink of her coffee and went to store it under the front counter. "I'm going to brush my teeth and touch up my makeup. It's almost time to unlock the door—not that I expect there to be much traffic today."

"One question, Hyacinth?" Brad paused with his polishing.

"That is?"

"If you really don't think anyone's coming in today, why are you back so far ahead of schedule?"

Good question. "I thought you said you expected me."

"I did. I usually know what you're going to do, but I almost never know why."

That made two of them, at least these days.

When Hyacinth unlocked the door at nine o'clock, she was fully prepared for no one to come through it. Under the best of circumstances, Trousseau wasn't Walmart, offering three-hundred-inch TVs for fifteen cents.

However, she was not prepared for Claire.

She should have been.

Hyacinth had known Claire from the days when Memaw used to sew for her, long before their Trousseau partnership. Even back then, Claire had seemed to know things no one else did. There was no chance she had missed Hyacinth's internet debut.

Hyacinth figured Claire to be somewhere between forty-five and fifty, but she looked younger. Statuesque, and pure class on a pair of high heels, she wore her blond hair in a messy low bun and her confidence like a crown. The emerald green silk wrap dress she wore today might be a vintage Diane von Furstenberg original or a thrift store find. It wouldn't have mattered to Claire. She did what she wanted—like Robbie, though she was certainly more prudent. The dress was exactly the color of Robbie's eyes.

"I brought y'all a little bite of breakfast for Black

Friday." Claire handed Hyacinth a basket covered with a black and white checked linen towel. "Just some sausage balls, a spinach and mushroom frittata, and some orange rolls."

Just? Claire wouldn't have made the food herself, but she would have had to collect it up and pack the baskets—plural—because Evans and Ava Grace and their staffs would be getting the same goodies.

"Thank you," Hyacinth said. "I appreciate it, and Brad and Patty will, too."

"I was surprised to see your car here. I thought you weren't coming back until midday."

Here it was. "That was the plan. But in view of what happened…"

Claire smiled. "That was quite the surprise, wasn't it?"

She was *smiling?* "I'll say."

"We must do something for them. A party, don't you think? Cocktails. You, Ava Grace, and me?"

Oh. She was talking about the elopement. Was it possible she didn't know about the video? That was bad news because Hyacinth would have to tell her, describe every wretched detail—probably bring it up on her phone to share, when she'd sworn she'd never watch it again.

"Of course, we need to find out what their families have planned," Claire went on.

Hyacinth willed herself to get with the present subject. She'd deal with the other later.

"Anna-Blair said something about a reception. Later on. Maybe when Jake has a break, or even after the season's over."

Claire nodded. "I'll call her."

They seemed to be finished with that, so time to face the music. "Did you see the video?"

Claire took a deep breath. "I read *The Face Off Grapevine* every morning." As part owner of the Yellowhammers, she would.

"I'm sorry."

"What are you apologizing for?" Claire truly looked puzzled. You didn't often see that.

"My part in putting Trousseau in jeopardy."

"Trousseau is *not* in jeopardy," Claire said. "You could lose some sales, I admit, but we're in good shape here. You are a far, far cry from losing this business."

Claire was the first one to admit that the video could impact Trousseau, so her assurance was somewhat of a comfort—however, though Claire knew she'd wanted to be on *All Dressed In White*, she didn't know how much it figured into Hyacinth's goals or how close she'd thought she'd been.

"I just wish so much it hadn't happened."

"So do I," Claire said sympathetically. "But I don't know what you could have done."

"I don't either, but something—stopped the video-ing, made Robbie leave."

Claire shook her head, laughed. "That Robbie." No. Surely to Lucifer and all his minions not. Was Claire—really the one person who somewhat understood—really amused and letting a fond expression take over her face? "There's no stopping him once he gets started. He's like a high-speed train leaving the station. It works on the ice, though." Another person under his spell.

Before Hyacinth could answer, Claire looked over Hyacinth's shoulder toward the front of the shop. "For crying out loud. Here comes Marvell Crenshaw. Do you mind if I go out the back?"

"Of course not." *After all, you do own the back door, the front door and everything in between.* Claire would never run away from a real conflict, but she would certainly move away from a mosquito she couldn't swat. And who could blame her?

Claire reached for the breakfast basket. "I'm on my way to Heirloom and Crust. I'll put this in your break room on my way out." She turned to go. "But, Hyacinth? Don't worry about the video. With those hockey players, it's something every day."

But she wasn't a hockey player and she wasn't used to something every day—or really hardly any days.

The bell above the door jingled. Because she couldn't swat or run, Hyacinth prepared to face the mosquito full-on.

Marvell was known for showing up with a plate of pralines, with servings of bad news and strong opinions on the side. It was a popular notion around town that her pralines were so good that it was worth enduring her nosy mean-spiritedness to get them. Hyacinth did not agree. She didn't like pralines that much.

"I saw you on the YouTube," Marvell declared, showing the plate she carried into Hyacinth's hands. There were about two dozen candies—twice what she usually gave out. She must have plenty to say. "If your grandmother was still alive, I wouldn't say this to you, but with her gone, I feel it's my duty."

If Memaw were still alive, you wouldn't say whatever you plan to say to me because she would run you out of Mt. Zion Missionary Baptist Church. She hadn't liked

Marvell any better than anyone else did. She'd called her Marvell Hacksaw and said Marvell was so smug that, if she sewed, she'd refuse to own a seam ripper. But she'd always insisted Hyacinth be polite, and that was a hard habit to break.

"Yes, ma'am?"

"I didn't like what I saw in that video."

Hyacinth took a deep breath and recited the speech she'd typed up at two a.m. this morning. "I was surprised as anyone to see that bridal appointment posted to social media. Neither I, nor my staff, would have compromised a client's privacy. However, it was their right to do so if they wished."

"I don't care two hoots about what Daisy Dubois wears when she gets married—*if* she gets married, after Brenda Buckner sees her boy's intended plastered all over kingdom come. It's you I'm talking about, Hyacinth"—she stabbed the air with her index finger in Hyacinth's direction—"and that hockey player you're messing with. You've always been a sensible girl. Austell said so all the time. You were a blessing to her. You don't need to be mixed up with some wild hockey player."

What the hell?

"I assure you I am not *messing with* that hockey player, nor am I mixed up with him." *But she had come close, so close.*

"I know what I saw, Hyacinth. I know fireworks when I see them."

"You're mistaken, Mrs. Crenshaw. Robbie and I are not one bit interested in each other." She couldn't bring herself to thank her for her concern as Ava Grace or Evans would have done.

"Robbie, is it? If he's not sniffing around you, what was he doing in your store?"

"You'd have to ask him that."

"And why didn't you make him leave, if you didn't want him here? And don't you bother telling me you tried. I've known you since you were twelve years old. When you set your mind to something, it happens."

Was that true? Had she not tried? It had sure felt like it.

"And what was it with that skirt? What man goes around wearing a skirt?"

"It wasn't a skirt." Hyacinth was surprised at the vehemence in her voice and her inclination to defend Robbie on this point. "It was a *kilt*. Robbie's a Scot."

Marvell looked confused for second. "Like Jamie? On *Outlander*?"

"Exactly like that."

"They still wear that? In Scotland?"

"Yes. That's all they wear. The men don't even own pants." That was a lie, but she was counting on Marvell not knowing any better.

"Okay then. If that's what he's used to. But he's here now and he ought to dress like an American, if you ask me."

Robbie wasn't likely to have anything dictated to him by anybody. She opened her mouth to say that, but closed it again, realizing it would have felt disloyal. Fat lot of sense that made. Unfortunately, the pause in the conversation allowed Marvell to sharpen her stinger.

"It's time you had a beau, Hyacinth, but it needs to be a nice American boy. Now, we've got a new youth director down at the church. I want you to come Sunday morning and I'll introduce you. He's good looking. Just one more year of seminary left. I've always thought a youth director needs a wife to help him herd those kids on their mission trips, lock-ins, and such."

Mother of pearl. Hyacinth hadn't been to Mt. Zion since Memaw died. She sometimes went to St. Ann's with Ava Grace, but she certainly wasn't going to herd kids, be they Baptist or Episcopalian.

"I'm too busy to date right now, Mrs. Crenshaw," she said firmly, "but I wish you luck in finding him a wife and herding partner. If you do, send her to me for a dress. I'll treat her right. As for Robbie, forget it. There's nothing there."

Marvell looked somewhat appeased, but not happy. Winning the battle wasn't good enough for her. She had to win the war and conquer the world, and she'd buzz around until she did it. But Hyacinth knew how to head her off.

"Now, I'm going to share something with you," Hyacinth said in a whisper.

"What's that?" Marvell looked intrigued. She loved new information.

"You granddaughter was in last week."

Her eyes bugged out of her head. "Valerie? *She's six-teen years old.* She's not getting married!"

"No, no. She was looking at dresses for the school Valentine dance and she found one she loved, but said it was too expensive. If you'd like to buy it for her—say for Christmas—it's priced at $499, but I'll let you have it for a hundred dollars." If it would get this woman out of here, it would be well worth it. Besides, it was last year's design and a shade of green that didn't play well on many people. She would have marked it down to two hundred after Christmas anyway.

Marvell looked torn. "I don't know. I don't really approve of dances and all those kids get up to..." Her voice trailed off. "But if she's going anyway... One hundred dollars, you say? Maybe." Marvell loved a bargain.

"It's sea foam green. Beautiful with her red hair. And she'd stand out, what with most of the girls wearing reds and pinks." Valerie's hair was about the same shade as Robbie's—sunshine on copper. A picture of him wearing the dress flashed through her brain. She bit her lip to keep from smiling. Crazy thoughts.

"Let me see it," Marvell said. "If it's decent and doesn't leave her half naked like what some of these girls are wearing, I'll consider it."

"Wonderful. Let me put these pralines away and I'll be right back with the dress."

When Marvell was at long last out the door, Hyacinth pulled Connie Millwood's file to make sure she hadn't missed anything. This was what she was supposed to be doing and it felt good.

"Do we have any Christmas paper?" she asked when she heard Brad come up behind her. "I promised Marvell Crenshaw we'd gift wrap the dress she bought her granddaughter. We have to deliver it, too."

"What's she got on you?" he asked around a mouth full of praline.

"Sometimes you do what you have to. I have to do the alterations after Christmas, too." She turned back to the file. "Connie's set on a jeweled belt and a tiara. She's small, and that's a lot to carry off. It needs to be one or the other, don't you think?"

"About that..."

"Now what? She turned to look at Brad.

"She just called and canceled."

"So it begins." All her nightmares were going to come true, starting with this.

"Now, hold on, Hyacinth. She said she'd call next week to reschedule."

"She won't. If she were going to, she would have done it when she called. Did she give a reason?"

"A good one." Brad nodded. "Her fiancé sprained his ankle yesterday playing backyard football."

"A sprained ankle! She said she was canceling over a *sprained ankle?* It's not like he's having brain surgery. And she's not a doctor." She waved the file in the air.

"It says right here she teaches kindergarten. Believe me, we won't hear from her again."

"Hyacinth, think about what you're saying. She said he was in a lot of pain and she didn't want to leave him. Would you leave the person you were in love with, if he were in pain?"

"I don't know." How could she? She'd never been in love.

Chapter Nine

"Is true?" Miklos Novak, Robbie's Czech teammate, sauntered up to him, naked as the day he was born. "Sparks has married Evans?" The word was out.

"That was the plan, as far as I know, and I haven't heard otherwise." Robbie bent over to tie his skates. "Do you have to strut around the locker room bare assed?"

"Was fast." Miklos ignored the reference to his undressed state. "Do you think she will have baby soon?"

"No, I think they got married because they love each other." Whatever that meant. You couldn't be in the wedding business without learning to recognize it when you saw it, but he'd yet to experience it firsthand. "Go put some clothes on."

"Too bad," Miklos said as he walked away. "I like babies."

Robbie hadn't considered that. While he would bet the castle that Evans was not pregnant, he supposed that would be next.

The whole thing left him feeling…lonely. Jake had been his carousing buddy, until he wasn't. It was probably natural that he would feel left behind—and it also explained his strange attraction to Hyacinth.

He and Jake had been on the same page about what

they wanted for a long time—hot women, loud parties, and late nights. It made sense that, subconsciously, Robbie wanted to get to the same place his best friend had landed. Hyacinth, being Evans's friend, was a handy candidate. He was sure, on some level, he had pictured the four of them playing cards, going on vacations, and teaching their kids to skate together.

That was the only thing that explained the attraction. Never had he been so off base about anybody. He'd laughed at her funny little ways and highhandedness, but never had he attributed it to the kind of cutthroat ambition she had. Sure, she'd had a rough go of it as a girl, but that was no excuse for caring more about being on a TV show than a friend's happiness.

All in all, it was disappointing, but not devastating. He still needed to pay her for the frock he'd ruined, and then she could have what she wanted—to never see him again.

The noise went up in the locker room with catcalls, whistles, and cheers. The groom was in the house.

Robbie rose and crossed the space to meet his friend halfway.

"So you did it?" Robbie asked as they embraced.

"Damn skippy!" Jake laughed. "First thing this morning. The minute she said yes, do you think I was stupid enough to let any grass grow under my feet? We didn't even have rings."

Robbie had to smile. Jake, with his good looks, hot hockey stick, and Southern charm had always been the pursued. Now he was at the mercy of a sweet girl with smiling eyes who loved to bake pies. And he wasn't just happy, he was entirely content.

Yeah. Robbie did want that. Now to find the right woman.

"I was afraid you'd be pissed I abandoned you in Mississippi," Jake said.

He had intended to give Jake a little good-natured hell about it, but the inclination evaporated. Maybe he could make up for Hyacinth's attitude. "It's not about me. It's about you and Evie."

In some small way, he thought, he ought to pity Hyacinth, because she would never understand that. He might not know much about romantic love, but he knew how to be a friend.

"I'd better get my gear," Jake said. "The Walleyes are coming, and we've got to be ready. I don't plan on losing in front of my wife."

Yes. He wanted that. It might take a while, but he intended to find it.

With Brad and Patty out the door to lunch, Hyacinth was removing the Pascal dress from the mannequin when the bell signaled that someone had entered the shop.

Though the streets were crowded with Black Friday shoppers, the bell had only chimed twice in the last hour. Once it was the mail carrier, the second time, a gaggle of teenagers wanting to try on wedding dresses—which happened every so often.

Hyacinth had handled that the way she always did, by giving them the exhaustive forms to fill out with style preferences, price range, wedding date, and venue. When she'd taken out her calendar and offered to make appointments for them, they'd left—like they always did.

Now, it was Evans who rushed through the door

carrying a pie box. Bright-eyed and pink-cheeked, she looked as happy as a puppy in a meatpacking plant.

"You're here!" Evans rushed toward her. "Mama said you left last night and I've been trying to call you."

"You have?" Hyacinth pulled her phone from her pocket. Dead. She had put it on the charger before going to bed—she *always* put it on the charger. But maybe she hadn't checked to be sure it was plugged in.

"This is for you and your staff." Evans held the pie out to her. "Penance for running out on you. It's not a Thanksgiving leftover, either. German chocolate with toasted coconut crust. It's still warm."

"Thank you." They might not make a single sale today—because, really, could she consider the green chiffon a sale, when she'd taken a loss?—but they could get a sugar high. "So you did it?" Hyacinth asked as she set the pie aside. She didn't even have to work to summon up a smile. It was impossible to look at Evans and not feel happy for her, regardless of *All Dressed in White.* "Are you Mrs. Champagne? Or maybe Ms. Pemberton-Champagne?"

"I did! And I don't know. Pemberton-Champagne is a big mouthful, and I want for us to have the same last name." She blushed prettily. "It's easier later for—you know. The kids."

Hyacinth realized too late that she should have held out her arms to Evans instead of the other way around, but she wasn't a hugger. At least she picked up on the cue really fast.

"I'm sorry about leaving you," Evans said when they separated. "That was the only thing that made me hesitate when Jake said we should just go for it. But he promised you'd get back in time and here you are. It was all right, wasn't it?"

"Of course." No point in belaboring what was done—and she *was* happy for Evans. She'd just had a little trouble remembering that. "Does everyone know? I wasn't sure if you were keeping it under wraps, so I haven't said anything."

"Yes. Jake's agent has already issued a statement. It's all over Twitter and *The Face Off Grapevine*." Evans winced a bit when she said that.

"That's something new for people to talk about." Hyacinth made a laughing sound that she didn't feel, but it was the best she could do.

"It'll all be fine." Evans reached out and squeezed her hand. "I promise." It was easy for Evans to believe that. It was clear that, right now, she felt like everything in the world was possible.

But that wasn't a discussion Hyacinth could have.

"Hey, what's this?" She caught sight of a huge gold, diamond and amethyst-encrusted ring suspended from a ribbon around Evans's neck. She captured it in her hand for a better look and spoke before she thought. "That's about the gaudiest thing I've ever seen."

Thankfully, Evans laughed. "Isn't it? It's Jake's championship ring from the Sound." That meant Robbie had one, too. She was surprised he didn't wear it. "We didn't have time to buy rings yet, so we used this. I love it!" She brought the ring to her face and rubbed it against her cheek.

Hyacinth's heart melted a little for her friend. "You love everything today." This time she initiated the hug.

"I do." Evans wiped her eyes. "Jake and I are leaving right after the game tomorrow afternoon. They're off

Sunday and he's been excused from practice Monday, so we're taking a quick trip to New Orleans."

"Good for you. That'll be fun." Or she assumed so. She'd never been to New Orleans.

"I can't wait. The game is tomorrow afternoon at three. I'd love it if you could come with Ava Grace and me. She's leaving Heirloom with Jen and Piper. Couldn't Brad and Patty handle things here?"

It was hard telling Evans no, and Hyacinth knew, since Claire had given them all season tickets, she was going to have to go to one of those Yellowhammer games eventually. But it couldn't be tomorrow. She had reached her limit of hell-no for right now. If she had to add in a hockey game she had no interest in—let alone one with Robbie probably charging around like he was the god of ice—she might run screaming through the crowd toppling beer and popcorn as she went.

"I can't, Evans," she said. "I have things I have to do here." That might even be true. "But I promise," she added hastily, "when you get back, we'll do something to celebrate—you, Ava Grace, and me."

"That sounds great." Evans's smile was bright as the sun. There was no disappointing her today.

Almost as soon as Evans went out the front door, Brad and Patty came in the back.

"We brought you a chicken salad sandwich," Patty said, handing her a bag from Laurel Springs Apothecary.

"Thank you. Everybody's bringing food. It's getting to be like a Baptist funeral around here today. Evans brought us a pie."

"We just got wind that she and Jake got married this

morning," Brad said with a sigh. "I would have loved to have dressed her."

"You might still get to," Hyacinth said. "I think the plan is to have some big reception at some point."

"Sweet," Brad rubbed his hands together.

And it was. Just no *All Dressed in White*. "I'm going to go eat my sandwich," she said.

"I see we've got a naked mannequin," Brad said.

"Yeah. Let's hang the dress with the others for Connie—at least for a few days. In case she does call back."

"What do you want on the mannequin?" Patty asked.

"Whatever y'all think. Use your judgment."

Hyacinth entered her workroom and settled in. It was small, but it had everything she needed for now—cutting table, sewing machine, and a combination desk/drawing table. The organization system she had designed for fabric, trim, and sewing notions was brilliant, even if she did say so. Usually, this room reminded her of what she would one day have. Today, it depressed her. Despite her vow to get through this, it was hard to come back from the blow of the canceled appointment.

She stored her sketches in a large acetate envelope before unwrapping her sandwich. Remembering that her phone was dead, she put it on the charger before reaching for the latest Anastasia Valens catalog. She was halfway through her sandwich when she remembered her phone.

As soon as she turned it on, it started chiming like a handbell choir on Christmas Eve. Surely Evans hadn't been *that* intent on getting in touch with her. No. Two missed voice mails and a text from her. A text from Ava

Grace that said: CAN YOU BELIEVE IT!!!!!, no doubt in reference to their friend's recent nuptials. Not surprising.

But there was something totally unexpected—two missed calls from Alex Leman and the five texts that all said the same thing: Call me, Call me, Call me, Call me, Call me.

She didn't bother to listen to his messages. No doubt he'd seen the video and heard that Jake and Evans had eloped, so she knew what he was going to say: "It was a nice thought, but adios, adieu, and aloha."

No future in putting it off.

He answered on the first ring. "Hyacinth? Where have you been?"

"My phone was dead. I guess you've heard about Jake and Evans. I'm really sorry. I had no idea they would do this."

"Ha! Forget Jake and Evans. We've got something better."

"We do?"

"Much better. You're going to be on *All Dressed in White*."

Chapter Ten

"Do what?" He hadn't said what Hyacinth thought she'd heard. It wasn't possible.

"You're going to be on *All Dressed in White*. But we have a time crunch. We have to shoot soon—twelve days."

"What . . . how?"

"You know who Jules Perry is."

It was a statement. Of course she knew. Everyone did. She'd been the reigning princess-next-door of the rom-com until a few years ago when she'd played a war correspondent in that blockbuster movie about Vietnam. She'd won the Oscar. Since then she'd been in a lot of movies, on a lot of magazine covers, and gotten a fair number of little statues. Hyacinth didn't keep up with pop culture much, but even she had seen *Secret Muse*, where Perry had played Helga Testorf, who modeled for Andrew Wyeth for years without either of their spouses knowing.

But there was something else.

"Isn't she getting married?"

"Yes. To Reynolds Fallon. Plays for the San Francisco 49ers. Born with a platinum dot com spoon in his mouth. Silicon Valley billionaire parents."

Hyacinth's heart raced. Jules Perry, here? It couldn't be.

"What has this got to do with me?"

"She's getting married mid-December. Some big-time French designer was making her dress—" She remembered reading that now. "Marius Marchand."

"Yeah, her," Alex said.

"Him," Hyacinth corrected.

"Whatever. Anyway, he leaked the design to the press, and she fired him. We got a call from her people. She was furious. Said if the world was going to know what her dress looked like, she'd go on television and pick one out, share it with her fans. Said she'd never thought she was too good for off the rack, anyway, that this Marchand person had been someone else's idea. It's yours if you want it, if you can do it on short notice. We need to air it on December sixteenth, an hour before the wedding."

"Want it? How could I not want it?" Everything else aside, Jules Perry would be a dream to dress—tall, trim, elegant, with just enough in the bust and booty. She could wear anything—and that was good, because it would truly have to be off the rack. Hyacinth could do the alterations, but there was no time to order anything. "I'd do it today if I had to. But why me?"

Then she remembered and a black veil dropped. Might as well shut it down now before they found out.

"Wait, Alex. There's something you don't know. There's this video. It's gone viral. I'm betting you'll change your mind when you see it."

Alex laughed. "Are you kidding? *When* I see it? Everybody at *All Dressed in White* has seen it so many times we can act it out."

She felt positively light-headed. "I don't understand. How did you make this happen?"

"I didn't. Don't you get it? Jules Perry saw the video and asked for you—asked for Trousseau."

She had to be in the best dream ever.

"Are you going to get to direct?"

He hesitated. "No. That would be unrealistic. It *is* Jules Perry. But I told them you and I have a working relationship, so I'm assisting Deb Carmichael."

"You'll be here?"

"Yes."

"Sounds perfect." She would have carried on without Alex, but the idea of a friendly face—or more accurately, voice—was a plus.

"There's this one thing," Alex said.

There always was, but that was fine, great even. She could do *one thing. One thing* was her specialty. Two, if need be.

"Anything. I'll give her the dress."

"No. You won't. Jules Perry doesn't need anybody to give her a dress. It's against the show's policy anyway, unless it's one of those specials where the bride's house burned down or she lost a limb in Afghanistan. You'll charge Jules Perry what you'd charge anyone."

"All right. What, then?"

"Robbie McTavish."

"What?" And her hell-no day turned into hell *fucking* no.

"She knows Robbie. He played in some celebrity golf tournament with Reynolds. They like him."

"Everybody does," she said flatly.

"They—Jules and Reynolds—thought the video was funny—looked fun."

"Oh, it was," Hyacinth said. "*So much fun.* I especially liked the part where he spilled his ice cream on an eight-thousand-dollar Rayna Kwan dress. That didn't make it on the video."

"Too bad. That would have been hilarious."

"Yes, so funny. I'm still laughing."

Her tone must have said it all because Alex's elation evaporated. "It's a deal breaker, Hyacinth. It's what she's asked for."

"But why?"

He sighed. "Why do stars do anything? But it works. It's what the brass around here wants, too. The chemistry between you two is staggering."

"There's *not* any chemistry between us. We don't even really like each other."

"Debatable," Alex said, "but not important. Can you be ready in time?"

"Yes. Absolutely. I'll be ready whenever you say."

"You decorate for Christmas, don't you? Deb wants decorations."

"Of course," she said with more assurance than she felt. She did decorate—more or less, emphasis on less. In fact, she'd already done it. Fake wreath on the front door. The retro silver tree covered in tiaras, bridal jewelry, and sparkling belts. Christmas tree paper napkins with the champagne and cheese straws. The poinsettia Claire sent on the front counter. She would have to do more.

"Good. We'll send someone the day before to check it out." Just more wouldn't do. It would have to be better.

"I'll need to meet with Jules."

"No," Alex said adamantly. "No meeting."

"It doesn't have to be in person. We can Zoom or

FaceTime. I need some idea of what she has in mind. I have preliminary meetings with all my brides."

"Not this time. We don't script and we want pure, organic interaction from beginning to end. It might take a while, but don't worry. We'll edit out the slow parts."

She didn't like the sound of that, but what could she say? "All right. I'm sure you know what you're doing."

"You can deliver Robbie McTavish, can't you?"

"Yes," she said with confidence she didn't feel. "I can deliver him."

"Good. Let's talk about the particulars."

When Robbie came out of practice, still running on hormones and adrenaline, he wanted food, sex, and a nap—not necessarily in that order. In fact, his preference would be sex, then food, then nap, but that wasn't happening.

"Who wants to go to Hammer Time?" Logan Jensen asked. Luka, Miklos, Wingo, and Christophe made affirmative noises, while Able Killen begged off, saying he had a date later. Robbie was jealous that Able had wanted to go out with Ariel. She was sweet, but about as spacey as they came.

"How about you, Scotty?" Logan waved his phone in the air. "I'm calling to tell them how many. You want to go?"

Robbie did not. He'd eaten his way through Hammer Time's menu twice in the past three weeks and he was tired of it. But then again, it was easy.

"Sure. Count me in."

Cold rain was coming down when he left the lobby of the iceplex. He looked at the sky, searching for signs of a tornado. They didn't get tornadoes much in Scotland, but he'd seen what they could do since moving to the South, and he was scared to death of them. At least Hammer Time would be warm and predictable. Was there a basement? He'd have to ask.

He rounded the corner to the lot where his car was parked and stopped abruptly.

There, parked beside his silver Corvette, was one of those ridiculous toy cars—a Mini Cooper, school bus yellow with black stripes on the hood. And if he wasn't mistaken, it was the same one that had been on Hyacinth's parking pad when he'd dropped her off last night. It had to be her. Surely, there weren't two people in Laurel Springs fool enough to buy a Hot Wheels car that wouldn't hold a bag of groceries—especially one that color.

What was she doing here? He jogged over and looked in her window. She had her head leaned back, eyes closed. She looked pretty and, as long as her mouth was shut, nothing would come out of it that would hurt his feelings or disappoint him. If it hadn't been raining, he might have looked at her longer, but it was. Lightning streaked across the sky, startling him.

"Hey!" He rapped on her window and her head jerked up. "Did you know you're parked by my car?"

She rolled down her window. "Yes. Brad told me what you drive and when you were likely to get through with practice."

"For somebody who was foaming at the mouth to get back to Trousseau, you don't seem to be there."

"No. The bride canceled her appointment. I want to talk to you."

He'd figured out that much, but what about? Maybe

she'd been thinking over the past few days and she'd come to apologize for the hateful things she'd said to him; maybe she'd say she was horrified that it sounded like she cared more about being on *All Dressed in White* than Evie and Jake.

Maybe she was thinking about that almost kiss and she wanted to wipe away the bad things that had happened after.

He could get on board with that. A little sorry went a long way with him, always had.

"Could you get in?" she asked.

He gave the car a once-over. "You're kidding, right? My hockey bag is bigger than this Matchbox car."

"Good thing you don't have your hockey bag with you. Come on. Get in. You're getting wet." She came across with a smile and he liked that she cared that he was getting wet. "It's got more leg room than it looks like."

He hesitated, almost suggested they go to the coffee shop. Then it thundered and he ran around and folded himself into the tuna can on wheels.

Chapter Eleven

It was close quarters in the car. Robbie smelled like soap with a little underlying sweat.

It wasn't unappealing.

"What is it you're after, la—" He let his voice trail off. "Hyacinth." This was the second time he'd almost called her *lass* after she'd told him not to, and he'd corrected himself both times. It made her sad. She remembered why she'd done it, but it seemed stupid now. Childish.

"Hyacinth?" He shifted in the seat, trying to get comfortable.

"Right. You're friends with Jules Perry? And her fiancé? What's his name?"

"Reynolds Fallon. Aye. I know them. More friendly acquaintances than friends like you'd call to get you out of jail—not that I've been in jail. But you never know. Pleasant folks." He looked up, like he was reading something on the roof of the car. "I played in a golf tournament with Reynolds. He's a fair golfer, but not as good as me. I won. Golf was invented in Scotland. A lot of people don't know that. After golfing, we went out for sushi—which I didn't want to do. Raw fish, you know.

But Jules wanted to, and you know what? It wasn't half bad. I had—"

Mother of pearl. Hyacinth snapped her fingers. "Robbie! You've gone down a bunny trail. Come back."

"More like a sushi trail, but all right. What about them?"

"They're getting married."

He nodded. "Aye. I was invited, but I had to send my regrets. Too bad, I have a game. It would have been a right good time. I had my agent send a present." It thundered and he looked at the sky. "Not sure what." He looked heavenward again, totally distracted. For once, she didn't mind because she was still trying to figure out how to proceed. She wasn't used to asking for favors. But then he snapped back. "Did you come here to talk about Reynolds and Jules?"

"No." But was that true? "Or yes, but not exactly."

"Get on with it, woman. I'm hungry. The guys are waiting on me."

He was telling *her* to get on with it? That was rich, but it probably wouldn't do her cause any good to say so. "Sorry. I'll be quick."

He widened his eyes and inclined his head toward her, waiting.

"Here's the thing. Jules's designer leaked her wedding dress design to the press. She fired him. She's coming to Trousseau to find a dress. And we're going to be on *All Dressed in White*."

"Fancy that." He laughed and nodded. "Didn't see that coming. Good on you. You're getting what you want."

"Almost. Maybe. Depending…" she said quietly. "What's that? Depending on what?"

"You." She said it quickly.

"Me? What's it to do with me?"

Okay. She'd said the hard part. She was good at recounting and explaining.

"They—she and Reynolds saw the video. They liked it. Jules decided if she couldn't keep her dress a secret, she'd share it with the world. She called *All Dressed in White*. Or her people did. You know. Like your agent sent the gift." She was headed down a bunny trail of her own. "Anyway. It needs to happen fast. In a little over a week. But the condition is you have to be on the show.'"

His expression went from mildly interested to surprised to…something else, something she couldn't read. He closed his eyes and laughed out loud, shaking his head.

"Let's get this straight," he said carefully. "The video that you hated so much, that you blamed me for, the one that was going to ruin your business, your future, your whole life, ended up getting you exactly what you want."

It sounded so much worse than it was. "Well, yes. Depending. Like I said."

He crossed his arms over his chest. "On me? Being willing to go on the show? To help you out? Tell me, Hyacinth. Where would this show take place?"

"Trousseau, of course."

"Ah. Too bad." He lightly punched his left palm with his right fist. "I won't be able to help you out with that. Two reasons. The *helping*. Can't do that. And I can't go in your shop. You said so."

She wanted to scream. He didn't even care that she knew he was enjoying this.

"Okay, Robbie. I have that coming. And more. I admit it. Don't make me beg."

"I think I will. I think that's exactly what I want you to do." He narrowed his eyes.

She took a deep breath. "Robbie, please do this for me. It's Wednesday, December sixth. It would all be over in about eight hours. They're going to air the show the day of the wedding."

He shook his head. "Got practice. And I fly out to LA that night."

"It starts early. It would be done before you have to leave. And you always have practice. Couldn't you be excused just once? Evans said Jake was excused Monday so they can go on their honeymoon."

He shrugged. "I could ask, if I wanted. But I don't. I like to practice."

"You'd be on TV."

He was playing with her. They both knew it. She sighed. "What's it going to take?"

"Oh?" He feigned surprise. "You mean there could be something in it for me?"

"Please." He rolled his eyes. "I'm on TV all the time. You're the one who cares about that."

"Then why don't you tell me what you want?" Though she couldn't imagine anything she could do for him.

He sat for a full minute, thinking. Just when she thought he wasn't going to answer, he held up one finger.

"First, I want to be absolved from ruining that dress."

Relief washed over her. "Done. That's easy. You don't owe me a cent."

"Not so fast." He drummed his fingers on the dash. "I'm not talking about money. I'm paying for the frock.

I take responsibility and I pay what I owe. No. I want you to let it *go*. Complete absolution. I don't want to hear about it again. I don't want to see you think about it. I damn sure don't want you to whine about it to anybody else." She'd never whined in her life, but she wasn't in the position to say so. "All that comes after you admit it was an accident, that it could have happened to anybody."

That was harder, but okay. "All right. Done."

"Not by a long shot. Say it," he demanded.

"Say what?"

"If you don't know, I can't help you."

"You didn't mean to do it. It could have happened to anyone." What was it he was always saying to defend himself? "You meant well. You were only trying to help." He nodded and looked somewhat pleased. She rushed on and added for good measure, "I'm partly to blame. I should have asked you to get rid of your ice cream as soon as you walked in. You would have done it."

"I would have. All you had to do was be nice." He smiled. "Brilliant. I'll come by and pay for the dress; then it will be a closed subject."

He'd said he would come in the shop. That was progress. "Yes. And I'm glad. I want it behind us." She could taste the finish line.

He held up two fingers. "Number two." Hell. Now there was a number two? And he had a long way to go before he ran out of fingers. "I want you to come to all of the Yellowhammer home games."

"Why?" It slipped out before she thought.

"Does it matter? Maybe I want you to do something

you don't want to as penitence. Maybe I want to make a hockey fan out of you. Either way, that's my price."

"I'll start as soon as we get the taping of the show behind us."

"You'll start tomorrow," he said.

She opened her mouth to argue, then closed it again. She had so much to do and she could already feel it bearing down on her, but she'd have to work it out.

Apparently, she hesitated too long. "Have it your own way." He reached for the door handle. "See you around, Hyacinth."

"Wait! All right. I'll be there. Tomorrow, and every other home game for the rest of the season." She'd get through it somehow. Maybe take some hand sewing to work on. "Are those all the terms of your blackmail?"

He opened his mouth and raised his eyebrows in mock surprise. "Oh, ho, ho. *Blackmail*, you say? Such an ugly word. Hmm. I don't believe I will..."

And just then an ear-splitting siren screamed from his pocket and a look of pure terror came over Robbie's face.

"There's a tornado coming!" He fumbled in his pocket, brought out his phone, and promptly dropped it at Hyacinth's feet.

"What? Tornado?" she said, reaching for his phone.

"No."

He dove for his phone in the same instant and their heads collided with a loud crack.

"Ouch!" Hyacinth rubbed her temple. "You hurt my head!"

"You've got bigger problems than that, woman,

and so have I!" He fiddled with his phone. "Where is Daphne?"

"Daphne who?"

"A city…a town."

"South Alabama. What's *wrong* with you?"

"I told you! There's a tornado."

"No," Hyacinth said. "There's no severe weather predicted. I listen every morning." Just then there was a flash of lightning, followed by a loud roar of thunder.

Wild-eyed, he pointed to the sky. "Isn't that prediction enough? We need to get out of here. This tin can car can't be a good thing. Worse than Dorothy's house. Should we go in the rink?"

Something in her turned. He was truly petrified.

"Calm down, Robbie." She spoke quietly and took his phone. "Let me see about this."

"This is no time to calm down. I've seen pictures of what happens."

She had the same weather app and hers hadn't gone off. "Oh. Here's the problem."

"The problem is out there!" The lightning flashed again.

"You've got the settings all wrong," she said. "You only need to be alerted if there's a tornado watch in our area. You don't need to know there's a flash flood warning two hundred miles from here—which is what's going on in Daphne."

"I thought that was safer. If there's a tornado watch, it's too late."

"No, it's not. A tornado watch means conditions are right for a tornado to form. A tornado warning means there *is* a tornado, though it doesn't necessarily mean it's on the ground. A tornado emergency means get your bug-out bag and get the hell out of Dodge."

He looked skeptical. "How do you know all that?"

"I'm a child of the South, raised on the god of all meteorologists, James Spann. Let's see what he has to say." She found what she was looking for on his phone and turned it so Robbie could see it. "Okay, look here at the radar, Robbie. The storm is coming in from Mississippi, moving east. A tornado could come out of it, but it looks like it's turned and is going south of us. All we're going to get is some rain and thunderstorms."

"What if it doesn't? What if we get a tornado?"

"Then we would go to the safe room on the ground floor of your building."

"There's a safe room where I live? How do you know about that and I don't?"

"I know because Claire told me about it when she was renovating the building and said I'd always be welcome there. You probably don't know because you didn't read the paperwork you were given when you signed your lease."

He sighed, but he looked calmer. "That is possible; it sounds like me. Camp was starting. I had to buy a bed. And some phone chargers."

She didn't intend to lay her hand on his arm, but she did. "Do you feel better?" Despite the aggravation he'd caused her, she didn't want him to be afraid. Fear was a terrible feeling, even when it was mostly unfounded.

"Yeah. Thanks for the weather lesson."

"You're welcome. I'm changing the settings on your phone."

"Thanks." He closed his eyes and wrinkled his forehead, like he was deep in thought, hopefully about *All*

Dressed in White. Should she bring it up again or wait for him?

"Hyacinth?" He sounded serious.

"Yes?"

"What's a bug-out bag?"

Of all the things she'd said, he remembered that?

"A bag with essentials in case I need to evacuate in a disaster like a chemical spill, fire, or tornado."

"What do you keep in it?"

"Insurance information, a list of phone numbers, safety deposit box key, a hatchet, my prescription allergy medicine, a toothbrush, change of underwear and socks, phone charger, protein bars, bottled water, fifty dollars in cash." She hesitated. "I also have a roll of tin foil."

"That must be a big bag."

"I like to be prepared."

"What's the foil for?"

"Nothing, really. Evans and Ava Grace gave it to me for a joke when they found out about my bug-out bag. They said it was to make a hat in case of an alien invasion."

He laughed, but there was no mockery in it. "And you actually put it in your bag? Do you believe in aliens?"

"No, but there was room in the bag, so why not? I mean, you never know."

"Your friends may yuk it up now, but if that invasion comes, they'll be looking for you and your bag."

"That's what I think."

He smiled. "You wouldn't be a bad one to have around in case of a tornado."

So now they were back to tornados. Time to reel it

in. "You wouldn't be a bad one to have around for *All Dressed in White*. Where are we on that?"

His sweet smile morphed to a grin with a little devil in it. "I was blackmailing you—or so you said."

"I'm at your mercy." Might as well admit it.

"I have to buy two tickets and attend some Christmas party in December."

"The Christmas Gala at Fairvale, Ava Grace's house. It benefits the historical society."

"Yes, that. I want you to go with me."

"Fine." She was going anyway. Everyone said Skip was finally going to propose to Ava Grace there this year. Even if that wasn't true, it wasn't like she had a choice.

"And also out to Hammer Time with me after the hockey games."

"All right. But you have to pay. And I'm going to eat a lot. Maybe get takeout for later."

"You wound me. You think I would let a woman—even one who is about Satan's business—pay for her own food? I'm a gentleman."

"The epitome, I'm sure. A gentleman and a golfer. And a blackmailer. What else do you want?"

He thought for a few seconds. "That's it. We have a deal."

Finally. She let out a breath she didn't know she'd been holding.

"I assume there will be releases and such to sign. Tell the TV people to get in touch with my agent, Miles Gentry. I'll send you his contact information."

What now? Did he think he was getting paid? "There's no money involved."

"Doesn't matter. Everything goes through Miles. He's also my lawyer."

Then he tilted his head and gave her a look she couldn't read, but she felt a ripple down her spine that radiated out all the way to her fingers and toes.

Stop it, Hyacinth! Don't let him make you feel special. You're not.

Without another word, he got out of her car and into his.

Still shaken from the whole ordeal and weak with confusion and relief, she sat motionless until he drove away.

Then she picked up her phone and dialed. "Ava Grace? Evans said you were going to the hockey game tomorrow. I'd like to meet you there. And I need a favor. Do you think you could help me with some Christmas decorations for Trousseau? You'll never believe what's happened."

Chapter Twelve

"Good game, Scotty," Logan Jensen said as he and Robbie emerged from the locker room together and headed to the area where players' families and friends waited. Robbie hated that place. "The best you've played all season."

"Thanks," Robbie said. "A lucky night, it was."

"The more you practice, the luckier you get."

Before Robbie could answer, "Daddy!" rang out through the air and Logan whipped his head in the direction of the little voice.

"Hey, pal!" Logan took the little boy from a middle-aged woman who Robbie assumed was the nanny.

"Thanks, Mrs. Houston. See you Monday."

The boy—Alexander—looked older than two, but not three yet. Robbie was a good judge of that, from his nieces and nephews. Logan had someone who had come to watch him play, even if it was a kid who couldn't know what was going on and the woman who'd been hired to bring him.

Hyacinth had not come. He'd left her a ticket, but the seat had remained empty. He'd been sure she'd come. She'd been so sweet to him about the storm that he'd decided he'd judged her too harshly over the whole ambition versus Jake and Evans thing—but come to think of it, one didn't have anything to do with the other. He had to stop letting her confuse him; more than that, he had to stop letting her hurt his feelings. That ought to be easy enough. After he paid her for the dress, avoiding her would be easy because he wouldn't be doing *All Dressed in White*.

It was just as well. He shouldn't have asked all those things of her anyway. He hadn't meant to. At first, he was only going to make her let go of that ruined dress business. Then he'd added on the games, curious if she would agree. Then she'd seemed to expect more, and he'd gotten carried away. But a bargain was a bargain and she hadn't kept her end.

Maybe they'd do the show without him and maybe they wouldn't. Not his problem.

But, still, disappointing. Logan was right. He'd had a good game—one of his best and, damn it, he'd wanted her to see it. Not because he was like some horny fifteen-year-old trying to get in her pants, either. It was a matter of pride. It was clear she thought he was a mindless buffoon with no discipline, talent, or skills. He'd wanted to show her she was wrong.

Alexander threw his arms around Logan's neck and kissed him on the cheek, causing Logan to laugh as he hugged him and patted his bottom.

"Hey there, laddie." Robbie took a puck from his jacket pocket and held it out. "Would you like this?" Robbie always took a game-used puck to give to a fan in the autograph line.

The boy looked from Robbie to the puck and back. Then he grinned, snatched the puck out of Robbie's hand, and hit Logan in the head with it.

"Hey!" Logan said. "No hitting." But he laughed.

"Coming out to Hammer Time?" Robbie asked.

"I wish. I could use some ribs, but I need to get him home. I guess it's leftover chili for us." He caught Alexander's wrist before the boy could hit him again.

"Guess I'll sign a few autographs and head out. See you, Scotty."

He was about to walk away when he saw her. Hyacinth. She was in a three-way embrace with Evans and Ava Grace while Jake looked on.

What the hell? Was she going to try to pretend she'd come to the game? He knew better, knew where her seat was, and he'd kept an eye on it even after he'd realized she wasn't coming.

He approached the group. Jake caught his eye and shrugged. "Come on, ladies," he said. "We're not going to the South Pole. I'm only taking her to New Orleans for two days."

"It's just that we're so happy for y'all," Hyacinth said. That's when Robbie realized she was teary. So were Ava Grace and Evans. Wiping their eyes, they disengaged.

"Even if I didn't get you on *All Dressed in White?*" Evans teased. She was teasing, wasn't she? Seemed like it.

"I forgive you," Hyacinth said. "Leaving me stranded in Mississippi is something else again."

Stranded? Really? He wouldn't have left her.

All the women were laughing and hugging again.

"I accept your reprimand and repent," Evans said.

"You do not," Ava Grace said. "You have to be sorry before you repent and you're not."

"No comment . . ." Evans looked at Jake like he was the best piece of chocolate in a heart-shaped box.

"I wouldn't have it any other way." Hyacinth's voice was all soft and she laid her hand on Evans's cheek. "Totally worth it to see the look on your face."

She sounded sincere; maybe she was. Damn it. Every single time he thought he had something figured out, she confused him again. Anyway, nothing changed that she'd stood him up.

"We're going to have the best party ever for y'all," Ava Grace said.

"We are." Hyacinth nodded.

"I hate to break up this love fest," Jake said. "Except I don't. Evie, we need to go." There was another round of hugs, with Robbie getting his share this time.

"I'll walk out with you," Ava Grace said. "Hyacinth, I'll see you tomorrow, like we talked about."

Hyacinth wiped her eyes again as they left.

She turned to Robbie. "Congratulations on the win. I don't know anything about hockey, but Evans said you had a great game."

The nerve of this woman. "Evans said, did she? I guess that's the only way you'd know."

Hyacinth nodded. "Everything moves so fast. It's hard to tell who's doing what all the time."

"It's easier to tell if you're actually at the game."

Hyacinth frowned. "What are you talking about? I was at the game. I'm right here."

"You weren't in your seat. I looked. A couple of times."

"How do you know where my seat was?" She looked puzzled—and annoyed.

"I left you a ticket."

"You didn't tell me that."

Hadn't he? Surely. But maybe not. He'd picked up

his phone to text her. He remembered that. But then, his mum called. The next plan was to call her at Trousseau, but something else had distracted him. Distraction had always been a particular problem of his.

This was downright embarrassing, but he wasn't admitting it. "I would have thought it was a given."

"Why would you think that?"

A reasonable question, but he still wasn't convinced she hadn't snuck in here after the game.

"Who did we play?" he demanded.

She shrugged. "I don't know the name, but their outfits were red and blue."

Those were the colors of the Montreal Caribous, but it could have been a lucky guess. Red and blue were good colors, some of the best. "What was the final score?"

Her whisky eyes went mean. "You think I drove all the way downtown to trick you into thinking I came to the game? I'm not answering any more questions. You made me come and I'm here. You did *not* tell me you were leaving me a ticket. If you had, I would have told you I've got my own damn tickets. Claire gave them to me. I was sitting in one of those little box things with Ava Grace. Evans was there part of the time, too. The rest of the time, she was where the wives sit. Ask them if you want, but I'm not getting a note from them or my mommy."

She'd have been sitting in a VIP suite then—way better than the ticket he'd left her. And failed to tell her about.

So she had come to see him play, even if it had been under duress, but had no idea what she'd seen. He could not win with this woman.

"Sorry." The apology came easy. He'd had plenty of practice over the years, often due to that distraction problem.

She stared him down for a beat or two and nodded.

"I got two goals and an assist. Did you see me?"

"I don't even know what an assist is. Are we going to eat? I'm hungry."

"Yeah. Almost. I have to hit the autograph line for a bit first."

"I'll meet you there."

"Why don't you come with me?" It wasn't late, but it was dark and he wasn't sure how safe this part of town was. "The autograph line is fun." He took her arm and guided her toward the exit. "Then I'll follow you back to Laurel Springs and we'll drop your car off at home before going to Hammer Time. The parking after games there is tight."

She wanted to argue with him; he could see it in her eyes. But she just set her jaw and gave him a half nod.

"Robbie! Over here!" came a voice as they neared the autograph line. He glanced to see if she'd heard it. Unfortunately, he couldn't tell.

Chapter Thirteen

"You have got to be kidding me!" Hyacinth closed her eyes and looked again. Surely she had misread the sign—but no.

The parking spot that Robbie had pulled into at Hammer Time had a sign that read Reserved for Yellowhammer Robbie McTavish, #5. "Is this why you insisted on taking my car to my house first? So I would see that you have your own parking place?" She shouldn't be surprised. He'd wanted her to see him signing autographs, too. She didn't know whether to be annoyed or flattered. But he had been sweet to the fans—especially the children.

He gave her a sidelong look. "The first star of the game gets the parking place until the next game. This is the first time I've had it."

She supposed the first star meant the best player that night.

She had lied to him earlier, though what she'd said was close enough to the truth that she could rationalize it. She *didn't* know anything about hockey, and the fast-moving game *was* hard to follow—but she hadn't needed Evans to tell her he'd had a good game. Even she could tell when he put the puck in the net, which he'd done twice. She wasn't as clear on that thing called assist, but that slamming opponents up against the sides of the rink… That happened a lot and it was exciting. It woke something almost primal in her and for the first time she understood why the girls in high school wanted the guy who could throw a football fifty yards or knock a baseball over the fence. It made her uneasy—especially in herself—but she understood it.

However, she wasn't going to praise him. He didn't need her praise; he had a sign and a parking place for that.

"Good thing I didn't drive," she said breezily. "If I'd have seen this, I would have parked here. I might come back tomorrow and do it. I might leave my car here all week."

"Yeah? Claire gave me this space. Are you willing to cross her?"

"I might. I guess you'll know when you come here and try to park." She reached to unbuckle her seat belt and he was there opening her door before she could do it herself.

Holding his hand out to help her from the low-sitting vehicle was such a benign gesture, but then her hand was in his and it felt anything but.

"Your hands are cold. Don't you have gloves?" He didn't let go of her hand, even when she was on her feet beside him.

"You don't have gloves," she pointed out.

"My hands aren't cold."

And they weren't. He took her other hand, folded them together, and rubbed them between his.

The feeling was dizzying. It shouldn't have been. It was just hands on hands. It shouldn't have meant anything—and it didn't. Not to him. But there was something about his hands. She had the unexplained, insane desire to kiss his palms, first one and then the other. Crazy. She had to stop.

"Thanks. That's better." She withdrew her hands and put them in her coat pockets.

And damn if he didn't put one of those hands on the small of her back to guide her into the restaurant. She needed a Kevlar bodysuit.

When they stepped inside the door, cheers went up. Robbie waved to his public.

"That's because I'm first star," he whispered in her ear. "That's important."

"I got that, what with the parking place and all."

The restaurant was packed. He put an arm around her shoulders to steer her past the bar toward the back room. "I have to enjoy it while I can. It'll be somebody else next week."

"Maybe not. Maybe you'll be first star again."

He shrugged. "That's the way of it. You're up. You're down. In between, people are asking, 'What have you done for me lately?'"

"It's not like you to be cynical."

"That's not cynical. It's just life, la—I mean, Hyacinth."

An icicle ripped through her. Why, why, why had she told him to never call her lass?

Their progress across the room was slow. Every two steps, someone stopped Robbie for a handshake, back slap, or selfie. Sometimes all three. She wondered idly if they looked like a couple or just a man running a woman through a crowd like a trolling motor on a bass boat.

"Here we are." He pulled out a chair for her at a

long table full of hockey players—some with women, some not.

Robbie took off his jacket, slung it over the back of his chair, and loosened his tie.

"I'm surprised you aren't wearing your kilt," Hyacinth said.

"Aye. So am I." His mouth went to a grim line. "I wore a dress kilt to my first game my rookie year and got fined. Prejudicial dress code, if you ask me, but no one did." He slipped into the seat beside her.

"You didn't fight it?"

"Not a hill I'm willing to die on. Anyway. Sorry about the crowd and all the stops." He wasn't; she could tell. "We're fair game until we sit. Then they don't approach us."

"How's that?"

He looked puzzled. "I don't rightly know. Claire said that was how it would be and it is."

"She has her ways."

"She scares people." He took a sip from his water glass. "She scares me."

"How can that be, Scotty?" asked the guy at the end of the table, whose first language was clearly not English. He had large dark eyes. "You say you are scared of nothing." He slung his arm around the blonde in the seat beside him.

"Just Claire," Robbie said. "If you're smart you will be, too." He unbuttoned his top shirt button and rubbed his neck. She looked away, but not before a shiver ran through her.

"You should fear being rude, for not making introductions." Big Dark Eyes turned to Hyacinth. "Hi. I am Miklos. This is Brittany." Brittany wore a Yellowhammer jersey, as had Evans today. That must be a badge of honor. Most of the women at the table also wore jerseys. It made for an odd look, given that the men wore suits and ties.

"Holy family and all the wise men, magic man," Robbie said. "Give a fellow time. Everyone, this is Hyacinth. She is a friend of Jake's girl, Evans."

"Wouldn't that be wife?" asked the dark-headed man with a Russian accent next to Miklos.

"Right," Robbie said. "Hyacinth, this is Luka. And next to him, Able Killen, with Ariel."

"I know Ariel," Hyacinth said. She was one of Evans's assistants. She walked around in an ethereal fog, but was apparently an inspired baker.

Hyacinth greeted everyone, and Robbie introduced the others around the long table, but she didn't pay much attention to the names of anyone except the five in her conversation range.

The waitress appeared with some sort of beer that looked like coffee for Robbie and he ordered a glass of prosecco for her without asking—which might have annoyed her if it hadn't been her favorite. But how had he known that? She remembered having some at Thanksgiving lunch, but how could he have noticed? He'd been barely speaking to her.

"They know what I like to drink here," he said, taking a sip of his drink. "Harviestoun Ola Dubh ale. They keep it for me special."

"Maybe they do," Luka said. "Maybe you have the parking spot for the moment, but do I see your jersey on the wall?" He pointed to where two jerseys were displayed. "I do not."

"I don't see yours either."

"Bah! I care not," Luka said. "It not like it's Olympic Gold Medal."

"You have to earn a spot on the wall," Ariel said in a soft little voice. "Able's was the first one up." She looked up at him with her lilac-colored eyes and rubbed against him like a happy kitten. He dropped a brief kiss on her lips.

"I'm the luckiest guy here, for sure," Able said. Hyacinth got the feeling he wasn't talking about the jersey.

"*Blyad!*" Luka said. "Here comes other Mr. Jersey Wall."

Hyacinth looked up to see a tall sandy-haired guy approach with a girl on each arm. He looked more like a boy than a man and seemed incredibly pleased with himself.

"Our esteemed goalie approaches," Robbie said quietly to Hyacinth. "Dietrich Wingo. Try to ignore him. He loves himself."

Pot, kettle. Hyacinth didn't say it, but she couldn't stop herself from laughing.

"What?" Robbie said.

She didn't have to answer because the goalie stepped up behind Robbie. "Hello, everyone! Meet Andrea and Shelly."

"Shelby." One of the girls corrected him.

He laughed. "Sorry, babe. I knew that. My tongue got tangled up. Now, Ryan," he said to the guy on the other side of Robbie. "I'm just going to need you to move down so we can slide in here. Yeah. That's right. One more." Everyone from Robbie down shifted.

"Why do they obey him like that?" Luka said none too quietly. "I will beat him to a bloody pulp yet."

"They do it because they don't skate first line," Miklos said, "and he had shutout tonight."

"*We had* shutout," Luka corrected.

"Able's the captain," Ariel said, as if that were pertinent, and traced the *C* on the shoulder of the jersey she wore.

"Use some of that captain luck to summon up a server," Miklos said. "Luka should eat before he commits cannibalism with our goalie, yes?"

And like magic, she appeared. "Is everyone ready to order? The soup tonight is chili, the appetizer is barbecue nachos, and we have fresh salmon with a balsamic glaze served with roasted baby rainbow carrots and lemon parmesan couscous."

Oh, yum. Salmon was Hyacinth's favorite and she loved anything with a balsamic glaze. But she wouldn't order it. She had talked big about what it would cost Robbie to feed her, but she would never be someone who ordered expensive specials when someone else was paying. She opened the menu. Maybe the chili and a salad—though she was really hungry. The grilled chicken sandwich came with fries, and a small salad was only five dollars extra. That wasn't likely to cost more than what he ate.

"I'll have two cheeseburgers, medium well, with double fries," Robbie said. "And the lady will have the salmon."

What? "No," she said, but by then Able was already ordering a rack of ribs and lasagna for himself and a grilled cheese sandwich for Ariel. "Robbie, I wasn't going to order that."

"Really? You wanted it."

"No."

"Oh. Sorry. I misread you. I thought you looked like you'd opened your best Christmas present when she was talking about it. I'll get her back." He started to raise his hand.

She found her voice. "No. I'll eat it."

"I'll not have you eat what you don't want."

"I do want it," she admitted.

He looked confused. "But you said you didn't."

"I want it now. All the talk about it…"

"If you're sure."

First the wine, now this. Had he really been paying such close attention? She looked at the table where he was resting his hands. One of his knuckles was swollen and bruised.

"It's always like this."

Hyacinth looked up. It was Brittany, the girl with Miklos, who had spoken.

"Like what?"

"This." Brittany gestured to the table, where the noise level had gone up, with the guys talking to each other all at once. "They get you settled, square you away with something to eat and drink—sort of like putting out Purina Dog Chow and a bowl of water. Then they're done with you because they've got some glory moments to relive with each other. Or not so glory moments. But don't worry. He'll remember you well enough once he's had some food, told all his stories three times, and wants some comfort."

This took Hyacinth aback. Brittany looked to be no more than twenty-two or -three. She seemed more cynical than sad—which was sad within itself. "No. It's not like that with us. Robbie and I are—" What were they?

Brittany laughed. "That's the way of it. You never know what you are."

Beside her, Miklos stood up and spoke excitedly about something. Between the hockey terms and the Czech he lapsed into, Hyacinth had no idea what. Brittany gave him a fond look that he didn't notice.

"Have you and Miklos been together long?"

Brittany gave her a wry smile. "Now and then. Here and there. I live in St. Louis. I see him when he plays there. If he wants to see me somewhere else, he flies me in." She shrugged. "It's not exclusive. I like hockey players. What can I say?"

Hyacinth got it. Brittany was one of those women Evans had mentioned—a puck bunny. To each her own, but if it was making her unhappy, why did she do it? Had it started out fun, but she'd stumbled onto the one she was in love with, who just wanted to have a good time? Was it possible to stumble into love?

"It's good that you know what you like," Hyacinth said. "But really, Robbie and I are friends…have mutual friends. Look, here's our food."

As Robbie shook ketchup on his fries, he turned to her. "Got everything you need there? Did you want a salad? Or some extra bread?"

"No, I've got a gracious plenty."

"Oh, but your glass is empty." He picked it up and held it where the server could see it. "Stacy. Lass, when you get chance. Prosecco."

Here a lass, there a lass, everywhere a lass, lass. He was about to say something else to her, but got distracted by Dietrich Wingo instead. "I've told you before, Wings. Keep your hands out of my plate."

An argument over fries ensued and Hyacinth settled

back to eat and watch Ariel. She'd never seen anyone eat a grilled sandwich like that before.

An hour later, their food was gone. Hyacinth had turned down dessert, and had chatted with Brittany about the weather, airplane flights, and their Christmas shopping. Robbie had stopped drinking after his second beer, but the rowdy festivity around them showed no signs of slowing down. How many times had they relived the game? How many times would they?

She'd had enough and she had some work to do. "I'm going to go now," she said in Robbie's ear as she stood. "But you stay."

His head whirled around. "No. How can you? I drove you."

"Then you know it's about a five-minute walk to my house."

"Not happening, not at night." He rose. "I'll go, too."

"It's not even nine o'clock."

"Criminals don't care about clocks." He put on his jacket and drank the last bit of water in his glass.

"Hold on there, Biscotti," Wingo said. "You can't go."

"I bloody well can."

But just then Claire sashayed out with Soup Carter behind her carrying a large shadow box.

"Gentlemen, ladies," she said, and the table went silent. "As you may know, here at Hammer Time a jersey doesn't go on the wall until it's earned. Dietrich, Able, join me, please."

They went to stand with her under their jerseys. "Robbie McTavish earned his place on the wall of excellence today and earned it well. Robbie, join us."

Much hooting and hollering commenced. There

would be no living with him now, for sure. Cameras came out. Pictures were taken.

Hyacinth might have taken a few herself.

Just for something to do.

Well, it had turned out to be a right fine night. Robbie had thought Luka's jersey would be next, or maybe Jake's.

Plus, Hyacinth hadn't given him any hell tonight—or much. Just about the parking space, and that was all in good fun.

"You really don't have to leave," she said as they stepped onto the sidewalk. "You should go back to your teammates. It's a short walk and it's well lit. I don't need a ride."

"Truly?" he asked. "You don't mind walking?"

"I do it all the time."

He took her arm. "Then let's walk. Helps me get the kinks out. I'll walk back and get my car."

"Alone? At night?" she said in mock horror. "I can't allow that. Too dangerous. I'll have to walk you back."

"And then I'll have to walk *you* back again." They proceeded down the street. All the stores had Christmas decorations and there were fairy lights in the trees.

She laughed. "We'll keep it up until one of us dies on the sidewalk."

"We'll be known in the record books as the couple who walked each other home to death."

"We aren't a couple," she said a little too quickly.

Not that he thought they were.

"Sure we are—in that there are two of us and that equals a couple—but a couple that never quite made it home. Just went round and round, back and forth."

"Until death. Which one of us do you think would die first?" she asked.

"You, of course."

"Me? Why me?"

"I'm an athlete. My endurance has got to be a hundred—maybe even a thousand—times what yours is."

"Who's to say what would kill us? Maybe we'd starve to death, or die of dehydration."

"Nah. We could stop and drink from people's garden hoses. Pretty soon people would stand on the street and give us food. We'd be famous."

"You're already famous," she pointed out.

"Not so much. Only in the hockey world. Did you know who I was?"

She laughed. "I'm still not sure I do."

"Ah. That's the way I like it. A man of mystery. Tell you what. Ask me a question. Anything. I'll answer."

"Hmm. That's hard." But he could tell she was interested.

"Take your time. You said it was a five-minute walk. You have at least three more minutes."

"Okay. Why were you and Wingo arguing about French fries?"

He stopped in the middle of the street they were crossing. "You have got to be kidding me. I give you carte blanche and that's what you ask?"

"What did you think I would ask?"

"I don't know. If I believe in God."

"I know you do. You've already talked about what a good Catholic boy you are. Good Catholic boys tend to believe in God."

"Well, then, if I've ever been in jail."

"You've already told me you haven't."

He had? "When?"

"When you were nattering on about what kind of relationship you had with Jules and her fiancé. You said they weren't the kind of friends you'd call to get you out of jail, but you hadn't been in jail."

"Oh, right. I guess I did. You *have* been paying attention."

She got the oddest look on her face, one he couldn't begin to read.

"What?" he asked.

"Nothing." When women said *nothing*, that was never true. Was he in trouble? He didn't see how.

She took his hand and pulled him onto the sidewalk. "Here comes a car. I'm curious about the French fries—not how your brains would look scattered on the pavement."

"That's disgusting."

"So about the French fries?"

"That. Wingo. Holy family and all the wise men. He's a great goalie; can't deny it. But he is a cross to bear. He's a rookie. He was cock of the walk in college—won the National Championship last year. He can't get over himself, knows he's handsome. He's always strutting around talking about how much weight he can press, and how his body is his temple, and he never puts anything bad in it—no red meat, simple carbs, sugar. God forbid anything fried. But the minute he sits down by somebody at a table, he starts eating off their plate. Bad stuff. Some of the guys put up with it, but I will not. As for Luka. Well. I don't think Wings will try it again with him. At least I didn't stab the back of his hand with my fork."

To Robbie's surprise, Hyacinth began to laugh—and not just a little chuckle. She bent double, held her sides, and laughed from the depths of her soul.

He caught his breath. When had he ever enjoyed a sight and sound more?

She finally straightened up and wiped her eyes.

"Y'all are like a bunch of junior high puppies."

"I didn't know puppies went to junior high."

She tucked her hand into his arm and started to walk again. "Maybe Wings brought two girls so he'd have two more plates to eat from."

Robbie shuddered in spite of himself. "I hope so. I had considered another reason. I don't want to think about that."

"Oh? Nothing that wild for you?"

"No. I am old-fashioned in my own way."

"I'm sure you are."

They had arrived at her little house faster than he had expected.

"Here we are," she said, reaching into her pocketbook for her keys.

He took them from her. "Let me get that for you."

He stepped inside first and turned on the lights. Everything looked fine, so he stepped aside and let her enter.

When she closed the door behind her, he thought she'd ask him to sit down, but she didn't.

"Thank you for dinner," she said. "And for walking me home. You should go back and celebrate with your team."

He'd been thinking he might, but that was before he'd seen her laugh. "I'll probably just go collect my car and head home."

She grinned. "I could give you a ride home so you can leave your car in the space."

"But then I'd have to follow you back."

"And on it would go." She reached for the knob to open the door, and he caught her scent. She smelled like she had the night he'd almost kissed her.

He considered it. She looked at him with a bit of expectation in her eyes, but she was probably wondering why he was still standing here when she had opened the door for him to leave. Kissing had come easier at fourteen, thirteen, even. But he had to wonder. Had those girls—and the women since—kissed *him*, or a hockey player?

It had been a good night. He didn't want to ruin it with a wrong answer to that question.

He reached for his wallet, but changed his mind. He had fully intended to pay her for the ruined frock tonight, but what would it hurt to have an excuse to see her again?

"Goodnight," he said. "Be sure to lock the door."

Chapter Fourteen

"This is the last one." Brad came in the front door of Trousseau with yet another plastic tote of Christmas decorations. "An even dozen." Ava Grace had sent them over and she didn't do anything halfway when it came to decorating.

"I appreciate that you gave up your Sunday morning to help me," Hyacinth said.

"Happy to. I put the boxes of live garlands and wreaths outside the back door."

Just thinking about it all made Hyacinth want to lie down and sleep until February. It wasn't even noon and she was already exhausted. After the hockey game, the command appearance at Hammer Time, and searching for the leaked photos of Jules Perry's original dress design, she hadn't gone to bed until way after midnight. Then, she got up at six so she could pull dresses for Jules with the same clean lines and understated elegance.

Since Alex had nixed her talking with Jules, finding that design was the best she could do to prepare. She understood that they wanted the dress selection to be spontaneous and natural, but she didn't do spontaneous and she didn't know what natural was. Despite Alex's assurances, she was worried. How could she not be, and how could she not get a head start with the leaked photos? The chore had worn her out, but she had six dresses that perfectly matched the look and two more that might do, but they had a bit of lace and beading that she suspected was too much for Jules's taste.

She needed to find her second wind because Ava Grace would be here soon to decorate the shop for Christmas.

"Are you sure you don't want me to stick around and help?" Brad asked.

Hyacinth eyed the stack of boxed decorations that had to be in place before Trousseau opened tomorrow morning, and almost took him up on his offer. But Ava Grace had been adamant that Brad was not to stay. As the son of Fairvale's household manager, Brad had grown up there, and he and Ava Grace were practically siblings. According to her, Brad always went overboard and would take elegant to gaudy when no one was looking.

"No, Brad. It's enough that you hauled all this in and got the tree in the stand." She stroked a branch of the eight-foot-tall Fraser fir. "We've got it from here. Ava Grace is coming as soon as she gets out of church. Go enjoy your afternoon."

"If you're sure. But I should warn you. Ava Grace's style is a little on the Spartan side. Don't be surprised if we have to bump everything up a notch or six to make it pop for the cameras."

"We'll cross that bridge if we have to."

Brad looked out the door. "There she is now." Ava Grace pulled her Jaguar into the spot beside Brad's truck. "Can you believe she's got the top down? It's forty degrees."

Hyacinth could believe it, which was one of the reasons she didn't like to ride with her.

"You're still here," Ava Grace said to Brad as she breezed in the door, carrying the large wicker basket she always used to ferry stuff around. Ava Grace did not believe in sacks.

"I love you, too," Brad said, and they air kissed as he made his exit.

"I can't thank you enough for doing this," Hyacinth said once Brad was gone.

"Nonsense. I enjoy it. I would have skipped church if I hadn't had to teach Sunday school."

"I needed to do other things this morning anyway."

"We'll get started soon, but we're going to eat first." She set her basket on the coffee table in front of the sofa.

"I picked us up some shrimp and grits from the country club. I bet you haven't eaten this morning."

"That's a bet you'd win." As much as Hyacinth wanted to get this chore behind her, the food that Ava Grace was unpacking smelled wonderful. She sunk down on the sofa and accepted a paper cup of iced tea. It was her inclination to offer to pay for the food, but she knew from experience Ava Grace would have put it on her daddy's tab and would refuse.

"If I know you, you didn't eat last night either." Ava Grace handed her a disposable bowl of steaming shrimp and grits.

Mother of pearl. Here it comes. "You do know me, but I did eat last night." Hyacinth wasn't above withholding information, but there was a point where evasiveness slid into a lie. "I had salmon at Hammer Time after the game."

Ava Grace's eyes snapped wide. "You went to Hammer Time alone?"

"No. Not alone." She put a shrimp in her mouth and took an extra-long time chewing it. Digestion began in the mouth and one could never be too careful about gastronomic issues. "This is good."

"Not alone?" Ava Grace was about as likely to let it go as she was to wear a burlap sack and go without makeup to a Junior League meeting.

"I went with Robbie McTavish—and some of his teammates."

"Well, well, well..." Ava Grace grinned.

"Three holes in the ground." Hyacinth knew what was coming. Ava Grace would see romance between a church mouse and a flea.

"You and Robbie."

"No." Hyacinth stabbed a shrimp. "It's not like that."

"Sounds like it to me."

"I tell you, it's not. You know how I told you Robbie's going to be on *All Dressed in White?* The show stipulated that. No Robbie, no show. I had to promise I'd go to all the home games and then out to Hammer Time before he would agree." *Among other things.* But Hyacinth wasn't going into the Christmas Gala date. It was a date, wasn't it? No matter. Either way, Ava Grace would see that as a guarantee that they were headed for the altar, or at least to bed.

"He must really like you."

"I wouldn't say that."

"Why else would he blackmail you into going out with him?"

"He wants to annoy me; it's his hobby." It struck her that that was a bit unfair. Last night had turned out to be pleasant—if confusing.

"I doubt that's true," Ava Grace said. "Even if it is, maybe he's like an eight-year-old pulling a girl's pigtails to get her attention."

"No. You can't put a romantic slant on everything." "No romance at all?"

"None."

And that was almost true. Or maybe totally true. Who the hell knew? There was the walk home, the wine, the salmon. When he'd seen her inside her house, she'd thought he was going to try to kiss her. She was still trying to decide how she would handle it when he said, "Be sure to lock the door." And those hands.

No way was she telling Ava Grace any of that. Best to change the subject. "The most interesting thing was Ariel. She was there with Able Killen, the captain."

"Ariel, as in Evans's assistant baker?"

"Same. She had a grilled cheese sandwich and she took tiny, tiny random bites of it all the way around. It was the weirdest thing. Then I realized she was—*sculpting*? I don't know if that's the right word, but she ate until there was nothing left except something that looked like the Yellowhammer logo. Then she ate that and started in on the other half. This time she made a heart and handed it to Able. He kissed her like she'd presented him with the Holy Grail. I thought they were going to have sex right there on the table."

"Oh, my." Hot damn. She'd finally distracted Ava Grace. "Do you think that shape eating is some sort of art? Do you suppose she learned it or made it up?"

"I don't know. I could probably do the heart, but that

Yellowhammer was impressive. I bet she had to practice. Maybe there's a YouTube video."

"Hey!" Ava Grace reached for an aluminum foil package on the table. "I forgot. We've got garlic bread. We could try—" She stopped abruptly and looked toward the front of the shop. "Well, well, well. Look who's come calling."

"Who?" Hyacinth asked but she knew, even before she looked around to see Robbie knocking on the glass door.

"Not interested, you say?" Ava Grace said.

"Stop it, Ava Grace." Hyacinth stomped toward the door.

"When you weren't home, I figured I'd find you here," he said when she unlocked the door. "I don't have any food and I have business. May I enter?"

So they were back to the old banter. Somewhat disappointing, but at least Hyacinth understood that—unlike their interaction last night.

"What are you? Some kind of vampire who has to be invited in?" To Hyacinth's surprise, he was wearing pants—sweatpants, but pants nonetheless. His gray hoodie had a stain that looked like coffee.

"It's a fair question," he said. "Considering you banned me from here."

"What's this business you speak of?" She stood aside to let him in. "Don't tell me you need a wedding dress."

"I need to pay for one." He glanced around and walked toward the seating area. "Hi, Ava Grace, I see you've got food. Don't spill it on a dress. That will get you in trouble, and not ordinary trouble—Old Testament caliber trouble."

"What are you talking about?"

"Hyacinth didn't tell you that I soiled a dress with ice cream?"

"Tell her? I most assuredly did not," Hyacinth said. "You said I had to let it go. You said not to talk about it. And I haven't."

"*Somebody* had better tell me," Ava Grace said.

"It won't be me. Robbie can talk about it if he wants." Robbie cracked his knuckles and stood taller—getting ready for his audience. "Did you see the video, lass?"

Lass, lass, lass. Everybody was lass but her. Though she'd brought that on herself.

Ava Grace looked sheepish. "Yes. I did. A few times."

Traitor! She'd probably laughed, too.

"During all that, I dropped my ice cream—mocha praline fudge, it was from Double Scoop."

"I love that. Constance calls me whenever she makes it."

The whole world was ice cream crazy.

"Anyway, a dress got in the way and the results were not what one might have hoped for."

The *dress* got in the way? Hyacinth opened her mouth to point out that it wasn't the dress that was at fault, but closed it again. She wasn't supposed to talk about it, and she would not.

"That's unfortunate." Ava Grace put the top on her food. That was like her—to refuse to eat in front of Robbie when she had none to offer him.

Unfortunate doesn't begin to describe it." Robbie plopped down in one of the club chairs. "This was like the Mt. Vesuvius of unfortunate."

Hyacinth sat back down on the sofa and resumed eating. Let him bait her; let Ava Grace starve herself. She was going to eat and then she was going to decorate this shop—alone if necessary. No whining either—not even in her head. *Tired, tired, tired!* So what if she was tired? She was lucky she had work to do.

"It's just a dress," Ava Grace said. "It's not like anybody died." Ava Grace would think that. She lived in a world of stained glass, silver spoons, and caviar.

"That remains to be seen." Robbie turned to Hyacinth. "I've come to pay for the frock." He reached into the pocket of his hoodie and brought out his wallet.

Hyacinth was torn. The prideful part of her wanted to refuse payment, to insist she could take the loss, no problem. But the logical part of her knew how it was going to end. Robbie had a lion's share of pride himself. What was it he'd said? *I take responsibility and I pay what I owe.* Also, it was an eight-thousand-dollar dress. Taking that kind of loss wouldn't get her any closer to her goal.

She put her fork aside. "I'll go check on the exact price."

"No need," Robbie said, opening his wallet. "I looked at the tag that day and calculated the tax."

"Then I'll get my iPad and card reader."

"No need of that either."

And to Hyacinth's amazement—and horror—Robbie opened his wallet and began to peel off bills like they were playing cards.

"There." He patted the stack of money. "Eight thousand, eight hundred dollars. Count it if you like."

Hyacinth put her hands over her face and shook her head.

"Robbie. Robbie." She waved her hands in the air, aware that she never waved her hands. "You can't go around carrying that kind of money."

"I'm not going around with it. I gave it to you."

"But you had to get it at some point, I assume from the bank, right in plain sight. You can't get that much money from an ATM. You couldn't have gotten it yesterday or today. They're closed. Please tell me you haven't been walking around with nearly nine thousand dollars in your pocket since Friday."

He widened his eyes and shrugged. "Well, a bit more actually, with my spending money."

"You're lucky somebody didn't follow you and slit your throat."

He leaned in toward her and her mouth went dry. "Slit my throat?" He stroked his neck. She didn't want to remember how that neck had felt pressed against her face when they had danced—how it had smelled, like pine-scented soap with a little sweat mixed in. "Surely not."

Surely not was right. She didn't need to be thinking like this.

"You're going to do what you're going to do." She picked up the money and shuffled it into a neat stack. "Ava Grace, do you think we should start decorating outside first? Since we can work on the inside after dark."

Robbie perked up. "Decorating for Christmas?"

"Yes," Ava Grace said. "Exactly what I thought. We'll get the garland and wreaths up and go from there."

Robbie stood. "Great. I'm in. Where's your ladder?"

What? No. She was too confused to have him around—climbing on ladders, sweating, calling Ava Grace *lass*. Plus, she couldn't ignore the disaster factor. These decorations did not belong to her and they had not come from the Dollar Tree.

"That's all right, Robbie. We've got this," Hyacinth said.

"Come now. You don't want to miss out on an expert like me. I have decked the halls of Wyndloch many a time. Nobody hangs lights and garland better than me. I'm your man. And I fair love Christmas."

"Great," Ava Grace said before Hyacinth could protest further. "We'd love the help."

She should put her foot down. Maybe she would have if she hadn't caught sight of the stacks of boxes waiting to be opened and dealt with.

"All right." With visions of broken ornaments, crooked garland, and tangled light strings dancing in her head, Hyacinth led him to the storeroom where the ladder was kept.

Ten hours, hundreds of ornaments, and thousands of twinkle lights later, Trousseau was a white and silver fairyland inside and out. The front window featured a bride in a dreamy, sparkling dress standing among snowy, fairy-lit trees, with woodland animals about. Robbie had been disappointed that none of Emma Frances Fairchild's animals were animated.

Ava Grace frowned and adjusted a crystal star on the tree until it was facing forward. "There. That's better."

"It's perfect," Hyacinth said.

"Are you sure you're happy?" Ava Grace asked.

"I couldn't be happier. You've saved my life. I could never have afforded to buy these decorations, much less make all this happen."

"It was nothing," Ava Grace collected her floral wire, craft snips, and bits of ribbon and packed them in her basket. "My mother has a different theme every year. All I had to do was go to the attic and find the boxes labeled Christmas Gala 2009. Winter Wonderland."

"We decorate the same every year at Wyndloch," Robbie said. "Pine boughs and holly that we collect from the woods. Berries, ribbons and lots of lights. You have to get the lights distributed just so, without a lot of bright spots. You want a twinkle effect. Like the sky." He gestured to the light-festooned garland around the window. "And you don't want to see the strings. The lights are my specialty—or they were. My brother-in-law does them now. But not as good."

He looked wistful and Hyacinth wondered how long it had been since he'd been home for Christmas and where he spent it when he didn't go. When she'd put the Yellowhammer games on her calendar, she'd noticed they only paused three days for the holidays.

"I don't know what we would have done without you, Robbie," Ava Grace said.

Hyacinth had to admit it was true. Robbie had been fast and proficient without breaking anything. Too bad Hyacinth couldn't claim the same. She'd broken a half dozen silver glass balls and a crystal snowflake. The snowflake debacle had occurred when Robbie, having ditched his hoodie, was on the ladder reaching over his head to hang garland. His T-shirt had ridden up just enough to show a narrow strip of muscled skin above his waistband. The snowflake had jumped from her hand.

She shook her head to clear it. There was a conversation going on here.

"I do appreciate all you've done, Robbie," Hyacinth said. "You were a godsend." It was only fair. "Come dawn, Ava Grace and I would have still been at it."

"A godsend, you say?" He looked at her all warm. "Can't say I've ever been called that before."

"We'd better not let my mother get wind of your light-hanging skills," Ava Grace said. "She'll figure out a way to put you to work decorating for the gala."

"Then don't tell Claire," Robbie said. "She, for certain, would send me over. I swear that woman will have us picking up trash on the side of the road before the season's over."

"She's a force of nature." Ava Grace picked up her basket with an eye toward the door.

Hyacinth had an eye toward the door, too. She might be able to wrap things up here and get in bed by midnight.

"I can't thank you two enough," she said.

"I've a mind to get a pizza," Robbie said. "Would you lasses like some?"

No. She didn't want a pizza. She wanted to double-check that the special-order veil that had arrived yesterday was the right one, take a shower, and go to bed.

But he'd called her *lass*. Sort of. And how could she say no, when he'd worked like a dog for her for ten hours?

"None for me, thanks," Ava Grace said, moving toward the door. "Skip's in Tulsa and I want to call him before bedtime. Y'all eat my part."

Ever the matchmaker, at least she was being subtle. It was entirely reasonable that she would want to talk to her almost fiancé.

But then, when she got to the front door, Ava Grace paused and flipped the light switch. "I wanted to see how it all looks with the lights off." There, the subtlety ended. Ava Grace closed the door behind her, leaving them in the glow of fairy lights—as if Hyacinth would fall into Robbie's arms just because they were in a dim setting that smelled like Christmas. It was a thousand wonders she hadn't found a way to pipe in a Fifty Songs to Have Sex To playlist.

But Robbie hadn't noticed how blatant she'd been. He was too busy staring in wonder at the tree and the shimmering garland that lined the crown molding, doors, and front window.

"Looks like the stars in the sky." He pronounced *stars* like a cross between *stirs* and *stairs*. *Déjà vu.* He'd done that before and she'd thought the same thing. It was charming.

"I wouldn't say exactly like the sky," she said.

"No?" He smiled and her stomach turned over.

Don't look at him, Hyacinth! He's a mess. He'll turn your life upside down, and break your heart. No. Not her heart. That wasn't up for grabs. It was her sanity that was in danger and that was worse. She could control her heart. She was going to run, run to the light switch and turn it on.

But then he put an arm around her shoulders and pointed to the garland above the tree. "Dream a little, Hyacinth. Don't you see the Big Dipper just there?"

And he slid a hand down her arm.

She was lost—right back where she'd been the night before Thanksgiving at Evans's house, with her heart pounding and a million stars shooting through her, warming and electrifying every part of her being.

All because of this haphazard, unpredictable man.

He felt it too. His arm tightened around her at the same moment that he brought his green, green eyes to melt into hers. There was a question in them, a question she was going to say yes to. He was going to kiss her and she was not only going to let him, she was going to revel in it. She wouldn't fool herself into believing it was just a kiss. It would be more—the beginning of something. She wouldn't fool herself into believing it would end well either, but right now she didn't care. So what if he wasn't a forever kind of guy? Sometimes right now mattered; this was one of those times.

He leaned in and parted his lips, testing the waters.

In answer, she raised her face and let her hand drift to his cheek.

Then his mouth was on hers, his hands caressing her back, her cheeks, her neck. Their tongues tangled and Hyacinth's stomach turned over and crashed against her heart like a storm at sea. The longer they kissed, the tighter he held her until she wasn't sure where he left off and she began. She raked his hair back and ran her hand down the back of his neck.

He leaned into her hand. "Ah, la... Hyacinth," he said, breathing hard.

She tightened her arms around his neck. "Call me lass. Always call me *lass*."

He buried his face against her neck. *"Lass, lass, lass."*

And he kissed her again and again and again as the storm inside her raged on.

When they broke for a breath, he whispered against her ear, "I think we're having a moment, lass."

"Several."

"More good than bad?"

"Excellent," she admitted. "Beyond excellent."

"And our next moment?" he asked.

Good question. Did he expect them to move straight for bed? Probably. Maybe the storm inside her liked that idea, too, but that's not who she was.

Just then, his stomach growled, providing her with an answer.

"Pizza?" she said.

He laughed, low and sweet, and pushed her hair off her face. "Pizza would be outstanding."

"What do you like?" she asked. "I'll order."

"Order? Oh, no, no, lass. You won't catch me with tomato sauce around all this." He gestured to the racks of dresses. "I've learned my lesson. It's the Brick Oven for us. It's a right fine night. We can walk."

When he stopped her halfway down the block to kiss her again, it struck her. A kiss was not just a vehicle to the next step for Robbie. He liked kissing—and people were almost always good at what they liked.

Perfect—a perfect day with perfect pacing.

As for later—this one time in her life, she'd worry about later when later came.

Chapter Fifteen

Fresh from the locker room shower, Robbie whistled as he made his way to his stall.

"You're mighty happy today, Scotty," Able said.

"What have I got to not be happy about?" he asked. "Great practice today and my jersey's on the wall at Hammer Time."

And I spent some quality time with a soft, gorgeous woman wrapped in my arms last night.

There was a time he would have said that out loud, but not today, and not about Hyacinth. She might be buttoned up and wound tighter than an eight day clock in her day-to-day comings and goings, but she had a fire in her—a slow burning one, but that was all right with him. Of course he wanted her, but she wasn't ready, and the journey would be sweet.

When she'd asked him to call her lass, it had gone straight to his heart, as if it cleared away all the bad things they'd said to each other.

"Did you hear me, Scotty?" Able shook his shoulder. "You're acting like you're on another planet."

Planet Hyacinth, and he couldn't wait to go back.

"Do you want to go to Crust with me?" Able asked. "Meat pies were on the lunch menu today, but Ariel put some back and she'll bake them for us."

"Sounds good, but no. I have somewhere else to be."

He was meeting Hyacinth at the Waffle House out by the highway. Though the taping was over a week away, she claimed they needed to make plans for the *All Dressed in White* shoot and there wouldn't be many distractions at Waffle House. He didn't really understand why they needed to make plans. It seemed like all they had to do was show Jules some dresses and be themselves, but Hyacinth liked plans.

This morning he'd lain awake thinking about her.

Maybe he'd been too hard on her about the whole Jake and Evans thing. Clearly, she did care about them, even if their happiness wasn't her first thought after getting word of the elopement. Who was he to judge? She was coming from a different place and had to worry more about her future.

If he blew out his knee tomorrow and could never skate again, he'd be fine. He could go back to Wyndloch and spend the rest of his days making wedding cakes, hanging Christmas lights, and pinch-hitting at the piano for the odd wedding music emergency. And, though losing hockey would be a blow, he'd be happy. Besides, he'd already earned enough money to live well for the rest of his life.

Hyacinth didn't have any of that—no family, no fortune made from playing hockey, no one who'd have her back if she failed.

No one…unless, maybe, he could be that for her. An idea began to take root.

Hyacinth sat in a back booth and laid out her laptop, calendar, and printouts.

She'd chosen Waffle House because, one, it would be relatively quiet. Two. Coming straight from practice,

Robbie would need food. Three. Since it was unlikely there'd be anyone here they knew, there would be fewer distractions. When she'd told Robbie this last night over pizza, he'd said it would be completely quiet and unin- habited at her place or his, so why not that?

She'd only given him a pointed look. Since he was holding her hand across the table and their mouths were swollen from kissing, he got it.

"Right. Distractions. That's what you're trying to avoid.'" And he'd kissed her nose.

She closed her eyes and relived that moment—the nose kiss. Certainly not the main event of their time together, but a sweet moment and that was a surprise.

She fought back the inclination to wonder where this was going, or if it should be going anywhere. No. This one time, she would not plan. She would just enjoy it while it was happening. Later, when whatever this was with Robbie was done, she'd have her plans to fall back on—continuing to build her business and hoping for a permanent relationship with someone who was a good fit.

Her stomach knotted in rebellion at that last part, but she didn't want to think about that.

"Ma'am? Take your order?"

This was a safer—and easier—subject.

"Iced tea and BLT for me, water, two cheeseburgers, and double hash browns for my—"

Her what? He wasn't her fling. She wasn't a fling kind of person. Besides, they hadn't had sex and a fling involved sex. Didn't it? But he wasn't her boyfriend— if women her age even had boyfriends. Maybe he was her interlude. Yes. She liked the sound of that. But you didn't go around saying that to Waffle House waitresses. A sobering thought washed over her. What if it was nothing? Just some kissing among the Christmas lights, some pizza, and pizza flavored kisses on her doorstep? She had assumed she was in control and would drive this bus where she wanted it to go. Could it be that *he* was in control and hadn't given a second thought to last night?

"Ma'am?" The waitress prompted her.

"My friend. The burgers and hash browns are for my friend. He should be here soon."

Chapter Sixteen

At the Waffle House, Hyacinth was dressed in a blue sweater and her hair was down. Robbie wondered if she'd done that for him.

"Hello, lass." He didn't mean for his tone to go soft when he called her that, but the memory that went with it snuck into his voice. She must be remembering, too, because her cheeks turned a pretty pink. He didn't think he'd be calling anyone else *lass* ever again.

Without a thought, natural as could be, he cupped her cheek and gave her a quick hello kiss—and stopped short. He'd never done that before, given a kiss that was more affection than passion. He'd seen it done a thousand times between his mum and da, sisters and brothers-in-law, cousins, aunts and uncles.

"Is something wrong?" Hyacinth asked.

"No." He settled into the booth across from her. *For the first time, something might be right.* "What's all this?" He gestured to her equipment and stacks of paper.

"Things we need to talk about. We'll go over it while we eat."

"Right. I'm hungry." He looked at the menu printed on the plastic placemat. "I'm going to have two cheeseburgers and hash browns, since I don't see fries."

"Just what I ordered for you," she said. "And here it is. I got you water. They don't serve beer here."

"How did you know what I wanted?" he asked after the waitress had gone.

She shrugged, pushed her sandwich to the side, and opened her laptop. "You said that was your go-to meal after skating. And it's what you ate at Hammer Time after the game."

She remembered that when he didn't even remember saying it. That had to be a good sign, didn't it?

She handed him a stack of papers and turned her computer so they could both see the screen. "Can you eat and talk about this at the same time?"

"Sure." He didn't see why not. She would be doing most of the talking. He squirted ketchup on his hash browns and, in the process, dribbled some on the papers she'd given him. "Sorry."

"This is a printout of the PowerPoint I've made." She wiped at the stain on the top page, which was a calendar. "Follow along with me. Stop me if you need to make notes."

"Aye. I will." He took a bite of his burger.

"Do you have a pen?" she asked.

"No. I don't usually travel with one."

"No problem." She, quick as a wink, produced one and set it by his water glass. He supposed he ought to try to make some notes, but he doubted if she had left anything out.

She pointed to the calendar on her laptop screen. "Today is Monday."

"Yes. All day long."

"Tomorrow is Tuesday." She pointed to the Tuesday block on her calendar.

He was tempted to ask her how dumb she thought he

was that he needed a PowerPoint to tell him the days of the week, but he just nodded and ate some hash browns.

"You have away games on Wednesday and Thursday." At last, something he could comment on. "The Big Apples. Thursday is a matinee. I'll be back that night."

"Right." She nodded. "You have home games Saturday and Sunday, then another home game on Tuesday."

"Minnesota. Anaheim," he said.

"The taping is the next day. Wednesday, the sixth. Trousseau will be closed all day. The show will air on the sixteenth, a week and a half later. That's also Jules and Reynolds's wedding. You have a game that night."

"The Sound. Away, but we don't spend the night in Nashville."

She nodded. "Now back to the taping." She scrolled to a page with a list of bullet points. "You'll find this on your second page." He started to flip the page, but she stopped him. "Let me. You have mustard on your hand."

"It would go with the ketchup. Might try for relish on the third." Saying that kind of thing had gotten him in trouble in the past, but she didn't seem bothered. Either she liked him better now, or she didn't have time to be mad, what with all the bullet points.

"Some of the production staff is coming on Tuesday afternoon to bring equipment, move things if necessary, and make sure the Christmas decorations are up to par."

"Why wouldn't they be?" They'd nearly killed themselves decorating that shop and those TV people damn well better like it.

"I don't have any reason to think they won't. I'm only telling you what's going to happen. You don't need to be there Tuesday."

"Good thing. I have a game."

"I know. Anaheim. Seven o'clock. But you do have

to be there Wednesday morning at seven o'clock. I've told them you have to be at the rink at seven that night to go to the airport. They said we should be done in plenty of time."

That was a lot of sevens. "It's going to take all day? To make an hour-long show?"

"Probably. They film everything and will edit it down to an hour. This is the order of how things will happen. Jules will have Reynolds, her mother, and her sister, who's also her maid-of-honor, with her. There will be some meet and greet with us. Next, Reynolds will leave. Then, with any luck, we'll find Jules a dress. I'm to treat it like any other bridal appointment. I have some dresses put aside that I think will work. You'll bring them out and I'll talk to her about them. Patty and Brad will be there in the background to help, but they won't be on camera. Alex said it gets confusing if there are too many people trying to interact."

"Who's Alex?"

"Alex Leman, the assistant director. Deb Carmichael is the director, but Alex is my contact."

He wondered what kind of contact they'd had. "Is it Alex as in Alexandria, or Alexander?"

"Alexander. Why?"

"No reason. What am I to do during all this? Besides being a dress holder?"

"Unlike a lot of reality TV, *All Dressed in White* isn't scripted. They said act natural, be yourself. Comment on the dresses. Talk to the mother and sister. Brad will hand off the dresses to bring out. He knows the order I want them shown."

"That should be easy enough. I know how to be Robbie." He smiled at her and picked up his second burger.

She smiled back, but then it faded away. "Yes, you

do. But that's one of the things I want to talk about." She reached under the table and brought out a large shopping bag. "I sent Brad downtown to get you some clothes."

"What the hell!? I have clothes," he said.

She opened the bag and pulled out a pair of khakis, a blue button-down shirt, a leather and canvas belt, and a pair of loafers—in other words, the Southern Fraternity Boy uniform.

"Brad says they'll fit. He's never wrong."

"If you were going to dress me up like Brad or Jake Champagne, why didn't you just have them do it?"

"Robbie, please." Her eyes begged and he suspected that was the only begging Hyacinth ever did.

"Okay. All right. If it'll make you happy, I'll wear the preppy mama's boy outfit." He *did* want her to be happy. At least there was no tie.

"Thank you. Roll the sleeves up to right below your elbows. On second thought, don't, I'll do it for you."

"Anything else?" He wasn't cutting his hair. He liked some flow out the back of his helmet.

"Yes. One thing. I know Alex said for us to be ourselves, but I'd like you to be a little *less* yourself, if you know what I mean?"

He put his burger down. "No, I don't think I do."

"A little more low-key. Not quite so charming."

He was torn between being annoyed because she didn't want him to be himself and taking pleasure in her admission that he was charming. Reminding himself that he was going to try to make this go like she wanted, he decided to go with the latter.

"You think I'm charming, do you, now?" He smiled and reached across the table and took her hand. "How charming am I, lass?" He made sure *lass* sounded like a caress.

She jerked her hand away. "Stop it, Robbie. That's what I'm talking about. Don't take over. I need this to go smoothly. This has to be dignified and elegant."

He almost asked her how dare she accuse him of being undignified, but he saw the look of terror on her face and took a deep breath. Nobody ought to have to be that terrified of making a little TV show.

Maybe he ought to tell her the idea he'd had to give her a way out. He hadn't thought it all the way through, but that seldom stopped him in the past, so why now?

"You don't have to do this, lass."

Her head snapped up in surprise. "Do what?"

"This show, not like this."

"No, I don't have to. There aren't that many things in life we *have* to do, but I've told you about my goals. I love my shop. But I want to create."

"Do something for me. If you could be doing any-thing—*anything*—in the world on that Wednesday, what would it be?"

"I don't know what you mean."

"Come on. It's not hard. If you had a wish and could wish up your life for that day, what would you be doing? I'll tell you what I'd be doing. I'd be getting on a plane headed to LA to play the Angels." *And I'd be with you.* "That *is* what you're doing. After taping the show."

"Not about me. What would *you* be doing?"

She closed her eyes for a second. When she opened them again, they were sparkling with happiness. "Okay. I'd be in my workroom, making a wedding dress of my own design while other people mostly ran Trousseau. But I would have some bridal appointments on my cal-endar because I'd have at least two assistants to help with the sewing and embellishments. I never want to go to an ivory tower. I love my brides." A little of the sparkle went out of her eyes. "But I can't do that, so I'm doing the next best thing. I'm pursuing my short-term goal that's a step toward my long-term goal."

"I'm not saying don't do the show and I'm not trying to get out of it. You're committed. I'm committed. But you don't have to live and die by it. We could just have fun and get Jules in a pretty dress. You can have your long-term goal right now."

"And how is that? Do you have a wish tucked into the waistband of your kilt?"

"Sort of. You could let me help you."

Her mouth went hard and she knew he'd said it all wrong.

"You mean *give* me money?"

"No, no." He waved like jazz hands at half-mast. "I put it poorly. I mean, you could let me *invest*. All legal, with a share of the profits coming my way. And I swear to you it has nothing to do with what passed between us last night and what might happen between us in the future. *Nothing*, lass. I have invested in small businesses in my village back home—a tearoom, a wool shop, and a craft beer pub. And I promise you, there has been nothing romantic between any of the proprietors and me. I saw hardworking, talented people with a dream. And that's what you are, lass. And I have to say, it was a right smart move for me, too. Those investments have served me—and them—well."

Some of the thunder went out of her face. "Thank you for the compliment, but no."

"Claire is an investor," he pointed out.

"Claire owns the building and went looking for me. I've given her what she asked for—a nice, up-to-date bridal shop to replace one that was stuck in 1992. I have to get to the next level on my own."

He didn't always know when to quit, but this time he did.

"If you're sure."

"I am."

"The offer doesn't have an expiration date."

"I appreciate it, but no."

"All right." He let out an exaggerated sigh. "When you're all fancy, with dresses in Paris and the like, I will have to say to folks, 'I tried to be part of that, but she wouldn't have me.'"

For once, the right words had come out of his mouth, because her smile was like a sunrise.

He reached across the table and took her hand again.

"So, tonight?"

"It's coming." She nodded.

"How about we go downtown Birmingham and get some food? Then find a neighborhood with some nice Christmas lights?"

She smiled. "Do you promise, if you see lights that aren't hung to your liking, that you won't go on private property and try to fix them?"

"Aye. It will be hard, but I can make you that promise—though it won't be a question of *if*. Most assuredly, there will be improvements that should be made."

They sat quietly for a moment, their hands still intertwined.

Then, she did the most amazing thing. She turned his hand over, raised it to her mouth, and kissed his palm.

Who knew such a simple thing could bring his manly parts to attention so fast? He found himself wishing she would lick where she had kissed.

Yes. This was going to be a sweet journey.

Chapter Seventeen

The dining room of the historic Laurel Springs Inn had an old-fashioned, elegant, country-club feel to it—not that Hyacinth had been to many country clubs. But along the way, she'd had occasion to attend the wedding receptions of a few particularly special brides who had included her, and the food was never much to write home about. Probably country clubs cared more about liquor and golf than food. Lots of people ate at the inn regularly, but for her and Memaw, it had been a strictly special occasion place—and that's how she still thought of it.

Or she had until last night, when she'd learned a whole different level of special occasion.

The place Robbie had taken her—Sideboard—was definitely not what she would have considered a Monday night impulse. When he'd suggested they get some food, she'd pictured driving until they ran up on some barbecue or Italian. But no. Seems Robbie had gone online and picked the place—even made a reservation, something that seemed out of character for him. They weren't dressed for it; she knew it the second she saw the valet parking, but Robbie didn't care. He walked in wearing his kilt and light-up shoes like he owned the place and five more just like it. Nobody blinked. She wasn't sure if it was because they were hockey fans and knew who he was or because he was just that sure of himself. She was rather proud of herself for taking it in stride. That wasn't something she'd had a lot of practice at, but recognized she'd better get used to if she were going to spend time with Robbie.

After all, he had meant well. And her grass-fed-locally-sourced-salted-with-unicorn-tears plate of food had been amazing. For once, she hadn't worried about the price of the food. She couldn't. There hadn't been any prices on her menu.

"Hello, Hyacinth," Lila Cokesberry said. Miss Lila had been the hostess at the inn since the Earth cooled. Memaw had sewed for her and Hyacinth still did her alterations. "You're meeting Ava Grace for lunch?"

"Yes, and Evans. We're having a little celebration. Evans got married."

Lila frowned. "I heard. I was surprised she married one of those hockey players. She couldn't have known him long."

"Actually, they grew up together."

"Well. That's good, anyway. Those hockey people sure are a boisterous bunch. We get a lot of the families here for the games, and those boys are always underfoot when their people are here. We've even got one living in the Bryant suite full-time. Though I have to say, he's quiet. Doesn't give us any trouble. Just eats his food then goes about his business."

No doubt; Lila ran a tight ship.

"Ava Grace said we'd be by the French doors overlooking the terrace. I'll just make my way back."

"Yes. She was very specific. She brought her own

centerpiece. I had to move what we had on the table. Not that I minded." Miss Lila sighed loud and long.

When Hyacinth reached the table, she found that Ava Grace had not only brought the centerpiece—a nosegay of pink sweetheart roses lying on a silver tray with pearls scattered around it—but had set up a crystal cake stand with pink and white petit fours.

"Wow," Hyacinth said. "I had no idea you'd bring your own dessert."

"They do, if you don't ask," Ava Grace said. "Evans hardly ever eats dessert, but she does like a petit four."

Hyacinth would never have had the nerve to do that. She laid her gift on the table. "Ava Grace? Is this your china and silver from home?"

"Maybe." She smiled a half smile, reached into her basket, and brought out some crystal glasses. "I only brought waters and iced teas. I figured we wouldn't drink wine since we all have to go back to work."

All this made Hyacinth wonder why they hadn't just had this lunch at Ava Grace's house—but she knew how this had evolved, knew how Ava Grace's mind worked. First, she would have thought of the flowers, which led to the full centerpiece. Then, she would have decided petit fours would be nice and, of course, they called for the cake stand, which made her think of the dishes. And on and on. Given another day and she would have had a wicker table and chairs brought in.

"Is there anything I can do to help you?" Hyacinth asked.

Ava Grace straightened a pink linen napkin that had been folded into the shape of a heart. "No, I think that's it." She picked up her basket. "I'm just going to stash this in the cloakroom."

Hyacinth slid into her seat. She knew she should put her napkin in her lap, but she hated to mess up the table.

"Now," Ava Grace said when she returned. "I've directed the kitchen to plate our food on clear plates and treat the china dinner plate like a charger."

"What? You didn't bring the food?" Hyacinth asked.

"No, but I ordered for all of us—smoked salmon and brie tarts, cranberry pink arctic salad, and sesame dill muffins. Do you think that's okay? I tried to call you last night to ask what you thought, but I couldn't get you."

"Oh. Sorry." She had turned off her phone in the restaurant and didn't remember until this morning. Robbie had insisted on driving through Cook Out for eggnog milkshakes to have while looking at not one, but two, decorated neighborhoods—one classic and elegant and one that looked like a neon jungle. *"Because you ought to have eggnog when looking at Christmas lights."* They had laughed and laughed. Eggnog kisses were sweet, as was the time on her sofa later—but confusing. How was it possible to want something so much, but not feel ready for it? From all indications, Robbie wanted things to go further, though he had not pushed her. In fact, he seemed happy with the status quo. But how long would that last? What if she still wasn't ready before his patience gave out? Not that he had shown any signs of impatience. The trouble was she'd never slept with anyone who wasn't a Could've Been Maybe.

"So is it all okay?" Ava Grace asked.

Good question. Maybe Ava Grace could give her some insight. She'd been with Skip for years. She searched for the right phrasing.

"I almost added some crostini for an appetizer, but that seemed like a lot."

Mother of pearl! Ava Grace was talking about the *food*, and Hyacinth had almost given herself away. She had to get Robbie and the sex question off her mind.

"It sounds delicious, Ava Grace, and just enough. And you know what? If we want something more, we can order it." Robbie had taught her that last night when he'd pronounced the food at Sideboard tasty, but skimpy, and ordered a second entrée.

"Oh! This is so nice!" Evans appeared beside Ava Grace.

"It's the bride!" Ava Grace and Evans landed in an embrace and Hyacinth rose to join them. There sure was a lot of hugging going on lately.

They had been settled in their seats no more than forty-five seconds before their food and iced tea appeared. Ava Grace had a talent, for sure. Hyacinth just wasn't so sure it was for selling antiques.

"So, tell us about New Orleans," Ava Grace said. *Ava Grace, are you nuts? They were on their honeymoon. They didn't see New Orleans. In fact, I don't know why they went.*

"Well," Evans said, "we stayed at the Bourbon Orleans. I've always wanted to stay there. It's supposed to be haunted. We didn't see any ghosts, but we did take a ghost tour."

A ghost tour? Really?

"I took Jake to meet my instructors from culinary school. We went to the Mardi Gras museum and the French market. Rode the streetcar down to the Garden District. Oh! We took a cooking class."

"A cooking class?" Ava Grace sounded aghast—and

why not? Who took a cooking class on their honeymoon? "You, of all people, do not need a cooking class. I, on the other hand, could use one. Or twelve." Ava Grace sipped her tea.

"But it was fun to cook with Jake," Evans said. "Besides, now he knows how to make crawfish etouffee and bananas Foster. That will come in handy. Other than that, we did a little shopping, ate a lot of good food, and danced in every bar on Bourbon Street."

"You sure packed a lot into two days," Hyacinth said.

"It was so fun," Evans said. "We're going back when the season's over. We might stay a week. There's so much to do."

Apparently sex had not been utmost on their minds. But, then, they'd been sleeping together for a while. Maybe they were tired of sex. She sure had gotten tired of it with her Could've Been Maybes. Though, with Robbie, things felt different; maybe that was typical of an interlude.

"Enough about me." Evans took a bite of her tart. "What's been going on with y'all?"

"Nothing exciting for me," Ava Grace said. "Just work and helping my mother get ready for the gala." She gave Hyacinth a sly little smile. "Hyacinth, however, has been a busy little bee. She has quite a lot to report."

"I do?" She wasn't sure she was ready to go into this.

"Sure," Ava Grace said. "You haven't even told her about *All Dressed in White*."

Right. There had been no time. "Trousseau is going to be on *All Dressed in White*."

"Hyacinth!" Evans said. "This is huge! Tell me all about it."

"The video—you remember the video?"

"Hard to forget."

"Well, Jules Perry found herself in need of a wedding dress. She saw the video and asked to come to Trousseau. So it's happening. A week from tomorrow."

Evans's eyes widened with each word Hyacinth spoke. "I'm so proud of you." She leaned over and hugged Hyacinth. "And to think, you thought that video was the end of the world."

"I got lucky," Hyacinth admitted.

"Tell her the rest," Ava Grace urged.

"The rest?"

"Tell her who's doing the show with you."

"Oh, that." Hyacinth split her muffin and buttered it. "Robbie."

"Robbie *McTavish*?" Evans said.

"Yes. How many Robbies do you think I know?"

"Well, I don't know, Hyacinth. I don't know everybody you know. And the last time I checked in, you were pretty mad at him."

"It wasn't exactly my idea."

"Whose idea was it, then?" Evans asked.

"To be honest, it wasn't so much an idea as a requirement—by Jules and the *All Dressed in White* people."

"But he agreed to do it?" Evans said. "I told you he was a good guy."

"The agreement didn't come easy and it didn't come free," Hyacinth said. "He was pretty mad at me, too."

"He's *charging you*?" Evans gasped. "Money? That doesn't sound like Robbie."

"Not money," Ava Grace chimed in. "But he had some demands. She can't talk about the chocolate ice cream and the ruined dress ever again. Plus, she has to go to all the Yellowhammer home games and out to Hammer Time with him after."

And the gala. Not going to point that out.

Evans parted her mouth and dropped her eyes, like she was trying to work something out. "He blackmailed you?"

"*Blackmail* is such an ugly word." Seemed like she'd had this conversation before.

"He must really like you to blackmail you into going out with him," Evans said.

"That's what I said," Ava Grace said. "And, Evans, you should see them together. He helped us decorate Trousseau for Christmas. It's all fire and ice, get away from me, come here. Eyes snapping. Everybody blushing. I've never seen anything like it."

"Well." Evans touched her pink napkin to her lips. "I didn't expect to come home to this, but I love you both, so what a gift."

"Wait," Hyacinth said. "Hold on. It's not like that."

"Then how is it?" Evans asked.

Excellent question.

"It's exactly like that," Ava Grace said. "Own up. How could she own up, when she didn't know what she was owning up to?

"Who are you now, Ava Grace?" Hyacinth said. "Some kind of Match.com oracle?"

"Have you seen him since we decorated?" Ava Grace said, like she knew the answer.

"We had to get together to talk about *All Dressed in White*. Yesterday. After practice. It was business."

"And come to think of it, last night? When I couldn't get you on the phone? It wasn't dead, was it?"

Hyacinth took a long drink of her tea. "It was no

big deal. We got something to eat and looked at some Christmas lights."

"Ah, Christmas lights," Ava Grace and Evans nodded and said it together.

"I bet you held hands while you drove around."

She would neither confirm nor deny. "Look." She laid her hands—along with her cards—on the table. "I don't know what's going on with Robbie and me. We've spent some time together, yes. But we're very different. We had a date. I don't know if there will even be another. Can we just not make a huge deal of this? Can you, please, not tell anyone—and Evans, that means Jake, too, especially Jake—that there's something going on with us? Because I don't know that there is."

"Sure," Evans says. "I'm not one of those women who thinks she has to report every little detail to her husband. But don't expect me to stay quiet about it to you."

"That would be too much to hope for," Hyacinth sighed. It was hard to say if she was sighing or hugging more these days.

"Where did you eat?" Evans asked, like that mattered.

"Sideboard. Downtown." Maybe they didn't know it.

"Ah, Sideboard." Again, in stereo. They knew it.

"That must have cost him a couple of hundred, minimum," Evans said. "Wouldn't you say, Ava Grace?"

"More if she got the lamb. Did you get the lamb, Hyacinth?"

"I got the lamb." How was she supposed to know what it cost with that crazy menu?

"He got two entrees," Hyacinth said defensively. "Beef tenderloin and some kind of pork belly situation."

"I don't know, Ava Grace," Evans said in a sing-song voice. "But I think he might have spent just a *little* money and gone to a *little* trouble to show her a good time. Do you think he did?"

"I think he may have."

No way was she telling about those milkshakes. She'd had enough of this.

"Why don't you open your gifts, Evans?" Hyacinth said. "After all, this lunch is supposed to be about you—not me."

"All right, all right. Ava Grace, we've tortured her enough." Evans reached for the smaller of the two packages—Ava Grace's gift.

Hyacinth's stomach went cold as soon as she saw what was inside—a sterling silver snowflake Christmas ornament. Leave it to Ava Grace to get the most perfect gift on the planet—supremely significant, but understated.

There was nothing understated about Hyacinth's gift. She had chosen not just poorly; she had taken poorly to a level previously unseen by animal, vegetable, or mineral.

"Oh, Ava Grace, it's lovely." Evans held the snowflake up to let it catch the light.

"For your first Christmas tree. The snowflake is for the snow Jake's skates make on the ice."

That wasn't snow. It was ice shavings. Snow fell from the sky, not off the blades of hockey skates.

Not that it mattered to Evans. "I'll treasure it always." She put it back in its little velvet bag.

Hyacinth had a brief fantasy where she grabbed her gift and ran for the mountains, but Evans was already reaching for it. Besides, there weren't any mountains within running distance.

"Let's see what this is." Evans gave her a teasing look as she untied the ribbon.

What had she been thinking? Ava Grace and Evans were going to have a field day with this.

She'd had no idea what to buy or much time to buy it after leaving Waffle House yesterday before she needed to be back at work. She'd wandered aimlessly around Powells, Laurel Springs's little jewel of a department store, hoping for an idea for the perfect gift for Evans— something personal, that said congratulations. It wasn't like she could get her a cheese grater.

And then she'd happened on the lingerie department and inspiration had hit.

She should have gotten the cheese grater. They were going to laugh their asses off and accuse her of having sex on her mind when she'd bought it.

Surprise crossed Evans face as she lifted the little confection of champagne-colored silk with strategically placed lace panels from the nest of tissue. It had seemed classy with a little bit of sexy in the store, but maybe it wasn't. Here in this elegant room where Lila Cokesberry could swoop in any second, it seemed more on the trashy side. But what did she know? She'd never bothered to buy a nightgown to wear for the Could've Been Maybes, which might have been part of the problem. Damn it, she was in the bridal business, she ought to know this stuff.

"Hyacinth, this is exquisite." Evans stroked the seed pearls at the neck.

"It is," Ava Grace agreed. "It will look beautiful on you."

Evans laughed and a pretty little blush landed on her cheeks. "You know what Jake says?" she whispered.

"That looks great, but it'll look better on the floor.'"

Relief settled on Hyacinth as they all laughed together. They weren't going to circle back to her on this.

And they'd never know she'd bought one for herself. In black.

"So." Evans met her eyes across the table. "The team flies out this afternoon for New York."

Yes. To play the Big Apples. "That might have been mentioned." Hyacinth ate a bite of her salad.

"We have all the hockey channels. They play Thursday during the day, but would you like to come over and watch the game tomorrow night?" Evans looked at Ava Grace. "You, too, Ava Grace, if you're interested."

"Sure," Ava Grace said. "I don't have anything else to do. Besides, I'm kind of getting into this hockey thing. I went at first because Claire gave us tickets, but it's fun."

"Great," Evans said. "Puck drop is at seven tomorrow night. I'll make chili and bring home a pie from Crust."

It was only later that Hyacinth realized she'd never answered Evans. They had just assumed she would want to come.

Which she did.

Chapter Eighteen

Robbie climbed into the passenger seat of Brad's pickup truck.

"Thanks for taking me to the rink," he said. "I don't like leaving my car there while I'm on the road. I usually get a ride with Jake, but our schedules didn't jive today."

Their schedules hadn't jived because Jake insisted on being at the rink to catch the bus for the airport at least an hour before they needed to be. Usually Robbie just went with it, but he'd decided at the last minute to pop into Trousseau and ask Hyacinth to take him—only to find she'd gone to lunch with Ava Grace and Evans.

He wondered if she was talking about him.

"Glad to do it," Brad said.

They were cutting it close, what with having to wait for Patty to get back from the post office and dropping the Corvette at home. Could be Hyacinth was right. A little forethought and planning would have come in handy today. Maybe if he'd made a few calls, he would have gotten to see her before he left. But how could you make a call about something you hadn't thought of yet?

"Do you need to be picked up when you get back?" Brad asked.

"Nah. I can catch a ride with Jake."

"Stop messing with your tie, Robbie," Brad said as he pulled out of the parking garage. "I swear only you can turn a Brooks Brothers suit and Turnbull and Asser tie into a walking disaster."

"Is that what I've got here? How about that? *Asser!* What a brilliant name for a tie. That about summed up his thinking on the matter of ties.

"Yes. I know about these things. How can you *not* know where you got your clothes?"

"My agent got some style person to collect them up for me after I got in trouble for showing up in my dress kilt for my first pro game."

"Did they let you wear a kilt in juniors and college?" Brad asked.

"What? Since when are you an authority on sports dress codes?"

"Did they?" he repeated.

"No." He might as well admit it. Brad wasn't one to let up.

"But you thought you'd try it after you turned pro."

"A man has to be proud of his homeland. And speaking of—*your* homeland, not mine—I *really* appreciate the Southern pretty boy outfit. Not my style."

"Just doing what the boss told me. Does it fit?"

"I suppose."

"You're a week away from wearing that for the taping of a top rated TV show. Don't tell me you didn't try it on."

He shrugged. "Hyacinth said you're good at guessing sizes."

"I am, but you need to be sure."

"I'll do it when I get back." Maybe the clothes wouldn't fit. But wait. No. Hyacinth wanted him in those clothes. Maybe she'd like him in them enough that she'd want him *out* of them. One could hope.

Or not.

There was a tiny thing that had begun to niggle at him. He wanted her, sure. Holy family and all the wise men, what that woman could do with her mouth—and that was just on his public parts. There hadn't been any private exploration, though he'd thought about it plenty. In fact, just thinking of it now… Last night tangled up with her on her couch had just about been his undoing. Still. There was a part of him—the part north of his waistband—that was relieved she wasn't ready. What if it was just sex he wanted, and not sex with Hyacinth? He couldn't do that to her.

Odd.

That was a new thought for him. When thinking along these lines, it was usually to wonder about things like if a woman's bra closed in the front or back and if dirty talk would turn her on or put her off.

"Roll the shirt sleeves up to just below your elbows," Brad said.

He was still nattering on about those TV clothes. "Hyacinth said not to, that she'd do it." He liked the idea of her neat, cool, little hands with the short nails efficiently rolling up his sleeves—then stroking his forearms. And then his face. And neck…and on southward. He really hoped it was Hyacinth, herself, that was making him so crazy and not what he'd been doing without.

"Brad?"

"Robbie." Brad pulled into the iceplex parking lot. "Did Hyacinth tell you we went out last night?" Brad's surprised expression answered the question.

"No. Where did you go?"

"A place called Sideways."

Brad frowned as he pulled up to the curb outside the entrance. "Where is that?"

"Downtown. Near a big fountain."

"Do you mean Sideboard? In Five Points?" Was that it? "Maybe so. Yeah."

"Nice." Brad looked impressed then slashed him with his laser eyes. "What," he asked, "did you wear?"

That again. "I don't remember. Thanks for the ride."

He jumped out of the truck and retrieved his luggage before Brad could ask what he'd packed.

It was only when he was entering the building that it occurred to him that Hyacinth hadn't mentioned their date to Brad. Didn't women usually talk about stuff like that? At least if they were excited about it?

That bore pondering.

He just wasn't sure he had the right kind of brain to work it out.

After helping Ava Grace pack up her dishes, and after more hugging, Hyacinth hurried down the street. She needed to get back and let Brad and Patty go to lunch, but she had time to make a quick stop at Laurel Wreath Books.

It would have been easier to download what she needed on her iPad, but she was committed to buying local. Besides, she liked the owners, Jeff and Donna Proctor.

"Hey, Hyacinth," Jeff said when she went in. "How's the wedding business?"

"As near as I can tell, people haven't given up on marriage. How's the book business?"

"I can't complain. Can I help you or do you want to browse?"

"I need a little help. Do you have a book about hockey? Maybe one of those for idiots or dummies?"

He stepped out from behind the counter. "I don't have those, but I have something with the basics."

She followed as he moved toward the sports section. "Caught Yellowhammer fever, have you?"

Had she? No. Not really. But if she was going to watch the game, she wanted to understand it. "Better than the flu."

He laughed. "That's a good one." He handed her two books. "These are the ones I show new hockey fans. People seem to like both."

Just then the shop phone rang.

"Go ahead and get that, Jeff," she said. "I'll look at these two and decide on one."

She had just started to glance through the thicker of the two books when the sign for the next aisle caught her eye.

Sex and Sexuality.

She hesitated. She glanced to the front of the store where Jeff was still on the phone before nonchalantly wandering over, perusing the display as she went. Most of the books seemed to be how-tos on technique, but then, one with a soft pink cover with swirls of hearts and clouds caught her eye. *Intimacy: How to Know if You're Ready and How to Get There if You're Not.* She needed that, needed it in the worst way. She didn't need any pointers on the mechanics; it was the head part she couldn't work out.

But no way was she buying this book from Jeff Proctor. If Donna were here manning the register, maybe, but probably not. It would have to be an ebook. She discreetly took out her phone and snapped a picture of the cover.

"You're very welcome," Jeff was saying into the phone. "I'll order it today."

She hurried to the register.

"Did you decide?" Jeff asked.

"I'll take both." That would make up for the book she wasn't buying from him.

"Are you sure? It's probably pretty much the same information."

She handed him the books and reached for her debit card.

"I'm sure. I've got a lot to learn."

Robbie was sorting his ties and hanging up his suits in his hotel room when a text came though.

Maybe it was Hyacinth. He grabbed the phone. No.

Not Hyacinth.

Melinda.

He would have known he'd hear from her if he'd thought about it. He always heard from her when he was in New York, had ever since his rookie year when they'd met in the autograph line.

He liked Melinda. She was fun. Great in bed. Celebrated when he won, sympathized when he lost. And he never, ever heard from her—nor did she expect to hear from him—between road trips to play the Big Apples.

But he was hearing from her now.

Hey, sexy, what's up? her text read.

And she deserved to hear back from him.

Just got in. Team dinner later. Early curfew.

Feel like some company between dinner and curfew?

This was quite the crossroads. Though he hadn't thought about her on the way here, the fact was he *did* want some company; he wanted to have sex.

Not just a crossroads, a crossroads with caution signs, sirens, and flashing lights.

Better not. Big game, he typed, then hesitated. Do you have some time now?

Always. What's your room number?

He hesitated again. Meet in the hotel Starbucks? Fifteen minutes?

You know it, baby!

He didn't know it. That was the problem.

Standing before the barista, no matter how hard he tried to remember, he didn't know what Melinda wanted to drink, or even if he'd ever bought her a coffee. Damn, damn, damn. So many women. So many cups of coffee.

In the end, he ordered a venti eggnog latte with three pumps for himself and a grande nonfat mocha latte for Melinda. Once when they'd had coffee together, that's what Brad had ordered to take back to Trousseau for Hyacinth.

He'd just collected the coffees when he heard a voice behind him. "I know you love your coffee, but I was surprised you wanted to meet in the coffee shop."

And here she was. "Hello, Melinda. You look good."

It was true. Tall. Blond. White fluffy coat and boots.

"Thanks." She raised her face, expectantly, and he dropped a kiss on her cheek.

"Sure. Just stating the obvious."

"Let's sit down." She took the coffee he held out to her. "Let's get the bad news out of the way."

"Bad news?"

She slid into a chair at a table by the window and he sat across from her. "Certainly bad news. We aren't going to see each other anymore."

Was she psychic? He hadn't even figured out the words yet. "How?"

"First, the coffee shop meetup. Then, the cheek kiss. Now, you're sitting across from me at a table in a public place instead of walking me to the elevator."

"You should be a private investigator."

She took a sip of her coffee, frowned, and set it down. "I *am* a private investigator."

Oh, fuck. She was. That must be why the deep part of his brain had thrown that out of his mouth.

"I'm sorry, Melinda. It slipped my mind."

"Don't apologize. If you weren't a hockey player, I wouldn't know your occupation."

"Look." He spread his hands on the table. "I'm sorry. It's just that I think I've found the real thing. But I wanted to tell you in person." His brain—or maybe it was his heart—threw those words out, too, but they were true.

She nodded. "That was nice, but you're deceiving yourself—at least partially. You called me here to test yourself—to see what you would do. And now you know."

She might be right. And he did know. What he didn't know was how things would end up with Hyacinth. He'd never wondered that before.

Melinda rose smoothly and he scrambled to his feet to stand in front of her. "I'm sorry, Melinda."

"Don't be." She pulled her leather gloves from her pocket and put them on. "We had a good time."

"We did. Without a doubt."

"And regardless of your motivation, thank you for the face-to-face. I think you would have done that even if you weren't testing yourself. You are a gentleman, Robbie McTavish."

"A gentleman and a golfer. And a blackmailer." These words, too, fell off his tongue of their own accord.

"What?" She looked perplexed. "A blackmailer?"

"Nothing," he said. "Just something someone said to me recently."

And she left, leaving behind her almost untouched coffee.

She laughed and laid a hand on his cheek. "You *have* got it bad. Tell her she's a fortunate lady. Good luck on the ice—and off, number five."

It took more than luck on the ice. It took work. For the first time, that might be true for life off the ice, too. He was going to work harder at pleasing Hyacinth than he'd ever worked at anything in his existence. Meaning well wasn't going to be good enough. He needed to think more, consider what she wanted more—or what he thought she wanted. Sometimes that was hard to figure out, but he was going to try.

He sat down again and picked up his phone. To hell with five o'clock closing times. She didn't have to answer if she was busy.

But she did.

"Hello, lass." He propped his feet in the chair that had been Melinda's. "I'm just sitting here drinking eggnog coffee and thinking about you. Are you thinking about me?"

Chapter Nineteen

Thursday night. Eleven p.m. and it was pouring down rain.

Hyacinth wondered if the Yellowhammers' plane had been able to land in the storm. Though he'd called twice and texted numerous times while in New York, she hadn't heard from Robbie since the loss this afternoon—which she'd kept tabs on the best she could via Twitter, during a final fitting.

They had won the game Hyacinth had watched with Evans and Ava Grace. Thinking back, she smiled. It had been a good time, even with Ava Grace and Evans teasing her the one time Robbie had scored and both times he'd gone to the penalty box. To Hyacinth's and Evans's utter shock, Ava Grace had turned into a full-fledged, bloodthirsty hockey fan, screaming words that Hyacinth would have sworn she didn't know. She'd also been able to explain icing and offside better than the hockey books Hyacinth had bought.

Too bad Ava Grace couldn't help her with that other book.

Fresh from the shower, she pulled on her oldest, softest flannel nightgown. Memaw had made it right before Hyacinth left for design school. In the weeks that followed Memaw's funeral, Hyacinth had wrapped it around herself like a security blanket, even on nights it was too hot for it. Now, it had been washed so many times, the nap was gone and it was worn so thin that it wouldn't provide much warmth on this damp, cold night. But she'd reached for it anyway, as she was inclined to do when she was in a quandary.

Which she was.

She missed Robbie. She'd found herself incessantly checking her phone in case she'd missed a call or a text. He made her laugh, but so had her parents. No one could claim they hadn't been fun; fun was a mark of a free spirit—but so was a haphazard lifestyle and the unpleasant surprises that came with it. And she couldn't go back—not that Robbie was asking her to.

When it came down to it, they'd shared a couple of meals, looked at Christmas lights, and had some outstanding kisses. Not so much, in the scheme of things.

Of course, there were his hands. Mother of pearl, those hands....

Might as well face it. She wanted them on her.

The book basically said if you're an adult, do what you want.

Hyacinth had read it cover to cover and some parts twice. There was some talk about losing virginity and not being pressured, which did not apply to her. She also didn't need lessons on safe sex, birth control, or how to tell if someone was lying about being single.

So, yeah, that was it. Two hundred twenty-four pages and the upshot was, do what you want—be it a hookup, one night stand, fling, friends with benefits, road to commitment, or complete commitment. None of that was who she was, not with Robbie.

But then, she'd definitely been on the road to commitment with the Could've Been Maybes and look how that had turned out. The whole thing made her head hurt.

She should go to bed. She made her way to the living room to turn off the lights.

Luckily, she didn't have to worry about any of this tonight. Robbie had once mentioned that he was inclined to sleep most of the day after a road trip. She might not even see him until Saturday night after the home game against Minnesota for the command attendance at Hammer Time.

If he still wanted her to go. He might be done with her. After all, she hadn't heard from him since this morning.

The thunder boomed. She wondered if he was afraid. There was no severe weather predicted, but fear didn't have much of a relationship with reason.

But the plane... Tornadic weather or not, it was storming. She would have heard if something bad had happened. Jake was on that plane, too. It wasn't reasonable to think the team wasn't entirely safe, but she reached for her iPad to check the news anyway.

That's when the knock came at the door—pounding, really. Demanding, almost violent pounding. *Dear God, help me.*

The plane had crashed and Ava Grace had come to tell her.

Probably for the first time in her oh, so careful life, she threw open the door without checking to see who was there.

And there he stood—not dead in a plane crash, not done with her. He was wet and wearing only a ragged kilt, Yellowhammers T-shirt, and those flashing shoes, but he was no worse for wear.

He stepped inside and she threw herself into his arms.

His mouth captured hers and she grabbed handfuls of his T-shirt to pull him closer. Between her worn nightgown and his thin kilt, there wasn't much between them. He lifted her just so, and there was no question of his desire.

Hers either. It had landed like an atomic bomb on the heels of the worst kind of terror and she never wanted to let him go.

"Ah, lass." He ran his tongue along her cheekbone and bit her neck beneath her ear. "I missed you so."

"Were you afraid?" She rolled her pelvis against his, just in case he didn't know what was on her mind. "Of the storm?"

He groaned and answered her pelvis with his. "Only afraid you wouldn't be here—or that you wouldn't let me in."

This was the moment. He pulled back and his green eyes danced their way into hers, questioning, hoping.

"I _am_ here," she said. "And I _am_ letting you in."

"Aye, you are." He buried his face in her neck and whispered something in what she assumed was Scots Gaelic.

"What?" Even in this state it wasn't like her to not have to know.

"I want you here and now." And he ran those hands down her sides, cupped her bottom, and molded her to him.

She shivered. "Not here, but definitely now."

"Why not here?" He moved her against the wall.

"You're ready; I'm ready. Past ready."

"Because I'm not an up-against-the-wall kind of girl."

He laughed into her neck, pulled up his kilt so she could feel him better, and notched his arousal between her thighs. "Sure about that?" He pressed her closer against the wall and suckled her neck. "Are you a couch kind of girl, then? It's close by."

"I'm a bed kind of girl. And it's not that far."

"Then take me there."

Though there hadn't been much between them before, soon there was nothing—except their differences.

Her nipples pebbled against his palms. "Your hands are cold," she said.

"Will you warm me?"

"If you'll warm—me." Her words came out in gasps because he was doing magical things with those wonderful hands.

"Aye, lass, I will—inside and out."

Inside was a miraculous thing. Her orgasm was immediate and violently strong. It had to be. The pressure was too great for anything else. Seconds later he cried out and collapsed against her.

They both fought to catch their breath.

Finally, he spoke. "Well, lass, some men might apologize for it being over too fast, but I'd say we lasted a long time. We've had the most enduring foreplay in the history of time."

He was so right about that. "Who says it's over?" she teased.

"Ah, woman, you read my mind." He shifted, rolled her to face him, and gently began to kiss her breasts.

She stroked him up one thigh, then the other, and settled her hand in the softness in between.

"You *did* read my mind," he said with a moan.

The softness didn't last long.

And so it went.

Before the night was over, Hyacinth learned she *was* an up-against-the wall kind of girl, after all.

With his hands on her, his sweet voice in her ear whispering, sometimes in that hypnotic lyrical language, and bringing her to heights she'd never known, their differences didn't seem to matter so much.

But she was a realist. She knew they were still there.

The next morning, after quietly reading herself for work, Hyacinth pulled the blanket tighter over Robbie's sleeping form.

He stirred and reached for her. "Come back to bed, lass," he said without opening his eyes.

"I can't." She dropped a brief kiss on his mouth. "I have work. But you sleep as long as you want. I know you're tired." And not just from hockey and travel. It had been a night to remember.

He opened one eye. "Will you come back? After work?"

"Of course. It's my house."

"Can I be here?"

"Yes, Robbie. You can be here." Hopefully, still in bed. He nodded and yawned, asleep again before she walked away.

She thought about the book and laughed a little to herself. If he wanted to be here when she came home, this wasn't a one night stand or a hookup.

That's when she realized she'd unwittingly landed right in the middle of a fling.

Ah, well. She didn't know how long it would last, but she was an adult and she wanted to be here—just like the book said.

The book hadn't said how long a fling could last. Could it be months? Years, even?

Did it ever turn into…more? Not that this could.

Nothing could change how different they were.

But she liked the sound of months—and months could turn into a year.

Chapter Twenty

When Robbie skated out with the rest of the starting line, he raised his stick in Hyacinth's direction.

"He's waving at you," Ava Grace said.

"Or you. He's your garland and Christmas light buddy."

"You should wave back," Ava Grace said, but she didn't. He might be waving at some kid behind her.

Despite the development between them, Hyacinth was a little iffy on how to act in public. In the four days since he'd returned from New York, they had spent most of their time together, but none of it in public. After the weekend games, he'd wanted to opt out of the Hammer Time gatherings, preferring to pick up burgers and go back to his place or hers.

Tonight, with the taping tomorrow, it would be his condo. That had been her choice because it would be easier to manage Robbie for the morning from his own house. She'd have to leave extra early and go home before going to Trousseau, but she'd worked it all out. She could iron and lay out his new clothes tonight, raising the odds that he would be on time.

The second period ended with the Yellowhammers ahead 1-0.

Hyacinth still didn't know much about what was going on, but she was beginning to get the hang of it—especially when Robbie was on the ice.

Claire slipped into the seat beside Ava Grace that would have been Evans's, had she not graduated to the wives and girlfriends' suite.

Hyacinth wondered if there was a players' flings' suite and how many it would need to seat. Probably not as many as the one-night-stand suite—at least she hoped not. Thankfully, she wouldn't belong there.

"Are you girls enjoying the game?" Claire asked.

"I am," Ava Grace said. "I'll love it better when we win. Hockey is almost as good as football."

Hyacinth nodded in agreement, though she wasn't sure exactly which parts she was agreeing to.

"Is everything ready for *All Dressed in White* tomorrow, Hyacinth?" Claire asked. Hyacinth had texted her the news as soon as she knew it was happening.

"Yes. The advance crew from the show came this afternoon and approved the Christmas decorations and set up their equipment. Thank you for the Moet and Chandon Champagne and petit fours you sent. They were delivered right before I left today."

When those things had arrived, a bolt of fear had gone through Hyacinth. She was usually so careful about every detail, but she would have served the same cheap champagne that she bought by the case. Maybe she should have been thinking about that when she was sleeping with Robbie, or when she was at Gus Mayer's buying underwear. She had gone there only intending to pick up the dress she'd left to be altered, since she hadn't had time to do it herself. She hadn't had time to shop either, but she'd had to walk past the lingerie department, and the rest was very expensive history. Maybe as expensive as the wine Claire had sent. It was actually from Champagne, France.

"You're very welcome. I don't know how you pulled this off, but I'm proud of you. Is there anything I can do to help you?"

"No. Brad's going to make some finger sandwiches and I have fresh cheese straws. Ava Grace lent me a silver tray, some linen cocktail napkins, and little china plates." Plus, Ava Grace had insisted on bringing over some of her mother's Waterford flutes, though Hyacinth had no intention of using them. No doubt Robbie and broken crystal went together like salt and pepper. His dishes were plastic, but he'd broken two plates and a coffee cup at her house in the past four days. At this rate she wouldn't have a dish left by the end of the month, if they were still doing this by then. She still didn't know how long a fling could last, but waking up with him on Christmas might be nice.

"I knew you'd have it all in hand, but call if you need me."

"Thank you. I will."

Claire removed her old-fashioned leather planner from her purse and opened it—which was Hyacinth's cue to open her calendar app.

"There's something else we need to talk about." Claire uncapped her honest to God fountain pen with the gold nib. "I finally got an answer from Evans's mother about their schedule. They aren't planning to have a reception until hockey season is over, but I thought we should go ahead with our party for Jake and Evans sooner. We can have it at my house."

"Wonderful," Hyacinth said, and she meant it. Claire

was going to be in charge and that was great news. Hyacinth didn't even know how to give the kind of parties Claire, Ava Grace, and Evans were used to. Witness the cheap champagne and paper napkins. She had grown up on punch and cake showers in the church fellowship hall.

"Yes," Ava Grace said. "What are your thoughts?"

"Cocktails, like we talked about. Naturally, a couple's party. Here's the sticky part. I've spoken with Evans and it needs to be this coming Saturday, December ninth. I know that's less than a week, but if anybody can pull it off, we can."

Hyacinth supposed if Claire said so, that was true—though she was concerned about what would be expected of her. She couldn't do anything until this taping was over.

"This was really the only time to have it if we're going to do it this year," Claire went on. "The Yellowhammers are in town, but they play in the afternoon. That's two weeks before the gala, so there wouldn't be parties on back-to-back weekends for a lot of the same people."

Hyacinth keyed it into her phone. At least *All Dressed in White* would be behind her.

"I thought if Ava Grace could take care of sending the invitations, I'll take care of the catering and decorations," Claire said.

"I can do that," Ava Grace said, "but there's no time for printing and mailing. It'll have to be email. I can put together something from one of those online invitation websites and send it out tomorrow." Her grimace showed what she thought of that plan.

Claire nodded. "I hate email invitations, too, but

there's no other way. I'll send you the Yellowhammer contacts as soon as I get home tonight."

"And I'll get a list from Evans," Ava Grace said.

"I guess there's nothing left for me to do except wash dishes," Hyacinth joked. "But I'm a champion dishwasher."

"About that," Claire said. "I know you have your hands full with *All Dressed in White*, but do you think you have time to arrange for some music? I was hoping for a jazz trio or quartet. With all your wedding contacts, I was sure you'd know the perfect one."

That was a huge relief. The easiest job ever.

"Shouldn't be a problem at all. December isn't a hot wedding month and I'm sure someone will be glad for the work. I'll get on it." She'd call the Jazz Notes first, with Heart on a String as plan B. Catgut could be plan C, if it got that far. They were fabulous musicians despite their unfortunate name.

"Great." Claire stood. "I feel sure we'll have a good turnout, in spite of the short notice."

True. Nobody turned up a nose at an invitation from Claire. Hyacinth wasn't a big party person, but this would be fun—plus she would be leaving with Robbie after.

"She didn't waste any time," Ava Grace said after Claire had gone.

"She never does."

Soon after the third period began, Anaheim tied up the game. Then there was a lot of skating and puckshooting for a long time with no change on the scoreboard. Players on both sides went to the penalty box, but not Robbie. Then, with two minutes to go, Luka Zadorov scored. Hyacinth was relieved. They had won both games over the weekend and she didn't know if there would be no living with Robbie if they lost. That second loss in New York hadn't seemed to bother him, but that was a unique circumstance.

The relief didn't last long. One of the Anaheim players skated into the Yellowhammer net, collided with the goalie, and all hell broke loose.

"Oh, dear," Ava Grace said. "Robbie threw his gloves and helmet on the ice. Not good."

That was an understatement. He jumped on the Anaheim guy like a duck on a june bug. Then the Anaheim guy's gloves and helmet went flying and he proceeded to beat the daylights out of Robbie—right on the face.

The crowd was cheering like they loved it, but Hyacinth damn sure didn't. Everyone on the ice—including the refs—just stood back and watched them.

"Why don't they stop them?" Hyacinth demanded from Ava Grace.

"They will. Soon—after the crowd gets to enjoy it a little."

Not soon enough. If people wanted to see fighting, they ought to watch boxing. Now there was blood—on both faces, though it looked like Robbie had gotten the best of Mr. Anaheim.

Even after the ref finally separated them, Robbie continued to punch the air and yell. She expected him to go to the penalty box, but he skated off the ice and disappeared behind the bench.

"Where did he go?" Hyacinth demanded. "Do you think they're taking him to the hospital?"

Ava Grace shook her head. "I've seen this before. He's gone to the locker room. The penalty for fighting is five minutes and since there's less than two minutes

left in the game, he went straight to the locker room."
She patted Hyacinth's arm. "Don't worry, Hyacinth.
He's not really hurt. They'll clean him up."

"I'm not worried," Hyacinth said, though her heart
had turned into a drum. "I mean, naturally, I don't want
him hurt. I don't want anyone to get hurt."

"So you say," Ava Grace gave her a sidelong glance.
"He's fine. But his face is going to be a real mess for
All Dressed in White tomorrow."

Hell. She hadn't even thought of that.

"Hey! Stop." Robbie was seated on his new couch, with
Hyacinth looming over him, wielding the first aid kit
she'd produced from her purse. "That stings." He caught
her wrist before she could press that alcohol-soaked cotton ball against the cut under his eye again. Hoping to
distract her, he kissed the inside of her wrist, but that
didn't slow her down a bit.

She jerked out of his grasp and did it anyway. "You
should have thought about that before you declared war
on the ice tonight."

"I didn't start it," Robbie said. "He started it when
he touched my goalie. Don't touch my goalie—ever."
She put the cotton ball aside.

"Can't say I ever knew anybody who carries a first
aid kit around," he said.

"I like to be prepared. I have a sewing kit, too."

"I guess I should expect nothing less from a woman
with a bug-out bag. Got a fire extinguisher in there?"

"Make fun of me if you want, but there may come a
day you'll be glad I'm prepared. In fact, you ought to
be glad today." She dove into her bag and brought out
a tube of Neosporin.

He liked that she alluded to the future, no matter how vague. "Aye, lass. I am glad." It wasn't just sex he wanted her—all of her. He stroked her cheek. "Maybe I'll bring you my jersey from tonight—the one I bled on."

She nodded emphatically. "Do that. I'm a cracker-jack stain remover. Blood is a tough one, but hydrogen peroxide usually does the trick. I can probably make it good as new."

He worked not to laugh at her. "I was going to bring it to you for wearing, not cleaning. You wouldn't want to get the blood out. That's a badge of proof that it's game-worn. The blood is beyond bonus. That's what everyone wants."

A look of horror took over her face. "*I* don't. That's disgusting. Are all you people so bloodthirsty?"

She didn't want his jersey? That stung a bit, but then he remembered the women who'd drifted through his bed for the express purpose of obtaining a jersey. He'd given a fair number away, too, because he liked to make people happy—though he'd never given his blood away. Apparently, it was going to take more than that to make this woman happy.

"Hyacinth, Hyacinth, Hyacinth. You do not know the ways of hockey."

"Make me a list." She tapped the tube of Neosporin against her palm for emphasis. That seemed to make her remember it. She squirted some onto her finger. "Hold still."

"I told you the team doctor took care of me."

She smeared it on his cut. "And *I* told *you*, you can't be too careful about infection. Since then, you've walked around the arena, signed autographs for people who could have been carrying God only knows what, driven through Burger King, and I'll bet you've been to the restroom. No telling what germs you've picked up."

"Probably the black plague. Maybe salmonella."

She sighed. "I still don't understand why you did that. You don't even like Dietrich Wingo."

"I don't exactly dislike him. He just annoys the shit out of me. But none of that matters. If you go after the goalie, you're going to get your ass beat. Every hockey player knows that."

"Seems like it was more face than ass." She was going after his split lip with her Neosporin now.

"Hey! Don't do that." He jerked his head back. "It tastes bad."

"You don't have to taste it. It's on the outside of your mouth."

"Ah, lass." He circled her waist with his arms. "It's you I was worried about tasting it." As unnecessary as all this medical ministration was, the attention was nice.

"Not sure your mouth is up for kissing. You're going to have a black eye, too. That ought to play great on TV."

"Ah." He pulled her into his lap. "Sorry about that, lass, but—"

"I know. I know. Don't touch your goalie." She slipped her arms around his neck.

"I was the closest one. Had to do it."

She ran her finger alongside his swollen eye. "Maybe they'll cover it with makeup."

He bristled a bit inwardly, but let it go. He was going to do everything he could to make this go like she wanted and if that included wearing makeup, so be it. He was so committed that he'd spent all day making a little surprise for tomorrow. She was going to be thrilled.

And right now, he wanted to thrill her in a different way—and let her thrill him. They'd eaten the food he'd picked up, she'd played doctor, and now…

"Cuddle into me like this." He turned her so that she was straddling him, just so.

She smiled a little like Mona Lisa. "That's a cuddle?" Her whisky eyes went a shade darker; she wanted him, too.

"The best kind." He pulled her tighter against him and kissed her neck.

"I need to iron your new clothes," she said, but she didn't sound very committed.

"Do you, now? More than you need this?" He moved his hips against hers until she answered his strokes with her own.

"I don't want to hurt your face. And shouldn't we put an ice pack on your eye?"

"I'm not worried about my face. Let's do this instead." He pulled her sweater over her head and got the surprise of the week—which was saying plenty.

Until now, she had only worn plain white bras without so much as a whisper of lace. Not that he cared. He was more interested in what was beneath. But he had to admit that wispy little red thing with the sparkles was right enticing. The idea that she might have bought it with him in mind was even more enticing.

"Well, lass, I didn't see that coming." He ran his hands over the silky cups. She was so lush, so beautiful. "Is it new?"

"Yes. Do you like it?" Her cheeks were almost as

red as the barely there, transparent lace. She placed her hands on top of his and moved them against her.

"Aye. Quite a lot—almost as much as that little black nightie." Then he had another thought. He ran his finger under the bra strap. "Any chance this has a matching companion below?"

Her blush deepened. "Maybe."

He swung her into a reclining position. Knickers would be quite acceptable, a thong almost too much to hope for. But he was going to find out. Good thing he'd bought a large couch. There was no time to get to the bed.

"I guess I could iron your clothes in the morning."

It was a sweet time there on that couch and a sweet time later in his bed.

Chapter Twenty-One

"Everything looks great, Hyacinth. No glitches." Alex took a sip of the latte Brad had brought in. "Deb's happy with the way things are shaping up."

"I'm glad. Let me know if there's anything that needs tweaking." Though they probably wouldn't let her do anything about it, even if there was. They had insisted on doing her makeup and having someone stage the M & C Champagne and snacks for Jules and her posse. Hyacinth was trying to be grateful for the help, rather than feeling out of control.

Deb Carmichael joined them. "We appreciate you getting here so early."

"I was happy to do it." It hadn't been hard, since she'd barely slept, even after Robbie had passed out from exhaustion.

She had met Brad, Patty, and the production crew here at five thirty; it was almost seven now—the time she'd told Robbie to be here. They weren't scheduled to begin taping until eight, but she wouldn't breathe easy until he was here. Plan B was to send Brad to get him. "Robbie should be here any minute," she said to reassure herself.

"Jules and company should be here by seven thirty," Alex said.

Deb added, "Jules brought her own hair and makeup people, so they'll be good to go when they arrive."

"I suppose I ought to mention this," Hyacinth said with dread. "Robbie got into a fight last night on the ice. Your makeup people might need to do some work on him. His face is pretty messy." If possible, his face had looked worse this morning than last night. She should have insisted on the ice pack.

Alex and Deb exchanged glances and looked positively gleeful. Strange.

"Black eye?" Did Alex sound hopeful?

"I'm afraid so. Split lip. Cut under his eye."

Alex and Deb high-fived. What the hell? "Can you believe the luck?" Deb said.

Luck? "Excuse me?" Hyacinth said.

"Sorry," Alex said. "It's too bad he got hurt, but it'll contribute to the whole hockey player vibe. We even played with the idea of having the makeup people give him a black eye."

"But we wouldn't really do that," Deb hurried to add. "We don't script or deceive. It was just wishful-thinking talk on the plane."

That didn't set well with Hyacinth, but there was nothing to be done about it. It wasn't like they had battered Robbie's face themselves.

Before she had to respond, the bell jingled and Hyacinth turned to see Robbie coming through the door.

Damn.

Hell.

Where to start, where to start?

It wasn't his appearance. No. He was wearing the freshly pressed clothes and new shoes and he'd shaved. His hair was even combed.

But he was carrying a wedding cake. *A wedding cake*—albeit a small one—three tiered, with swirls, rosettes, and a garden of multicolored icing flowers. It was exquisite, but what the hell? She had not specially said to him, "Robbie, don't bring a wedding cake," but wasn't that a given?

"Hello, lass." He beamed at her. "Will I do? I need you to roll my sleeves like you want them."

Had he not noticed he was carrying a wedding cake? "Where did you get that?" *And why do you have it?*

"This?" He held up the cake and beamed, so proud of himself. "I made it."

Deb and Alex closed in. "Robbie, I'm Deb Carmichael. This is my assistant, Alex Leman. I'd offer to shake hands, but—" She gestured to the cake. "You made that? Really?"

"He didn't. He couldn't have." Her tone was sharper than she had intended. "He's kidding you." *But why?*

"Aye. I did bake it. Yesterday. Hyacinth didn't know I can make wedding cakes. I wanted to surprise her."

"You certainly achieved that." What alternate universe had she landed in?

"This is surprising," Deb said.

"As Hyacinth knows, my family is in the wedding business. I started helping my granny with the cakes when I was a lad. Now I can make a whole cake on my own and not just a wee one like this—one that will feed three hundred people, but I don't have those pans. Not that I have any pans. Not here. I borrowed these little ones from Kristin at the bakery. The decorating bags and tips, too."

Bunny trail, but Hyacinth did not have the wherewithal to reel him in. She didn't know what bowled her over more—that he was a cake decorator or that he'd had the nerve to borrow equipment from Kristin so he could make what she sold.

"I could have borrowed big pans from Kristin, but the cake had to fit in my car. It's a Corvette. Not made to transport a cake for three hundred, to be sure. Anyway, we, we don't need that big today."

We don't need one at all. I have tea sandwiches, petit fours, cheese straws, and French Champagne. That was the plan!

"I brought it to celebrate Jules and Reynolds, since I can't attend their wedding. I thought it would be a right nice treat for the whole crew here. I bake a tasty cake, if I do say so."

Hyacinth still couldn't speak, but Deb could and she looked even more elated by this latest development than she was over his battered face.

"This is fabulous!" Deb said. "We can definitely use this."

"Use it?" Robbie wrinkled his brow. "In what way?" Deb and Alex looked at each other for a beat.

"How about this?" Alex said. "You leave and come back in with the cake after Jules and Reynolds are here. We'll get their surprise on camera. This is great stuff."

Not great and not the beginning Hyacinth had pictured. She'd thought there would be introductions, small talk, and a toast to finding Jules the perfect dress. After all, this was a show about finding a wedding dress, not a hockey player making wedding cakes.

"I thought you didn't script." Hyacinth finally found her voice.

"We don't," Deb said. "This is providing an opportunity for spontaneous interaction. It would be scripting if we'd brought the cake and told Robbie what to say."

"At the end of the day," Alex said, "after Jules has settled on a dress, Reynolds can come back and we can cut the cake to celebrate."

"I like it," Deb said. "Are you all right with that, Robbie?"

No! What about, *Are you all right with it, Hyacinth? After all, this is your shop and nobody warned you about a cake party.* She didn't have any cake plates or forks—just the four china appetizer plates Ava Grace had brought over. And what about something to drink? Coffee? She only had a Keurig and disposable cups. Champagne? Claire had only sent three bottles of the good stuff. She had some of her standard in the fridge, but not enough flutes unless she broke out Emma Frances Fairchild's Waterford—*broke out* being the appropriate phrase because that's what would happen.

"Am I all right with it?" Robbie glanced at Hyacinth.

He was willing her to give him an answer. She knew all she had to do was shake her head and he would say he wasn't okay with it, but she nodded instead. What else could she do? Now that they'd seen it, Alex and Deb were practically salivating.

"I suppose," Robbie said. "My teammates—most of them—don't know I can make wedding cakes. But I can take a little ribbing if it'll make this a better show. That's what I'm here for."

"I'm glad to hear that," Alex said. "There's one other thing. This wasn't quite the look we envisioned for you."

"No?" He looked down at his clothes. "What's wrong?"

"You look nice," Deb said, "but we were hoping for the same look from the viral video."

Oh damn. Oh fuck. This was turning into an out of control merry-go-round, switching between clockwise and counterclockwise rotation. No wonder she was feeling queasy.

"I'm not sure." Robbie glanced at Hyacinth again. "I mean, I don't remember what I was wearing…though I guess I could find the video."

"A kilt," Deb said. "An I heart New York T-shirt and light-up running shoes. It doesn't have to be the exact garments—but a kilt and T-shirt. No vulgar words on the shirt."

He looked at Hyacinth with a question in his eyes. She nodded. Again, what else was she to do? Deep breaths. While he should not have brought that cake without consulting her, the clothes were a different matter. He'd done exactly what she'd asked.

"Do I have time to go change?" he asked.

"We'll wait for you." Alex stepped forward and took the cake. "Let me take this. When you get back, can you go around back? We'll let you know when we're ready for you. You can come in carrying the cake—like before, but wearing a kilt."

The merry-go-round was in hell, with Satan himself at the controls. Not a Wonder Woman golden lasso in sight.

Robbie had returned wearing a kilt that he might have plucked from the dirty clothes, a faded black T-shirt with Runrig—whatever that was—plastered across the front, mismatched socks, and those blinking shoes. Somewhere along the way he'd messed up his hair. Or maybe not. Maybe Deb had instructed someone on her staff to do it. Either way, it was falling in his eyes, which was attractive when he was lying over her, coming in for a kiss. For national television, not so much.

You'd have thought with all the hugging, kissing, and carrying on, that Robbie, Reynolds, and Jules were triplets who'd bonded in the womb and were lost without each other. As for the cake—he might as well have handed them his first born and a yacht.

The sister—Leslie, who was almost as good-looking as Jules—got in on the hugging, too. So did Shelia, the mom. Robbie had not called any of them lass. That was something.

They were all very nice, but everything seemed wrong. Here, at Trousseau, she usually felt like queen of her domain, confident, professional, and effective. Today, she was a shop girl, bowing and scraping to her betters.

But she would get things on track. She'd checked to make sure the dresses she'd put aside were in pristine condition and sent Patty to Heirloom to ask Ava Grace for forks and cake plates. Robbie had been working the crowd, making everybody love him, but he hadn't destroyed anything. Now, Reynolds was gone and the women were settled on the sofa with full glasses of champagne.

It was time to get on with what they were here for, time to show that she and her shop were elegant and dignified. Brad would hand off the dresses to Robbie and, one by one, he would bring them out for Jules to see. With any luck, they would have some for her to try on in the next few minutes.

"Jules, we haven't discussed what you're looking for," Hyacinth said. "I thought it would be fun to show you some gowns I've put aside, get your reaction, and go from there."

"That sounds perfect," Jules said. "Truthfully, I don't

know what I want, though I do think with my coloring, pure white is a better choice than off white or candle-light."

"I agree." There could be no showing her a candle-light dress, with a plan to order it in white. No time.

"With your figure, you can wear anything. Shall we start the fun?" Wouldn't Jules be surprised that Hyacinth had hit the mark so close to what she had originally commissioned?

Robbie brought out the first dress. It wasn't outside the realm of possibility that she might even choose this one. "This Abele Lombardi is elegant and sophisticated," Hyacinth said. "As you can see, it doesn't have a lot of embellishment. The star of the show, after the bride, of course, is the cut of the gown and the flow of the shantung silk fabric."

Jules pursed her lips and exchanged looks with her mother and sister. Hyacinth's heart sank; she could practically hear foreboding music playing. She'd been so sure Jules would love this one.

"I know I said I don't know what I want," Jules said slowly, "but I do know what *I don't* want. As the whole world knows, I had commissioned Marius Marchand to make my dress and he leaked the design. That is a lovely gown, but it reminds me of Marchand's design and I want nothing to do with that look. I want something completely different."

Bad. How had she miscalculated so badly? She never miscalculated.

Worse. She'd been so certain, there was no plan B. She always had a plan B.

Worst. Jules had just dogged out one of the biggest names in bridal design in her shop on national television. The merry-go-round was on fire.

Chapter Twenty-Two

Robbie stood beside Hyacinth holding up a dress for Jules's inspection. The frock didn't look like much to him, at least not for a wedding. Too plain. A bride ought to be decked out in all manner of flounces, bows, and sparkles. When else would she ever get to dress like that again? But he held his tongue. He was trying his best to be low-key, like Hyacinth had asked. She had been so good to him lately and he was determined to make this all she wanted it to be.

They were about an hour into shooting now and, all in all, things were going okay. Not much excitement, but that's what Hyacinth was aiming for. The cake had been a good idea, though. Jules, Reynolds, and the TV people loved it, so that was good for Hyacinth. He didn't imagine that she had been happy about the whole clothes change, but that wasn't his fault. He'd cooperated.

Hyacinth looked fantastic. She was wearing black, like usual, but her look was less Professor McGonagall goes to a funeral, and more classy, sexy woman out on the town. Her dress had a tight waist and was long enough to be ladylike, but short enough to show her legs. She'd also spiffed it up with some silver jewelry. As for the hair—it was up in the prim little bun, but he'd decided he didn't like everybody else seeing it like he saw it in bed, curling around her face this way and that.

Too bad he had to go to LA tonight but since he did, his most fervent wish was that this dog and pony show would be over in time for him to take that dress off her and that hair down. Maybe she was wearing some more of that sexy underwear.

If only he could entice her to meet him in the workroom. That would liven things up, especially if the camera followed them.

Uh-oh. Jules didn't like this dress. Right smart of her, and that was okay—though he could feel the tension radiating from Hyacinth.

"I'll get the next one," he said cheerfully. "Lots of bonny dresses to be had." He said that last part to remind Hyacinth that she had all those dresses on that rack that Brad was minding and many more in the shop. Hundreds, at least.

Hyacinth turned to him and said in a whisper, "Tell Brad to send the Anna Carrey. And tell him to pull some different styles—fast. No sheaths."

Had he heard her right? He opened his mouth to ask for clarification, but she turned, plucked the champagne out of the bucket and began to pour another round. He hoped they weren't going to be drunk before noon. He could barely imagine Hyacinth's reaction if someone threw up on a dress. Ice cream was nothing beside that.

He raced to the back room, where Brad was already holding a dress out to him.

"She said the Anna somebody."

Brad looked confused. "Anna Carrey? But that was the *last* choice."

"That's what she said. And she said to pull some different styles—fast. No sheets."

"Sheets?" Brad asked, but then nodded with understanding. "That explains it."

It explained nothing, but he didn't need to understand. His job was to carry dresses without dropping, soiling, or tripping over them—and to be low-key.

And probably to evade the camera that was following him right now. But there was nothing to be done about that. He rushed back to Hyacinth's side.

"Is this more like it?" Hyacinth asked as Robbie held up the dress. He was feeling a little like a game show assistant.

Jules cocked her head to the side and studied the dress. "Closer. I like the lace and the beading. There's just not enough of it."

Ah. It was becoming clearer. Hyacinth had picked plain dresses like a regal queen would wear, but Jules wanted to be a princess.

"Do you think you'd like to try something like this?" Hyacinth's tone was begging her to say yes.

He needed to help her out. Hyacinth wanted Jules to put this dress on and he was going to see to it if possible.

Robbie smiled a cheesy smile and swooped his hand the length of the dress the way he'd seen those game show women gesture to washing machines and vacuum cleaners.

Jules, Shelia, and Leslie laughed like he was a clown at the circus. Maybe they *were* drunk. It wasn't that funny. But some of the tension did go out of the room, so that was good. He glanced at Hyacinth. Not happy.

"How about it, Jules?" He gave her a little wink.

"Want to try it on?" He wiggled the dress. "Show it who's boss?"

"Robbie, you could sell a glacier in Antarctica," Jules said. "You make me almost want to, but no. It would be a waste of time. That's not my dress. I want to see something not so straight—a bigger skirt. And more bling."

He'd failed and Hyacinth was panicking. He could taste it in the air. He had to do something. She wouldn't like him diverting from the plan, but the plan wasn't working and she didn't like that either—though that wouldn't stop her from locking down and stubbornly carrying on with what she had mapped out.

Also, he'd learned a secret about Hyacinth that she probably didn't know herself. There was something she would hate worse than not having the plan followed: failure. She got so wrapped up in the process that she sometimes lost sight of the goal. He knew what it was like to be laid low by a bad practice and forget that there was something worse—a lost game.

He could make this better, stop it from tanking. He watched *All Dressed in White* religiously. It didn't happen often, but sometimes brides did leave without a dress. This was headed that way, as sure as fighting would get you five. He couldn't let that happen to Hyacinth. He just had to give her a minute to breathe and get back to the place where she remembered how competent she was.

"Excuse me, ladies," he said. "I'll be right back. I saw just the thing."

Really, he'd seen no such thing, but he could find her some dresses. And this one dress at a time wasn't cutting it, not if the day was going to end like Hyacinth wanted.

He could only hope Hyacinth would see that was more important than the plan—like for him to be low-key and Jules to pick a dress from that rack. After all, the clothes she picked for him hadn't worked out so well.

Damn it all to hell, it was happening again. Hyacinth had been so sure that since they knew each other better—*intimately*—this would not be a repeat of the Daisy debacle. And she had been so clear about what she expected. He'd seemed equally willing to comply. But here she was in Déjà vu Land. Only this time Hyacinth knew the world would see it, and she couldn't chase Robbie down to stop him. Maybe Brad would head him off.

Now she had to figure out something to say to these women. She couldn't ask about the wedding venue. That was a secret. She couldn't ask about the honeymoon. That was also a secret.

Veils. Usually she didn't discuss that until the dress was chosen, but sometimes the reverse worked. If a bride had her heart set on a particular type of head-piece, that could dictate the style of the gown. And let's face it, beyond a bigger skirt with some embellishment, Hyacinth had absolutely no idea what this woman wanted to wear.

She opened her mouth to ask the question, but Jules spoke first, addressing her mother and sister.

"Robbie is adorable. We had the best time with him when he and Reynolds played in that charity golf tournament a couple of years ago. He played in a kilt."

"Not a bad look." Leslie reached for a petit four and popped the whole thing in her mouth, which annoyed

Hyacinth. Just because something would fit in your mouth didn't mean you ought to eat it in one bite.

"He's a cutie," Jules said. "Don't you think so, Leslie? He's not attached."

"It's too bad he can't come to the wedding," Shelia said.

But he is. Wasn't he? They hadn't discussed it. Did fling equal attachment? At least for the time being?

"Are you sure?" Leslie asked. Had they changed shows on her? Was this *Getting to Know You?*

"Pretty sure." Jules turned to Hyacinth. "Hyacinth, do you know if Robbie's dating anyone in town?"

"I, uh..."

"Frocks!" Mother of pearl. Robbie rounded the corner with dresses pilled so high in his arms you could barely see a few red curls bouncing around above a mound of white. "I think I got the best ones."

He had to have a dozen. Where was he even going to put them?

He laid them on the floor.

"Not the floor!" she burst out before she could stop herself.

"It'll be fine, lass. Your floor's cleaner than anything I own." He turned to Jules and held up an Amelia Carson fit and flare. "This?"

"No," Jules said. "Still too straight."

"Gone." Robbie started a reject stack. "This is shiny." It was the Giorgio Sabelli sequin and crystal encrusted mermaid.

"Mm. No. I like the beading, but the sequins are a little much. And it doesn't look comfortable. I want something I can dance in."

And it went on and on—ball gown, empire, long

train, short train, no train, backless, strapless, tea length, high-low, and even a jumpsuit with an over-skirt. Robbie presented dresses and Jules rejected them, while Hyacinth stood by mute and helpless, looking stupid with Robbie going to collect more dresses now and then. All she could do was mentally take note of what Jules did and didn't like, refill glasses, and try to make small talk.

Meanwhile, her showroom looked like a yard sale. She tried to discreetly pick a dress up from the floor, but Alex caught her eye and shook his head.

If she'd had a golden rope, she might have hanged herself.

"How about this?" Robbie held up the Odette Pascal A-line with the cap sleeves and crystal medallions.

"Not so fluffy as the ball gown, but still a lot of bottom. Looks comfy. I think you could dance in it." He danced a few steps, holding the dress like it was his partner.

His audience loved him. No surprise there.

And for the first time, Jules looked intrigued. "Not that exactly. I don't like the sleeves, but I think we're on to something. It has a pretty shape without looking like a parade float."

Finally, Hyacinth had something to contribute. "We have some beautiful A-lines with different sleeves. Would you like to try this, just to see if you're happy with the silhouette, while I pull some?"

"Yes. I believe I would," Jules rose.

"Great." Hyacinth took the dress from Robbie. "Let's get you in the dressing room, where Patty's waiting to help you. Robbie, why don't you pour Leslie and She-lia some more champagne? And have some yourself." Maybe he would pass out.

He laid his hand on her arm and gave it a squeeze. "Sure thing, lass." He made *lass* sound like a caress, but she didn't have time for that. She was doing good to hang on to the blazing merry-go-round.

As she escorted Jules away, Hyacinth heard Leslie say, "Robbie, tell us about your home in Scotland and your family's wedding business."

She was about to get an earful, complete with bunny trails. It would go nicely with the eyeful she'd already helped herself to.

Jules stood on the pedestal looking at herself in the three-way mirror.

Maybe there was light at the end of the tunnel. Hyacinth might have recaptured some of her credibility by pulling a selection of A-lines according to Jules's preferences: no sequins, no train, no strapless, but lots of crystal beads and lace.

After trying a dozen or more gowns, Jules had narrowed her choice to two. Thank God Robbie had simmered down. At the moment, he was standing quietly by holding the other dress.

"I love the top." Jules ran her hands over the crystal embellished lace bodice of dress number one. "The sweetheart neckline and the roses on the shoulders. I wish the skirt was fuller—like that one." She pointed at the Simone Donatella that Robbie held. "I don't mean to be difficult, Hyacinth." She looked a little teary-eyed.

Hyacinth was good at this part. She took Jules's hand. "You aren't being difficult. You're a bride. You should have the dress you want and deserve. And we are going to find that dress."

"Thank you," Jules said, and looked lovingly at the

three-dimensional appliquéd roses on the shoulders of the dress she wore.

"Maybe you should try on the other one again," Shelia suggested.

"Maybe..." Jules turned to look at herself at a different angle. "But the top of that one is so plain. I love the sparkle of this one—and the roses. Especially the roses. See the little pearls?"

"Then pick that one," Leslie said. "You've got to decide. You're getting married in eleven days and it still has to be altered."

True, though the alterations would be simple. A nip here and tuck there was all either gown would need. Thank goodness neither needed to be shortened. Since the hems were embellished, that would entail taking the dress apart at the waist, cutting down the top of the skirt, and putting it back together—not an easy or fast task.

"It's so hard!" Jules was getting more and more frustrated. "I don't like how this skirt moves at all. Why can't I have this bodice and that skirt? That's what I'd really love. And as long as I'm wishing for what I can't have, I'd like some of these roses scattered on the skirt."

Everyone was quiet for a moment.

"Maybe she can have that," Shelia said. "Or almost that. Maybe not the roses on the skirt."

"How?" Jules asked.

"It's a wild idea," Shelia said. "But what if we bought both dresses?"

"What good is that?" Leslie asked. "Is she going to change at halftime and be happy with the top some of the time and happy with the skirt the rest?"

"No," Shelia said. "Is it possible to take the skirt from one dress and attach it to the bodice of another?"

All eyes were on Hyacinth and she hated that she was going to have to give them unhappy news.

"That *is* possible in some cases. I've done it once." This almost never came up. Most people were doing good to pay for one dress, never mind two. "But some designers don't allow the look of their dresses to be significantly altered. Simone Donatella is one of them. I'm sorry."

"Was there another skirt you liked, Jules?" Shelia asked. "Maybe one by a designer who doesn't have that rule?"

"Not that moved like that one."

"Then get cracking," Leslie said. "Times a-wasting. Suck it up, Jules. One or the other."

Jules looked ready to cry. "Easy for you to say. You have your dress."

Hyacinth sympathized, but Leslie had a point.

"Leslie, you aren't helping," Shelia said.

"Mother, someone has to get tough with her. She's got to have a dress and this is the last chance stop. She can't get married in Reynolds's football jersey."

Hyacinth suddenly felt sick. Probably because the burning merry-go-round had sped up. She'd never considered that Jules would leave without a dress.

Leslie and Shelia started to talk at once. Hyacinth picked up a few phrases. *Maybe look somewhere else. Not too late to call Marchand. What about Aunt Ivy's dress?*

This was a nightmare—and it was all being recorded for posterity. The footage of Hyacinth Dawson's Epic Fail would probably be included in the biographic prospective of Jules Perry that would be made on the fiftieth anniversary of her first Academy Award.

Then Robbie's voice rang out, "Ladies, I might have a right fine solution."

Everyone stopped and looked at him—probably more because he was Robbie than because they thought he had an answer. But who knew? He was full of surprises. Hyacinth was willing to listen; she sure didn't have any ideas.

He took the Simone Donatella off the hanger, folded the bodice over, and held the skirt up to Jules. "This is what you want, Jules? That would make you happy?"

"Yes, but I can't have that. You heard Hyacinth."

"Aye. I did, but perhaps you can." He winked at Hyacinth. "Hyacinth is a right fine designer herself and you'll find nobody better with a needle. Maybe she can make something like the south side of this frock and attach it to the top of that one? Plus, she can sew little rosies on the skirt. Can you do that, lass?"

The merry-go-round spun faster and burned hotter. It would have melted her Wonder Woman rope into a pool of gold if she'd had one.

Eleven days. Thousands of crystal beads, at least thirty pearl-embellished fabric roses, the voluminous skirt that would have to be hemmed by hand.

Impossible. And saying *no* with the cameras rolling and the three women looking so hopeful was not an option.

"Yes," she said calmly. "I can do that." And she could—if she had a month and nothing else to do.

Everyone in the room applauded and cheered.

The merry-go-round exploded into a million pieces.

Chapter Twenty-Three

Thanks be to the holy family and all the wise men, too.

It was nearly over. Robbie was proud of himself for solving that not so wee problem. Jules was getting the dress she wanted and—bonus—Hyacinth would get a head start on that dressmaking business she was so keen to have. Surely that would offset the alternate route he took.

Best of all, he was packed with his suitcase in the car, so there would be time to say a proper goodbye to Hyacinth—that is, if they would get on with it.

"Would you like to talk about jewelry and a veil now?" Hyacinth asked Jules.

"Actually, I'm going to wear my grandmother's pearls and I don't want a veil. Harry Winston has offered to lend me a tiara. Do you think that will be all right? That the dress won't look wrong without a veil?"

"Absolutely not," Hyacinth said. "It will be perfectly beautiful."

Robbie didn't know who this Harry fellow was or why he dealt in tiaras, but he was grateful to him if it would help wind this up.

Hyacinth took the big-skirt dress that Jules was still holding and offered her a hand. "We need to get you out of this and let me get some measurements."

As Jules took off for the dressing room, Hyacinth handed the big-skirt dress to him and stepped so close he could smell her lemony soap. "Hang this up. Do you know how to cut a wedding cake?"

"Of course, I do, lass. I'm an expert. First, you take off the top layer and then—"

"I don't have time for a bunny trail and I don't need to know." Still tense, but that was understandable. Sometimes, after a game, he didn't come down for hours—though that hadn't happened since he'd had Hyacinth to give him some care and comfort. Hopefully, soon, he could help her relax in the same way. "Plan on serving the cake when we're done. And try to find a knife. Look in the break room." And she trotted after Jules.

It took him a while, but he finally found the perfect thing—that skeleton cake serving set she'd used on that haunted house cake at the fall fest. Lucky thing, too. Those plastic ones that came with takeaway food wouldn't get the job done.

Hyacinth made her way from the break room to the showroom with a tray of Waterford flutes filled with the cheap champagne.

For better or worse—and most assuredly worse—it was almost over. It *would* be over if Robbie hadn't brought that damned cake. Reynolds was back, and they were all assembled in the seating area, with Robbie holding court.

Again, she'd looked like a fool, though this time, a frozen, mute fool instead of running around like a chicken with her head cut off. She didn't know which was worse.

"I can't wait to taste your cake, Robbie," Shelia said as

Hyacinth picked her way around the dresses still strewn on the floor like a bunch of dead brides. She'd like nothing more than to hurl the tray—Emma Frances's fancy flutes with it—against the wall and set her shop to rights. "Did you use a mix or make it from scratch?"

"A mix? Oh, no, no. My granny would be scandalized. This is her own recipe, flavored with orange, brandy, and almond. It's a nod to the traditional fruitcakes from long ago, but people don't like that so much anymore."

Next, Alex and Deb would want to bring in a stove and have him demonstrate. And why not? Every reality show ever made rolled into one. *All Dressed in White, Getting to Know You,* and one of those cake shows everybody was so crazy about. All they'd need was a singing and dancing show. Robbie could probably take care of that, too.

Robbie looked up, caught her eye, and jumped to his feet. "Ah, lass! That tray looks heavy. Let me help you."

He started to step forward, but Reynolds made it there first. "I've got it."

Reynolds passed around the champagne and went to perch on the sofa arm beside Jules. "Have my chair, Hyacinth."

Why had she not realized there weren't enough seats? Oh, right. Because she hadn't known there would be a cake party.

"Who wants cake?" Robbie asked.

"I know I do," Jules said. "After all our hard work today, we've earned it."

"That's an interesting knife you've got there, Robbie," Leslie said.

Hell. He had the skeleton cake server.

"It's right festive, don't you think?" And he held it

up for the world to see. Nothing like a Halloween prop in the midst of Christmas splendor.

"Cool," Reynolds said. "Maybe we could borrow that for the wedding."

"Uh, no," Jules said. "We've got that covered."

Robbie proceeded to cut the cake and pass it out, like he'd been doing it for years—which he probably had. "When I get married, I've a mind to use a hockey stick to cut my cake."

When he got married? That shouldn't have surprised her. Of course he would get married. Someday. Just because he wasn't husband material for her didn't mean he wouldn't suit someone. He'd be happy, of course—and so would his wife. It would be a fun, if disorganized, life. Willy-nilly or not, Robbie spread joy wherever he went. What would it be like to live with that kind of joy forever?

"I don't know, bro," Reynolds said. "I've smelled those hockey sticks. Might run everybody off."

"I endorse Ice Time. They'll give me a new one tailor made for the purpose."

As he handed a plate to Leslie, she said, "I'd love to see you play sometime."

What?

"Would you now?" He looked as pleased as a pig with an ear of corn. "The team is flying to LA tonight. Game tomorrow night."

"I don't live in LA. That's just Jules. I live in Denver."

He held out a plate to Hyacinth. "Here you are, lass."

He turned back to Leslie. "We play the Mavericks next month. I'll leave you a ticket."

"Great! We'll get together about the details," Leslie said.

Yes, Leslie. Be sure and do that. He's not so good

on the fine point of things, but at least he told you he's leaving the ticket for you.

Once everyone had cake, Jules stood up and raised her glass. "Before we all dig in, I'd like to propose a toast. First, to my groom, who loves me, even when I'm unlovable. To my mother and sister, who have been with me through every step of this wedding planning process and administered a soft touch and tough love in equal parts. To Robbie, who has made this day more fun than I could have imagined. And last, to Hyacinth, who has shown us the epitome of Southern hospitality and—most important—made my dream dress come true, when I thought it wasn't possible."

I haven't done it yet, sister. How do you feel about a half-hemmed skirt with no roses and no beading? She could see the headlines now: Bridal Shop Owner Doesn't Deliver on Promise and Ruins Academy Award winner Jules Perry's Wedding Day. There would be a picture of a weeping Jules wearing a football jersey and clutching a bouquet.

"Thank you from the bottom of my heart. To you all," Jules sipped her champagne and everyone followed suit and cheered.

"Cut!" Deb bellowed. "And that's a wrap."

Done. People were eating cake and Robbie was slicing more cake and handing it out to the crew. There was backslapping, hand shaking, and Alex and Deb kept saying, "Great stuff, great stuff."

As people finished their champagne, Hyacinth discreetly collected Emma Frances's Waterford flutes and ferried them out of harm's way.

If she could return them intact, she would have done one thing right.

Chapter Twenty-Four

"Sure thing, Alex," Robbie said as the last of the *All Dressed in White* people exited. "I'd love to grab dinner. I'll call you next time we play in New York."

Thank the blessed virgin they were finally finished. Darkness had set in, but he still had a little over an hour before he was due to catch the bus for the airport. Not quite enough time to make love to Hyacinth the way he wanted to, but it would do nicely enough.

He crossed the room to where she was picking up dresses from the floor and hanging them on a rolling rack.

"That was fair brilliant, lass." He tried to take her in his arms, but she pulled away.

"I need to get these dresses off the floor, Robbie." She sounded weary.

"Sorry about that," he said. "I should have fetched that rolling rack thing, but I didn't think about it."

She paused. "No. I don't imagine you did. That wasn't part of the plan."

Ah, the plan. She was disgruntled—tired, probably hungry. Soon, she'd realize what a success the day had been. He could sweeten her up though. He was randy and he wanted her, but what he really longed for was afterward, when she would lie with her head on his chest and idly play with his St. Sebastian medal while he stroked her hair. Those were lovely times.

"It's all over now," he said. "Don't go getting yourself all wound up. You were great."

"Robbie," Patty said from where she was clearing the cake plates, "what do you want me to do with the rest of this cake?"

"I meant to send it with Jules and Reynolds, I forgot. Take it home to your family, unless Hyacinth wants it."

"I promise you I do *not*."

Well, hell. He didn't expect her to want it, but did she have to be so adamant, and act like she wanted no part of the cake he'd worked hard on to make her day go better? He'd even gone the extra mile and made buttercream orchids. Those were a pain.

Brad came from the back, rolling another rack. "Hyacinth, go home," he said. "Patty and I have already discussed this. We're going to clean up."

Yay! Brad to the rescue.

"Yes," Patty chimed in. "You're exhausted."

"You've been here as long as I have," Hyacinth said, picking up another frock.

"Maybe," Brad said, "but you are also emotionally used up. We're going out to grab some quick dinner and come right back. We won't leave until everything is in tip-top shape—dresses steamed, floor vacuumed, dishes packed and ready to go back to Ava Grace. Let us do this for you."

"Yes, lass. Let them do it for you." Robbie dug into his sporran and brought out a hundred dollar bill. "Here, Brad. Dinner's on me for you and Patty."

Brad grinned and took the bill without hesitating.

"Patty, looks like it's steak at the Laurel Springs Inn instead of burgers at Hammer Time."

"I should have done that," Hyacinth said after they'd gone. "Treated them to dinner. They've worked hard."

"Probably wasn't on your list," he teased and tried to take her in his arms again.

Again, she pulled away.

"A lot of things happened today that weren't on my list."

He shouldn't have mentioned the list. Maybe he could make light of it. "Sometimes that's the way of life. Things happen. You didn't see the puck coming, but there it is—right in front of you. Next thing you know, you've knocked it in."

"I don't think it's sometimes with you. I think it's all the time. And I certainly didn't score today."

Teasing wasn't working. "But you did," he said quietly. "You did great."

"Don't patronize me."

She was officially Miss Crabby Pants, but he wasn't going to take it personally.

"You're tired and hungry." They didn't have to have sex. "Why don't you let me take you for something to eat?"

"Or cheese crackers and a ride?" she sneered.

It was getting harder to not take it personally. He'd known she wouldn't like that he'd gone off the plan, but she ought to know him well enough to know that he had done it for her.

So let her be disgruntled; he would not give it any energy. "I was hoping to give you a ride to your house for some quality time before I go, but I'd rather feed you if that's what you need."

She closed her eyes and shook her head. When she opened them again, her whisky eyes were all Tennessee rotgut and not a bit of Scottish smooth smoke. It had been a while since she'd given him the evil eye.

"What I need is to not have an impossible task before me—one that I probably will fail at."

"I don't understand, lass. What task would that be?"

He really was confused now.

She looked heavenward and leaned on the rack. It rolled and she would have fallen if he hadn't caught her. She jerked out of his grasp.

"What made you tell Jules that I could make a whole new skirt for her dress?"

For someone who was wound tight about the most insignificant of details, she had a way of reinventing past conversations.

"I didn't tell her that. After I heard it was possible to put two dresses together, I asked if you could make the bottom part. You're the one who said you could."

"I couldn't very well go on television in front of millions of people and say I couldn't."

"Millions? That many?" He wouldn't have thought so large an audience.

"I don't know. But a lot. And that's not the point. It would still be plenty of people. I couldn't admit I wasn't capable of making that skirt."

"I don't know why not. If you can't, you should have said so. If someone asked me on TV if I could fly, I'd say no. Or even not on TV. Anywhere. I'd still say no. Because I can't. Not without an airplane."

She clenched her fists and let out a little scream. "It's not the same and you know it."

"It's exactly the same. I don't have the skill to fly. You don't have the skill to make the skirt. Just say so."

"I *do* have the skill. That's no problem. It's the time, Robbie. She's getting married in eleven days. She's flying back here in nine days for a final fitting and to take the dress back. Alex and a cameraman are coming to get a final shot. I'll never get it done. Things like this take weeks. Besides making the skirt and attaching it, there's beading, and let's not forget the roses you promised her."

Unfair, all unfair. Again, he had promised nothing. He had only come up with the idea. Hyacinth had done the promising. Frankly, he was getting a little tired of this. But she was overwrought and he was going to let it go. He didn't want to leave for California on bad terms. Besides, he had another idea.

"I'm sorry, lass. I thought it was a good thing. I thought you wanted to make frocks and this would be a leg up. But if it's a matter of time, not skill, all isn't lost. Maybe I can help."

"Oh?" She picked at her thumbnail. "How's that? Can you sew as well as you can decorate cakes? Can you stitch seed pearls onto I don't know how many fabric roses? Because that's what it's going to take."

"No. I can't do that, but here's an idea: I could help Brad and Patty out here in the shop, so you could sew full time. I'd still have to go to practice, but I could have all your meals sent in and—"

"No, no! Stop, stop!" She moved her hands in front of her like she was trying to push a car out of the mud. "That's all I need. You—coming up in here, scattering thousands of dollars' worth of dresses all over the floor." She swung her arm in a wide arc. "And having unplanned parties with your stupid cake."

That hit him where he lived. "I was trying to help," he said quietly. "I'd never told you I can make wedding cakes. I thought the cake would be a good surprise for you. People love cake. I meant to make people happy so you'd have a good day of it. I didn't know your good pal Alex would want to have the cake on the show, let alone eat it. I thought the crew would snack on it and Jules and Reynolds would take the rest home with them."

"You thought they would take that cake on a *plane?* Where would they even put it?"

"I did, and they'd put it anywhere they liked. Reynolds Fallon doesn't fly commercial and wouldn't even if he wasn't a big football star. He flies in his Silicon Valley billionaire parents' private plane." She would have only flown commercial, probably coach. He would like to change that, take her to Scotland, first class all the way. "You can believe me or not, but I did it to make your day go better."

Some of the wind went out of her sails and she nodded. "Okay. I appreciate the thought, but surprises are never good."

It must have been a sad life she'd lived to think that. His heart hurt for her.

"Sometimes they are. I thought, by now, you trusted me enough to not mind a surprise from me. I thought you knew I only want good things for you."

She bit her lip, seemed to deflate a bit more. Relief washed over him.

"But what about the dresses?" And she was off and running again. Premature relief. "I had a plan, and you went off road like a dirt bike with a mind of its own."

He'd tried to be patient, to take into account that she was stressed, but he was past tired of it. Maybe it was time to tell her some hard truths.

"Yes, you had a plan, and it wasn't working. That's your problem, Hyacinth. You get locked into your plan so tight, you try to make everybody step-to until they see it your way. It was like you dressing me up like some fraternity boy on his way to the country club. They didn't like it. Same with Jules. She wasn't going to wear any of those dresses you picked."

"I know! I miscalculated. On both things. Badly. That's why I told you to have Brad gather some other styles. But you took over—"

"And a good thing for it, too. Your dress-picking wasn't all that wasn't working."

"What do you mean?"

"I mean the whole show was a mess. It was about as dry as a nun's retirement party. Were you just going to stand around and quote Bible verses while Brad took his sweet time about gathering frocks? I love the man, but he's slow to make a decision of any kind. If you don't know that about him, you haven't been paying attention. It takes him twenty minutes to decide what flavor of wings he wants. We'd still be in the middle of it all if we were waiting on Brad."

She looked like he'd struck her, and he wanted to strike himself. He'd gone too far.

"Look, lass." He put a hand on her cheek. "After we got you on the right track with that one kind of dress—"

"A-line."

"Yes. That. You took it from there and you got comfortable. All you needed was a wee bit of help moving things in that direction. You knew what to do then and you did it in grand style."

"We'll have to agree to disagree on that. But even if it were true, I'm still obligated to have that dress ready in nine days."

"You'll do it. I have faith in you." This time she let him fold her against him, allowed him to offer her comfort.

"Well. Maybe. At least I don't need to order fabric. I have a bolt of silk taffeta for the skirt in my workroom."

"See there? My Hyacinth, always prepared. Let's get you home. I have a little time before I have to leave. We can order a pizza, maybe. Or not. Whatever you like." She stiffened in his arms and jerked away.

Pizza—that was another thing.

Hyacinth's head was spinning. Robbie was right. She was tired, hungry, and stressed. But how much of that was because of him?

"If you want pizza, why don't you go catch up with Leslie before they leave town? I heard them say they were going to the Brick Oven before they set off. You can kill two birds with one stone."

He wrinkled his brow. "What two birds would that be?"

"Have pizza and work out the details for meeting up with Leslie in Denver."

He shook his head. "If you must know, they invited me and I turned them down because I wanted to be with you. You aren't making sense. What details do I need to work out with Leslie?"

"The ticket you're going to leave her. For your game when you play Denver."

"*That* bothered you?" Ass. He almost smiled. He thought she was jealous.

"I didn't say it bothered me. It doesn't."

"I was not making a date with her. I was being nice to the sister of my friend. I leave tickets for people all the time. I promised Alex some as well."

"Nice to know you're leaving tickets for people you aren't trying to punish."

His face went blank and he stared at her without blinking. "That's what coming to my games is for you? A punishment? Still?"

Shame washed over her, but not enough to make her admit to him that she was beginning to understand hockey and that she loved watching him play.

She sighed. "I'm sorry. You're right. I'm stressed and tired. I shouldn't have made that crack about Leslie. You should see who you want to see."

"I am seeing who I want to see. I see you, only you."

Was he for real? "Look, Robbie. Let's not pretend."

"Pretend what? We have something here, you and me—the beginning of something, anyway."

"What we're having is a fling."

His jaw went hard. "A fling? That's what you think this is?"

"Don't pretend like you're above it."

"I'm not. I'm just above it where you're concerned."

Why, oh why, had she gone there? Why hadn't she had the sense to just let it play out until it was over? How was she supposed to know the first rule of flings must be don't talk about flings? The book hadn't said so. But she was into it now.

"Look, Robbie. Look around us. Could we be more different? I'm set in my ways. You make it up as you go. Suppose we were in this for the long haul. Suppose it even led to something permanent."

"I can think of worse things," he said.

"I can't live a haphazard life. I can't live with un-paid power bills and children missing the school bus. I can't get up in the morning to find strangers asleep on my living room floor."

He frowned more with every word she spoke. "I don't understand. My bills are paid by automatic bank draft and if my children missed the bus, I'd just drive them to school." He stopped and looked upward and to the right like he always did when he was going to go down a bunny trail. "But I'd need a different car. Maybe a Tahoe. Red." She thought the conversation was over, because she wasn't bringing him back from that bunny trail this time. But, then, he snapped his eyes back to meet hers. "As for strangers asleep in the living room—in what world would that ever happen?"

Not your perfect world, where everything was happy brides, wedding cakes with icing roses, and family dinners around the table.

She put up a hand to stop him. "You're missing the point." They could have probably made a Broadway musical about his childhood. He'd never gone without, never even lived in a blue collar world where payday meant trips to the grocery store and a fast food restaurant, where people overcompensated at Christmas and spent the rest of the year paying it off—the very life most people tried to escape, but she'd longed for until going to live with Memaw, when she finally got it.

"Then explain it to me," he said.

"I don't think I can. We're too different."

"You're saying a fling is all this is? A roll in the hay and goodbye when you're tired of it?"

When put like that, it sounded so sad. He waited for her answer, but she remained silent.

After what seemed like forever, he sighed and ran his hand over his face. "Tell you what, Hyacinth. I can at least give you back a little time that you'll need to work on the frock that I so thoughtlessly and selfishly caused you to commit to."

Damn. He was hurt now. She hadn't meant that. "Robbie, I didn't—"

"No, no, hear me out. You're absolved from attending my games. Same for going out to Hammer Time with the guys and me afterward. Same for the Christmas Gala. No more punishment."

That wasn't what she wanted. "No. I made a commitment and I keep my commitments. I'll be there."

"Yeah? Then, how about this? I don't want you there."

Gutted. She was gutted like a catfish on a riverbank, but what could she say to that? That she would call back the day and do things differently if she could? Or, though there was no future for them, she wanted this fling, wanted to lie in his arms for a while yet? Wanted to wake up with him Christmas morning?

But none of that would do.

"I'm going home," she said. Because where else did one go to lick her wounds?

He followed her out silently and waited until she set the alarm and locked the door.

She had driven a block down the street when she noticed that Robbie was following her. That might be good news. He'd proven he was slow to anger and quick to forgive. They could put this behind them. Nothing had changed about the possibility of a future for them, but maybe they could have a little more of each other. She needed time to make up for the hurtful things she'd said.

She was hopeful when he parked behind her and got out of the car.

"Come in?" she asked. He nodded and followed her into the house. After switching the light on, she turned to him. "Robbie, I'm sorry. I said things I shouldn't have, didn't give you credit where it was due."

"I'm not here for your apology," he said. "I think we have established where we are."

"Then why are you here?"

"To make sure you're safely home."

"Why wouldn't I be?"

"I don't know, Hyacinth. There are all kinds of people in the world, a lot of them bad—thieves, murderers, rapists, and sociopaths who imprison people and cut them up for the pure pleasure of it. Maybe, with all your other bad opinions of me, you think I'm chauvinistic or some kind of fuddy-duddy fool from days gone by to want to see you home safely. But it's how I was raised. The men in my family revere, cherish, and protect the women in our lives. I wouldn't let anything happen to you, no matter what you think of me, and I don't need a list or a spreadsheet to remind me. Old-fashioned or not, I come from a world where I pay for dinner, open doors, and do my best to please. I admit I fall short on that last one when my good intentions get ahead of my brain, but I've been trying to work on that. That's who I am. Take it or leave it." His sweet mouth went to a hard line and he shook his head. "But I guess we've seen that you've decided to leave it."

Her world bottomed out. Such a good man, with such a good heart, and she had hurt him to the core. She'd never had a man who wanted to look out for her before. If he had lived to see her old enough to drive, would her father have been reluctant to let her out on her own? Sadly, she knew the answer. When he had a daughter—and he would—Robbie would probably want to lock her in a tower. Lucky girl and she wouldn't even know it.

Everything had gone so wrong. She had not meant to end things.

"Oh, Robbie." She reached out to him.

He stepped back. "Don't touch me, lass. Don't ever touch me again. You were right. We are too different, but not for the reasons you claim. You were having a fling and I was having a relationship." And he was gone.

Hyacinth stood completely still for what must have been a full five minutes, willing her heart not to tune into what her brain was saying.

Then she got in her car and drove back to Trousseau. There were dresses to hang and champagne flutes to return.

After all, they were something borrowed—just like Robbie.

Chapter Twenty-Five

Despite the 3-2 loss to the Angels, Robbie had loved being on the ice tonight even more than usual. It was easy to know why. He hadn't thought about Hyacinth a single time.

Unfortunately, after the final buzzer sounded, it all came rushing back like a plateful of fish gone bad. He still couldn't figure out if he was mad or hurt.

"They've put out food for us in the atrium," Clay Dempsey said as they entered the hotel.

"I'll be along," Robbie said. "I'm hot. I want to change clothes."

"I know," Clay said. "Welcome to La La Land. People were saying it's unseasonably warm even for here."

Summertime in December—another thing that wasn't right.

It was his intention to slip into a kilt and join his teammates, but the kilt he'd packed was the one Hyacinth had mended. Usually, wearing it gave him a good feeling, but no more. He hid it in the bottom of the suitcase and found a pair of shorts instead. He was casting about for a Yellowhammer T-shirt when it became too much effort.

To hell with it. He wasn't hungry anyway. He crawled

into bed and closed his eyes. Maybe he'd stay here until morning when they had to go make some commercial for literacy before flying back.

Robbie hated conflict, especially within himself, but that's what he was living with. He wanted to call Hyacinth, but at the same time, never wanted to talk to her again.

Maybe she was right. Maybe all it had been was sex, but it hadn't felt that way, and he ought to know. After losing his virginity at age sixteen to an eighteen-year-old bridesmaid at Wyndloch, casual sex had been the story of his life.

Maybe that was why this was happening to him— punishment for past sins. Had he made someone feel the way he felt now? There was a knock at the door. He didn't wonder, or much care, who it was. He knew who it wasn't—Hyacinth come to shoot more black lightning bolts at him.

"You okay?" Jake said when Robbie opened the door.

"Fine. Why?" He stood aside so Jake could enter.

"When you didn't show up to eat, I assumed you were with Mia since you've never been one to brood over a loss."

Ah, yes. Mia. He and Jake had charming companions in almost every hockey city in North America, but he was surprised that Jake thought he would have called her. Now that he thought about it, Jake might not know he'd been seeing Hyacinth. Though it sometimes felt like he'd been with her forever, it had actually been a very short time. They hadn't been seen out together much, opting for more private pleasures. Hard to believe he hadn't said anything to Jake, but maybe he hadn't.

Well. He wasn't going to say anything now. No point in visiting a moot point.

"But then Clay said you were coming to eat," Jake went on.

"I did say I was, but I got distracted. Apparently that's a particular problem of mine."

Jake laughed. "Not usually where your stomach is concerned." He took off his jacket and tie, threw them on the bed, and sat down on the couch.

"I would have thought you'd be back at your room talking to Evie."

"I've already talked to her. She's asleep by now. Remember it's two hours later there."

"Right." Hyacinth was probably still up sewing on that dress. "Sparks?"

"Yes?" Jake said.

"About Mia—"

"What about her?"

"I know you'd never call Angelique while you're here." Robbie named Jake's LA charming companion.

"I should hope you do know that." Jake's face clouded over.

"Hold your horses, man. I said I knew you wouldn't." Why, why, why did people have to reinvent what he said? "My question is this: Why? I know you wouldn't because you're married, and that's not who you are. You have a standard."

"Damn right I do. And I've got Evie."

"Let's say you didn't have that standard. Would you do it?"

"What kind of question is that?" Jake said.

"Hypothetical. And one I'd like an answer to."

Jake bit his bottom lip, considering. "It's hard to even

wrap my head around that, but no. I wouldn't. It's not only about my moral code. I don't want to be with anyone else. I love Evie. She's my whole world. Anyone else would just be...empty."

"Ah." Did that explain why he hadn't thought of calling Mia? Or Melinda in New York?

"Why do you want to know?" Jake asked.

"Just curious. Do you think we mistreated those women?" He thought of Maya in Winnipeg, who volunteered at the animal shelter, and sweet Nicole in Phoenix who could make him laugh even after a loss. Rayne in North Carolina always brought him fudge. He'd miss that fudge, but not Rayne, and what kind of man did that make him? "Do you think we acted like we were just using them for sex?"

Jake looked at him for a long moment. "No, Robbie, I don't. We were careful about that. Everyone knew what was what. We didn't live where they lived and they never indicated they wanted more than seeing us when we played in their cities. Remember, those girls were not sitting around waiting for us. They wanted to have fun and be a little wild, like we did—which was their right as much as it was ours."

"What you're saying is, these girls wanted a fling and nothing more."

"Exactly. Like us."

And like Hyacinth. What if nobody ever wanted him forever?

Robbie sighed. "Thanks. I wouldn't have wanted to lead anyone astray."

"I never saw any evidence that you did. But you know what I find interesting?"

"What's that?"

"That you're talking about this carousing in the past tense—and not just for me. For yourself, too."

"Am I? I wasn't aware. Doesn't mean anything." Maybe. But deep down, he knew. He wouldn't see any of those girls again. If he heard from them, he wouldn't ghost them, but he had no desire for that life anymore.

"If you say so," Jake said.

"I want to ask you something else. What would you do if you found that you had fallen for someone who hadn't fallen for you? Someone who could be down-right mean to you?"

Jake laughed. "You say that like I haven't been there. In my case, I guess I'd buy her a giant engagement ring and a McMansion. I'd marry her and take her to Paris, where I'd buy her a king's ransom in jewelry and a bunch of clothes. And then, she'd throw me out of the house and marry somebody else before the ink was dry on the divorce papers."

"Right. Sorry, mate. I guess I forgot there for a minute you were married to Channing before Evans." Though he didn't see how; he'd been with Jake through every minute of that hell ride.

"Excellent idea. Let's all forget about Channing." Then Jake's face went serious. "What's going on with you, Robbie? Who did this to you?"

"No one," he lied. If he told Jake what had passed between himself and Hyacinth, Jake would be indignant on Robbie's behalf. That could make for a strained relationship between Hyacinth and Evie and maybe a point of contention between Evie and Jake. He wouldn't do that to his friends.

"If you want to talk, I'm right here."

"Thanks. I'll keep that in mind."

But he would never tell and he might as well face why. It was Hyacinth he was looking out for, more than Jake and Evie. He didn't want them mad at her.

Robbie turned on the television. "How about some *Sports Center*?"

"Sure. Let's see what they have to say about us getting our asses handed to us."

Robbie had never had his ass handed to him twice in three days' time before. One, he would come back from. The other, he wasn't so sure.

Behind the closed doors of her workroom, Hyacinth sewed the final seed pearl on another silk organza rose and laid it on the worktable with the others. They were lovely, and this work would have been relaxing and satisfying, if not for the giant, invisible clock ticking above her head.

She'd constructed the skirt and had been working on the roses for two days now—ever since that ghastly day of scattered dresses, cake crumbs, and thoughtless words. Not for the first time, she wondered if it would be more efficient to carry on with completing them one by one or to make all the roses first and then go back and embellish them.

She hoped to be well into beading the skirt by Saturday—when she wouldn't be watching Robbie at a home game against Detroit. Because he didn't want her there. Ghosts of the times when he had wanted her swirled around her head.

Hand sewing gave a person time to think—too much.

There was a knock on the workroom door. Probably Brad trying to get her to eat again.

"Come in."

"Hello, Hyacinth." Not Brad, but Claire who stepped through the door.

Shock waves went through Hyacinth. It was only then that she realized she had not called Claire to report on the taping.

"Hello, Claire." Hyacinth stood up. "I've been meaning to call to tell you how it went with *All Dressed in White*." Not quite a lie. She would have if she'd thought of it. But she hadn't. Claire had not crossed her mind since that awful day, though plenty else had—stuff that, unlike her relationship with Claire, didn't affect her at all. She knew the Yellowhammers had lost to LA and Robbie had gotten a goal and an assist. She knew that if he'd kept company with a woman in California, *The Face Off Grapevine* didn't know about it.

All that—and the roses—had taken a lot of energy, so there had been none left for Claire.

Claire would give her a pass; she deserved it. She had always been spot-on about keeping her apprised.

Claire nodded. "How was it with *All Dressed in White*? I can't wait to see it."

"Some good, some bad. Hopefully, the bad will end up on the cutting room floor." Maybe admitting that there was bad would somewhat prepare Claire for what would be the mortification of the decade. "Jules wasn't completely satisfied with a dress so I'm getting to make a skirt for the bodice she liked."

Getting to? She could scarcely believe those words had come out of her mouth.

Claire smiled. "Hyacinth, that's wonderful. I know how much you want to create. One step closer."

That much was true, if only she could finish.

"I had no doubt it had gone splendidly," Claire went

on. "But I really stopped by to ask about the music for the party."

Party?

Oh, fuck. Oh, damn. Oh, every bad word that hadn't been invented yet. The party for Jake and Evans—the one that was supposed to happen after *All Dressed in White* was behind her, that was supposed to be fun, that she was supposed to leave from with Robbie.

That she was supposed to have lined up the music for!

The party that was tomorrow!

Her legs turned to water and she dropped heavily into her chair.

Claire looked concerned. "Hyacinth, are you all right? I realized this morning that you had not answered me when I emailed you yesterday to ask the name of the group you had booked. You always respond, even if it's only to say you received the email."

That was true. She did. Always. Every time, no matter what. But she had not received the email because she hadn't read her email since the taping—never even thought of it.

Who was she? Who ignored their email in this day and age? Especially a business owner, who communicated almost exclusively with her clients that way?

She'd spent too much time with Robbie. He had rubbed off on her.

There's no such thing as too much time with Robbie, a silent, inward voice whispered.

But too late, way too late for that. Too late for everything.

She's coming unglued. Hyacinth had heard the expression, but never understood it and certainly never thought she'd live it. But here she was, glueless, clueless, and doomed to—to what, she didn't know. Maybe just doomed.

She looked up at Claire. "Claire, I'm sorry. I forgot. It's just that I've been so caught up." She picked up a silk rose and waved it in the air like Claire was supposed to know what that meant.

"It's all right, Hyacinth. Just tell me now who you found."

"No. I don't mean I forgot to answer your email. I forgot to book the music." *Kill me now!*

"This isn't like you, Hyacinth." Claire's expression was surprised, but her tone was kind. Concerned. Hyacinth wasn't used to people needing to be concerned for her—like Robbie was concerned that she would get home safely.

That slapped her in the face again. She covered her eyes with her hands in an effort to escape.

"Hyacinth?"

Right. Claire. Music. The thoughts in her head were like jazz tunes, going off into twenty directions. Mother of pearl! Her head was full of bunny trails, with no one to get her back on track—no one but herself.

She had to concentrate.

"I'm so sorry. I was going to take care of it first thing yesterday, but I never even thought of it."

"Did you have someone in mind?" Claire asked.

"I did. Do. I had plan *A*, *B*, and *C*." Nobody ever had to follow up with Hyacinth. She didn't need them. She had her lists, spreadsheets, and diagrams to keep her straight. But where were they now? Gone, like Robbie was gone.

"Calm down," Claire said. "Maybe we can still get someone."

A lifeline! "Yes. If they weren't booked yesterday, they won't be today. I'll call."

"If it doesn't work out, well, I have decent speakers. I can make a playlist."

Plan D? She could tell by the look on Claire's face this was even worse than email invitations.

"Let me make some calls first."

"Would you like me to do it?" Claire asked. "You seem to have your hands full."

Full hands. Empty bed. Empty brain.

Empty heart.

"No," Hyacinth said. Turning her obligation over to anyone, let alone Claire, would be the ultimate in failure. "I'll make the calls. I'll do it right now. And I'll text you as soon as it's taken care of."

"If you're sure," Claire said.

"I am." Hyacinth stood again.

"Then I'll get out of your hair. Call me if you need help."

When she'd gone, Hyacinth pushed aside the roses and opened her laptop.

Then part two of the nightmare hit. She would be expected to attend this party, hours and hours of time she couldn't spare.

But she could get back to work as soon as it was over. She wouldn't be leaving with Robbie.

That thought chased away all the panic inside her. Trouble was, emptiness replaced it—and she'd take panic over empty any day.

Chapter Twenty-Six

Robbie leaned against the wall of Claire's crowded living room and sipped his scotch. Most of his teammates were in the dining room gathered around the food. He'd been headed there, too, before stopping to have a look around.

He knew Hyacinth would be at this party. She was one of the hostesses; it had said so right on the invitation. While he'd been prepared to see her, he was not prepared for her to float in looking like an angel.

And that wasn't just starry-eyed talk; she really did look like an angel. She wore a filmy dress the color of rich cream that wouldn't have been amiss in a nativity play. It hit her at mid-calf and had silver sparkles along the neck, sleeves, and waist that put him in mind of stars swirling about her.

All she needed was a halo and wings—though a halo would probably be lost in that magnificent hair tumbling around her face and shoulders.

He would do well to remember she wasn't an angel, but that was hard now that his anger had gone, leaving him with only his hurt and longing. He supposed eventually the hurt would go away, too.

He hoped it took the longing with it.

He wished he didn't remember how her hair smelled.

"Don't you look magnificent in your kilt? And you looked almost as good on the ice this afternoon."

Robbie turned to find Christine Champagne at his elbow. Sweet relief washed over him at the welcome distraction. He took her hand and kissed it. "Quite a compliment coming from the loveliest woman in the room."

She laughed. "You're very kind, but I think my new daughter-in-law has that distinction."

Robbie followed her gaze to where Jake and Evans stood in the large foyer greeting well-wishers as they entered the house—but his eyes didn't linger there very long. They were drawn to a whirl of cream and silver behind the happy couple.

Naturally, she would be in a whirl. She had a hand in giving this shindig. It would follow that she would be sorting appetizer picks by color or instructing the bartender to iron the paper napkins.

"Ah, there's that smile," Christine said. "The one I love to see." He hadn't realized he was smiling. "They *do* look so happy, don't they?" She gestured to Jake and Evans.

He wasn't likely to tell her it wasn't the bride and groom who had made him smile, but a woman he was never going to have and ought not even want.

Despite the short notice, the party was overrun with people—Yellowhammers, people from around town, Jake's and Evans's families, and people Hyacinth suspected were party crashers, hoping for some good booze and food. They were getting it, too. Claire had not scrimped. In addition to the ever revolving wait-staff carrying trays of fancy little bites, there was a prime rib carving station, a sushi bar, and a selection of pasta. The star of the dessert table was a huge chocolate, tiered cake that wasn't nearly as nice as what Robbie could have made.

And thanks be to God—literally—sweet music floated through the house. The Jazz Notes had not only been available, but happy for the job.

Hyacinth leaned in between Jake and Evans and said as quietly as possible, "Are you two doing all right? Can I get you anything? Refresh your drinks?"

"We're fine." Evans turned to smile at her, "This is a wonderful party, Hyacinth. Thank you."

"Our pleasure." It felt deceptive to accept thanks when she hadn't done anything except nearly botch the music, but she didn't have the energy to set them straight, and they didn't care anyway.

"Show her your ring, Evie," Jake said.

Hyacinth extended her hand to accept Evans's. "You did get a ring. No more championship ring around your neck?"

"I gave it to her right before coming here," Jake said.

He was awfully proud of himself for what it was. It was nice enough, but ordinary—a gold band with diamonds all around and not very big ones at that.

"It's lovely, Evans."

"Wait until you see," Evans said excitedly. "It's got a secret." She slipped the ring off her finger and brought her hand to the pendant she wore—a huge diamond surrounded by four circles, all set with smaller diamonds. That *was* impressive, if it was real.

"Nice," Hyacinth said. "Is that new, too?"

"It came with the ring." And she popped the ring on

the pendant, creating a fifth circle. "For when I have my hands in pie dough. Jake had it made."

Boy, she'd pegged that wrong, but what else was new?

"It's perfect for her, Jake," Hyacinth said sincerely. "I don't know if I have ever seen anything as thoughtful."

And to think she'd thought there was nothing special about it. What would it be like to have someone willing to go to such lengths for you?

You mean like giving up a whole day to do a TV show just because you asked? She'd gotten used to that inward voice bitching at her night and day, telling her it was her own damn fault when she woke up lonely, and was sneering at her when she went over how she could have done things differently, all the while chanting *too late, too late, too late.*

Claire chose that moment to appear like a genie out of a bottle. "All well here?" she asked. "Jake, Evans, do you need a drink?"

"No, thanks," Jake said. "Hyacinth was just checking on us."

"Good, then. Hyacinth, would you mind going to the kitchen and telling Renee the horseradish sauce is getting low?"

"Happy to." Relieved for a task she couldn't possibly make a mess of, Hyacinth made a beeline through the living room, only to have her progress impeded when a voice called her name.

"Hyacinth, darling." It was Jake's mom, and she was standing in a huddle with none other than Robbie in his full Scottish formal attire.

Hyacinth gave a little wave and tried to move on, but

Christine Champagne was having none of it. "Come see me, precious." She held out her hand.

There was nothing Hyacinth could do but close the distance between them and take her hand.

"It's so good to see you again." Christine kissed her cheek. "I'm sorry our visit was cut short at Thanksgiving, but I guess we have my impulsive son to thank for that." She tried and failed to look disgruntled.

"It seems to be an impulse that suited all concerned," Hyacinth said. She could feel Robbie's stare bearing down on her. She needed to get away—away to attend to the horseradish emergency. But Christine still had her by the hand like a dog chained to a spike in the yard.

"This party is so nice. Thank you for doing it for them. You will come to the reception Anna-Blair and Keith are having when the hockey season ends, won't you?"

"I wouldn't miss it for the world." *Let me go before I go jump off the roof or—worse—cry.*

"I was trying to convince Robbie to come to us for Christmas, but I can't get him to commit. See what you can do to persuade him. And you'll come, too, I hope."

"I, uh—"

"Oh, there's my cousin Troy. I need to go." At long last, Christine released Hyacinth's hand, but not before she gave it a squeeze and said, "Now, I'm expecting you for Christmas, honey, and for you to convince Robbie. Marc and I have already called dibs on Evie and Jake and there's plenty of room for you and Robbie, too. Robbie, I'll see you later."

And she was gone with a swish of silk and the subtle scent of her perfume.

"You should go to the Champagnes' for Christmas,"

Hyacinth said without inflection or emotion. "They want you there." And didn't everyone? She and Robbie probably wouldn't have been together for the holiday anyway, considering the nature of flings.

He gave her a half smile. His face looked better, but wasn't well by any means. How was that possible? It seemed years since she'd seen him.

"Was that your attempt to persuade me?"

She shrugged. "For some reason, I feel compelled to do what that woman commands."

"Most do," he said.

"Did it work?" she asked.

"I don't know what I'm doing in an hour, never mind Christmas."

She would have excused herself then, had he not spoken.

"How goes the frock, lass?" *Lass.* How could that one word, spoken as only he could say it, lift her heart and wreck her soul all in the same instant?

"Well enough." The construction and roses were done, but it wasn't hemmed and she'd barely started the beading. Five days before Jules flew in on the Fallon family jet and Alex swooped in from the North with his cameraman. Her heart raced.

"Will you finish?"

"Yes," she said defiantly. "I might not sleep, and Brad is taking my bridal appointments so I may have some unhappy clients who expected to have me, but it will be done."

He looked sad. "Lass, for what it's worth, I meant well. I know that's a broken record between us, but I did. I would never have done that—or brought the cake, or any of it—if I had known it would put you in distress. That's not what I wanted for you."

If she had been less tired, she might not have melted so completely. She badly wanted to touch him, but he'd told her to never touch him again. Was it possible she could change that?

"I know that, Robbie, and I'm only sorry I didn't let myself see it at the time. The things I said to you—I am sorry. I can't even say how much. And this isn't like the last time I apologized to you. We both know I said what I had to so I could get what I wanted. Not this time. I've played what I said to you over in my head a million times and every time, I've hated myself."

He studied her for a long moment. "Don't you think hating yourself is a mite overkill?" He lifted one corner of his mouth. "If I say I forgive you, can you stop that particular bit of foolishness?"

She felt lighter than she'd felt in days. Maybe this could be over, after all. "Can we put it behind us?"

"By that, do you mean pick back up where we left off?"

It cost her to bare her soul, but there was only one answer. "I'd like that."

"You mean with the fling, as you say?"

"Yes." A million times yes, even if she never finished Jules's dress and was tarred and feathered for it.

"Then, no. I forgive you, but I can't put it behind me." Turns out, there were things worse than being tarred and feathered.

His expression went to weary. "I've had flings, too many to count, but I'll have no more of it."

She couldn't move her feet, her mouth, or her mind.

"I don't mean to hurt your feelings, but I can't do it anymore. You don't know what it's like."

"Do you think I haven't had flings?"

"No. I don't think you have. You may think you have in hindsight, but I'd wager you always went into any potential relationship with hope for the future. Until me. I'm betting any prospect you considered in the past kept lists. And, as you rightly pointed out, that's never going to be me. I don't even have a pen." There was nothing but kindness in his tone and eyes when he spoke. But then Robbie was a kind man—and, apparently, an intuitive one. It was amazing how right he was. "You see, Hyacinth, I find that I want a real relationship. A wife. Children." He nodded in the direction of Jake and Evans. "I want what they have, what my mum and da have—though not *so* many children."

"You can't mean," she said slowly, "that you're offering that to me after this short time."

He hesitated. "Maybe not, not yet. But I want the possibility. You can't offer me that, and I can't offer you a fling. That's where we are, lass. No changing that."

She was hollow, but he was right.

He looked as though he was going to speak, then stopped and shook his head.

"What?" She had to know what he wanted to say.

"Nothing."

"Please."

"All right. Much of the time, I'm not a wise man, but I've thought about this a lot. We've not talked about it since that night we drove back from Mississippi together, but I haven't forgotten you had a tough go of it with your parents—what with them dying and not paying attention to the finer details of life. But, Hyacinth, you can't make everybody you encounter pay for how your parents lived their lives."

"They weren't bad people. They loved me, and their neglect was never intentional."

He nodded. "You said as much before. Just free spirits who didn't make a lot of plans—unsuited to the way you're wired up. Like me."

She heard the words, but she didn't process them—refused to process them.

"I have to see about some horseradish sauce," she said.

Later that night, after the party was over, when she got in her car to head for home, a silver Corvette pulled behind her.

This time, she knew better than to hope.

He would see her inside and leave her with ten thousand Swarovski crystals to sew on to a silk taffeta skirt.

Chapter Twenty-Seven

Robbie boarded the team bus and slipped into the seat beside Jake. They were headed to Nashville to play their old team, the Sound.

"Like the old days," Jake said. "Traveling to a game by bus."

"Not even close," Robbie said. "At least I never rode a bus this nice in juniors or college."

"It's strange having another team so close."

"I'm happy I can wake up in my own bed tomorrow." *Happy* wasn't the right word. A bed without Hyacinth wasn't a happy bed, but he might as well get used to it. It had been a week now since he'd even seen her, longer since she'd been in his bed. At least four years.

"Too bad you can't watch your star performance on that wedding dress show tonight. Did you DVR it?"

"I might stream it later." Ah, hell. Who was he kidding with the emotional drama? There was no *might* about it. He'd probably watch it twenty times in a row.

"Evie set up to record it. She doesn't trust streaming, says you never know when someone will take offense at something and they'll take it down. Isn't that ridiculous?" He smiled as if he found that the most endearing thing since baby lambs.

"That so? She's not watching it when it comes on?" He would have thought Evans would watch with Hyacinth and Ava Grace.

"No. She's coming to the game tonight."

"In Nashville?"

"Yes, dunce. In Nashville. She's coming to see me play."

Must be nice. "Alone?" Maybe Hyacinth was coming with her. Sure, he'd told her not to, but Hyacinth did as she pleased, though it probably wouldn't please her to come to his hockey game instead of watching *All Dressed in White* the second it aired.

"Yes, Robbie. Alone. In her car. Probably listening to a podcast. Or singing. She can't sing a note, you know."

"You should have gotten Glaz to let her come on the bus with us."

"Seriously? Do you really think there's a chance that would ever happen?"

"I guess not," Robbie admitted.

"Anyway, did it occur to you that she might not want to ride on a bus with a bunch of hockey players?"

"I don't know why not. We're a fun lot. Me, especially." He took his water bottle out of his backpack and took a drink.

"Evie isn't always enchanted by our kind of fun. Junior high antics, she calls it."

Hyacinth had once said something similar. "You should tell Glaz you're riding home with Evie and that's that. If we win, he'll probably let you. You don't want her out alone that late." That's what he would have done if it were Hyacinth.

"Not a bad idea. I like her company better than yours.

I'll think on it. Give me some of that." He reached for Robbie's water.

"Get your own." But he handed the bottle over. "Don't spit in it."

"If you have to have a woman who'll let you tell her she can't drive herself where she wants to go, you are going to lead a sad, lonely life."

Yeah, well. What else was new? "If you found one who'll put up with you in all matters, I don't think I'll have any trouble."

Though, come to think of it, for all that he annoyed her on every other level, Hyacinth had never seemed to mind when he followed her home. Considering she was out and about on her own all the time, it made no sense that he felt compelled to see her home when they were in the same place at the same time.

He could see it now. In fifteen years, he'd see her at the market with her three identically dressed, perfectly groomed kiddies—each equipped with a notepad, pen, and megaphone for shouting orders. After Hyacinth bagged her groceries in alphabetical order, he'd follow her home. The husband would catch sight of him and chase him, screaming, "Stalker!" The police would be called. It would be on *The Face Off Grapevine*. Glaz would throw him off the team.

Asinine thinking. He wouldn't be living in Laurel Springs in fifteen years. Hockey was a young man's sport and he wouldn't be sticking around after he retired. Almost nobody had a career that long anymore. Now, in the old days… He halted his thinking. If he'd been speaking and Hyacinth were here, she'd be shouting about bunny trails and reeling him back in to the subject at hand. He needed to stop following her, but he didn't know how.

He tuned back in to what Jake was saying.

"It'll be good to see some of the Sound guys—Bryant, Jarrett, Emile, Thor."

"Aye. And good to see them beaten into oblivion."

"Maybe Emile will be off his game," Jake said. "I hear Amy's pregnant."

"Probably just pump him up."

Robbie's stomach turned queasy. A baby. He loved babies—children and teens, too. He'd always assumed he'd have them, but had never imagined who their mother would be until now—and he needed to stop imagining that because it was off the table. Or, more true, had never been on the table. Just as well.

A whole forest would have to be sacrificed for the amount of paper it would take for Hyacinth to make baby lists. Ridiculous, she was about that.

But it was as endearing as baby lambs.

Driving up to Ava Grace's palatial home always made Hyacinth want to run. But then she would remember Ava Grace was inside, and not someone who would treat her like she was out of their league.

Out of habit, she reached for the bag that contained her hand sewing. But there was no bag. The dress was done and gone. She'd cut it close, only finished the hem minutes before Jules, Shelia, and Leslie arrived for the final fitting. Hyacinth had had to stall while Brad and Patty steamed it.

Yet, she had been calm. Or maybe she'd been too exhausted to get "wound up," as Robbie would have said. *Robbie.* Alex and the women had been disappointed that he wasn't there for the reveal shoot, but Hyacinth hadn't cared. It wasn't as if Trousseau was going to be a repeat venue for the show anyway. She had reminded them that he was, after all, a professional hockey player and she had already asked him to miss one practice for the show and hadn't been inclined to do it a second time.

Consequently, what would be the last few minutes of the show had been anticlimactic.

The dress had been a perfect fit. A stunning Jules had cried and declared Hyacinth a miracle worker. Shelia and Leslie had cooed and tricked Jules out in the pearls and tiara she'd brought. Finally, Jules had sparkled for the camera, spread her arms wide as if she were embracing all of mankind, and performed the classic closing line like the Oscar winner she was, "And here I am. All dressed in white!"

Alex had yelled, "Cut," and hadn't even asked for a second take. After getting Jules in the dress, the whole thing had taken no more than twenty minutes.

Had Robbie come, they might still be there. He would have probably brought an ice cream truck, a pipe band, and an elephant.

Come to think of it, riding an elephant while eating ice cream might have been fun. She could tolerate a pipe band if she had to. Crazy thinking.

"Looks like it's just the two of us," Ava Grace said when she opened the door for Hyacinth.

At that, relief washed over Hyacinth. She had never wanted this watching party that Ava Grace had insisted on putting together. Humiliation was always best done alone, but Ava Grace could dig her heels in when she was of a mind to. Hyacinth had, however, been adamant that the guest list be severely limited.

In the end, it had worked out. Claire and Evans were in Nashville with the team, Patty had a family birthday, and Brad had gone to Atlanta to meet a friend at the last minute. But she had thought Skip was supposed to be in town.

Hyacinth asked, "Why no Skip?" She liked him fine, but didn't know him well enough to relish sitting through this particular episode of *All Dressed in White* with him.

Ava Grace frowned. "He had to stay in Atlanta through the weekend." She brightened. "But he's coming in Wednesday in time for the gala."

"And your hand will be a little heavier this time next week," Hyacinth teased her.

"I do think you're right. This *is* the year. Adele wasn't supposed to tell me, but he called and asked her to get their grandmother's jewelry from the safety deposit box."

"I'm so happy for you, Ava Grace."

"Let's not talk about me. This is your night, and here I am making you stand at the front door. I've set us up in the library. It's cozier in there."

Hyacinth followed her down the hall, thankful that they weren't going to the cavernous media room with the screen the size of a movie theater.

"Don't expect too much," Hyacinth said. "It didn't go that well."

"I'm expecting everything," Ava Grace said as they settled in on the deep, butter soft sofa. "It's going to be wonderful—you're going to be wonderful!"

"Don't count on it."

There was a bottle of wine, some crackers, a brick of cream cheese with pepper jelly, and some cheese straws on a tray on the coffee table. Ava Grace removed the lid from a crystal dish of nuts and poured them each a glass of wine.

"Dorothea made a light supper for us to have after, but help yourself to a little nibble."

As if she could eat. "Thanks." She sipped the wine and waited for the death knell as Ava Grace turned on the television.

The show opened as it always did, with a shot of the outside of the featured bridal shop and a voice-over from someone the audience had never seen. It was bizarre after all her wishing and hoping—and pleading and harassing—to see Trousseau in that shot.

"Today we're at Trousseau, a charming shop in a suburb of Birmingham, Alabama," the familiar voice said. "Let's see if owner Hyacinth Dawson can send our bride away today happy and all dressed in white, or if she'll have to leave disappointed and still have nothing to wear for the most important day of her life."

Most important day of her life? Really? What about birth? And the day it all clicks and she realizes she can read? Graduations? Giving birth? And come to think of it, what could be more important than the day she uses the bathroom on her own for the first time? That might be the top thing, right there. She wouldn't say any of that to Ava Grace since that other important day was on the horizon for her.

"Does that ever happen on this show?" Ava Grace asked. "Do they ever leave without a dress?"

"Occasionally. It's always awful—drama, crying, and handwringing. And that's just from the shop owner."

"Were you afraid that would happen?"

"No," Hyacinth admitted. "But I should have been. It almost did."

The show opened with Hyacinth opening the door for Reynolds, Jules, Shelia, and Leslie with the disembodied voice identifying everyone.

"You look great, Hyacinth," Ava Grace said. "Is that a new dress?"

"Yes. The latest in a long line of shrouds."

"What?"

"Never mind." Maybe she'd rethink her work clothes. Sure, she needed to be subdued, but did she have to go to the extreme? Wearing some neutrals, with a few plain pastels thrown in here and there, would be a welcome relief.

Ah, the arrival of Robbie—and the noise in the room went up.

"Has Robbie got a *cake?*" Ava Grace gasped.

"Yes. And he made it. I guess we haven't talked much." That had been intentional on Hyacinth's part, even after Jules's dress was finished. She didn't want to talk about what had happened with Robbie until she had to.

On the screen, the love fest ensued, accompanied by tight shots of the cake and all the exclamations over Robbie's off the ice talent.

"Wow. I would not have seen that coming. He really made it himself?" Ava Grace said.

"Believe me, I didn't see it coming either, but apparently he did; he borrowed the equipment from Kristin."

"How sweet." She grinned. "Amazing what he's willing to do for you."

For you. Funny that Ava Grace saw it that way. That was exactly what Robbie had insisted.

Next, there was a short segment of Reynolds and Jules sitting on stools holding hands and talking about how they met and Reynolds's proposal—all with the magical Christmas decorations twinkling in the background. Nice, but standard stuff.

"Our decorations look great," Ava Grace said.

"They're perfect," Hyacinth agreed. "Thanks to you. It was your vision."

"Don't sell Robbie short," Ava Grace said. "He had some great ideas."

Too late, too late, too late, her inward voice whispered. Now, Reynolds was kissing Jules goodbye and it was time to get down to dress business—and the humiliation that was coming as sure as the sun was going to rise tomorrow.

It started out well enough. Hyacinth's speech about showing Jules different dresses to get an idea of what she wanted was good. Professional and poised, even. The irony was, she hadn't pulled different styles—only a different take on that same sheath over and over again.

But the worst was about to set in—Jules's rejection of the dress and Hyacinth's utter panic. But wait. What was this?

The camera homed in on Jules's rejection, her interaction with Shelia and Leslie, and only switched back to Hyacinth and Robbie when they were presenting the slightly more elaborate, but still plain, sheath that was meant to buy time. It showed none of Hyacinth's discomfort or long, silent pauses. Then Robbie clowned with the dress, pretending to be a game show hostess but, again, Hyacinth's pained reaction wasn't revealed.

Maybe humiliation wasn't coming. Somewhere, she'd gotten the idea this show was going to be about her, picking apart all her flaws and incompetence. The audience didn't care about her! And that was great news. They cared about the bride, especially since it was Jules Perry. And they cared about Robbie to a lesser degree, because he was unpredictable and funny. The *All Dressed in White* folks knew that and that's what they were showing.

The scene with the tossing of the dresses was blessedly short. The show got the comic relief they wanted, a slice of Robbie's charm, and none of Hyacinth's reaction. They showed the moment where Hyacinth zeroed in on the style Jules liked and went from there to Jules trying on A-line dresses, without showing any of the downtime while Hyacinth gathered the selections. Alex had told her they would edit out the downtimes, but she had lost sight of that.

"You're coming across just right," Ava Grace said. "Knowledgeable. Professional."

It was true. One might even say dignified and classy. But she wasn't out of the woods, not by a long shot. The worst moment of the day was coming and there was still plenty of time for her to look like a fool.

And here they were. Jules in a panic over wanting one skirt and another bodice, Leslie telling Jules to suck it up, Shelia suggesting that maybe they needed to go another way. That came across much more drama-filled than it had been.

None of this was about Hyacinth—until it was. Robbie's fateful speech. *"Hyacinth is a right fine designer herself and you'll find nobody better with a needle. Maybe she can make something like the south side of this frock and attach it to the top of that one?*

Plus, she can sew little rosies on the skirt. Can you do that, lass?"

The camera only showed a slight hesitation on her part. None of her inner turmoil and panic came out in her expression. There was just her agreement to the plan and the joy that followed from Jules and her posse.

Except for one thing. For the barest moment, right after Hyacinth agreed and Jules cried with joy, the camera focused in tight on Robbie's face. He was looking at her all soft and proud, with the most radiant smile Hyacinth had ever seen.

Hyacinth caught her breath. In that split second, his expression told a story for the ages, with nothing left out.

Also in that moment, Hyacinth knew for certain what was the most important day in a woman's life, and it wasn't any of those other things she'd thought of. It was the day the person she was going to love forever looked at her like she was everything in the world.

Ava Grace hit pause and met Hyacinth's eyes. There was no teasing or humor there this time. It was a heavy moment.

It was hard, but Hyacinth found her voice. "Let's finish." The rest was a blur, and fairly unremarkable. The cake and champagne, the happy couple, Jules's toast. Then on to the reveal scene, with Jules so radiant and happy, full of praise for Hyacinth.

Finally, with Jules's pronouncement that she was "all dressed in white," it was over. Trousseau and Hyacinth could not have come across in a better light.

She should have been pleased, elated even. Maybe she was, or would have been if she hadn't been in emotional overload.

"Do you want me to back it up to that part again?" Ava Grace asked quietly.

There was no question in either of their minds which part Ava Grace meant.

"Please."

Ava Grace showed it twice and might have for a third time, had Hyacinth not put up a hand to stop her.

"Oh, Ava Grace," she said. "What have I done?"

"I don't know, Hyacinth. What *have* you done?" Ava Grace moved to sit close to her.

"I thought I was having a fling, but I wasn't."

Ava Grace smoothed her hair and slipped an arm around her. "I wouldn't have imagined that you were."

"I was in love!"

"Tell me," Ava Grace said.

And Hyacinth told her everything while all the angels in heaven wept the tears she was too empty to shed.

Chapter Twenty-Eight

After Monday practice and loading up on carbs at the Brick Oven with some of the guys, Robbie wearily let himself down on the couch with an armload of mail—two weeks' worth. When the pile got so high it fell over, taking a game controller, a coffee mug, and bottle of Scotch with it, it was time to sort it.

Hyacinth was right. It would do him well to have a few systems in place.

Hockey equipment catalogs, mattress sales flyers, and people who wanted to give him a credit card. Nothing interesting. There were some bills, but they were only duplicates of what he could access online. He communicated with his family by email, phone, and texts, so there would be no letters. Come time for his birthday, there would be cards, but that was three months away.

Ah, a Christmas card. That was nice. He ripped it open. It was from his insurance agent. Maybe he'd just chuck it all. Bored and tired of the chore, he shoved the pile to the floor and lay down on the couch.

The last time he'd lain on this couch, Hyacinth had just doctored his hurt face and then lain over him and they'd made magic. At least it had felt like magic to him. The memory of that projected him into the land of the horny and the abandoned. Maybe he should have taken her up on her offer and slid back into the fling. At least it would have taken care of the horny and delayed the abandoned.

He was cold now. There was a blanket on the end of the couch, but he couldn't reach it. He ought to hire somebody to sort mail and cover him up.

His phone rang and he groaned. Maybe he could reach it there on the coffee table if he stretched a little more...ah, hell no. He was going to have to sit up.

It was his agent.

"Hi, there, Miles. What you got?" Because Miles always had something. He was a busy, busy man—way too busy for casual hellos and bunny trails.

"Too bad about the loss to the Sound on Saturday, but congrats on the win Sunday. It was a close one." Yet, he always made a wee bit of small talk.

"I'd say. Three to two win in OT?"

"It's looking good for you guys this year, especially for a debut year."

Robbie agreed, but he didn't speak of such things out loud. Glaz, the most superstitious man who had ever walked the earth, didn't allow it. Glaz wasn't here, of course, but he always seemed to know everything. Robbie wasn't taking any chances.

"Easy, Miles. It's only December. Miles to go before we sleep." Then he laughed out loud at his accidental pun. "I didn't know I was going to say that.' "

Miles laughed, too. "I've had a call..."

"You usually have."

"From the *All Dressed in White* people."

That. He'd watched the episode, not twenty times, but more than five, less than ten. Hyacinth ought to be pleased, but what did he know? He'd thought he'd begun to understand her feelings, but he'd been wrong.

"What about them?"

"They have an offer for you."

"What could they want with me?"

"The ratings were off the charts for your episode and, according to the social media feedback, it wasn't only due to Jules Perry and Reynolds Fallon. People loved the shop, the shop owner—"

"Hyacinth," Robbie said. "That's her name."

"All right. Hyacinth. They loved her. And you. The network wants to contract with you and her for two shows next year, with an option to renew."

They were offering what Hyacinth wanted so badly— for Trousseau to be a repeat venue for the show. It was tempting to accept. Not only would it get her what she wanted, it would give him time with her. But time with her was the reason he had to say no. He had to give up on her, and the more time they spent together, the more impossible that would become.

"No, Miles. Thanks for the information, but I've peddled my last wedding dress."

"Are you sure? You wouldn't be doing it for free this time. Don't you want to know what they're offering?"

"No. I know what the Yellowhammers pay. I know what Ice Time and Glendale Scotch Whisky pay for me to say their products are the best in all the land. Thanks to you, all that will suffice for me." And then some. But what would suffice for Hyacinth?

"Okay. I'll let them know."

He almost told him to stall a bit to give him time to tell Hyacinth he wasn't going to sign that contract. No doubt, she had gotten the call by now and would be hoping he would agree. He hated the thought of her disappointment served up by phone from someone who didn't care about her. Damn, he hated that she would have to be disappointed at all.

Maybe there was a way around it.

"Why do they have to have me, anyway?" Robbie asked. "Can't they let Hyacinth do it on her own?"

"Not happening," Miles said. "They like her; the viewers like her. She's knowledgeable and was sincerely warm and sympathetic when Jules got upset, but she's the straight man. She needs someone who'll pack in some energy and fun."

He was afraid of that. There was no way to save it for her. Unless... A germ of an idea took hold.

"Miles, wait."

"Second thoughts?"

"No. Not for me. But if I were you, I'd try to sell them on that new boy of yours."

Miles paused before speaking. "Clancy or Cartwright?"

"Clancy. From the Sound. The one they call Rapunzel. I met him when we played them over the weekend."

"I don't know, Robbie. They were set on you. It's not like Clancy goes around in a kilt and has a Scottish accent. They want some quirky."

"Come on, man. This isn't like you. Get out of the box. Clancy *is* quirky. He's got all that blond hair, practically to his ass, that he wears in a braid. He had red streaks in it on Saturday and green on Sunday. Plus he's good looking and has a big personality. I liked him."

Miles laughed. "You like everybody."

"Aye. I'll give you that. But Luka Zadorov liked him."

"That *is* a recommendation."

"Plus, he's a fan favorite. The team likes him. He's in Nashville, an easy drive to Trousseau."

Miles hesitated. "The idea has possibilities. Robbie, are you sure you don't want to do this yourself?"

No. I'm sure I do, but I can't. "I'm sure."

"I'll give it a go."

"Give it your best go."

"Why do you care?"

"I have my reasons." The doorbell rang. "Got to go, Miles. My public beckons."

Since you had to have the codes to get in the building and use the elevator, "his public" would be one of his teammates who lived here, probably come to razz him some more about *All Dressed in White* and being a cake decorator.

But he opened the door to find Hyacinth there. Evans would have given her the codes or let her in. Not wearing black today. She had dressed up in a checked skirt that showed some leg and a soft looking green sweater to ask him to do the show.

It was going to be hard to look into those whisky eyes and tell her no, but he had to.

"Ah, lass. Come in."

It had taken Hyacinth two days to gather the courage to come here.

She'd vacillated between accepting what she'd done and living with it, and desperately wanting to correct it. She supposed that on some level she'd made her decision when she confessed all to Ava Grace. Ava Grace wasn't the kind to let up until Hyacinth ripped her heart out and laid it at Robbie's feet.

And here she was to do just that. His eyes were soft

and he'd called her *lass* in that husky whisper that made her want to throw her arms around him and cling there forever.

To be honest, everything made her want to do that, but she mustn't. Not yet. Her last directive had been to never touch him again, but she was here to change that. The way he was looking at her was encouraging.

"Come in. You look lovely."

What a mess his condo was, what a lovely mess. She had to smile. He had a cleaning service, so it wasn't dirty, just tumbled like he was. There was mail on the floor under the coffee table and two half-full Gatorades and an empty beer bottle on the baby grand piano. No coasters. There was a time when she would have wanted to set the scattered, dog-eared sheet music into a neat stack. Maybe a small part of her still did, but all that didn't seem to matter much—at least not right now. She knew herself too well to think she could live with a mess. She was too far into leopard-hood to change those spots, but maybe she could earn the right to set things straight.

"Can I get you anything?" he asked.

If this had been a rom-com movie, she would have said, "Just you," and they would have fallen into each other's arms. But it wasn't going to be that easy.

"No thanks. I suppose you're wondering why I'm here."

He smiled. "Not so much." Maybe this was a rom-com. Maybe they were on the same page. "Let's sit down."

He sat on the sofa and it was tempting to sit beside him, to be close, but she took the one chair in the room. Better to sit across from him so she could look him squarely in the eye when she said what she needed to say.

She took a deep breath. "This isn't going to be easy."

He nodded with understanding. Sweet. He was the sweetest man alive. How could she not have seen that? Why had it mattered so much that he always seemed to have ketchup on his shirt?

"I'm not one to bare my soul, but there are some things I need to say to you. You were right. I make everyone around me pay for how my parents were—no one more than you. I haven't always been kind to you and you're the kindest man I know."

He laughed a little. "I can be a cross to bear. I've not always made your life easy."

"But you've made it interesting." She took a deep breath. "And I'd like you to keep on making it interesting."

He frowned and shook his head. "Lass, I don't think—"

She put up a hand. "Hear me out, Robbie. That's all I ask."

He nodded. "All right. That's fair."

"I know I said we were too different. I know I said I couldn't live with someone so haphazard. But I misspoke. I didn't understand myself. It's irresponsibility I can't live with. *Haphazard* doesn't equal *irresponsible.* My parents were irresponsible, but you're not. Your socks might not always match and you might get distracted, but you do what you need to. You have accomplished what a million little boys with a hockey stick hope to, but hardly any do. You pay your bills. You get to practice on time. You work out every day. But most of all, you're *there*—there for your team, your friends, and you've been there for me. Even if I haven't appreciated you."

"But, still—"

"Please. Let me finish. This is hard and I have to say what I came here to say."

"All right." His face was a study of sweet concern and sorrow. Maybe she could make that sorrow go away.

"I don't want a fling. I want what you want. I want a real relationship. I can't promise I won't try to get you in matching socks. I might drive you crazy with my list making. I can't change my whole being, but I won't expect you to change yours either. I can celebrate what makes you who you are. I hope you can do the same." She took a deep, deep breath. This was going to be the hardest part. "The fact is, I love you."

He set his elbows on his knees and dropped his face into his hands, but not before she caught a glimpse of the warmth draining from his face and the stony mask that took its place.

Something had taken a wrong turn. She felt it in her racing heart and knotted gut. "Robbie?"

He slowly raised his head and froze her with his icy stare. "Just when I think I'm wrong," he said almost to himself.

"I don't understand."

"If you had come here and said all this to me an hour ago, I'd have you in my arms dancing a jig. I guess I should be grateful you came when you did so I can know the truth."

So many emotions crashed and burned against each other—the certainty that she had been offering him what he wanted, the image of him dancing her across the room, the cold words he spoke.

"I don't understand," she stammered. "What could happen in an hour?"

"Don't pretend you don't know, Hyacinth."

"I *don't* know."

He sat back, put one ankle on his knee, and crossed his arms across his chest. His shoe must have hit his knee in just the right place because it started to blink. He gave the shoe a sour look and let out a mean laugh.

That laugh broke her heart. His laugh was always so joyful.

"You must think I'm the biggest fool to ever walk the streets. I *know*, Hyacinth. Miles called me."

"Your agent? But why? What's it to do with me—us? Are you getting traded?"

"There is no us. Okay. We'll play it your way. Miles called to tell me *All Dressed in White* wants to contract us for two shows next year."

"They want to do *what*?" Impossible.

"You heard me and don't pretend like you didn't already know it. That's what you're here for."

"No. That's not true. I don't know anything about this. I came here because I realized how I feel about you."

"At first, I thought you'd come to ask me to do the show—honest and forthright. And it was tearing me up that I was going to have to tell you no, when I know you want it so much."

"No. I came here for *you*."

"Don't lie to me, Hyacinth. Do you know why I was going to tell you no? Because, for whatever reason, I wanted you so much that it was killing me to be around you when all you wanted was a fling."

"Robbie, I swear to you—"

"But instead, you come here pretending like you want me." His eyes were huge and full of rage and pain. "How much can one man be expected to take, Hyacinth? Tell me that."

Calm. She had to be calm and reason with him.

"Robbie, listen to me," she said quietly. "I have not heard from *All Dressed in White*. Not a word. I don't know anything about this offer. Everything I said to you is true. When I watched the episode, I saw something—something in the way you looked at me. That changed everything and made me face how I was feeling, too. All I want is a chance with you."

He sat back and rubbed his eyes, all the energy gone out of him.

"Wouldn't it be something if that were true?"

"Have I ever lied to you?" she asked. "Have I ever given you any reason to think I would?"

He shook his head. "I don't know. I don't have any reason to think you wouldn't, seeing how important your *short-term* and your *long-term goals* are to you."

He spat the words out. That hurt.

She felt at least as flat as he looked. She knew when she'd been beat. She always had.

"If you're not going to believe me, there's nothing left for me to say. I guess I'll go."

"Aye," he said. "You should do that."

She walked slowly to the door, hoping he would stop her, but he didn't. With her hand on the knob, she turned and spoke again. "I have an answer to the question you asked that night we danced at the fish restaurant."

He didn't answer, but he looked curious.

"It's true," she said. "What Bonnie Raitt sang about. Love has no pride."

As soon as she quietly closed the door behind her,

she heard a crash. He'd broken something, only this time it hadn't been an accident.

Hyacinth had just climbed in the car and was reaching for her keys when the phone rang.

She was in no mood, but she looked at the screen, just in case.

No. Not Robbie, but might as well answer.

"Hello, Alex."

"Great news, Hyacinth! We're offering you and Robbie a contract for a two-episode deal, with an option to renew. Deb has already called Robbie's agent, but I wanted to tell you myself."

"Yeah," she said. "I wish you'd called an hour ago."

Chapter Twenty-Nine

Robbie sat in a back booth of Laurel Springs Apothecary with a cup of coffee and three slices of pie—lemon icebox, chocolate, and pecan—lined up in front of him like soldiers.

He'd discovered the apothecary had a soda fountain and grill when he'd come in for condoms during the happy days of Hyacinth. You'd never see such in chemist shops back home. He'd been fascinated and asked a thousand questions.

But it wasn't fascination or, God knows, the need for condoms that brought him back today. It was the need to escape from the setting of Hyacinth's final betrayal to somewhere he was unlikely to know anyone. Oh, the place was popping, but it was the high school set who'd taken it over, and they weren't interested in the likes of him. It would take a Laurel Springs High letter jacket to get a second look here, so he might as well be alone—which was the order of the day. That and the pie.

He methodically continued to eat his way through the pie, taking a bite of each, one after the other—lemon, chocolate, and pecan in that order. Hyacinth would be proud of him for not chaotically mixing it up, taking two bites of pecan and skipping the lemon to go to the chocolate. If he followed the plan and took precise bites, he would finish all the slices in the same round.

"What have we here? Do I need to call your best bud and tell him you're cheating on his wife's pie shop?"

Ah, hell. Brad. Nothing personal. Anyone would have gotten an ah, hell.

"What brings you here?" Robbie asked.

"Picking up my mother's prescription." Without being invited, he sat down across from Robbie and pointed to the pie. "They buy that stuff off a truck, you know. But they have great milkshakes and patty melts."

"No such thing as bad pie." It was chocolate's turn. "Just better and best pie."

"No cherry?"

"This was all they had." He ate a bite of pecan.

"Hyacinth wouldn't eat at all today, and here you are binging yourself into a sugar coma. I have to wonder if there's a connection."

"There is no connection of any kind between Hyacinth and me."

"Funny that, I could have sworn there was something going on there."

"Yeah. Me, too. But I was wrong."

"You sure?"

He paused his fork over the lemon. "I am that. She lied to me."

Brad's face went sour, but he never missed a beat. "She didn't lie to you."

"You know all about it? She told you, did she?"

"I don't know all about it, whatever it is. But I know some things about Hyacinth. She didn't lie to you, because she doesn't lie."

"She said she could make the frock for Jules on time when she didn't think she could," Robbie pointed out.

Brad shook his head. "That's different. The answer was unknown. Besides, she got it done. I'm talking about lying about something that matters to someone who matters to her. She doesn't even know how."

"If that was ever true, but she's gotten past it. No surprise. She's a quick study. Besides, I'm not someone who matters to her."

"Could have fooled me."

"Maybe you're easily fooled."

"Look, Robbie." Brad spread his hands out in front of him on the table. "You've been a good friend to me. I'm only going to say this one time. I don't know what happened to send you both into a funk, but whatever it is, it's not worth it."

"You might disagree if you knew the particulars."

Yet, some twisted, misplaced brand of loyalty stopped him from enumerating them.

Brad shook his head. "I don't need to know. She's not a liar. Not to say she's a saint. She's got her faults—and plenty of them. About half of what comes out of her mouth shouldn't."

That wasn't *quite* true. Half was going a little heavy. It was more like a quarter. Or maybe an eighth.

"She's the most inflexible creature in five universes," Brad went on.

He could see where Brad might think that, but she could soften up. Sometimes. Under the right circumstances. Under him, with her arms tight around him and her face buried in his neck.

Fuck. He had to stop.

Brad went on, "You'd better get out of her way when

things aren't going like she wants, unless you're some kind of masochist who wants the rough side of her tongue. Man, she can hurl some balls of barbed wire that will scar you into the next life."

That was a little on the dramatic side. And unfair, mean, even. Brad ought to know it mostly happened when she was stressed and tired.

"One might say"—Brad leaned in so he could whisper—"that she can be a real *bitch*."

Robbie's mouth went dry. He slammed his fist on the table and pointed a finger in Brad's face. "That's enough!"

"Yeah." Brad got up. He had an evil, but almost amused glint in his eyes. "I thought it might be. I'm just going to leave it right there." He patted the table and left.

Robbie defiantly pushed the lemon and chocolate slices away and set about finishing off the pecan.

He didn't need Hyacinth to be proud of him.

"I want to take in these straps a tiny bit more. Turn your back to me." Hyacinth put the pins in place. Her life might be a mess, but she could make damn sure Ava Grace's dress for the Christmas Gala was perfect. "How's that? I don't want them to be too tight, but you don't want them falling off your shoulders either."

Ava Grace flexed her shoulders. "Perfect." The pale silvery blue dress fell right above Ava Grace's knees and was scattered with just enough crystals to give it a soft glow. "You're sure it's not too much? That it's not too tight?" This was not the first time Ava Grace had asked these questions.

Nor the first time Hyacinth had reassured her.

"Never too much or too tight with a figure like yours. You're beautiful."

Ava Grace nodded, but she didn't look convinced.

"Thank you for doing this after hours. It's probably silly of me to not want anyone to see my dress before the party."

"I don't mind at all." Besides, where else did she have to be? "And it's not silly. It's a big night for you."

Ava Grace frowned. "Maybe. But Skip's been home for two days and he hasn't said anything about getting engaged."

"You know better than I do that the Landry men always propose in public at that gala. This is your year." Though it did seem odd to Hyacinth that two people who'd been together as long as Skip and Ava Grace seemed to communicate so poorly. But who was she to judge, considering the mess she'd made?

"I keep telling myself that. He's finally transferring to the Birmingham office and moving home, so it makes sense. I guess I'm anxious because I'm tired of waiting."

"Don't forget he had Adele get the jewelry from the bank."

Ava Grace brightened. "That's true. I'm just a nervous Nellie."

"Any idea what your ring will look like?"

Ava Grace smiled wide and followed it with a laugh. "I don't. Not for sure. I hope it's the sapphire and diamond one that his grandmother always wore on her right hand. I've loved it from the time I was a little girl. But she had some other lovely things. I'll be happy with whatever he decides."

Hyacinth removed her wrist pin cushion. "You'll

probably get it eventually anyway. I would think if Adele wanted it, she'd already have it."

"Maybe. She got the engagement ring. But it doesn't matter. I love Adele. She should have it if she wants it."

Hyacinth had never thought about what she would want for an engagement ring. Odd, since she had admired so many on so many hands. Did Scots give engagement rings? She cringed inwardly at the thought. Why would she even wonder that? Everyone gave engagement rings. Anyway, it didn't matter.

When she looked up, Ava Grace was staring at her.

"I'm sorry, Hyacinth. Here I am going on and on about a stupid ring after what you've just been through."

She'd had little choice but to tell Ava Grace what happened.

"It's not a stupid ring, Ava Grace. It's going to be your engagement ring, and I want to celebrate every second of it with you." In an attempt to veer her away from what had gone on with Robbie, Hyacinth gave Ava Grace a little wink and said, "Even if I can't dress you for your wedding."

Ava Grace rolled her eyes. "Believe me, World War III would break out if I refused to wear my great-grandmother's dress. It's important for the portrait wall, you know—same dress, same pose, same smile."

"Is that what you want?" Hyacinth asked. "To wear that dress?"

"I want it more than I want to hear for the rest of my years how I ruined everyone's life by breaking tradition."

"I guess there's something to be said for not having a bunch of family heirlooms. You can get married in what you like."

Ava Grace frowned. Damn. She shouldn't have said that. No matter how weak, the reference to herself and a wedding dress took Ava Grace right back. "Have you told Evans what happened with you and Robbie?"

"No. And I'm not going to. And don't you tell her either, or anybody else. He's Jake's best friend. And Evans loves him, too. When it comes up, I'll say I got too busy. I won't cause trouble for him."

"But, Hyacinth! He deserves for them to know; he doesn't deserve your protection. He accused you of lying to him! And after you opened your heart to him. How dare he? I'd have him uninvited to the gala if the Yellowhammers weren't required to attend."

"And your reaction is exactly why I'm not telling Evans or anybody else. Let's not forget that I made some missteps along the way. It wasn't only a matter of bad timing. I earned some of what happened."

"Maybe. But who hasn't? He had no right to treat you like that."

Suddenly, Hyacinth was exhausted. This was not the first time she and Ava Grace had had this conversation and she couldn't talk about it another second.

"It's water under the bridge, Ava Grace. Let's get you out of that dress and think about how gorgeous you're going to look in the pictures when you get your ring."

After Ava Grace left, Hyacinth had just sat down to alter the dress straps when the Trousseau landline rang. She considered letting it go to voice mail, but if it was something that needed dealing with, she might as well do it tonight. There would be procrastinators who would rush in tomorrow, frantic for a gala dress. It happened every year.

She picked up the phone. "Trousseau. Hyacinth Dawson speaking."

"This is Pitch."

The woman sounded like she expected Hyacinth to know who she was. Had she talked to a bride who might have that nickname? Or maybe it was a last name. She searched her memory, but came up with nothing.

"I'm sorry. Pitch who?"

"Just Pitch." The woman hesitated, allowing time for the lightning bolt of knowledge to strike Hyacinth. When Hyacinth said nothing, the woman carried on, "I style for Aubrey Jamison."

That was a name Hyacinth did know—everybody did. She turned out hit country songs like a mama rabbit turned out babies.

"I see," Hyacinth said, though she didn't.

"As you've no doubt heard, she's engaged."

She hadn't heard, but this was getting interesting.

"Yes?"

"She was at Jules Perry's wedding Saturday. Aubrey fell in love with Jules's dress and she'd like you to design and make hers."

Hyacinth's heart beat a little faster—an opportunity to design. This was the first good news she'd had in what seemed like forever. If it was good news.

"When is the wedding?" That mattered. Never again would she commit to something with an unreasonable deadline. It wasn't worth it.

"October."

Ten months. Almost a year. Entirely doable, even if she needed specially made materials.

"I can commit to that," Hyacinth said evenly. She had been dying to use handmade lace made by artisan

Hélène-Louise Soileau, but it would be expensive and it would take time. This might be the perfect opportunity—if the bride wanted lace. "I'll need to meet with Ms. Jamison sooner rather than later."

"Aubrey doesn't take these kinds of meetings," Pitch said. "I would act on her behalf."

Hell, no. She'd gone down that road with Jules because *All Dressed in White* had insisted, but never again. Yet, this was quite the coup. She didn't want to mess it up.

"I'll make it easy for her," Hyacinth said. "I'm happy to come to Nashville or meet her wherever she likes."

"You don't understand. It's not the convenience. She doesn't need to meet with you. I'll know what she wants."

Hyacinth hesitated. She could do the easy thing and roll over. This had been a tough week and she deserved this break. It wouldn't be her fault if Aubrey Jamison ended up with a dress she didn't like.

But the words of a Scot in a ragged kilt came barreling back at her. *The dress was all wrong for the girl. In the wedding business, your reputation is everything.*

He'd been right. He'd been right about so much.

"All due respect, Pitch, but I find that, even if they think they do, most brides don't really know what they want."

"Are you questioning my professionalism?" Pitch asked.

"Are you questioning mine?" Hyacinth was proud of herself for not expounding on bended knee how thankful she was for the opportunity.

"I deal with the people who supply her wardrobe. I have for years."

"A wedding dress isn't just another piece of a wardrobe. It's the manifestation of a dream."

Where had that come from? She didn't use flowery phrases. But she knew. It was time spent with a man who lived on dreamy talk. Time would pass and would sweep away the memories of that, like it would make her forget how he smelled, tasted, and felt wrapped around her.

"This is my final word on the matter," Pitch said. "You will meet with me. I will be the go-between. You won't deal directly with Aubrey until it's time for a dress fitting."

Hyacinth never hesitated. "Then I won't deal with her—or you—at all. Best of luck with finding her dream dress." Too bad she hadn't been able to save this, but on the other hand, she found that she just really didn't give a shit.

Hyacinth had her finger on the button to end the call when Pitch spoke again.

"Wait." Big sigh. "Hold on. Let me look at the calendar. You'll come to Nashville, you say?"

"I'll be happy to." After setting up the meeting, Hyacinth hung up and waited for the happiness to set in. It didn't, but she supposed she was as pleased about this lucky break as she could be about anything.

She might have pondered that until the next morning if her cell phone hadn't rung. What now? It couldn't be Pitch. She didn't have this number.

Alex. Again, what now? There couldn't be anything else left to say.

"What is it, Alex?"

"I've got great news for you. Do you know Bret Clancy? From the Nashville Sound?"

Chapter Thirty

Valet parking was available at the Christmas Gala, but Robbie opted out for two reasons. One, he had no intention of turning his Corvette over to a high school kid who believed faster was better; and two, he didn't want to take a chance on getting blocked in, because he was getting out of here as soon as humanly possible—if he was lucky, before he had to see Hyacinth. Seeing her all dressed up in party clothes was more than he could stand right now. Considering their last meeting, he could only imagine the awkwardness. Besides, it was only fair that the make himself scarce. This was her turf. He was only here because he had to be.

He hadn't forgotten he'd blackmailed her into being his date tonight and then fired her from the job. The last few days, his sins had preyed on his mind, while he'd hardly thought of hers at all.

Where to park? The Fairchilds probably didn't hold with cars on their grass, but there was a big white tent set up on the lawn between the side terrace and the tree line. His car couldn't do the grass any more harm than the tent. He pulled in behind it and killed the engine.

As he was getting out, Luka roared up on his Harley-Davidson and parked behind Robbie.

"I see you found my secret place," he told Luka. "Don't block me in."

"I left you room to get out," Luka said. "Anyway, I'll be gone before you will, party boy that you are."

"Don't bet on it."

"Why *are* we here?" Luka asked.

"You were in the same room I was when Claire laid down the law."

"I try not to listen to Claire."

"Good luck with that." Robbie took a deep breath and attempted to imitate Claire. "It's important for the Yellowhammers to not just be perceived as part of the community, but to *be* part of the community. The Christmas Gala has been a tradition in Laurel Springs since nineteen-something, whatever. It isn't enough to purchase the tickets; attendance is also mandatory. There will be a silent auction that, like the gala itself, will benefit the historical society. While not mandatory, it would be nice to support that as well."

They moved toward the house. "They are nickel and diming us to death," Luka said.

"More like five hundred dollaring and thousand dollaring us to death. How about the price of these tickets?" He wondered if Hyacinth had had to buy a ticket or if, as Ava Grace's friend, she got to come free. The decent thing would have been to send her his second ticket, since he had asked her and fired her.

"Do we go in the tent or the house?" Luka asked.

"No idea. But wait. Jake and Evans just pulled up." They parked in the circle drive and got out. "They're going in the house."

"I cannot believe Sparks is handing over the keys to his Lamborghini to that kid," Luka said.

"My thoughts exactly."

The Fairchilds were lined up at the door, along with a woman Mrs. Fairchild introduced as the president of the historical society.

"No kilt tonight, Robbie?" Mrs. Fairchild said.

He was wearing one of his standard to-the-arena-and-back suits. "My dress shirt was dirty." That was probably true. It usually was, but that had never stopped him before, since it was hidden under the jacket. The truth was he just wanted to blend in and be done.

He reached for Ava Grace's hand. "Ava Grace, aren't you the bonny one tonight?"

"Am I?" She shot ice daggers from her eyes at him.

Before he could react, she jerked her hand away and extended it to Luka, looking all happy again. "Luka. So glad you came. A pleasure to see you again."

He probably had the same reception coming from Evans.

They moved into one of the big parlors.

It was a damned forest. What the hell? Had Ava Grace's mother run out of decorating themes? She'd have done better to have gone to the attic and gotten something from last century. There was a banner that said A Woodland Christmas, and it was that. Trees, birds, little furry animals—bunnies, foxes, deer, and the like. Not a piece of glitter or a light in sight, but plenty of mistletoe and fake snow. Didn't these people know mistletoe was poisonous? If they ate it, the little birds and bunnies would probably die. If they were real. Oh, well. Not what he would have done, but nobody asked him. He wouldn't have to look at it long.

"Luka, I'm going to talk to Jake and Evans." It had to happen eventually.

"I'm going to find food. I'm hungry. For what we paid, they should feed us well."

"You do know it's only a dessert buffet, don't you?"

Luka's nostrils flared. "All I get is cookies?"

"There's probably cake and pie."

"Could this party get any worse?" Luka said as he stomped away.

Yes, it could.

And it was probably about to, at least for him. Jake and Evans were talking to Glaz and his wife, Noel. Might as well get it all over with all at once—let Glaz see that he was here, get frozen out by Evans, and watch Jake side with his wife. And Jake should do that, just like Ava Grace and Evans should side with their friend.

Why did there have to be sides? It wasn't fair, but life almost never considered what was fair. He advanced, ready to take his medicine.

But when Robbie approached the group, Evans was the first to notice him and she broke into a smile.

"Hello, honey." She held her arms out to him the way she always did. Apparently, Hyacinth had told Ava Grace, but not Evans. Why was that?

"I'm surprised you haven't gone straight for the desserts," Jake said.

"I was headed there."

"You eat terrible, McTavish," Glaz said. "Too much sugar. I should put you on diet."

"Nickolai," Noel said. "It's a party. Be a guest, not a coach."

Jake put an arm around Evans and beamed at her.

"Evie made pies for this soiree. All kinds, but the lemon chess is the best."

"I have to have some of that," Noel said.

"And you will, my love." Glaz looked at her like she was the last, best thing on Earth. "All you want. We must find a place for you to sit and I will bring to you." Then he put his hand on her stomach and said, "We only today find out. My Noel will have another baby—a little brother or sister for Anna Lillian."

And there was hugging, handshaking, and pronouncements of congratulations. Robbie participated, but he felt like he was having an out-of-body experience.

What was that old song? "What Becomes of the Brokenhearted?" He could answer that question. They had to stand around in a poisonous forest and watch the happy get happier.

Brokenhearted was brokenhearted. It didn't matter what was said, who was at fault, or how it ended up like it did. It was hell, all around hell.

He would have to watch the happy get happier. No doubt about that since he wasn't going to live on an island with monkeys, who, by the way would probably be happy, too. So, in Hyacinth speak, there was no way to escape the blissful in the long-term plan, but for tonight, he'd stood all he intended to. Leaving was the short-term plan.

"Evie, do you know where that silent auction is?" he asked.

"In the tent outside."

Good. Near his car. He would go place an outrageous bid on something he probably wouldn't want. Maybe there would be a lamp and he could replace the one he'd thrown against the wall the last time he saw Hyacinth. Then he was out of here—hopefully before he caught sight of her. Surely the universe could at least spare him that.

Chapter Thirty-One

Hyacinth sat alone at a small table at the entrance of the tent. She was not in a partying mood and had wanted to fall down and kiss Emma Frances Fairchild's feet when she asked her to be in charge of the silent auction. "The numbers and names got mixed up last year and it was such a chore getting it straightened out," Emma Frances had said. "I know you'll keep everything in order."

Kylie Beth Cathcart was supposed to be helping her but so far, the other chair at the table remained empty. Hyacinth was all right with that. It was a simple job and she didn't need Kylie Beth until later tonight when it came time to collect the payments. The party had barely started, and the few bidders who'd been in had come and gone. In fact, she was completely alone in the tent, unless you counted Dub Edwards, the off duty policeman who Emma Frances had hired to guard the auction items. And he could hardly be counted, considering he was clear at the other end of the tent with his earbuds in and his phone.

Ah, the tent door opened. Another customer. She reached for her logbook and started her speech without looking up. "Here's your bid number." She handed off the card after making sure the number was the next one in the book. "You'll find a sheet by each item. When you write down your bid, use your number, not your name, to identify it. I'll take your name down and the winners will be announced at eleven thirty tonight."

Then, she looked up into the greenest eyes she'd ever seen, and they might also be the saddest.

"Hello, lass."

Her heart flamed up and turned to ashes.

She did not write his name down. She did not advise him that if he planned to leave before the winners were announced to leave a number where he could be reached. She did not tell him payments could be made via card, Venmo, PayPal, check, or cash.

She just looked at him. And he looked back.

She thought she'd be safe here. It had never occurred to her that Robbie would be in the least interested in diamond earrings from Hasting Jewelers, a week at the Landry's beach house, or a basket of bath products from the Gift Emporium.

"You look nice." When you didn't know what else to say, that would always do. She would have thought he'd be wearing his dress kilt. It made her sad that he wasn't.

"As do you. Different frock from the party for Jake and Evie. All bronzy. Nice with your hair."

"Thank you." She'd picked the dress from Trousseau's inventory because it was a little shopworn. If it was flattering, it was a happy accident. "How's the party?"

He shrugged. "Fine, I guess. Lots of people." His mouth turned down. "Ava Grace isn't my biggest fan, it seems, for all that we bonded over Christmas lights."

"Sorry about that. She was there when I had my...

epiphany, so to speak. I kind of had to tell her the follow-up. I didn't sugarcoat my part in things, but—"

"I get it. She's your friend. Loyal, like."

"Yes. I didn't tell anyone else." She needed him to know that.

"No. Me neither—anyone at all. Couldn't see the reason in it."

There didn't seem to be anything else to say, yet he stood there like someone had sunk his feet into cement.

Then he spoke again. "I guess congratulations are in order for you."

Was he being snide? It didn't seem so. Besides, Robbie didn't do snide. That was her.

"For what?" He wouldn't know about the Aubrey Jamison appointment. She'd told no one. That was for Aubrey Jamison to divulge if and when she chose to.

He looked confused. *All Dressed in White*, of course."

Oh, that. Kind of ancient history at this point, but this was probably as awkward for him as it was for her.

"Yes, thank you. It did turn out so much better than I thought, and you were a big part of that. So congratulations to you, too."

He wrinkled his forehead and shook his head. "I didn't mean that. I meant the ones to come."

"There aren't any more to come." But he must know about Alex's most recent call to her.

"You didn't get the offer to do two episodes with Bret Clancy?"

Her heart slammed into her ribs and her head spun.

"You suggested Clancy? You did that for me? Why?"

She nodded. "I did. How did you know?"

"Miles sent me a case of ale to thank me for the suggestion. Clancy's his client, too."

He hesitated and looked heavenward, but she got the feeling he wasn't about to go down a bunny trail this time. He was looking for words. Finally, he brought his eyes back to hers.

"Because, lass, no matter what's gone wrong between us, no matter what words were said and who said them, I want you to succeed." Then he tilted his head, as if he had a new thought. "But wait. You said there wouldn't be any more *All Dressed in White*. What happened? Did Clancy back out? Did the network?"

"No. I turned it down."

She turned it down?

He pointed to the empty chair beside her. "Do you mind if I sit?" This was turning into a longer conversation than he had anticipated and it didn't seem right to tower over her.

"Sure."

"You turned it down? I don't understand."

She shrugged and looked at her hands. "I found that I didn't want to do it. The day we taped was a horrible day. I was a miserable, nervous wreck. My behavior was abominable." She met his eyes and her voice went soft. "I said terrible things to the person who has been nicer to me than anyone ever has."

The horrible truth hit him. Brad had tried to tell him. He should have known. She had not lied to him. She *wasn't* willing to say or do anything for *All Dressed in White*, else she wouldn't have turned down the offer.

"You didn't know about the offer for us—that day you came to me." It wasn't a question.

"No. Alex called as I was leaving."

"Oh, hell..." Everything she'd said to him, she'd

meant. She hadn't been trying to manipulate him. She'd been trying to make a relationship with him; she'd said she loved him—what he'd wanted above all else. And he'd thrown it away. It was too late now.

She nodded. "I know. Great timing, huh?"

"Lass, I'm sorry."

She put a hand up. "Don't. I'd already done a spectacular job of proving that I would do whatever was necessary to get what I wanted. It's not a stretch to think I would have done that, too."

"But you wouldn't have."

"No, I wouldn't. Not that. Still, understandable that you would think what you did."

"But the things I said…"

"We both said plenty. All the things you did to please me, I threw back in your face."

"It doesn't matter who said what," he said. "In the end a broken heart is a broken heart."

"And our hearts are broken, aren't they?" she said.

Too broken to ever mend.

He swiped his hand over his face. "You're sure about *All Dressed in White?* You wanted it so much. And I wanted it for you. I just couldn't do it with you, doing all the wrong things, wanting what I couldn't have, making you miserable along the way."

"I'm sure. I learned some things from you on this journey. I'm not sure those things are worth what I squandered in the process, but at least there's that. And one of the things I learned from watching you is how important it is to achieve joy. You're the most joyful person I know. *All Dressed in White* did not bring me joy. I was so sure it would, but it didn't, and it made me rob you of yours."

He had to laugh at that. *Joy?* Right now, that was as foreign to him as the North Pole.

"But what about your long-term plan, your short-term plan, your designing?"

"I'll get there." She smiled a sad smile. "Or I won't. Either way, I have a beautiful shop I love where I sell happily ever after. Even if I never get to design as much as I'd like, I'll get to now and again. I already have a possibility. That's enough, Robbie. Sometimes you have to decide *enough* is sufficient and you're lucky to have it."

"But I want you to have everything you want. I want you to be happy."

"Do you?" she asked. "Really?"

"More than anything." *Because I love you, even if I can't have you.* He took a deep breath and spoke before his mind could talk his heart out of what he felt he had to say. "I'll do *All Dressed in White* with you. I'll call Miles and tell him to make it happen. I won't bring any cakes or do anything you're not expecting. I'll make sure it's not miserable for you. I'll make sure that—in the end—you're so famous that every bride this side of Eden will beg you to make her wedding frock. You'll have to turn ten people away every day. Brides will put off their weddings for years because your waiting list will be so long and they refuse to get married in anything except a Hyacinth Dawson original. I swear it."

He didn't know how he would do all that, but he would, or die trying. This was Hyacinth, who had his heart. As far as that went, it wouldn't matter. He'd never have her. Too much had happened. But she would have what she'd longed for and that was, as she'd said, enough—*sufficient*—for him.

His heart beat like he'd just done a skate 'til you puke, but he felt lighter.

"You'd do that?" Hyacinth laid a hand on his arm and he memorized the moment. It might be the last time she would ever touch him.

"Aye, lass. I will."

"No." She shook her head, but tightened her hand on his arm. "If you truly want to give me what I want, let me have you. It's hard for me to ask for what I want one time, let alone twice, but I'm going to ask again. Can't we please just put all the bad behind us and remember the good and loving times? And go from there?"

Just like that, a cool breeze blew through his soul.

"Not a fling?" That's what she'd said that day at his condo, but he had to be sure.

She shook her head. "Not a fling."

"Oh, lass. I thought I'd ruined it for all time."

"I thought *I* had." She leaned her forehead against his. It felt good. Was it possible that their broken hearts were fusing together and joining as one?

"I'm never going to make lists or have a spreadsheet." She had to be warned. "Or probably have a pen."

"You don't need to. I've got that covered. And I'll keep you safe if a tornado comes."

He shuddered at the thought. "What's in it for you?"

"Hmm." She played with the button on his shirt. "You'll make me laugh and remind me that life will go on without a list. Maybe you'll wave to me from the ice?"

Joy. The joy she'd spoken of rushed around him and into his heart. "At the beginning of every period."

"I want a game worn jersey, preferably with blood-stains. I hear those are the best."

"I'll sew it myself. And bleed on it. Probably from the sewing."

"I hope you'll make me a birthday cake every year."

"For years and years and years—until I'm so old I can't open the oven door. Then I'll buy you one." Oh, hell. He'd just offered her a lifetime. What if she didn't want that, wasn't ready to hear it?

But if she'd taken notice, she didn't seem to mind the idea.

"Then there are the Christmas lights and garland. I'm counting on you for that."

"You've got it. More lights than you can even imagine. I'll buy every string in four states."

"And then..." She dropped her head and looked up at him through her eyelashes. "There's that thing you do... You know the one."

"The one on the couch?" He took her hand and circled her palm with his index finger. "Or that other, from the shower?"

"Both, actually."

"I'm on it. I'll make a list—but only in my head."

"Or you could write it on a cake with frosting."

His heart burst into song at the sweetness of it all. He cupped her face in his hands. "Then it's possible that we don't have to keep being brokenhearted?"

"Mother of pearl, I hope not, because it's hard to sell happily ever after in the state I've been in."

They laughed together and she came into his arms and tucked her face into his neck—the thing he liked best. Almost best.

"It's hard to play hockey, too." He sprinkled kisses

into that fabulous hair that curled this way and that. "Or eat, drink, sleep, breathe…"

She lifted her face from his neck to meet his eyes.

"Is it hard to leave this party?"

"That might be the easiest thing I'll ever be called on to do, if I'm leaving with you." He stood up and pulled her to her feet. "My car's right outside. Just this one time, can you please ride with me? Not make me have to follow you?"

She laughed and hugged him. "We can come get my car tomorrow."

The next thing Robbie heard was the sound of bells. For one stupid second he thought they were coming from his heart. He was glad he didn't mention that because, then, a voice from the terrace called out, "Attention, everyone! You're all invited inside for a toast. Please make your way inside to the ballroom."

"There it is," Robbie said. "Ava Grace's engagement. Are you sure you don't want to go inside so you can see it?"

She pulled him by the hand toward the tent entrance. "Right now, all I want to see is you."

But then she stopped and her face went blank, then on to panic. Had she changed her mind? "Lass? What's wrong? Do you want to stay for Ava Grace, after all?"

"I need a second."

She ran to the other end of the tent and clapped her hands in front of the face of a policeman Robbie hadn't noticed until now.

"Dub, Dub!" She yanked an earbud from his ear. "Look alive! I'm leaving. And I'm not coming back." She pointed a finger in his face. "Now, you listen to me. Send word to Kylie Beth Cathcart that she needs to get up here. But send word. Do *not* go yourself. There's thousands of dollars' worth of stuff in this tent."

Robbie dissolved into laughter. Of course she wouldn't leave her post without giving some orders. She wouldn't be Hyacinth if she did. At least she wasn't taking the time to make a list with bullet points.

"I'm ready." She sounded breathless as she ran back to him. "If you are."

"Oh, yes, lass. I'm ready."

And not just to leave this place—for the rest of their lives.

Epilogue

Joy.

It was the first thing Hyacinth saw when she woke up on Christmas morning. Robbie had spelled out the word with Christmas lights over the door of her bedroom—multicolored lights. And they blinked. Memaw would have said it made her bedroom look like a honkytonk, though Hyacinth doubted if Memaw had ever been to a honkytonk in her life.

The Christmas tree—also in the bedroom—reached the ceiling and also blinked. All that, along with the matching garland, might have been a little excessive for Hyacinth's tastes, but Memaw had also taught her that life was about compromise.

That certainly had been true of this relationship. She moved closer to Robbie. He flopped an arm over her and snored in her ear. When she'd first imagined waking up with him on Christmas morning, she had envisioned it as a one-time occurrence, but once wasn't enough. She wanted to wake up with him for all her Christmases to come and she was going to make that happen if she could.

They were happy; they had joy.

It hadn't been all smooth sailing every minute of every day. It probably never would be.

What she thought of as his blister pack syndrome—where he left the packaging for whatever piece of electronic equipment or video game he'd bought lying a foot from a trash can—drove her crazy and she might have belabored the point more than she should have.

Then there was the time she'd thought she was doing him a favor when she'd sorted his T-shirts and purged the stained, holey ones that—to her mind—weren't fit to be seen in public. Yeah. That had gone well. When she'd defended herself by saying she was just trying to help him, he'd widened his eyes and given her a pointed look. It wasn't lost on her and she'd had plenty of time to ponder that as she dug through the trash.

He might have ambled into Trousseau a time or two during a bridal appointment and felt compelled to "help" her and the bride—but, to be honest, he'd had some good ideas and they'd been able to laugh about it.

The biggest row they'd had was when she needed to drive to Nashville for a night meeting with Aubrey Jamison and Pitch. He was headed out the door for a road trip to Minnesota when she told him and he'd set his jaw and told her she would *not* drive all the way there alone at night; she would wait until he returned and could take her. She had retaliated by saying she had a business to run and he was not the boss of her. Furthermore, she'd been taking care of herself for years.

This, too, ended in compromise. She'd promised to ask Evans to go with her and to call when she was home safely. He'd promised he wouldn't ask her to take someone else along again, if she'd do it this once. She suspected she'd always have to make that check-in call, but she was all right with that.

She laughed a little to herself.

Making a list of these things—even mentally—made it seem like their adjustments had been so much worse than they had been. Maybe he was right. There was such a thing as overthinking and too many lists.

As she'd hoped, they were learning to celebrate their differences. The good, by far, outweighed the prickly times—the laughing, the making love, the waking up with each other.

And speaking of that…

"Hey." She shook his shoulder. "Wake up, Robbie. It's Christmas. The electricity is back on." There had been an ice storm yesterday, stranding them together at her little house—but they wouldn't have wanted to be anywhere else anyway.

He smiled before he opened his eyes and her stomach turned over because that smile was just for her. Then he opened those beloved green eyes.

"Merry Christmas, lass." His voice was sleepy and sweet.

"Time to get up. We have celebrating to do."

He pulled her to him. "Eager for your presents, are you?"

"Yes." Might as well admit it. She was out of her mind wondering what was in the mysterious packages. "But I'm eager to make Christmas breakfast, too. And to open stockings and watch you open your gifts. And then to go to the Fairchilds' for lunch. I can't wait for them to see the cake you made."

"All that sounds fair brilliant," he said. "But I want to give you the first gift of Christmas right here in bed."

She expected him to reach for her and start making magic—Christmas magic—and that would have been fine with her. But he reached into the bedside table drawer and took something out.

"This is something you've been hoping for." He put a piece of paper in her hand.

"A receipt from Best Buy?" she asked. "For *Call of Duty?*"

"Oh, no, no, lass. That's not the present." He took the receipt, turned it over, and handed it back to her. "The present's on the back. I made a list," he said proudly.

"Probably the only one I'll ever make."

She read the words aloud, "Love and do my best to make Hyacinth happy for the rest of our lives." Hyacinth couldn't remember the last time she'd cried, but tears gathered in her eyes.

"It's a one item list," Robbie said. "One bullet point."

It wasn't just enough; it wasn't even more than enough. It was everything.

She went into his arms and they made Christmas magic.

* * * * *

About the Author

USA TODAY bestsellers Stephanie Jones and Jean Hovey write together as Alicia Hunter Pace. Stephanie lives in Tuscaloosa, AL, where she teaches school. She is a native Alabamian who likes football, American history, and people who follow the rules. She is happy to provide a list of said rules to anyone who needs them. Jean, a former public librarian, lives in Decatur, AL, with her husband in a hundred-year-old house that always wants something from her. She likes to cook but has discovered the joy of Mrs. Paul's fish fillets since becoming a writer. Stephanie and Jean are both active members in the romance writing community. They write contemporary romance. You can find them at:

www.AliciaHunterPace.com
https://www.facebook.com/AliciaHunterPace
https://twitter.com/AliciaHPace
email: aliciahunterpace@gmail.com

A pro hockey player learns that home is where the heart is in Sweet as Pie, the first book in the Good Southern Women series from USA TODAY bestselling author Alicia Hunter Pace.

Keep reading for an excerpt!

Prologue

Hell on Earth.

Pro hockey defenseman Jake Champagne understood the meaning of the phrase, but had never lived it until that March day at the end of his second season with the Nashville Sound.

He woke to the sound of pounding and the smell of hockey stench. At first, he thought the pounding was in his head but, as the fog cleared, he realized someone was intent on getting into his hotel room. When he opened his eyes, the first image he saw was a blurry half-empty bottle of Pappy Van Winkle bourbon. No wonder he couldn't see straight. He was usually a beer guy, but special nights called for special liquor and last night had been spectacular—though not in a good way.

Oh, no. Not at all. After hoisting the cup two years in a row, his team had gone four up and four down in the playoffs. Plus, it was cold here in Boston and he hated the cold, hated the snow. You wouldn't catch any snow on the ground in March in the Mississippi Delta—or any other time either. That was just one of the things he missed about home.

The pounding on the door became more intense just as a warm body rolled over next to him.

Hellfire and brimstone. It was all coming back now, and that was where the hockey stench was coming from. She was wearing his nasty jersey, had insisted on wearing it while they made love. He laughed under his breath. *Made love.* Ha.

He pulled on his sweatpants and caught sight of the clock as he crossed the room. Five forty-one freaking a.m.! The team plane didn't leave until ten o'clock. He was going to kill somebody—probably Robbie. His best friend most likely hadn't been to sleep yet. The last time he'd seen him, Robbie'd been doing shots with a red-head, the companion of the blonde in his own bed. He jerked open the door. "What do you want?"

Not Robbie. It was Sound staff member Oliver Kle-packi, who frowned at the tone of Jake's voice. "Sparks," He used Jake's nickname.

Dread washed over Jake. This man was not in the habit of knocking on hotel doors at this hour. In fact, from the looks of him, he had just rolled out himself.

"Sorry, Packi. Is something wrong?"

"You need to call your mother."

After closing the door, Jake reached for his phone with shaking hands. He'd turned it off last night, even before coming back to the room with his latest charming companion. Not wanting to talk to anyone who might want to commiserate over the loss to the Colonials or the minutes he'd spent in the penalty box because he'd showed his ass on the ice for no good reason, he'd taken the landline phone off the hook.

But that seemed small now. Something bad had hap-pened. Christine Jacob Champagne was a Mississippi Delta Southern belle who took breakfast in her room every morning at eight o'clock. She spoke to no one before then. In any case, she wasn't the type to hunt down her grown son like a dog who needed his worm medicine.

He didn't call right away. There had to be a clue on his phone, and he couldn't take another breath without knowing if his dad and sister were okay.

Fourteen missed calls, five voice mails, and six text messages later, he knew. His uncle Blake—the man who had put him on skates at four years old—had had a heart attack.

And he was dead. The texts and voice mails hadn't said so. His mother would never leave that in a message, but he had to be. Otherwise she wouldn't have hunted him down in Boston at this hour.

He started to call, but paused and looked down at the woman in his bed. His mother would probably know she was here, would probably be able to smell her through the phone. He went into the bathroom, quietly drawing the door shut behind him before he dialed.

"Darling boy," Christine answered immediately.

"Uncle Blake?" he said.

There were tears in her voice. "I know how you loved him."

Loved. Jake hadn't realized that he'd still held out a miniscule bit of hope until his mother spoke in the past tense. He had known before he even made the call, but—at the same time—how was it possible?

"So hard to believe…only forty-seven…" Christine's voice trailed off.

"Forty-six." Jake was very sure of that. Jake had been four and Blake twenty-five—just the age Jake would be come October—when Blake had moved to the Delta to work at Champagne Cotton Brokers. Not long after, he had married Christine's younger sister.

"Forty-six," Christine said. "You're right, of course. Would've been forty-seven in June."

Would've been. Cruel words.

There were things he should be saying, questions he should be asking to prove he wasn't an asshole. "Aunt Olivia?" He said the words, but his thoughts were on himself.

In a land where football was king and baseball crown prince, Blake had taught Jake to skate by standing behind him, hands on his waist. Blake claimed trainer walkers that beginning skaters typically used to steady themselves encouraged bad posture and technique.

"She's resting," Christine said. "At least I hope she is."

"I hope so, too." The words were hollow. *Hope* wasn't much of a word right now.

Blake had showed him the movie *Miracle on Ice* and bought him a souvenir 1980 U.S. Olympic Hockey Team puck. At the time Jake didn't understand that the puck had not been in the actual game—or for that matter, that *Miracle on Ice* wasn't actual footage of the famous Soviet/U.S. match, or that the game had been played years before his birth. And later it didn't matter. By then, the puck was his constant companion and good luck charm.

"Adam and Nicole?" Jake asked after his two teenage cousins. Even after Blake and Olivia had children, he had not forsaken his bond with Jake.

"About like you'd expect," Christine said.

But what was that? How did anyone know what to expect?

Expect. Things would be *expected* of him by people who seemed to instinctively know the correct behavior for every situation known to man. "Naturally, I'm coming home." For the first time today, his voice sounded sure and strong.

And suddenly, that was what he wanted, all he wanted—to be home in Cottonwood, Mississippi. He wanted to drive down Main Street, past the bakery, the hardware store, and the drugstore that still had a soda fountain. He wanted to go to the house that been home to three generations of Champagnes, sleep in his childhood room, and smell the bacon and coffee that Louella had made for his family every morning for thirty years. He wanted to take his grandmother to lunch at the Country Club and hit a bucket of balls with his dad.

But Christine was talking, interrupting the flow of his thoughts. "No, Jake. No."

"I don't need to wait until morning," he assured her. "I won't be too tired to drive. I'll pack a few things and get on the road as soon as I can. I'll get into Nashville around noon and be home by bedtime—well before." Certainly in time to stop at Fat Joe's and pick up a sack of famous Delta tamales.

"No, Jake! Listen to me." Christine began to speak very clearly as if she were speaking to a child. "Do *not* come home. We're all flying out tonight to Vermont. You need to go there."

"Vermont?" Did they have tamales in Vermont?

"Yes. You *do* remember that Blake is from Vermont, don't you?"

"Well, yes, but…" Of course he remembered. Vermont was the whole reason Blake had played hockey as a kid, the reason he'd taught Jake to love hockey. But it didn't make any sense. Cottonwood had become Blake's home.

Christine seemed to read his mind. "He has—*had* family there. His father is unwell and unable to travel under the best of circumstances. The funeral will be there. You need to go to Vermont. We've reserved a block of rooms."

So, no home. More cold weather. Probably snow. But there would be people from home. That was something.

"Who's going?" he asked. "Besides y'all, Olivia and the kids?"

"About who you would expect—your grandmother, your sister, Anna-Blair and Keith, your aunt—"

"Evie? Is Evie going?" He cut her off. The mention of his godparents, Anna-Blair and Keith Pemberton, naturally led to thoughts of their daughter.

"No," Christine said. "She can't get away from work."

Evie had opened a pie shop in a fancy-pants section of Birmingham, Alabama, a few years back. There had been a time when she would have—pie shop, or no pie shop—crawled over glass to get to him if he needed her. However, that was before he'd let life get in the way and hadn't bothered to take care of their friendship. But he couldn't think about that right now. He had to get to Vermont.

"Okay, Mama. I'll go there from here. Text me the particulars and I'll book a flight. Or rent a car and drive. Yeah. Probably that." It would be faster, and not nearly as annoying as dealing with a commercial airline.

"All right. Text me your ETA when you know. Your dad wants to talk to you. I love you, Jake."

"I love you, too, Mama."

"Son!" Marc Champagne's big booming voice was the next thing he heard. Jake could tell in that one spoken syllable that his dad was driving this heartbreak wagon, bossing everyone around, and making them like it. He couldn't fix it, but by damn, he would make it go as easy as he and his money could. If Marc had his way, he'd probably move Olivia and the kids into the Champagne ancestral home.

"Hello, Dad."

"This is bad business, Jake. Bad."

"As bad as it gets," Jake agreed.

"Listen." Marc always said that before he said something important, even when the person he was speaking to was already listening. "I'll buy you a plane ticket back to Nashville from Vermont."

Jake opened his mouth to remind his dad that he could afford his own ticket. But that wasn't necessary. Marc knew how much the Sound paid him.

"Sure, Dad. Thanks." Jake hung up and walked back out to the bedroom. He needed to get that woman—Meghan, if he recalled correctly—out of here. Good-time girls had no place in bad times.

It was when he put out a hand to shake her awake that he saw it—the glint of gold on the ring finger of her left hand. Just when he thought he couldn't feel any sicker, his stomach bottomed out. Since his divorce two years ago, he'd taken raising hell to a whole new art form, but there was one line he had never crossed: he did not sleep with married women.

"Hey." He poked her shoulder.

"What? Stop!" When she jerked the covers over her head, he saw that the ring was not a wedding band after all, but some kind of little birthstone ring that had turned around on her finger. He didn't feel much relief in that. He hadn't asked, hadn't even thought about it. That was a first. And if he had been willing to cross that line, what was next? His eyes darted to his bedside table. He was relieved to see an open box of condoms there, though it didn't negate the panic and shame coursing through him. "Hey, Meghan." He pulled the covers off her head. "You have to wake up."

She opened one mascara-smudged eye, seemed to consider, and decided to smile.

"Hello there, Southern boy. Come back to bed."

"I can't."

She sat up. "Sure you can. I want to see if you speak Southerner as good in the morning as you do at night."

She ran a hand up his thigh.

"No. Really. You've got to go." He moved her hand.

"Why? What time is it?" She frowned and picked up her phone. "What the fuck! Do you *know* what time it is?"

"I do. I'm sorry. But you have to go." He was repeating himself, but apparently it was necessary.

She pouted. "I thought you liked me."

"I did. I do. But you still have to go."

She threw her legs over the side of the bed. He thought he had won, but she was relentless. "All right," she said with a sigh. "I'm just going to jump in the shower. Why don't you order breakfast? I've never had room service before."

And he was done trying to trot out his Mississippi Delta Cotillion manners—not that he'd been very successful. "And you aren't going to have it now." She didn't deserve it, but he was out of time, out of patience, out of everything except the raw feelings marching through his head and heart. He reached for his wallet and peeled off two hundred-dollar bills. "Buy yourself some breakfast and an Uber."

Meghan looked at him like he was a snake recently escaped from a leprosy colony. He couldn't blame her.

She had signed up for a little uncomplicated fun and had woken up to a complicated situation.

When she didn't say anything, he peeled off another hundred. "Ubers are expensive."

"*You* are an asshole," she said.

He nodded. "I am that."

She snatched the money from his hand, gathered up her clothes and boots from the floor, and stomped to the door. With her hand on the knob she turned and hissed, "I'm keeping this jersey."

He nodded. "Please. I want you to have it." It was a good thing it reached her knees because apparently she couldn't stand him another second, not even long enough to put on her jeans.

Understandable. He couldn't stand himself.

Jake needed concrete evidence there was a time when he didn't drink a six-pack every night and sleep with women who were more interested in his jersey than in him—needed to remember a time before he'd lost so many pieces of himself that he didn't know who he was anymore.

He didn't want to be a man Uncle Blake would have been ashamed of.

But if things didn't change, he was going to become the kind of person that everyone hated as much as he was beginning to hate himself. He loved the Sound, loved his teammates, but it would be easier to start over somewhere else with people who didn't naturally assume he was going to raise hell.

His scalp prickled at the thought.

Start over. Leave Nashville.

Leave the Sound? Maybe he ought to. The team had enough heavy-hitting veteran players that he was still the new kid in town. It would be years before he skated first line in Nashville, and who knew if he had years?

Blake certainly hadn't.

Jake picked up his phone again and dialed his agent, Miles Gentry, who answered immediately, despite the early hour. "Jake! I was just—"

"Trade me," he blurted out.

"What?"

"Trade me. Hopefully to somewhere I can skate first line. But it *has* to be a place where I don't have to buy a snow shovel. I don't care where. California. Texas. Florida. Arizona. Just get me the hell out of Nashville."

"Are you sure about this?" Miles asked.

"As sure as the fact that death is coming for us all."

Miles was quiet for a moment. "How do you feel about that new expansion team down in Birmingham? The Alabama Yellowhammers."

Right. He hadn't considered the new Birmingham team. It was still in the South—and Evie lived there. Maybe he could get their friendship back on track. Those were pluses, but the team was an unknown quantity. "Talk to me," Jake said.

"They've asked about you. I was waiting until the playoffs were over to tell you."

"Playoffs aren't over. Just over for the Sound—and me."

"Semantics," Miles said. "So—Alabama. Brand-new state-of-the-art practice facility. Drew Kelty is the head coach." Jake didn't really know him other than by name, but Kelty had plenty of pro hockey experience—as a player and a coach. "From what they said, I would think first line is an excellent bet. Any interest?"

And Jake said something neither he, nor any other Ole Miss fan, had ever said before. "Roll Tide."

Chapter One

Five months later

Evans Pemberton considered the dough on the marble slab in front of her.

What was wrong with pie in this country was the crust. No one made quality crusts anymore or thought about which kind of crust went best with what pie. Butter crusts were wonderful with fruit pies, but too rich for pecan pies. Savory pies needed a sturdy crust, but it was important to get the right balance so as not to produce a soggy mess. A bit of bacon grease gave crusts for meat pies a smoky taste, and Evans liked to add a pinch of sage for chicken pot pies. Crumb crusts had their place, too.

As did Jake Champagne, she thought, as she gave the ball in front of her a vicious knead. And his place was now apparently *here*. He was going to land in town any day, any hour.

He hadn't spoken to her in almost three years. Sure, back in March, he had texted to thank her for the funeral flowers she'd sent when his uncle died and apologized for not making more of an effort to keep in touch. According to her business manager, Neva, he'd also stopped by the shop a month later when he'd come to Laurel Springs to sign a lease on a condo, but Evans had been in New York taking a mini puff pastry course.

She didn't know why she was thinking about him anyway. Who knew if he would even try to contact her again? He had abandoned her once after a lifetime of friendship. There was no reason to think, despite the text and drop-in, that anything would change.

"You're looking at that dough like you don't like it," said a woman behind her.

"I don't." She turned and handed her friend, Ava Grace Fairchild, an apron and chef's hat. Ava Grace was no chef, but Evans had given up on trying to keep her out of the pie shop kitchen, so she'd settled on doing what she could to make Ava Grace acceptable should the health inspector make a surprise visit to Crust. "Though I suppose it's not so much that I don't like it. I don't *know* it."

"I thought you knew every dough." Ava Grace tied the apron over her linen dress and perched the hat on the back of her head so as not to disturb her loose chestnut curls. She looked like a queen dressed as a chef for Halloween.

"I don't know this one." Evans placed her hand on the dough. Normally, she wouldn't think of putting her warm hand on pastry dough, but this was a hot water pastry so it was warm to begin with.

Ava Grace slid onto a stool and crossed her long, perfect legs. "What makes this one different?"

"It's for a handheld meat pie with rutabagas, potato, and onions. The crust has to be sturdy but not tough. That's tricky." She gave the dough another vicious slap. "They're called Upper Peninsula pasties, from Michigan."

"Never heard of them," Ava Grace said.

"Claire has, and she wants to feed them to the new hockey team on their first day of training camp tomorrow."

Ava Grace's mouth twisted into a grin. "For a silent partner, Claire isn't very quiet, is she?"

Evans laughed. Ava Grace would know. Claire was her "silent" partner, too. "Well, she never promised to be quiet."

"That's a promise she couldn't have kept. Why is she so set on these little pies?"

"You know as well as I do that Claire doesn't have to have a reason, but she says most of the team is from up North, so we should give them some Northern comfort food."

Evans had not pointed out to Claire that not all hockey players would associate these pasties with home. She knew of one in particular who would need barbecue pork, hot tamales, and Mississippi mud pie to make him think of home. Claire wasn't an easy woman to say no to, even if Evans had been willing. Saying no had never been Evans's strong suit, which was why she was catering this lunch when she just wanted to make pies.

Evans had thought it would be years before she could fulfill her dream of having her own shop, until Claire had taken her under her wing. Now Crust was thriving.

The old-money heiress had excelled in business, and successfully played the stock market rather than living off her inheritance. A few years ago she had decided to help young women start their own new businesses.

Evans and Ava Grace were two of Claire's girls, along with Hyacinth Dawson, who owned a local bridal shop.

"Claire must really like hockey," Ava Grace said.

"I don't think it's that, so much as she likes a project and loves the chase." Claire was one of several locals who owned a small part of the Yellowhammers. Her uncle and nephew had been the ones to bring the team here, but Claire had quickly formulated a plan to turn Laurel Springs into Yellowhammers Central.

"She knows a bunch of rich hockey players are going to live and spend their money somewhere and she wants it to be here." She had convinced the owners to build a state-of-the-art practice rink and workout facility in Laurel Springs, renovated the old mill into upscale condos, lobbied for more fine dining and chic shops, and turned the old Speake Department Store building into a sports bar and named it Hammer Time—all to welcome the new team.

"It looks like she's getting her way," Ava Grace said.

"Everywhere you look there's a gang of Lululemon-wearing men in Yellowhammer ball caps."

"We should be thankful for them," Evans said. "Sponsoring our businesses was part of her master plan to make the area appealing to the team. Had to be."

Ava Grace pulled at one of her curls. "I'm sure she knows what she's doing. I've lived here all my life, and I've never known Claire to fail," she said wryly.

"At least not yet." Of the three businesses Claire had backed, Ava Grace's antique and gift shop was the only one losing money. Claire insisted that was to be expected in the beginning, but it was still a sore subject. "Anyway," Ava Grace clapped her hands together like she always did when she wanted to change the subject. "Hockey in Birmingham. Hockey people here in our little corner of the world. I've never even been to a hockey game. Have you?"

And here it was. She'd never mentioned Jake to anyone in Laurel Springs, not even Ava Grace and Hyacinth, who were her best friends. And she was loath to do it now. What if he ignored her as he had the last few years?

"I have. A guy I've known all my life is a hockey player." She wasn't about to mention that he'd been the best-looking thing in Cottonwood, Mississippi—plus he had that hockey-mystique thing going for him in a world where most of the other boys played football and baseball. "His parents and mine are best friends, so we went to a lot of his games when I was growing up. After college, he went on to play for the Nashville Sound, but he's going to play for the Yellowhammers now."

Ava Grace widened her eyes. "Really? He's coming here?"

"If nothing has changed since the last time I talked to my mother. I haven't talked to him in a while." Technically not a lie—condolence texts didn't count as talking.

"Is he married?"

"Not anymore." She slammed her fist into the ball of dough.

Ava Grace's eyes lit up and Evans knew what was coming. Ava Grace was all but engaged and was always looking for romance for everyone else. "Is this an old boyfriend?"

"No! Of course not." She hadn't meant to sound so vehement.

Ava Grace narrowed her eyes. "You never went out with him a single time?"

"No. Never entered my mind." If she'd been Pinocchio, her nose would be out the front door. There had been this one time at a holiday party—for just a fraction of a minute—when Evans had thought he'd looked at her differently, when she'd been sure that Jake was finally going to ask her for a date. But they'd been interrupted, and the moment had passed. To this day, she never saw a sprig of holly or heard a Christmas bell without the memory of the humiliating disappointment slamming against her rib cage, driving the breath out of her.

"It's a new day," Ava Grace said. "I grew up with Skip, and look where we are. It could happen for you, too."

"Not likely." Evans floured her rolling pin. "A couple years back, my cousin Channing married and divorced him in the space of about seven months in the messiest way possible."

"Wow." Ava Grace raised her eyebrows. "Your cousin just up and stole your man, easy as you please? Why, you must've been madder than a wet hen!"

Evans shrugged. "He wasn't mine." She clenched her fist and the dough shot up between her fingers. "I doubt he would be open to romance with another Pemberton woman. Not that I would—be open to it, I mean."

The words had barely made their way out of her mouth when one of her assistant bakers ducked into the kitchen.

"Evans, there's a guy here to see you."

She stilled her rolling pin.

"I think I conjured up a man for you." Ava Grace laughed and removed her cap and apron. "See you tonight at Claire's house."

"Right." It was mentor dinner night with Claire,

something they did every few weeks where Evans, Ava Grace, and Hyacinth gave reports and swapped advice.

Ava Grace nodded. "I'll just slip out the back."

"Who is it, Ariel?" Please, God, not the rep from Hollingsworth Foods—a regional company that provided frozen foods to grocery stores. According to Claire, they were interested in mass-producing her maple pecan and peanut butter chocolate pies. So far, the rep had only tried to contact her by phone and it had been easy enough to elude his calls, allowing her to tell Claire that she hadn't heard from them.

Ariel shook her head and played with the crystal that hung around her neck. "I don't know."

Evans sighed. Of course she wouldn't have thought to ask. The female hadn't been born who was more suited to her name than Ariel—ethereal, dreamy, not of this world. But she could make a lemon curd that would make you cry.

"All right." Evans reached for a towel and wiped her hands. As tempting as it was to follow Ava Grace out the back door, she supposed it was time to deal with it. "Will you cover these and put them in the refrigerator?" She gestured to the sheet pans of oven-ready meat pies.

Ariel nodded. "I'll just get the plastic wrap." And she floated to the storeroom.

Evans still had a few meat pies, then peach cobblers to make for the Yellowhammer lunch tomorrow, so the quicker she sent him away, the better.

She hurried through the swinging door that led from the kitchen to the storefront—and looked right into the eyes of Jake Champagne.

Eyes.

He had eyes all night long and possibly into the next

day. Big, cobalt blue eyes with Bambi eyelashes. They weren't eyes a woman was likely to forget even if he turned out to be a man she had to walk away from. Still, Evans had thought the day was done when those eyes would make her forget her own name. *Evans. Evans. Blair Pemberton*, she reminded herself.

Jake widened those eyes. That was a willful act. She was sure of it because she'd spent years studying him—so she knew what it meant when Jake Champagne went all wide-eyed on someone. He understood the value of those eyes and the effect they had on people. When he widened them, he was either surprised or angling to get his way. This time he was surprised. If he'd been trying to get his way, he would have cocked his head to the side and smiled. If he wanted his way really bad, and it wasn't going well, he'd bite his bottom lip.

Speaking of what he wanted—what in the ever-loving hell was he doing here? She was pretty sure he had not gone to work for Hollingsworth Foods.

"You look great, Evie." She was suddenly sorry she'd studied him. Knowing he was surprised that she looked great wasn't the best for the ego.

Besides, she didn't look great. Her hair was in a messy ponytail, she was wearing an apron covered in flour, and any makeup she'd applied this morning was a memory. She only looked great compared to the last time he'd seen her—at the Pemberton family Thanks-giving two years ago, when she'd been coming off a bad haircut and sporting a moon crater of a cold sore. That had been five months after his wedding and two months before his divorce. Now, three years later, he could still send her on a one-way trip back to sixteen.

"Hotty Toddy, Jake!" Why had she said that—the

Ole Miss football battle cry? Neither of them had gone to Ole Miss, though most of their families had. They were fans, of course, but she didn't normally go around saying *Hotty Toddy.*

"Hotty Toddy, Evie. That's good to hear in Roll Tide country."

She stepped from behind the counter and the awkward hug they shared was softened by his laughter. Though she didn't say so, he really did look great—however, in his plaid shorts and pink polo, he looked more like a fraternity boy on spring break than a professional hockey player. Jake's eyes might be his best feature, but he was gorgeous from head to toe. His caramel blond hair was a little shaggy and his tan face clean-shaven.

They came out of the hug and she looked up at him—way up. He was over six feet tall to her barely five feet four.

"It's good to see you, Evie."

Evie, rhymed with *levy.* He'd christened her that—probably because it was easier for a toddler to say than Evans. "Only people from home call me Evie now," she babbled.

He raised one eyebrow and his mouth curved into a half smile. She'd forgotten about that half smile. "I *am* from home."

He had a point.

"Would you like some pie? I have Mississippi mud." His favorite. The meringue pie with a chocolate pastry crust and layers of dense brownie and chocolate custard was one of her most popular. She glanced around to see if one of the round marble tables was available. Though it was after one o'clock, a few people were still lingering over lunch, but there was a vacant table by the window.

"No, I don't think—" He stopped abruptly and narrowed his eyes. "Yes. I would. Can you sit with me? For just a bit?"

Of course she could. She was queen of this castle. She could do whatever she wanted. But did she want to? Ha! What a stupid question, even to herself.

"Sure." She might still be making cobblers at midnight, but that was nobody else's business. "Joy?" She turned to the girl behind the counter. "I'm going to take a break. Can you bring a slice of Mississippi mud and a glass of milk? And a black coffee for me." She met his eyes. "Unless you've started drinking coffee."

He looked a little pained and she wondered why.

"No. I still don't."

He held her chair before sitting himself down in the iron ice cream parlor chair opposite her. What had she been thinking when she'd bought these chairs? Apparently, not that hockey players—let alone this hockey player—would be settling in for pie. He looked like a man at a child's tea party. She laughed a little.

And in that instant, with the sun shining in the window turning his caramel hair golden, Jake came across with a smile that lit up the world. Good thing she'd packed up all those old feelings, right and tight, when he'd gotten involved with her cousin. Her stomach turned over—a muscle memory, no doubt.

"What's funny?" he asked.

"I was thinking I didn't choose these chairs with men in mind."

"You don't think it suits me?" He leaned back a bit.

"Maybe you could trade them for some La-Z-Boys."

"Not quite the look I was going for."

He looked around. "So this is your shop? All yours?"

"I have an investor, but yes. It's mine."

She loved the wood floors, the happy fruit-stenciled yellow walls, the gleaming glass cases filled with pies, and the huge wreath on the back wall made of antique pie tins of varying sizes. Five minutes ago, she'd loved the ice cream parlor chairs. She probably would again.

"I knew you had a shop." He looked around. "But I had no idea it was like *this*. So nice."

You might have, if you'd bothered to call me once in a while. Evans bit her tongue as if she'd actually spoken the words and wanted to call them back. Instead, she packed them up and shoved them to the back of her brain. Jake was here. She was glad to see him. That was all.

"I've had some good luck," she said.

His eyes settled on the table next to them. "You serve lunch, too?"

"Nothing elaborate. A choice of two savory pies with a simple green or fruit salad on the side. I would offer you some, but we sold out of the bacon and goat cheese tart and you wouldn't eat the spanakopita."

He frowned. "Spana-who?"

"Spanakopita. Spinach pie."

He shuddered. "No. Not for me, but I'm meeting my teammate Robbie soon for a late lunch anyway." She knew who Robbie was from *The Face Off Grapevine*, a pro hockey gossip blog she sometimes checked. They called him and Jake the Wild-Ass Twins, though they looked nothing alike. For whatever reason, this Robbie was coming to play for the Yellowhammers, too. Jake went on, "He's been in Scotland since the season ended and just got in this morning. We're going to a place down the street."

So I'm only a pit stop. "Hammer Time. Brand-new sports bar for a brand-new team."

He nodded. "I hope Hammer Time is half as nice as your shop. You obviously work really hard."

"I do. But I don't have to do it on skates." She held up her chef clog-clad foot. Why had she said that? Belittled herself?

He laughed like it was the best joke he'd ever heard. Ah, that was why. She'd do anything to make him laugh. She'd forgotten that about herself.

"Here you go, Evans." Joy set down the pie, milk, and a thick, retro mug decorated with cherries like the ones on the wall.

"No pie for you?" Jake picked up his fork.

She sipped her coffee. "No. I taste all day long. The last thing I want is a plateful of pie. Are you sure you want that? Aren't you about to eat lunch?"

"I want this more than I've wanted anything for a long time." He took a bite and closed his eyes. "Other people only think they've had pie."

If she never got another compliment about another thing, this one would do her until death. "Mississippi mud is a hit in Alabama."

"Don't tell her, but this is so much better than the one from your mother's bakery."

No kidding. Anna-Blair Pemberton was all about a shortcut. "If she'd had her way, I'd be back in Cottonwood, making cookies from mixes and icing cakes with buttercream from a five-gallon tub."

Jake laughed a little under his breath. "My mother might have mentioned that a time or six."

"No doubt." Christine Champagne and Evans's mother were best friends. When Evans had deserted her mother's bakery after graduating from the New Orleans Culinary Institute, it must have given them fodder for months.

"I, for one, am glad you're making pie here." Jake took another bite. "There's something about this… something different. And familiar." He wrinkled his brow. "But I can't place it."

Evans knew exactly what he meant, and it pleased her more than it should have that he'd noticed.

"Do you remember the Mississippi mud bars we used to get when we went to Fat Joe's for tamales?"

"Yes! That's it." He took another bite of pie. "We ate a ton of those things, sitting at that old picnic table outside. Didn't Joe's wife make them?"

"She did. I got her secret and her permission to use it. She used milk and dark chocolate, and she added a little instant coffee to the batter."

He stopped with his fork in midair. "Coffee? There's coffee in here?"

Evans laughed. "You've been eating Lola's for years without knowing." She reached for his plate. "But if you don't want it…"

"Leave my pie alone, woman." He pretended to stab at her with his fork. "Those were good times."

"They were. We did a lot of homework at that picnic table."

He grimaced. "Well, it wasn't the homework I was thinking about. I'd have never passed a math class without you."

"Oh, I don't know about that."

"*I* do." He shook his head and let his eyes wander to the ceiling like he always did when he wanted to change the subject. "What about the beach this summer. How was it?"

The question took Evans aback. Jake hadn't been on the annual Champagne-Pemberton beach trip since Channing came on the scene. She was surprised he even thought about them anymore.

"Sandy. Wet. Salty," she quipped. "Like always."

He grinned. "Must have been a little *too* sandy, wet, and salty for you. I hear you only stayed two days."

"Lots to do around here." She gestured to the shop.

He let his eyes go to a squint and his grin relaxed into that crooked smile. "Too much sorority talk?"

"I swear, it never stops." She slapped her palm against the table. All the women in that beach house—Evans's mother and two older sisters and Jake's mother and younger sister—were proud alumnae of Ole Miss and Omega Beta Gamma, the most revered and exclusive sorority on campus. Addison, Jake's sister, had recently made the ultimate commitment to her Omega sisters by taking a job at the sorority's national headquarters.

Jake took a sip of his milk and chuckled. "I hear you. Especially with rush coming up."

"It's like being in a room full of teachers who won't talk about anything except test scores and discipline problems. You just get tired of it." But it was more than that. Legacy or not, Evans would have never made the Omega cut had she gone to Ole Miss instead of culinary school. She wasn't tall, blond, and sparkly enough. She loved those women—every one of them—but she had always been a little out of step with them. Plus, living with all that sparkle could be hard on the nerves.

Jake laughed. "Well, they have to do their part to keep Omega on top, where it belongs."

"Sorority blood runs deep and thick in Mississippi," Evans said. "Sisters for life."

Jake went from amused to grim. "I don't think Mama and Addison feel very sisterly toward Channing anymore."

Channing had, of course, been the poster child for Omega. "For what it's worth, my mother and sisters don't either." *And I don't feel very cousinly toward her. Not that I ever did.*

He shrugged. "I've moved on—not quite as fast as she did, of course. Miss Mississippi, hockey wife, music producer wife, all in the space of eight months. I suppose you've heard she's pregnant?"

"Yes." The baby would probably have mud-colored eyes like Mr. Music Producer, when it could have had the bluest eyes in the world. Baffling.

"But I'm better off," Jake went on.

She studied his face and decided he meant it. "I'm glad you know it. You're better than that, Jake. You deserve better."

Jake looked at his pie, and back at her again. "You remembered my favorite pie and that I'm not a coffee drinker?"

Thank goodness for the change of subject. "How could I not remember? You always asked for Mississippi mud pie when you came into the bakery at home."

He took a deep breath. "I'm glad to see you, Evie."

"I'm glad to see *you*," she echoed. And she was. But something was niggling deep in her gut. It seemed Glad and Mad were running around inside her, neither one able to get complete control. She beat back Mad and embraced Glad. It was impossible to control most emotions, but mad wasn't one of them. She had always believed that if you didn't want to be mad, you didn't have to be. So what if he'd only come to see her because

Crust was near his lunch spot? They had history. That was what was important. And he'd been through a lot: divorce, Blake's death, a new town and team, and—well, she didn't know what else, but wasn't that enough?

"I probably don't deserve for you to be glad to see me, but I appreciate it." Oh, hell. He was going to try to get negative now, just when she'd talked herself into a good place. She would not allow it. The only thing she was better at than turning out a perfect puff pastry was turning a situation around.

"Why wouldn't I be glad to see you?" She smiled like she meant it, and she did. Everybody always said you had to clear the air before you could move on. As far as she was concerned, that was way overrated. Sometimes it was better to just let it go. Saying yes when others might say no sometimes made life go smoother.

"Let's not pretend I don't owe you an apology." He cocked his head to the side and widened his eyes. What was the point of that? She'd already forgiven him.

"Jake, there is no need for all of this."

"There is. I haven't been the friend to you I should have been. I guess when I met Channing, I didn't think about anything except her and hockey. I know I texted that to you a few months ago, but I wanted to say it in person." He lifted one corner of his mouth. "I did come by before I took Olivia and the kids to Europe, but you weren't here."

"I was in New York."

"I know. Please say you forgive me."

It would have been easier to downplay the whole thing and say it didn't matter. But no one was going to believe that, so she did the next best thing. "It's in the past. Our friendship goes back far and deep. It can withstand a storm or two." The truth of that lightened her heart.

Jake looked relieved, happy even. Maybe she did matter to him. "I shouldn't have let our friendship slip away—let you slip away."

The hair on the back of her neck stood up. *Slip away?* With that, Mad slammed a boxing glove into Glad's face and a foot on to its fallen body.

Why had he had to go and say that? She hadn't *slipped away*. She had gone kicking and screaming. It was true that she hadn't contacted him for a month after *that Christmas*—the Christmas of Channing—but wasn't she entitled to that, considering how things went down? And he damn sure hadn't bothered with her.

Evans had been home from culinary school for the holidays, and Jake from the University of North Dakota. They hadn't seen each other since summer, so they'd filled their plates with Anna-Blair's fancy canapés and found a corner to catch up—though catching up wasn't really necessary, because back then they talked and messaged each other at least three times a week. But they laughed and talked and she thought she'd finally seen the spark she'd felt for twenty years reflected in his eyes. He almost confirmed it when he said, "You know, Evie, my fraternity spring formal is going to be in New Orleans, and I was thinking that—"

But she'd never know for absolute certain what he had been thinking. Maybe he wasn't going to invite her. Maybe he was only going to ask her for a ride from the airport or advice about where to get the best gumbo.

Channing's family seldom made the trip from Memphis to Cottonwood and never for Christmas—but they had that year. And Channing chose that precise moment to sail in, looking like *Vogue* and smelling like Chanel. Or maybe it was Joy. Who the hell knew? It damned sure wasn't vanilla extract. Whatever it was,

Evans had gotten a good whiff when Channing swooped in and hugged her—something Evans could never recall happening before. Of course, Channing had never walked in on Evans in conversation with someone who looked like Jake before either. "Well, cousin, who do you have here?" Channing had asked. Evans had introduced them, and then it was all over but the crying.

And Evans had cried—for a month. But what purpose would it serve to go into all that with Jake? It was over. It didn't matter—except it did. Strange that it only occurred to her now that if Jake had been planning to ask her to the dance, maybe it was because she was going to school in New Orleans anyway—convenient.

"You know, Jake, I didn't slip away." She took down her ponytail and put it back up again. "I didn't go easily." After that month had passed, she'd batted back the humiliation and put on her big girl panties. Still, no matter how many times she'd called or texted, he never had time for her. Even if he answered, he was somewhere else. The next time she'd seen him had been in New Orleans the morning after that dance, when she'd met him and Channing at Brennan's for breakfast. Channing had brought the nosegay of white roses and succulents that Jake had bought her for the dance and held hands with him under the table. Evans had cursed herself for saying yes to that breakfast invitation, when she should have said no. It wasn't the first time, and it wouldn't be the last. "I fought for our friendship."

The moment the words cleared her mouth, she was sorry. He'd apologized. What more did she want? Jake's face went white and he put his fork down. Understandable. He probably didn't want to eat any more of her pie after what she'd said. Why hadn't she just left it alone?

"I'm sorry. I shouldn't have said that," she said hurriedly.

"Why? It's true." There was real hurt on his face.

"Nonetheless. You apologized, and I wasn't gracious about it. And after all you've been through. It's behind us. Let's move forward."

He looked skeptical, but nodded. "That's all I want. And you've been gracious to forgive me at all." Eyes wide. Head cocked. Lip bite. "I'll make it up to you."

He had never, as far as she could remember, had to get to the lip biting with her before. "There's nothing to make up."

He picked up his fork again. "I disagree, though it may not be possible. But I will say this: for a while there, I forgot what was important. After the divorce, I forgot my raising. But after Blake… It made me stop and think. I won't forget again. I'm going to be a better man—a better friend."

He covered her hand with his, and her heart dropped like a fallen star.

"We're good?" What was wrong with being convenient anyway?

Then he nodded and smiled like he was pleased. Pleasing Jake Champagne had once been her life's work. She supposed she was glad she had finally accomplished it.

Don't miss Sweet as Pie *by Alicia Hunter Pace, available now wherever books are sold.*

www.CarinaPress.com

Also available from Alicia Hunter Pace
Sweet Gone South

Welcome to Merritt, Alabama, where summers are lazy, tea is sweet, and guests are always welcome....

Luke Avery needs a wife to help raise his motherless three-year-old. Candy shop owner Lanie Heaven desires a child but can never have her own. When Luke moves into the apartment above Lanie's shop, she can't help falling for the sexy single dad and his sweet little girl.

Luke's not planning to fall in love ever again—but easing the ache of loneliness with pretty Lanie isn't falling in love. Still, proposing to her could solve all his problems and give his child what she needs. Lanie believes her dreams of love and family are finally coming true. Until she's faced with evidence that Luke's heart is locked away tight. Can Luke learn to slay his demons and put the past to rest? Or will he lose Lanie—and any hope he might've had for a sweet life—forever?